FALLING KINGDOMS

MORGAN RHODES

The moral right of the author has been asserted

Set in Fournier

Printed in Great Britain by Clays Ltd, St Ives plc

United States of America, this book is sold subject to the condition that it or otherwise, be lent, re-sold, hired out, or otherwise circulated without in any form of binding or cover other than that in which it is published condition including this condition being imposed on the subsequent pur

British Library Cataloguing in Publication Data
A CIP catalogue record for this book is available from the British Libr

PENGUIN BOOKS

PENGUIN BOOKS

Published by the Penguin Group
Penguin Books Ltd, 80 Strand, London WC2R ORL, England
Penguin Group (USA) Inc., 375 Hudson Street, New York, New York 10014, USA
Penguin Group (Canada), 90 Eglinton Avenue East, Suite 700, Toronto, Ontario, Canada M4P 2Y3
(a division of Pearson Penguin Canada Inc.)
Penguin Ireland, 25 St Stephen's Green, Dublin 2, Ireland (a division of Penguin Books Ltd)
Penguin Group (Australia), 707 Collins Street, Melbourne, Victoria 3008, Australia
(a division of Pearson Australia Group Pty Ltd)
Penguin Books India Pvt Ltd, 11 Community Centre, Panchsheel Park, New Delhi – 110 017, India
Penguin Group (NZ), 67 Apollo Drive, Rosedale, Auckland 0632, New Zealand
(a division of Pearson New Zealand Ltd)
Penguin Books (South Africa) (Pty) Ltd, Block D, Rosebank Office Park, 181 Jan Smuts Avenue,
Parktown North, Gauteng 2193, South Africa

Penguin Books Ltd, Registered Offices: 80 Strand, London WC2R ORL, England

penguinbooks.com

First published in the USA by Penguin Group (USA) Inc. 2012
Published in Great Britain by Penguin Books 2013

001

ISBN: 978-0-141-34615-1

www.greenpenguin.co.uk

MIX
Paper from
responsible sources
FSC
www.fsc.org   FSC™ C018179

Penguin Books is committed to a sustainable
future for our business, our readers and our planet.
This book is made from Forest Stewardship
Council™ certified paper.

ALWAYS LEARNING   **PEARSON**

Mytica

LIMEROS

PAELSIA

Forbidden Mountains

The Wildlands

AURANOS

THE

SILVER

SEA

CAST OF CHARACTERS

URANOS

Southern kingdom

CLEIONA (CLEO) BELLOS	Youngest Auranian princess
EMILIA BELLOS	Eldest Auranian princess
THEON RANUS	Cleo's bodyguard
SIMON RANUS	Theon's father
ARON LAGARIS	Court noble; Cleo's intended
CORVIN BELLOS	King of Auranos
ELENA BELLOS	Deceased queen of Auranos
NICOLO (NIC) CASSIAN	The king's squire
MIRA CASSIAN	Nic's sister and Emilia's lady-in-waiting
ROGERUS CASSIAN	Nic and Mira's late father
CLEIONA	Goddess of fire and air

PAELSIA
Middle kingdom

JONAS AGALLON	Youngest son of wine seller
TOMAS AGALLON	Jonas's older brother
SILAS AGALLON	Wine seller; Jonas's father
FELICIA AGALLON	Jonas's older sister
PAULO	Felicia's husband
BRION RADENOS	Jonas's best friend
EIRENE	Village woman
SERA	Eirene's granddaughter
HUGO BASILIUS	Paelsian leader/chieftain
LAELIA BASILIUS	Basilius's daughter
EVA	Original sorceress; Watcher

LIMEROS
Northern kingdom

MAGNUS DAMORA	Prince of Limeros
LUCIA DAMORA	Princess of Limeros
GAIUS DAMORA	King of Limeros
ALTHEA DAMORA	Queen of Limeros
SABINA MALLIUS	King's mistress
JANA	Sabina's sister
MICHOL TRICHAS	Lucia's bashful suitor
TOBIAS ARGYNOS	Gaius's bastard son
ANDREAS PSELLOS	Lucia's suitor; Magnus's rival
AMIA	Kitchen maid
VALORIA	Goddess of earth and water

WATCHERS

ALEXIUS	Young Watcher
TIMOTHEUS	Elder Watcher
PHAEDRA	Young Watcher
DANAUS	Elder Watcher

PROLOGUE

She'd never killed before tonight.

"Stay back," her sister hissed.

Jana pressed against the stone wall of the villa. She searched the shadows that surrounded them, briefly looking up at the stars, bright as diamonds against the black sky.

Squeezing her eyes shut, she prayed to the ancient sorceress. *Please, Eva, give me the magic I need tonight to find her.*

When she opened her eyes, fear shot through her. On the branch of a tree a dozen paces away sat a golden hawk.

"They're watching us," she whispered. "They know what we've done."

Sabina flicked a glance at the hawk. "We need to move. Now. There's no time to waste."

Keeping her face turned away from the hawk, Jana pushed away from the safety of the wall to follow her sister to the heavy oak and iron door of the villa. Sabina pressed her hands against it, channeling the magic that had been strengthened by the blood they'd spilled earlier. Jana noticed that Sabina's fingernails still bore traces of red in the cuticles, and she shuddered, remembering. Sabina's hands began to glow with amber light. A moment later, the door disintegrated into sawdust. Wood was no barricade against earth magic.

Sabina sent a victorious smile over her shoulder. Blood now trickled from her nose.

At her sister's gasp, Sabina's grin faded. She wiped it away and entered the large home. "It's nothing."

It wasn't nothing. Using too much of this temporarily enhanced magic could harm them. Could kill them if they weren't careful.

But Sabina Mallius was not known to be the cautious one. She hadn't paused earlier tonight in using her beauty to lead the unsuspecting man from the tavern to his fate, while Jana had hesitated far too long before her sharp blade finally found its mark in his heart.

Sabina was strong, passionate, and completely fearless. Heart in throat as she followed Sabina inside, Jana wished she could be more like her older sister. But she'd always been the careful one. The planner. The one who'd seen the signs in the stars because she'd studied the night skies all her life.

The prophesied child had been born and she was here in this large and luxurious villa—built of sturdy stone and wood compared to the small, poorer straw and mud cottages in the village nearby.

Jana was certain this was the right place.

She was knowledge. Sabina was action. Together they were unstoppable.

Sabina cried out as she turned the corner of the hallway up ahead. Jana quickened her pace, her heart pounding. In the dark hallway, lit only by wall-set torches that flickered their meager light on the stone walls, a guard had her sister by her throat.

Jana didn't think. She acted.

Thrusting out her hands, she summoned air magic. The guard lost his grip and flew back from Sabina, slamming into the wall behind her hard enough to crush his bones. He crumpled to the ground in a heap.

Sharp pain sliced through Jana's head, agonizing enough to make her whimper. She wiped at the warm, thick blood that now gushed from under her nose. Her hand trembled.

Sabina gingerly touched her injured throat. "Thank you, sister."

This fresh blood magic helped speed their steps and clear their vision in the darkness of the unfamiliar, narrow stone hallways. But it wouldn't last long.

"Where is she?" Sabina demanded.

"Close."

"I'm trusting you."

"The child is here. I know she is." They proceeded a few steps more down the dark hallway.

"Here." Jana stopped outside an unlocked door.

She pushed it open and the sisters moved toward the ornately carved wooden cradle inside the room. They looked down at the baby, swaddled in a soft rabbit's fur coverlet. Her skin was pale white with a healthy, rosy glow to her chubby cheeks.

Jana adored her instantly. The first smile she'd been capable of for days blossomed on her face. "Beautiful girl," she whispered, reaching into the cradle to gently pick up the newborn.

"You're certain it's her."

"Yes." More than anything else in her seventeen years of life, Jana was positive of this. The child she held in her arms, this small, beautiful baby with sky-blue eyes and a fuzz of hair that would one day be black as a raven's wing, was the one prophesied to possess the magic necessary to find the Kindred—four objects that contained the source of all *elementia*, elemental magic. Earth and water, fire and air.

The child's magic would be that of a sorceress, not a common witch like Jana and her sister. The first in a thousand years, since Eva herself had lived and breathed. There would be no need for blood or death to play any part in this child's magic.

Jana had seen her birth in the stars. Finding this child was her destiny.

"Put my daughter down," a voice snarled from the shadows. "Don't hurt her."

Jana spun around, clutching the infant to her chest. Her eyes fell on the dagger the woman pointed toward them. Its sharp edge glinted in the candlelight. Her heart sank. This was the moment she'd been dreading, had prayed wouldn't come to pass.

Sabina's eyes flashed. "Hurt her? That's not what we plan to do at all. You don't even know what she is, do you?"

The woman's brows drew together with confusion, but fury hardened her gaze. "I'll kill you before I allow you to leave this room with her."

"No"—Sabina raised her hands—"you won't."

The mother's eyes grew wide and her mouth opened, gasping. She couldn't breathe—Sabina was blocking the flow of air to her lungs. Jana turned away, face screwed up in misery. It was over in a moment. The woman's body fell to the ground, still twitching but lifeless, as the sisters sidestepped her and fled the room.

Jana gathered her loose cloak around the baby to hide her as they left the villa and ran into the forest. Sabina's nose bled profusely now from using so much destructive magic. Blood dripped to the snow-covered ground.

"Too much," Jana whispered as their steps finally slowed. "Too much death tonight. I hate it."

"She wouldn't have let us take her any other way. Let me see her."

Feeling oddly reluctant, Jana held the baby out.

Sabina took her and studied the child's face in the darkness. Her gaze flicked to Jana and she gave her sister a wicked grin. "We did it."

Jana felt a sudden rush of excitement, despite the difficulties they'd faced. "We did."

"You were incredible. I wish I could have visions like you do."

"Only with great effort and sacrifice can I have them."

"It's all a great effort and sacrifice." Sabina's voice twisted with sudden disdain. "Too much of it. But for this child, one day magic will be so easy. I envy her."

"We'll raise her together. We'll tutor her and be there for her and when the time comes for her to fulfill her destiny, we'll stand by her side every step of the way."

Sabina shook her head. "You won't. I'll take her from here."

Jana frowned. "What? Sabina, I thought we agreed to make all decisions together."

"Not this one. I have other plans for the child." Her expression hardened. "And apologies, sister, but they don't include you."

Staring into Sabina's suddenly cold eyes, Jana at first didn't feel the sharp tip of the dagger sink into her chest. She gasped as the pain began to penetrate.

They'd shared every day, every dream . . . every secret.

However, it would appear, not *every* secret. This was not something Jana would have ever thought to try to foresee.

"Why would you betray me like this?" she managed. "You're my *sister*."

Sabina wiped away the blood that still trickled from her nose. "For love."

When she yanked out the blade, Jana collapsed to her knees on the frozen ground.

Without a backward glance, Sabina swiftly walked away with the child and was soon swallowed by the dark forest.

Jana's vision dimmed and her heart slowed. She watched as the hawk she'd seen earlier flew away . . . leaving her to die alone.

CHAPTER 1

PAELSIA

SIXTEEN YEARS LATER

"A life without wine and beauty isn't worth living. Don't you agree, princess?" Aron slung his arm around Cleo's shoulders as the group of four walked along the dusty, rocky country path.

They'd been in port for less than two hours and he was already drunk, a fact not unduly startling when it came to Aron.

Cleo's glance fell on their accompanying palace guard. His eyes flashed with displeasure at Aron's proximity to the princess of Auranos. But the guard's concern wasn't necessary. Despite the fancy jeweled dagger Aron always wore on a sheath hanging from his belt, he was no more dangerous than a butterfly. A drunk butterfly.

"I couldn't agree more," she said, lying only a little.

"Are we almost there?" Mira asked. The beautiful girl with long, dark, reddish hair and smooth, flawless skin was both Cleo's friend and her older sister's lady-in-waiting. When Emilia decided to stay home due to a sudden headache, she'd insisted that Mira accompany Cleo on this trip. Once the ship arrived in the harbor, a dozen of their friends chose to remain comfortably on board while Cleo and Mira joined Aron on his journey to a nearby village to find the "perfect" bottle of wine. The palace wine cellars were stocked with thousands of bottles of wine from both Auranos and Paelsia, but Aron had heard of a particular vineyard whose output was supposedly unparalleled. At his request, Cleo booked one of her father's ships and invited many of their friends on the trip to Paelsia expressly in search of his ideal bottle.

"That would be a question for Aron. He's the one leading this particular quest." Cleo drew her fur-lined velvet cloak closer to block out the chill of the day. While the ground was clear, a few light snowflakes drifted across their rock-strewn path. Paelsia was farther north than Auranos, but the temperature here surprised her nonetheless. Auranos was warm and temperate, even in the bleakest winter months, with rolling green hills, sturdy olive trees, and acres upon acres of rich, temperate farmland. Paelsia, by contrast, seemed dusty and gray as far as the eye could see.

"Almost there?" Aron repeated. "Almost there? Mira, my peach, all good things come to those who wait. Remember that."

"My lord, I'm the most patient person I know. But my feet hurt." She tempered the complaint with a smile.

"It's a beautiful day and I'm lucky enough to be accompanied by two gorgeous girls. We must give thanks to the goddess for the splendor we've been greeted with here."

Watching the guard, Cleo saw him briefly roll his eyes. When he noticed that she had seen him, he didn't immediately look away as any other guard might. He held her gaze with a defiance that intrigued her. She realized she hadn't seen—or, at least, noticed—this guard before today.

"What's your name?" she addressed him.

"Theon Ranus, your highness."

"Well, Theon, do you have anything to add to our discussion about how far we've walked this afternoon?"

Aron chortled and swigged from his flask.

"No, princess."

"I'm surprised, since you are the one who'll be required to carry the cases of wine back to the ship."

"It's my duty and honor to serve you."

Cleo considered him for a moment. His hair was the color of dark bronze, his skin tanned and unlined. He looked as if he could be one of her rich friends waiting on the ship rather than a uniformed guard her father had insisted accompany them on this journey.

Aron must have been thinking the exact same thing. "You look young for a palace guard." His words slurred together drunkenly as he regarded Theon with a squint. "You can't be much older than I am."

"I'm eighteen, my lord."

Aron snorted. "I stand corrected. You are much older than me. Vastly."

"By one year," Cleo reminded him.

"A year can be a blissful eternity." Aron grinned. "I plan to cling to my youth and lack of responsibility for the year I have left."

Cleo ignored Aron, for the guard's name now rang a bell in her mind. She'd overheard her father as he exited one of his council meetings briefly discuss the Ranus family. Theon's father had died only a week ago—thrown from a horse. His neck had broken instantly.

"My sympathies for the loss of your father," she said with

sincerity. "Simon Ranus was well respected as my father's personal bodyguard."

Theon nodded stiffly. "It was a job he did with great pride. And one I hope to have the honor to be considered for when King Corvin chooses his replacement." Theon's brows drew together as if he hadn't expected her to know of his father's death. An edge of grief slid behind his dark eyes. "Thank you for your kind words, your highness."

Aron audibly snorted and Cleo shot him a withering look.

"Was he a good father?" she asked.

"The very best. He taught me everything I know from the moment I could hold a sword."

She nodded sympathetically. "Then his knowledge will continue to live on through you."

Now that the young guard's dark good looks had caught her attention, she found it increasingly difficult to return her gaze to Aron, whose slight frame and pale skin spoke of a life spent indoors. Theon's shoulders were broad, his arms and chest muscled, and he filled out the dark blue palace guard uniform better than she ever would have imagined possible.

Guiltily, she forced herself to return her attention to her friends. "Aron, you have another half hour before we head back to the ship. We're keeping the others waiting."

Auranians loved a good party, but they weren't known for their endless patience. However, since they'd been brought to the Paelsian docks by her father's ship, they'd have to keep waiting until Cleo was ready to leave.

"The market we're going to is up ahead," Aron said, gesturing. Cleo and Mira looked and saw a cluster of wooden stalls and colorful worn tents, perhaps another ten minutes' walk. It was the first sign of people they had seen since they'd passed a ragged band of children clustered around a fire an hour ago. "You'll soon see it was well worth the trip."

Paelsian wine was said to be a drink worthy of the goddess. Delicious, smooth, without equal in any other land, its effects did not lead to illness or headaches the next day, no matter how much was consumed. Some said that there was strong earth magic at work in the Paelsian soil and in the grapes themselves to make them so perfect in a land that held so many other imperfections.

Cleo wasn't planning to sample it. She didn't drink wine anymore—hadn't for many months. Before that, she'd consumed more than her share of Auranian wine, which didn't taste much better than vinegar. But people—at least, Cleo—didn't drink it for the taste; they drank it for the intoxicating results, the feeling of not a care in the world. Such a feeling, without an anchor to hold one close to shore, could lead one to drift into dangerous territory. And Cleo wasn't in any hurry to sip anything stronger than water or peach juice in the foreseeable future.

Cleo watched Aron drain his flask. He never failed to drink both her share and his and made no apologies for anything he did while under its influence. Despite his shortcomings, many in the court considered him the lord her father would choose as her future husband. The thought made Cleo shudder, yet she still kept him close at hand. For Aron knew a secret about Cleo. Even though he hadn't mentioned it in many months, she was certain he hadn't forgotten. Nor would he ever.

The revelation of this secret could destroy her.

Because of this, she tolerated him socially with a smile on her lips. No one would ever guess that she loathed him.

"Here we are," Aron finally announced as they entered the gates of the village market. Beyond the stalls, off to the right, Cleo saw some small farmhouses and cottages in the near distance. Though far less prosperous-looking than the farms she'd seen in the Auranian countryside, she noted with surprise that the small clay structures with their thatched roofs and little windows seemed neat and well kept, at odds with the impression she had of Paelsia. Paelsia was a land filled with poor peasants, ruled over not by a king, but a chieftain, who was rumored by some to be a powerful sorcerer. Despite Paelsia's proximity to Auranos, however, Cleo rarely gave her neighbors to the north much thought, other than an occasional vague interest in entertaining tales of the much more "savage" Paelsians.

Aron stopped in front of a stall draped in dark purple fabric that fell down to the dusty ground.

Mira sighed with relief. "Finally."

Cleo turned to her left only to be greeted by a pair of glittering black eyes in a tanned, lined face. She took an instinctive step back and felt Theon standing firm and comfortingly close behind her. The man looked rough, even dangerous, much like the few others who'd crossed their path since they'd arrived in Paelsia. The wine seller's front tooth was chipped but white in the bright sunlight. He wore simple clothes, made from linen and worn sheepskin, and a thick wool tunic for warmth. Feeling self-conscious, Cleo pulled her sable-lined cloak closer around her silk dress, pale blue and embroidered in gold.

Aron eyed the man with interest. "Are you Silas Agallon?"

"I am."

"Good. This is your lucky day, Silas. I've been told that your wine is the best in all of Paelsia."

"You were told right."

A lovely dark-haired girl emerged from the back of the stall. "My father is a gifted wine maker."

"This is Felicia, my daughter." Silas nodded at the girl. "A daughter who should be getting ready for her wedding right now."

She laughed. "And leave you to work all day lugging cases of wine? I've come to convince you to close shop early."

"Perhaps." The pleased glint in the wine seller's dark eyes shifted to disdain as he took in Aron's fine clothes. "And who might you be?"

"Both you and your lovely daughter have the great privilege to be acquainted with her royal highness Princess Cleiona Bellos of Auranos." Aron nodded toward her and then Mira. "This is Lady Mira Cassian. And I am Aron Lagaris. My father is lord of Elder's Pitch on the southern coast of Auranos."

The wine seller's daughter looked at Cleo, surprised, and lowered her head with respect. "An honor, your highness."

"Yes, quite an honor," Silas agreed, and Cleo couldn't detect sarcasm in his tone. "We rarely have royalty from either Auranos or Limeros visit our humble village. I can't remember the last time. I'd be honored to give you a sample to try before we discuss your purchase, your highness."

Cleo shook her head with a smile. "Aron's the one interested in your wares. I simply accompanied him here."

The wine seller looked disappointed, even a little hurt. "Even still, will you do me the great honor of tasting my wine—to toast my daughter's wedding?"

How could she refuse such a request? She nodded, trying to hide her reluctance. "Of course. It would be my pleasure."

The sooner she did, the sooner they could leave this market. While colorful and well populated, it smelled less than pleasant—

as if there was a cesspit nearby with no fragrant herbs or flowers to cover its stench. Despite Felicia's palpable excitement for her impending wedding, the poverty of this land and these people was distressing. Perhaps Cleo too should have stayed on the ship while Aron fetched the wine for their friends.

All she really knew about small, poor Paelsia was that it had one form of wealth that neither of the other two kingdoms flanking it could claim. Paelsian soil this close to the sea grew vineyards that put any other land's to shame. Many said that earth magic was responsible. She'd heard stories of grapevines stolen from the earth here that withered and died almost immediately once they crossed over the border.

"You'll be my last customers," Silas said. "Then I'll do as my daughter asks and close up shop for the day to prepare for her wedding at dusk."

"My congratulations to you both," Aron said with disinterest as he scanned the bottles on display, his lips pursed. "Do you have suitable glasses for our tasting?"

"Of course." Silas moved behind the cart and dug deep into a rickety wooden case. He pulled out three glasses that caught the sunlight and then uncorked a bottle of wine. Pale, amber-colored liquid trickled in the glasses, the first of which he handed to Cleo.

Theon was suddenly right next to Cleo, snatching the glass away from the wine seller before she touched it. Whatever dark look was on the guard's face made Silas take a shaky step backward and exchange a glance with his daughter.

Cleo gasped, startled. "What are you doing?"

"You would taste something a stranger offers you without any second thoughts?" Theon asked sharply.

"It's not poisoned."

He peered down into the glass. "Do you know that for sure?"

She looked at him impatiently. He thought someone might poison her? For what purpose? The peace between the lands had lasted more than a century. There was no threat here. Having a palace guard accompany her at all on this trip was more to appease her overprotective father than out of any true necessity.

"Fine." She flicked her hand at him. "Feel free to be my taster. I'll be sure not to drink any if you fall over dead from it."

"Oh, how ridiculous," Aron drawled. He tipped his glass back and drained it without a second thought.

Cleo looked at him for a moment. "Well? Are you dying now?"

He had his eyes shut, savoring. "Only from thirst."

Her attention returned to Theon and she smiled slightly mockingly. "May I have my glass back now? Or do you think this wine seller took the time to poison each one individually?"

"Of course not. Please, enjoy." He held the glass out for her to take it. Silas's dark-eyed gaze was now filled more with embarrassment than annoyance at the drama her guard had caused.

Cleo tried to shield her immediate appraisal of the glass's questionable cleanliness. "I'm sure it's delicious."

The wine seller looked grateful. Theon moved back to stand to the right side of the cart, at ease but watchful. And she thought her father was overprotective.

Out of the corner of her eye, she saw Aron tip his glass back and drain a second sampling the wine seller's daughter had poured for him.

"Incredible. Absolutely incredible, just as I'd heard it was."

Mira took a more ladylike sip before her brows went up with surprise. "It's wonderful."

Fine. Her turn. Cleo took a tentative taste of the liquid. The moment it touched her tongue, she found herself dismayed. Not because it was rancid, but because it was delicious—sweet, smooth, incomparable to anything she'd ever tried before. It stirred a longing inside her for more. Her heart began to pound faster. A few more sips was enough to empty her glass entirely, and she glanced around at her friends. The world suddenly seemed to shimmer with golden halos of light around each of them, making them appear even more beautiful than they were to begin with. Aron became marginally less loathsome to her.

And Theon—despite his overbearing behavior—looked incredibly beautiful too.

This wine was dangerous; there was no doubt about it. It was worth any amount of money this wine seller might ask for it. And Cleo had to be careful to stay away from it as much as possible, now and in the future.

"Your wine is very good," she said aloud, trying not to seem overly enthusiastic. She wanted to ask for another glass but swallowed back the words.

Silas beamed. "I'm so glad to hear that."

Felicia nodded. "Like I said, my father is a genius."

"Yes, I find your wine worthy of purchase," Aron slurred. He'd been drinking steadily during the trip here from the engraved golden flask he always kept with him. At this point, it was a surprise that he continued to stand upright without assistance. "I want four cases today and another dozen shipped to my villa."

Silas's eyes lit up. "That can certainly be arranged."

"I'll give you fifteen Auranian centimos per case."

The tanned skin of the wine seller paled. "But it's worth at least forty per case. I've received as much as fifty before."

Aron's lips thinned. "When? Five years ago? There are not enough buyers these days for you to make a living. Limeros hasn't been such a good customer over the past few years, have they? Importing expensive wine is at the bottom of their priority list given their current economic straits. That leaves Auranos, because everyone knows your goddess-forsaken countrymen don't have two coins to rub together. Fifteen per case is my final offer. Considering I want sixteen cases—and perhaps more in the near future—I'd say that's a good day's work. Wouldn't that be a nice gift of money to give your daughter on her wedding day? Felicia? Wouldn't that be better than closing up shop early and getting nothing?"

Felicia bit her bottom lip, her brows drawing together. "It is better than nothing. I know the wedding is costing too much as it is. But . . . I don't know. Father?"

Silas was about to say something but faltered. Cleo was only half watching, concentrating more on trying to resist the urge to sip from the glass that Silas had already refilled for her. Aron loved to barter. It was a hobby of his to get the best price possible, no matter what he was after.

"I mean no disrespect, of course," Silas said, wringing his hands. "Would you be willing to come up to twenty-five centimos per case?"

"No, I would not." Aron inspected his fingernails. "As good as your wine is, I know there are many other wine sellers at this busy market, as well as on our way back to the ship, who'd be more than happy to accept my offer. I can take my business to them if you'd prefer to lose this sale. Is that what you want?"

"No, I . . ." Silas swallowed, his forehead a furrow of wrinkles. "I do want to sell my wine. It's the reason I'm here. But for fifteen centimos . . ."

"I have a better idea. Why don't we make it *fourteen* centimos per case?" A glint of wickedness appeared in Aron's green eyes. "And you have to the count of ten to accept or my offer decreases by another centimo."

Mira looked away from the debate, embarrassed. Cleo opened her mouth—then, remembering what Aron could do with her secret if she chose, closed it. He was determined to get this wine for the lowest price he could. And it wasn't as if he couldn't afford to pay any more, since Cleo knew he had more than enough money on him to buy many cases even at the top price.

"Fine," Silas finally said through clenched teeth, although it seemed as if it deeply pained him. He flicked a glance at Felicia before returning his attention to Aron. "Fourteen per case for sixteen cases. I'll give my daughter the wedding she deserves."

"Excellent. As we Auranians have always assured you . . ." With a small smile of victory, Aron dug into his pocket to pull out a roll of notes, counting them off into the man's outstretched palm. It was now more than obvious that the total sum was only a small percentage of what Aron had with him. By the look of outrage in Silas's eyes, the insult wasn't missed. ". . . Grapes," Aron continued, "will never fail to feed your nation."

Two figures approached the stall from Cleo's left.

"Felicia," a deep voice asked. "What are you doing here? Shouldn't you be with your friends, getting all dressed up?"

"Soon, Tomas," she whispered. "We're about to finish up here."

Cleo glanced to her left. Both boys who'd approached the stall had dark hair, nearly black. Dark brows slashed over copper-brown eyes. They were tall and broad-shouldered and deeply tanned. Tomas, the older of the two, in his early twenties, studied his father and sister. "Is there something wrong?"

"Wrong?" Silas said through gritted teeth. "Of course not. I'm conducting a transaction, that's all."

"You're lying. You're upset right now. I can tell."

"I'm not."

The other boy cast a dark glare at Aron and then at Cleo and Mira. "Are these people trying to cheat you, Father?"

"Jonas," Silas said tiredly, "this isn't your business."

"This is my business, Father. How much did this boy"—Jonas's gaze swept the length of Aron with undisguised distaste—"agree to pay you?"

"Fourteen a case," Aron offered casually. "A fair price that your father was more than happy to accept."

"Fourteen?" Jonas sputtered. "You dare insult him like that?"

Tomas grabbed the back of Jonas's shirt and pulled him backward. "Calm down."

Jonas's dark eyes flashed. "When our father's being taken advantage of by some ridiculous silk-wearing bastard, I take offense."

"Bastard?" Aron's voice had turned to ice. "Who are you calling a bastard, *peasant*?"

Tomas turned slowly, anger brimming in his gaze. "My brother was calling *you* a bastard. *Bastard*."

And this, Cleo thought with a sinking feeling, was the absolute worst thing someone could ever call Aron. It wasn't common knowledge, but he *was* a bastard. Born of a pretty blond maid his father once took a liking to. Since Sebastien Lagaris's wife was barren, she had taken the baby on as her own from the moment he was born. The maid, Aron's real mother, had died soon after under mysterious circumstances that no one had dared to question either then or now. But there was still talk. And this talk was what had met Aron's ears when he was old enough to understand what it all meant.

"Princess?" Theon asked, as if looking for her command to intervene. She put her hand on his arm to stop him. This didn't need to become more of a scene than it already was.

"Let's go, Aron." She exchanged a worried look with Mira, who nervously set down her second glass of wine.

Aron's attention didn't leave Tomas. "How dare you insult me?"

"You should obey your little girlfriend and leave," Tomas advised. "The sooner the better."

"And as soon as your father fetches the cases of wine for me, I'd be more than happy to do just that."

"Forget the wine. Walk away and consider yourself lucky that I didn't make a bigger deal of your insult toward my father. He is trusting and willing to undersell himself. I am not."

Aron bristled, his previous calm now thrust aside by offense and inebriation, making him much braver than he should have been when faced with two tall, muscular Paelsians. "Do you have any idea who I am?"

"Do we care?" Jonas and his brother exchanged a glance.

"I am Aron Lagaris, son of Sebastien Lagaris, lord of Elder's Pitch. I stand here in your market accompanied by none other than Princess Cleiona Bellos of Auranos. Show respect to us both."

"This is ridiculous, Aron." Cleo hissed a small breath from between her teeth. She did wish that he wouldn't put on such airs. Mira slipped her arm through Cleo's and squeezed her hand. *Let's go,* she seemed to be signaling.

"Oh, your highness." Sarcasm dripped from Jonas's words as he mock-bowed. "Both of your highnesses. It is a true honor to be in your shining presence."

"I could have you beheaded for such disrespect," Aron slurred. "Both of you and your father. Your sister too."

"Leave my sister out of this," Tomas growled.

"Let me guess, if it's her wedding day, I'll assume she's already with child? I've heard Paelsian girls don't wait for marriage before they spread their legs to anyone with enough coin to pay." Aron glanced at Felicia, who looked mortified and indignant. "I have some money. Perhaps you might give me a half hour of your attentions before dusk."

"Aron!" Cleo snapped, appalled.

That she was totally ignored by him was no surprise. Jonas turned his furious gaze on her—so hot she felt singed by it.

Tomas, who seemed the marginally less hotheaded of the two brothers, turned the darkest, most venomous glare she'd ever seen in her life on Aron. "I could kill you for saying such a thing about my sister."

Aron gave him a thin smile. "Try it."

Cleo finally cast a look over her shoulder at a frustrated-looking Theon, whom she'd basically commanded not to intervene. It was clear to her now that she had no control over this situation. All she wanted to do was go back to the ship and leave all this unpleasantness far behind. But it was too late for that now.

Powered by the insult toward his sister, Tomas flew at Aron with fists clenched. Mira gasped and put her hands over her eyes. There was no doubt Tomas would easily win a fight between the two and beat the thinner Aron into a bloody pulp. But Aron had a weapon—the fashionable jeweled dagger he wore at his hip.

It was now in his grip.

Tomas didn't see the knife. When he drew closer and grabbed hold of Aron's shirt, Aron thrust his blade into Tomas's throat. The boy's hands shot up to his neck as the blood began to gush, his eyes wide with shock and pain. A moment later, he fell to his knees and then fully hit the ground. His hands clawed at his throat, the dagger still deeply embedded there. Blood swiftly formed a crimson puddle around the boy's head.

It had all happened so fast.

Cleo clamped her hand against her mouth to keep from screaming. Another did scream—Felicia let out a piercing wail of horror that turned Cleo's blood ice cold. And suddenly the rest of the market collectively took notice of what had happened.

Shouts sliced through the market. There was a sudden rush of bodies all around her, pushing and shoving. She shrieked. Theon clamped his arm around Cleo's waist and roughly yanked her backward. Jonas had started for her and Aron, grief and fury etched onto his face. Theon pushed Mira in front of him and pulled Cleo under his arm, Aron close behind. They fled the market while Jonas's enraged words pursued them.

"You're dead! I'll kill you for this! Both of you!"

"He deserved it," Aron growled. "He was going to try to kill me. I was defending myself."

"Keep going, your lordship," grunted Theon, sounding disgusted. They pushed their way through the crowd, making their stumbling way onto the road back to the ship.

Tomas would never live to see his sister get married. Felicia witnessed her brother's murder on her wedding day. The wine Cleo had drunk churned and soured in her stomach. She yanked away from Theon's grip and threw up on the path.

She could have had Theon stop this before it got so far out of control. But she hadn't.

No one seemed to be following them, and after a while it became clear that the Paelsians were letting them leave. They slowed to a fast stride. Cleo kept her head down, holding on to Mira for support. The foursome walked through the dusty landscape in absolute silence.

Cleo thought she'd never get the image of the boy's pain-filled eyes out of her mind.

CHAPTER 2

PAELSIA

Jonas collapsed to his knees and stared with horror at the ornate dagger sticking out of Tomas's throat. Tomas moved his hand as if to try to pull it out, but he couldn't manage it. Shaking, Jonas curled his hand around the hilt. It took effort to pull it free. Then he clamped his other hand down over the wound. Hot red blood gushed from between his fingers.

Felicia screamed behind him. "Tomas, no! Please!"

The life faded from Tomas's eyes with every slowing beat of his heart.

Jonas's thoughts were jumbled and unclear. It felt as if this moment froze in time for him as his brother's life drained away.

A wedding. There was a wedding today. Felicia's wedding. She'd agreed to marry a friend of theirs—Paulo. They'd jokingly given him a hard time when they had announced their engagement a month ago. At least, before they welcomed him into their family with open arms.

A big celebration was planned unlike anything their poor village would see again for a very long time. Food, drink . . . and plenty of Felicia's pretty friends for the Agallon brothers to choose from to help forget their daily troubles carving out an existence for their family in a dying land like Paelsia. The boys were the best of friends—and unbeatable in anything they attempted together.

Until now.

Panic swelled in Jonas's chest and he looked frantically around at the swarm of locals for someone to help. "Can't something be done? Is there a healer here?"

His hands were slick with Tomas's blood. His brother's body convulsed and he made a sickening gurgling sound as more blood gushed from his mouth.

"I don't understand." Jonas's voice broke. Felicia clutched his arm, her wails of panic and grief deafening. "It happened so fast. Why? Why did this happen?"

His father stood helplessly nearby, his face grief-stricken but stoic. "It's fate, son."

"Fate?" Jonas spat out, rage blazing bright inside him. "This is not fate! This was not meant to be. This—this was done at the hands of a Auranian royal who considers us dirt beneath his feet."

Paelsia had been in steady decline for generations, the land slowly wasting away, while their closest neighbors continued to live in luxury and excess, refusing them aid, refusing them even the right to hunt on their overstocked land when it was their fault in the first place that Paelsia lacked sufficient resources to feed its people. It had been the harshest winter on record. The days were tolerable, but the nights were frigid within the thin walls of their cottage. Dozens, at least, had frozen to death in their small homes or starved.

No one died from starvation or exposure to the elements in Auranos. The inequality had always sickened Jonas and Tomas. They hated Auranians—especially the royals. But it had been a formless and nameless hate, a random, overall distaste for a people Jonas had never been acquainted with before.

Now his hatred had substance. Now it had a name.

He stared down at the face of his older brother. Blood coated Tomas's tanned skin and lips. Jonas's eyes stung, but he forced himself not to cry. Tomas had to see him strong right now. He always insisted that his kid brother be strong. Even with only four years separating them, that's how he'd raised Jonas to be ever since their mother died ten years ago.

Tomas had taught him everything he knew—how to hunt, how to swear, how to behave around girls. Together they'd provided for their family. They'd stolen, they'd poached, they'd done whatever it took to survive while others in their village wasted away.

"If you want something," Tomas had always said, *"you have to take it. Because nobody's ever going to give it to you. Remember that, little brother."*

Jonas remembered. He'd *always* remember.

Tomas had stopped twitching and the blood—*so much blood*—had stopped flowing so quickly over Jonas's hands.

There was something in Tomas's eyes, past the pain. It was outrage.

Not only for the unfairness of his murder at the hands of an Auranian lord. No . . . also at the unfairness of a life spent fighting every day—to eat, to breathe, to survive. And how had they wound up this way?

A century ago, the Paelsian chief of the time had gone to the sovereigns of Limeros and Auranos, bordering lands to the north and south, and asked for help. Limeros declined assistance, saying that they had enough to contend with getting their own people back on their feet after a recently halted war with Auranos. Prosperous Auranos, however, struck an agreement with Paelsia. They subsidized the planting of vineyards over all the fertile farmland in Paelsia—land that could have been used to grow crops to feed its people and livestock. Instead, they promised to import Paelsian wine at favorable prices, which would in turn enable Paelsia to import Auranian crops at equally favorable prices. This would help both countries' economies, the then king of Auranos said, and the naive Paelsian chieftain shook hands on the deal.

But the bargain had a time limit. After fifty years, the set prices on imports and exports would expire. And expire they had. Now Paelsians could no longer afford to import Auranian food—not with the falling price of their wine since Auranos was their only customer and could ruthlessly set the cost, which they did, ever lower and lower. Paelsia lacked the ships to export to other kingdoms across the Silver Sea, and austere Limeros in the north was devout in its worship of a goddess who had frowned on drunkenness. The rest of the land continued to slowly die as it had for decades. And all Paelsians could do was watch it fade away.

The sound of his sister's sobs on the day that should have been the happiest of her life broke Jonas's heart.

"Fight," Jonas whispered to his brother. "Fight for me. Fight to live."

No, Tomas seemed to convey as the remaining light left his eyes. He couldn't speak. His larynx had been sliced clean through by the Auranian's blade. *Fight for Paelsia. For all of us. Don't let this be the end. Don't let them win.*

Jonas fought not to let out the sob he felt deep in his heart but failed. He wept, a broken and unfamiliar sound to his own ears.

And a dark, bottomless rage filled him where grief had so quickly carved out a deep, black hole.

Lord Aron Lagaris would pay for this.

And the fair-haired girl—Princess Cleiona. She stood by with a cold and amused smirk on her beautiful face and watched her friend murder Tomas. "I swear I'll avenge you, Tomas," Jonas managed through clenched teeth. "This is only the beginning."

His father touched his shoulder and Jonas tensed.

"He's gone, my son."

Jonas finally pulled his trembling, bloody hands away from his brother's ravaged throat. He'd been making promises to someone whose spirit had already departed for the everafter. Only Tomas's shell remained.

Jonas looked up at the cloudless blue sky above the market and let the harsh cry of grief escape his throat. A golden hawk flew from its perch on his father's wine stall above them.

CHAPTER 3

LIMEROS

L

Someone asked Magnus a question, but he hadn't been paying any attention. After a while, everyone at a banquet like this began to resemble a swarm of buzzing fruit flies. Annoying, but impossible to squash quickly and easily.

He pasted what he hoped was a pleasant expression on his face and turned to his left to face one of the more vocal of the insects. He took another bite of *kaana* and swallowed it without chewing in an attempt to evade the taste. He barely glanced at the salted beef next to it on his pewter plate. He was quickly losing his appetite.

"Apologies, my lady," he said. "I didn't quite hear that."

"Your sister, Lucia," Lady Sophia said, dabbing at the corner of her mouth with an embroidered jacquard napkin. "She's grown into a lovely young woman, hasn't she?"

Magnus blinked. Small talk was so taxing. "She has indeed."

"Tell me again, what age has she turned today?"

"Sixteen."

"Lovely girl. And so polite."

"She was raised well."

"Of course. Is she betrothed to anyone yet?"

"Not yet."

"Mmm. My son, Bernardo, is very accomplished, quite handsome, and what he lacks in height he more than makes up for in intelligence. I think they would make a fine match."

"This, my lady, is something I would suggest you speak to my father about."

Why had he been seated directly next to this woman? She was ancient and smelled of dust and also, for some bizarre reason, seaweed. Perhaps she had emerged from the Silver Sea and traveled up over the rocky cliffs to get to the frosty granite Limeros castle at the top rather than across the ice-covered land like everyone else.

Her husband, Lord Lenardo, leaned forward in his high-backed seat. "Enough about matchmaking, wife. I'm curious to know what the prince's thoughts are on the problems in Paelsia."

"Problems?" Magnus responded.

"The recent unrest caused by the murder of a poor wine seller's son at market a week ago in full sight of everyone."

Magnus slid his index finger casually around the edge of his goblet. "A murder of a poor wine seller's son. Pardon my seeming disinterest, but that doesn't sound like anything out of the ordinary. The Paelsians are a savage race, quick to violence. I've heard they'll happily eat their meat raw if their fires take too long to build."

Lord Lenardo gave him a crooked grin. "Indeed. But this is unusual since it was at the hands of a visiting royal from Auranos."

This was more interesting. Marginally. "Is that so? Who?"

"I don't know, but there are rumors that Princess Cleiona herself was involved in the altercation."

"Ah. I've found rumors have much in common with feathers. It's rare that either holds much weight."

Unless, of course, those rumors proved true.

Magnus was well aware of the youngest princess of Auranos. She was a great beauty the same age as his sister—he'd met her once when they were both small children. He felt no interest in going to Auranos again. Besides, his father severely disliked the Auranian king and as far as he knew, the feeling was mutual.

His gaze moved across the great hall and he locked eyes with his father, who stared back at him with cold disapproval. His father despised the look Magnus got when he was bored at a public function like this. He found it insolent. But it was such a struggle for Magnus to hide how he felt, although he had to admit, he didn't try all that hard.

Magnus raised his water goblet and toasted his father, King Gaius Damora of Limeros.

His father's lips thinned.

Irrelevant. It wasn't Magnus's job to ensure this celebration feast went well. It was all a sham anyway. His father was a bully who forced his people to follow his every rule—his favorite weapons were fear and violence, and he had a horde of knights and soldiers to impose his will and keep his subjects in line. He worked very hard to keep up appearances and show himself to be strong, capable, and vastly prosperous.

But Limeros had fallen on hard times in the dozen years since the iron-fisted Gaius, "King of Blood," had taken the throne from his father, the much loved King Davidus. The economic struggles had yet to directly affect anyone living at the palace, given that Limerian religion didn't encourage luxury in the first place, but the tightened straits in the kingdom at large were impossible to ignore. That the king had never addressed this publicly amused Magnus.

Still, the royals were served a portion of *kaana* with their meals—mushed-up yellow beans that tasted like paste—and expected to eat it. It was what many Limerians had been choking down to fill their bellies as the winter dragged on and on.

In addition, some of the more ornate tapestries and paintings had been removed from the castle walls and put into storage, leaving the walls bare and cold. Music was banned, as was singing and dancing. Only the most educational books were allowed within the Limeros palace, nothing that simply told a tale for entertainment's sake. King Gaius cared only for the Limerian ideals of *strength, faith,* and *wisdom*—not art, beauty, or pleasure.

Rumors circulated that Limeros had begun its decline—just as Paelsia had for several generations—due to the death of *elementia*, elemental magic. The essential magic that gave life to the world was drying up completely, much like a body of water in the middle of a desert.

Only traces of *elementia* had been left when the rival goddesses Cleiona and Valoria destroyed each other, centuries ago. But even those traces, whispered those who believed in the magic, were beginning to vanish. Limeros froze over each year, and its spring and summer were now only a couple short months long. Paelsia was withering away, its ground dry and parched. Only southern Auranos showed no outward sign of decay.

Limeros was a devoutly religious land whose people clung to their belief in the goddess Valoria, especially in hard times, but Magnus privately thought those who relied on their belief in the supernatural, in any form it took, showed an inner weakness.

Most of those who believed, anyway. He did make an exception for a precious few. He directed his gaze to the right of his father, where his sister sat dutifully, the guest of honor at this banquet touted as being in celebration of her birthday.

The dress she wore tonight was a pinkish orange shade that made him think of a sunset. It was a new dress, one he'd never seen her in before, and beautifully made, reflecting the image of eternal richness and perfection his father demanded the Damora family show—although even he had to admit he was surprised by how colorful it was in the sea of gray and black his father tended to prefer.

The princess had pale, flawless skin and long, silky, dark hair that, when it wasn't pulled into a tidy twist, fell to her waist in soft waves. Her eyes were the color of the clear blue sky. Her lips were full and naturally rosy. Lucia Eva Damora was the most beautiful girl in all of Limeros. Without a single exception.

Suddenly, the glass goblet in Magnus's tight grip shattered and cut his hand. He swore, then grabbed for a napkin to bind the wound. Lady Sophia and Lord Lenardo looked at him with alarm, as if disturbed that it might have been their conversation of betrothals and murder that had upset him.

It was not.

Stupid, so stupid.

The thought was reflected by the look on his father's face—he hadn't missed a thing. His mother, Queen Althea, seated to the king's left, also took notice. She immediately averted her cool gaze to continue the conversation with the woman seated next to her.

His father didn't look away. He glared at him as if embarrassed to be in the same room. Clumsy, insolent Prince Magnus, the king's heir. *For now, anyway,* Magnus thought sourly, his mind flashing briefly to Tobias, his father's . . . "right-hand man." Magnus wondered if there would ever come a day when his father would approve of him. He supposed he should be grateful the king even bothered to invite him to this event. Then again, he wanted to make it seem as if the royal family of Limeros was a tight-knit and strong unit—now and always.

What a laugh.

Magnus would have already left frigid, colorless Limeros to leisurely explore the other realms that lay across the Silver Sea, but there was one thing that kept him right where he was, even now that he was on the cusp of turning eighteen.

"Magnus!" Lucia had rushed to his side and knelt next to him. Her attention was fully focused on his hand. "You've hurt yourself."

"It's nothing," he said tightly. "Just a scratch."

Blood had already soaked through the meager binding. Her brows drew together with concern. "Just a scratch? I don't think so. Come with me and I'll help bandage it properly."

She pulled at his wrist.

"Go with her," Lady Sophia advised. "You don't want an infection to set in."

"No, wouldn't want that." His jaw set. The pain wasn't enough to bother him, but his embarrassment did sting. "Fine, my sister, the healer. I'll let you patch me up."

She gave him a comforting smile that made something inside him twist. Something he tried very hard to ignore.

Magnus didn't cast another glance at either his father or his mother as he left the banquet hall. Lucia led him into an adjoining room, one that was chillier without the body heat of the banquet guests. Hanging, muted tapestries did little to warm the cold stone walls. A bronze bust of King Gaius glared at him from a tall stand between granite pillars, judging him sternly even though he'd left his father's presence. She asked a palace maid to fetch a basin of water and bandages, then sat him down on a seat next to her and undid the napkin from his wound.

He let her.

"The glass was too fragile," he explained.

She raised an eyebrow. "So it just shattered for no reason at all, did it?"

"Exactly."

She sighed, then dipped a cloth in the water and began to gently clean the wound. Magnus barely noticed the pain anymore. "I know exactly why this happened."

He tensed. "You do?"

"It's Father." Her blue eyes flicked up to meet his. "You're angry with him."

"And you think I imagined his neck in place of the stem of the glass, like many of his subjects might?"

"Did you?" She pressed down firmly on his hand to help stop the flow of blood.

"I'm not angry with him. More like the other way around. He hates me."

"He doesn't hate you. He loves you."

"Then he would be the only one."

A smile lit up her expression. "Oh, Magnus. Don't be silly. I love you. More than anyone else in the whole world. You must know that, don't you?"

It felt as if someone had punched a hole through his chest and taken hold of his heart to squeeze it tightly. He cleared his throat and looked down at his hand. "Of course. And I love you too."

The words felt thick on his tongue. Lies always slid smooth as silk for him, but the truth was never quite so easy.

How he felt for Lucia was only the love of a brother for his sister.

That lie did feel smooth. Even when he told it to himself.

"There," she said, patting the bandage she'd wrapped around his hand. "All better."

"You really should be a healer."

"I don't think our parents would consider that an occupation befitting a princess."

"You're absolutely right. They wouldn't."

Her hand was still on his. "Thank the goddess you weren't hurt worse than this."

"Yes, thank the goddess," he said drily before his lips curved. "Your devotion to Valoria puts my own to shame. Always has."

She looked at him sharply, but her smile remained. "I know you think such strong beliefs in the unseen are silly."

"I'm not sure I'd use the word *silly*."

"Sometimes you need to try to believe in something bigger than yourself, Magnus. Something you can't see or touch. To allow your heart to have faith no matter what. It's what will give you strength in troubled times."

He watched her patiently. "If you say so."

Lucia's smile widened. His pessimism had always amused her. They'd had this discussion many times before. "One day you'll believe. I know you will."

"I believe in you. Isn't that enough?"

"Then I guess I should set a good example for my dear brother." She leaned forward and brushed her lips against his cheek. His breath ceased completely for a moment. "I must return to the banquet. After all, it is supposed to be in my honor. Mother will be angry if I just disappear and never return."

He nodded and touched his bandage. "Thank you for saving my life."

"Hardly. But try to be careful with your temper while around breakable things."

"I'll keep that in mind."

She gave him a last grin and hurried back into the great hall.

Magnus remained where he was for several more minutes, listening to the buzz of conversation from the crowd of nobles at the banquet. He couldn't seem to summon the energy or interest to go back in there. If anyone asked him tomorrow, he'd simply say that loss of blood had made him ill.

He did feel ill. The way he felt about Lucia was wrong. Unnatural. And it was growing by the day even though he fought to ignore it. For a whole year he'd barely been able to look at any other noble girl—now at a time when his father was pressing him to choose a future wife.

Soon the king would likely think that his son's romantic taste was not for girls at all. Quite frankly, Magnus didn't care much what he might think. Even if he did prefer boys, the king would still force him to marry someone of his choosing when his patience wore out.

It would not be Lucia, not even in Magnus's wildest fantasy. Such incestuous unions—even amongst royals—were forbidden by both law and religion. And if Lucia ever learned of the depth of his feelings for her, she'd be disgusted. He didn't want the light in her eyes when she looked at him diminished in any way. That light was the only thing that gave him any joy at all.

Everything else about this made him utterly miserable.

A pretty young maid passed him in the cool, shadowy hall and glanced at him, pausing. She had gray eyes and hair the color of chestnuts, bound into a bun. Her woolen dress was faded but neat and unwrinkled. "Prince Magnus, is there anything I can do for you tonight?"

While his beautiful sister's very presence tortured him, he did allow himself a few meaningless distractions. Amia was extremely useful, in countless ways.

"Not tonight, my sweet."

She moved closer, conspiratorially. "The king left the banquet and is meeting with Lady Mallius right now on the balcony, talking in hushed voices. Interesting, yes?"

"Perhaps."

Amia had proved a useful tool over the last few months to learn tidbits of information. She was Magnus's very willing eyes and ears here in the castle, and she had no qualms about eavesdropping for the prince whenever the opportunity called for it. The occasional kind word or the edge of a smile was enough to keep her loyal and eager to please. Amia believed he would keep her indefinitely as his mistress. In that she was destined to be disappointed. Unless the girl stood directly in front of him as she did right now, he tended to forget she existed.

Magnus patted her on the waist, dismissing her, and silently moved toward the stone balcony that overlooked the black sea and the rocky cliffs on which the castle and the Limeros capital perched. It was his father's favorite spot for reflection, despite the cutting winter chill on nights like this.

"Don't be ridiculous," the king hissed from the balcony. "It has nothing to do with such rumors. You're being superstitious."

"What other explanation could there be?" another familiar voice said. Lady Sabina Mallius, the widow of the king's former advisor. At least, that was her official title. Her unofficial title was the king's mistress, a position she'd held for nearly two decades. The king didn't keep this a secret from anyone, not the queen or his children.

Queen Althea wordlessly tolerated his infidelity. Magnus wasn't entirely sure the cold woman he called his mother cared one way or the other about what her husband did or whom he did it with.

"What other explanation for Limeros's difficulties?" the king said. "Plenty. And none of them are related to magic in any way."

Ah, Magnus thought. *It seems as if the talk of peasants has also become a discussion for kings.*

"You don't know that."

There was a long pause. "I know enough to doubt."

"If any of this strife is based in *elementia*, it means that we weren't wrong. That *I* wasn't wrong. That all these years haven't been a waste as we've waited patiently for a sign."

"You saw the sign years ago. The stars told you what you needed to know."

"My sister saw the signs, not me. But I know she was right."

"It's been sixteen years and nothing has happened. Only endlessly waiting. My disappointment grows with each day that passes."

She sighed. "I wish I knew for sure. All I have is my faith that you must only wait a short time longer."

The king laughed, but there was no humor to the sound. "How long should I wait before I choose to banish you to the forbidden mountains for such deception? Or perhaps I can think of a punishment more suitable to someone like you."

Sabina's voice chilled. "I would advise you never to even consider such a thing."

"Is that a threat?"

"It's a warning, my love. The prophecy holds as true today as it did all those years ago. I still believe. Do you?"

There was a long pause. "I believe. But my patience grows thin.

It won't be long before we've wasted away like Paelsia has and must also begin to live as poor peasants."

"Lucia is now sixteen. The time is drawing closer for her awakening, I know it is."

"Pray that you're right. I'll not take well to continued deception if you're wrong, even from you, Sabina. And you know very well how I deal with disappointment." There wasn't a sliver of warmth in the king's icy tone.

Nor was there in Sabina's. "I am right, my love. And you won't be disappointed."

Magnus pressed up against the cold stone wall behind him so he wouldn't be seen as his father left the balcony. His head was swimming with confusion over what he'd heard. This close to the balcony, his warm breath created frozen clouds in the cold night air. Sabina emerged shortly afterward and began to follow the king back to the banquet hall. But she stopped, tilted her head, then turned to look directly at Magnus.

A chill went down his spine, but he kept his expression neutral.

Sabina's beauty had yet to fade—long, sleek, dark hair, amber-colored eyes. She always dressed in shades of red, luxurious fabrics that hugged the curves of her body and that stood out amidst the more sober colors that most Limerians donned. Magnus had no idea how old a woman she was, nor did he give such issues much thought. She'd been around the palace since he was only an infant and always appeared exactly the same to him—cold, beautiful, timeless. Like a marble statue that lived and breathed, and expected the occasional tiresome conversation.

"Magnus, my sweet boy." A smile spread across her face. Her dark eyes, lined in black kohl, remained distrustful as if she'd guessed he'd been listening.

"Sabina."

"Aren't you enjoying yourself at the banquet?"

"Oh, you know me," he replied drily. "I always enjoy myself."

Her lips curved as her eyes moved over his face. He felt an unpleasant tingle in the scar that traced his cheekbone. "Of course you do."

"If you'll excuse me. I'm retiring for the evening to my chambers." She didn't move, and his eyes narrowed. "Go on, now. Wouldn't want to keep my father waiting."

"No, wouldn't want that. He hates to be disappointed."

He gave her a cold smile. "He does indeed."

Since she showed no signs of moving, Magnus turned from her and began walking leisurely down the hall. He felt her gaze hot on his back.

The conversation he'd overheard echoed in his ears. His father and Sabina had made no sense at all. He'd heard talk of magic and prophesies. And all of it sounded dangerous. What secret did the king and Sabina know about Lucia? What awakening did they speak of? Was it just a silly joke they'd made up to amuse themselves on the event of her birthday? If they'd sounded remotely amused, he might give weight to this theory. But they had not. They sounded tense and concerned and angry.

The same emotions swelled within Magnus's chest. He cared for nothing in the world except Lucia. While the depth of his true feelings could never be revealed, he would do everything he could to protect her from those with the potential to do her harm. And now he put his father, the king—the coldest, deadliest, and most dangerous man he'd ever known—firmly in that category.

CHAPTER 4

THE SANCTUARY

Alexius opened his eyes and took a deep breath of the sweet, warm air. The sun-warmed green grass worked well as his bed, and he pushed himself up into a sitting position. It took him a moment to come back fully into his own body since he'd been traveling without it for quite some time.

He looked down at his hands—skin had replaced feathers. Fingernails had replaced talons. It always took getting used to.

"What did you see?"

Perhaps he would not have as much time as he would like. Alexius craned his neck to look at the one waiting for his return. Timotheus sat nearby on a carved stone bench, his legs crossed, his flowing white cloaks impeccable as always.

"Nothing more than usual," Alexius said, although it was somewhat of a lie. He and the others who traveled from this realm in this manner had agreed to discuss with each other their findings before taking any important information to the elders, who themselves could no longer transform into hawks.

"No clues at all?"

"Of the Kindred themselves? Nothing. There are as hidden today as they were a millennium ago."

Timotheus's jaw clenched. "Our time grows shorter."

"I know." If they did not find the Kindred, the wasting away that the mortal realm was experiencing would soon bleed over into the Sanctuary as well.

The elders were uncertain how to proceed. So many centuries and nothing. No clues. No leads. Even paradise could become a prison if one had enough time to take notice of the walls.

"However, there is a girl," Alexius said a bit reluctantly.

This captured Timotheus's attention. "A girl?"

"She could be the one we've waited for. She has only now turned sixteen mortal years. I felt something from her—something is emerging that goes beyond anything I've sensed before."

"Magic?"

"I believe so."

"Who is she? Where is she?"

Alexius hesitated. Despite his agreement with the others, he was duty bound to tell the elders what they wished to know—and he trusted Timotheus. But something about this felt fragile, like a small seedling that hadn't yet taken root. If he was wrong, it would make him look a fool to raise an alarm. But if he was right, then the girl was incredibly precious and had to be treated gently.

"Leave it to me to learn more," Alexius said instead. "I will keep watch over her and report back anything I see. This means I must abandon my search for the Kindred."

"The others will focus on that." Timotheus's brow raised. "Yes, keep watch over this girl whose identity you wish to protect from me."

Alexius looked at him sharply. "I know you mean her no harm. Why would I wish to protect her from you?"

"This is a good question." A small smile touched the elder's lips. "Do you wish to leave the Sanctuary entirely to go to her side or continue to watch from afar?"

Alexius knew several who had become deeply enamored of the world of mortals and of those they watched, but to leave the Sanctuary meant one could never return.

"I'll stay right where I am," he said. "Why would I wish for anything other than to be here?"

"That is what your sister once said."

His heart gave a sharp twist. "She made a mistake."

"Perhaps. Do you ever visit her?"

"No. She made her choice. I don't need to witness the result. I prefer to remember her as she was—young forever. She would be an old woman now, fading away just as the land she loved more than this one fades away with only her precious seeds to keep her company."

With that, Alexius laid his head back against the soft, warm grass, closed his eyes, and transformed, returning by air to the cold and unforgiving world of mortals.

CHAPTER 5

AURANOS

"The birds are watching me," Cleo said as she paced back and forth in the palace courtyard.

"Really?" Emilia repressed a smile as she added another stroke of paint to her canvas. It was an image of the Auranos palace, well known for its façade of gold set into polished stone, which made it appear like a glittering jewel upon the lush green land that surrounded it. "Is my little sister paranoid or is she beginning to believe in old legends?"

"Maybe both." Cleo's citron-colored skirts swished as she shifted direction and pointed to the corner of the grassy enclosure. "But I swear that white dove in the peach tree has studied every move I've made since I came out here."

Emilia laughed and shared an amused look with Mira, who sat nearby working on her embroidery. "The Watchers are said to see through the eyes of hawks, not just any random bird."

A long-eared squirrel scurried up the tree trunk. The bird finally flew away. "If you say so. You're the expert on religion and myth in our family."

"Only because *you* refuse to study," Mira pointed out.

Cleo stuck her tongue out at her friend. "I have better things to do with my time than read."

For the last week, those "better things" had included much fretting and worrying while awake and nightmares while asleep. Even if she wanted to read, her eyes were bloodshot and sore.

Emilia finally put down her paintbrush to give Cleo her full attention. "We should go back inside, where you'll be safe from the beady eyes of spying birds."

"You can make fun of me as much as you like, sister, but I can't help how I feel."

"Indeed. Perhaps it's guilt over what happened in Paelsia that makes you feel this way."

Nausea welled within her. She turned her face up toward the sun, so very different from the coldness in Paelsia that had sunk down to her bones. The entire trip home she had shivered, unable to get warm. The chill had stayed with her for days afterward, even once she returned to the warmth of home. "Ridiculous," she lied. "I've already forgotten it."

"Do you know that is what Father is meeting with his council about today?"

"About what?"

"About . . . well, you. And Aron. And everything that happened that day."

Cleo felt the blood drain from her face. "What are they saying?"

"Nothing to be concerned with."

"If I wasn't to be concerned, you wouldn't have brought the subject up at all, would you?"

Emilia swung her legs around and rose from her chair. She

steadied herself for a moment and Mira looked up, concerned, and put down her needlework to come to her side. Emilia had been having some difficulty with headaches and dizziness the last couple of weeks.

"Tell me what you know," Cleo urged, watching Emilia worriedly.

"The death of the wine seller's son has apparently caused some political difficulties for Father. It's become a bit of a scandal, really. Everyone's talking about it and placing blame in various places. He's doing his best to ease any ill feelings this has raised. Even though Auranos imports a great deal of Paelsian wine, export of it has all but shut down until the crisis eases off. Many Paelsians refuse to deal with us. They're angry with us—and with Father for letting this happen. Of course, they're blowing everything completely out of proportion."

"It's all so horrible," Mira exclaimed. "I wish I could forget it ever happened."

That made two of them. Cleo wrung her hands, her dismay mirrored on Mira's face. "And how long will it take before everything goes back to normal?"

"I honestly don't know," Emilia replied.

Cleo despised politics mainly because she didn't understand them. But then, she didn't have to. Emilia was the heir to their father's throne. She would be the next queen, not Cleo.

Thank the goddess for that. There was no way that Cleo could deal with endless council meetings and being cordial and polite to those who hadn't earned it. Emilia had been raised from birth to be a perfect princess who could deal with any issues that arose. Cleo . . . well, she enjoyed sunning herself, taking her horse out for long rides in the countryside, and spending time with her friends.

She'd never been associated with such a scandal yet. Apart from the secret Aron kept, there was nothing scandalous anyone could say about Princess Cleiona. Until now, she realized anxiously.

"I need to talk to Father," Cleo said. "To find out what's going on."

Without another word spoken, she left Emilia and Mira in the courtyard and entered the castle, hurrying through the well-lit hallways until she came to the council room. Through the arched doorway, sunlight shone through the many windows, their wooden shutters wide open. A fire in the hearth also lent light to the large room. She had to wait until they were finished and all filed out before her father was alone. She paced outside the room, bristling with energy. Patience was a gift Cleo had never received.

Once everyone had left, she burst inside to find her father still seated at the head of a long, polished wooden table large enough to seat a hundred men. Cleo's great-grandfather had commissioned it from the wood of olive trees that grew outside the palace walls. A wide colorful tapestry hung on the far wall, detailing the history of Auranos. Cleo had spent many hours as a child staring at it in awe and admiring the great artwork of it. On the opposite wall was the Bellos family crest and one of many bright, sparkling mosaics depicting the Goddess Cleiona, for whom Cleo had been named.

"What's going on?" Cleo demanded.

Her father looked up at her from a stack of scrolls and paperwork. He was dressed casually, in leathers and a finely knit tunic. His neatly groomed brown beard was threaded with gray. Some said Cleo and her father's eyes were the exact same color of vivid blue-green, while her sister, Emilia, had inherited their late mother's brown ones. Both Emilia and Cleo, however, had been born with their mother's fair hair, unusual in Auranos, where the people tended to be darker-complected from the sun. Queen Elena had been the daughter of a wealthy landowner in the eastern hills of Auranos before King Corvin had seen and fallen in love with her on his coronation tour more than two decades before. Family lore had it that Elena's ancestors had emigrated from across the Silver Sea.

"Were your ears burning, daughter?" he asked. "Or did Emilia tell you of current events?"

"What difference does it make? If it concerns me, then I should be told. So tell me!"

He held her gaze easily, unmoved by her demands. The fiery nature of his youngest daughter was nothing new to him and he weathered it as he always did. Why wouldn't he? Cleo never caused more of a fuss than a few words spilled. She would grumble and rant but then swiftly forget about whatever troubled her as her attention caught on something else. The king recently compared her to a hummingbird flitting from flower to flower. She hadn't taken this as a compliment.

"Your trip to Paelsia last week is a topic of contention, Cleo. A growing one, I'm afraid."

Fear and guilt immediately crashed over her. Until today, she didn't realize he even knew about it. Except for unburdening herself to Emilia, she hadn't said a word about it from the moment she stepped on the ship in the Paelsia harbor. She'd hoped to put the murder of the wine seller's son out of her mind, but it hadn't worked very well. She relived it every night when she closed her eyes and fell asleep. Also, the murderous glare of the boy's brother—Jonas—as he threatened her life before she, Aron, and Mira ran away haunted her.

"Apologies." The words caught in her throat. "I didn't mean for any of this to happen."

"I believe you. But it seems as if trouble follows you wherever you go."

"Are you going to punish me?"

"Not precisely. However, these recent difficulties have made me decide that you will stay here at the palace from this day forward. I won't allow you to take my ship again on your explorations until further notice."

Despite her shame over the events in Paelsia, the very idea of this grounding made her bristle. "I can't just be expected to never leave, like some sort of prisoner."

"What happened is not acceptable, Cleo."

Her throat tightened. "Don't you think I feel horrible about it?"

"I'm sure you do. But it changes nothing."

"It shouldn't have happened."

"But it did. You shouldn't have been there at all. Paelsia is no place for a princess. It's too dangerous."

"But Aron—"

"Aron." Her father's eyes flashed. "He's the one who killed the peasant, correct?"

Aron's violent and unexpected turn in the market surprised even Cleo. Even though she harbored distrust for the boy, she was dismayed by his lack of guilt.

"He was," she confirmed.

The king was quiet for a long moment as Cleo held her breath, fearful of what he would say next.

"Thank the goddess he was there to protect you," he finally said. "I've never trusted the Paelsians and have encouraged the dissolution of trade between our nations. They're an unpredictable and savage people—quick to violence. I'd always admired

Lord Aron and his family, but this recent turn of events has confirmed that for me. I'm very proud of him, as I'm sure his father is too."

Cleo had to bite her tongue to keep from saying anything that might contradict her father's opinion.

"Still," the king continued, "I'm not happy that this unfortunate altercation happened in the midst of a large crowd. When you leave this palace, when you leave this kingdom, you must always remember that you are a representative of Auranos. I've been informed there is some unpleasantness now brewing in Paelsia. They're not happy with us right now, even less so than usual. They're already jealous of our resources while they've allowed their own to waste away to next to nothing. Of course, they'd see the murder of one of their own—no matter how it came about—as a statement of Auranian superiority."

Cleo swallowed hard. "A—a statement?"

He waved a hand dismissively. "It will blow over. Auranians must be very careful when traveling through Paelsia. Such poverty and desperation inevitably leads to robbery, mugging, assault . . ." His face tightened. "It's a dangerous place. And you are never to go there again for any reason."

"Not that I want to, believe me, but . . . never?"

"Never."

Overprotective, as usual. Cleo restrained herself from arguing. Much as she hated the idea that Aron had come out looking like a hero to the king for killing Tomas Agallon, she knew when to stop talking so she wouldn't get herself into any further trouble.

"I understand," she said instead.

He nodded and shifted through some of the papers before him. His next words struck her cold. "I've decided to announce your official engagement to Lord Aron very soon. It will clearly show that he killed the boy to protect you—his future bride."

She stared at him with horror. "What?"

"Do you have a problem with that?" There was something in the king's gaze that betrayed his otherwise casual manner this afternoon. Something restrained below the surface. Cleo's words of protest died on her lips. There was no way her father could know about her secret . . . could he?

Cleo forced a smile. "Of course, Father. Whatever you say." She would figure out a way to change his mind when things had blown over—and when she'd established for sure that he had no knowledge of that night. If he ever found out what she'd done, Cleo knew she would never be able to bear it.

He nodded. "Good girl."

She turned toward the archway, hoping to make a quick escape.

"One more thing, Cleo."

She froze and slowly turned back around. "Yes?"

"I'm assigning a full-time bodyguard to you, one whose main job is to keep my youngest daughter out of any future trouble."

Her horror intensified. "But there's no trouble here in Auranos. If I promise not to go back to Paelsia, what's the problem?"

"Peace of mind for your father, my darling. And, no, this is not negotiable. I'm appointing Theon Ranus to the job. I expect him here soon so I can inform him of his new position."

Theon. The guard who'd accompanied her to Paelsia. As handsome as she'd found him, that paled in comparison to the thought that he'd be around her at all hours of the day. No matter where she went. Leaving her no privacy or time to herself.

She looked at her father to see a very small glint of amusement now in his eyes. This, she realized, was part of her punishment for dragging Auranos's name through the mud and straining relations between the lands. She forced herself to remain calm and bowed her head slightly. "As you wish, Father."

"Very good. I knew you could be every bit as agreeable as your sister if you try hard enough."

Cleo was certain that Emilia had simply learned over the years to hold her tongue when it came to dealing with their father in order to be the perfect princess. Cleo wasn't that perfect. Nor had she ever wanted to be.

It was clear to her what she had to do. As soon as Theon presented himself to her for his newfound duty, she would simply relieve him of that duty. He could do what he wanted and she would do the same. The king, who usually only saw her at meals, would never know the difference.

Simple.

Her upcoming engagement to Aron was more of a problem. After what had happened in Paelsia, and Aron's ridiculously vain and selfish behavior during the trip back home when all he seemed concerned with was the fact he'd lost his precious dagger in the wine seller's son's throat and hadn't acquired any wine for his efforts, she'd decided that there was no way she would ever want to associate with him again, let alone *marry* him.

Not negotiable, indeed. Her father couldn't force her to do this.

What was she thinking? Of *course* he could force her to marry someone she didn't want to. He was the king! Nobody said no to the king, not even a princess.

She rushed away from the council room, through the courtyard, up a flight of stairs, and down a hall into an open corridor before she let out a harsh scream of frustration.

"Ouch. You have absolutely no consideration for my eardrums, do you, princess?"

Cleo spun around in shock, heart pounding—she'd thought she was alone. She let out a long sigh of relief to see who it was. And then she promptly burst into tears.

Nicolo Cassian leaned against the smooth marble wall, his arms crossed over his chest. The curious expression on his thin face fell and his brows drew together.

"Oh, no. Don't cry. Tears are not something I can deal with."

"My—my father is cruel and unfair," she sobbed, then collapsed into his arms. He gently patted her back.

"The cruelest ever. There has never been a crueler father than King Corvin. If he wasn't king, and if I wasn't his squire who had to follow his every order, I would strike him down, just for you."

Nic was the older brother of Mira. Only a year separated the siblings, making Nic seventeen. Where Mira's hair was dark with streaks of sun-kissed red, her figure warmly voluptuous, Nic's hair was unusual for Auranos: the color of a carrot, sticking up in every direction. His face was more gawky, sharp angles, and with a nose that tilted slightly to the left. And his skin was covered in freckles that only intensified the more time he spent outside in the sun. She could easily wrap her arms all the way around his waist as she buried her head in his chest and her tears sank into his wool tunic.

Nic and Mira had been the children of Sir Rogerus Cassian, a close friend of the king's who had died, alongside his wife, in a boating accident seven years ago. The king had given the orphaned children official positions at the palace, allowing them to live there and take meals side by side with him, Cleo, and Emilia and to be educated by the palace tutors. While Mira was the lady-in-waiting to Emilia, Nic had proved himself a very useful squire to the king himself—a position envied by many.

If Mira was Cleo's closest friend, then Nic was Cleo's closest friend who was a *boy*. She felt more comfortable in his company than anyone except her sister's—even Mira's, if she was being honest. And this was not the first time, nor did she think it would be the last, that she would cry on his shoulder.

"My kingdom for a handkerchief," he murmured. "There, there, Cleo. What's wrong?"

"My father plans to announce my engagement to Aron soon." Her breath hitched. "Officially!"

He grimaced. "Now I see why you're so upset. An engagement to a handsome lord. How horrible that must be for you."

She slapped his shoulder and tried not to laugh in the midst of her tears. "Stop it. You know I don't want to marry him."

"I know. But an engagement does not equal a marriage."

"Not yet."

He shrugged. "I suppose I might have a simple solution for you if you're really so upset about this."

She looked at him eagerly. "What?"

He raised an eyebrow. "Tell your father that you're madly in love with me and that you refuse to marry anyone else. And if he causes a problem, threaten to run away with me and elope."

This finally coaxed a true smile from her and she hugged him again. "Oh, Nic. I should have known you'd be able to cheer me up."

"Is that a yes?"

Cleo gazed up into his familiar face with a grin. "Stop being silly. As if you'd even have me. We're too good of friends to consider each other anything else."

He shrugged a bony shoulder. "Can't blame me for trying."

She let out a shaky sigh. "Besides, my father would have a fit at the very suggestion of it. You're not exactly royal."

"As unroyal as they come, actually." He gave her a lopsided grin. "And damn proud of it. You royals are such a stuffy bunch. Mira, however, wishes she was born royal every waking hour."

"Your sister is a handful."

"We'd better make sure she marries a man with large enough hands to deal with her."

"Does he exist?"

"I sincerely doubt it."

She heard footsteps coming toward them, heavy on the marble floors.

"Your highness." It was Theon, dressed in his stiff blue uniform, his expression dour. "The king sent me to find you."

She let out a long shaky sigh. *And so it begins.*

Nic looked between them. "Is there a problem?"

"This is Theon Ranus," she said. There was a tight look on his face right now that wasn't quite the same as the arrogant one she'd seen the other day in Paelsia. "Theon, you don't look very happy. Did my father ask you to do something that doesn't agree with you?"

The young guard kept his dark eyes straight forward. "I obey any command the king gives me."

"I see. And what did he want of you this time?" she asked knowingly.

Theon's jaw tensed. "He assigned me as your personal bodyguard."

"Hmm. How do you feel about that?"

"I feel . . . *honored.*" He gritted this out.

"Bodyguard?" Nic's eyebrows went up. "Why would you need a bodyguard?"

"My father feels that I will stay out of trouble if I have a full-time guard assigned to protect me. He means to stop me from having any fun."

"A death threat *was* uttered by the peasant's brother," Theon pointed out.

Cleo's stomach clenched at the memory, but she waved a hand. "I'm not afraid of him now that I'm back here. He'd never get past the palace walls."

"Well, this is amusing," Nic said. "A bodyguard. Even here at the palace."

"It's ridiculous and totally unnecessary," Cleo exclaimed. "Besides, Theon told me his career goal was to become my father's bodyguard, yet now he's been assigned to look after *me* instead. That must be incredibly disappointing for someone with such ambition, don't you think?"

"Utterly disappointing," Nic confirmed sympathetically, looking at Theon.

Theon's expression tensed, but he said nothing.

Cleo continued. "He'll have to watch over me when I'm out lounging in the sun. When I'm having a dress fitted. When I'm taking an art class. When a maid is braiding my hair. I'm sure he'll find this all incredibly fascinating."

"If he watches close enough, maybe he can help braid," Nic said lightly.

It looked as if every word twisted into Theon like a knife in his back.

"Does that sound fun to you, Theon?" she teased. "To accompany me on my many excursions and local adventures . . . for the rest of my life?"

He met her gaze and it stopped her dead in her tracks. She

expected distaste, but there was something else there. Something darker, yet slightly intrigued.

"As the king wishes, I obey," he said evenly.

"Will you obey *me*?"

"Within reason."

"What does that mean?" Nic asked.

His dark eyes shot to the redheaded boy. "It means that if the princess puts herself into harm's way, I'll intervene without a second thought. I won't have another incident like last week. That murder could have been avoided if I'd been given the chance to stop it."

Guilt had taken up a permanent place inside Cleo, burrowing deep into her heart. She dropped all teasing. "Aron never should have killed that boy."

He glared at her. "Good to know that we agree on something."

She held his intense gaze, wishing very hard that she didn't find this inconvenient guard so fascinating. But the look in his eyes—that challenging glare . . .

No guard had ever looked at her with such boldness. In fact, no one at all had ever looked at her this way. Angry and fierce and vastly unfriendly . . . but there was something else there. As if Cleo was the only girl in the entire world and now he owned a part of her.

"My, my." Nic's voice cut into her thoughts. "Perhaps you'd like me to leave the two of you alone so you can continue to stare at each other all day long?"

Heat came to her cheeks and she tore her gaze away from Theon. "Don't be ridiculous."

Nic laughed, but it wasn't filled with amusement like before. It was much drier and less pleasant this time. He leaned forward and whispered so Theon couldn't hear. "Just keep one thing in mind as you embark on this arrangement with your new bodyguard . . ."

She looked at him sharply. "What's that?"

He held her gaze. "He's not royal either."

CHAPTER 6

PAELSIA

Jonas had cleaned the dagger's blade twice, but it was as if he could still see his brother's blood on it. He tucked it into the leather sheath at his hip and surveyed the border between Paelsia and Auranos, a thick tangle of forest known as the Wildlands that only the bravest—or most unwise—would consider traversing. Travel between the three lands was conducted along the western shore by ship, rarely with exception. It was the "civilized" way of travel.

Despite its intrinsic dangers—sharp-toothed carniverous animals, brutal terrain, and thieves and murderers who'd taken to the forest to hide, to name but a few—the border was monitored. Auranian guards were assigned to keep watch over it from the Silver Sea in the west and across to the mountains in the east. Stealthy guards, since they couldn't easily be seen—unless you knew what to look for.

Jonas knew. He'd been taught by the best—by Tomas. The first time he'd ever come close to this dangerous area was when he was only ten years old, his brother fourteen. Tomas had a secret, one he'd never shared with anyone until he decided to share it with his younger brother. He braved the forest and the grassy fields beyond to poach from their neighbors. It was a crime with an immediate death sentence if they were ever caught, but he'd thought it was worth it to keep their family healthy and alive. Jonas agreed.

Paelsia was once a land of gardens, lush forests, and hundreds of rivers filled with fish, a land filled to overflowing with wild animals to hunt. That had begun to change three generations ago. Slowly, from the snow-capped mountains in the east and across toward the ocean in the west, Paelsia had become less fertile, less able to sustain life. It all began to die, leaving behind brown grass, gray rock, and death. A wasteland. Closer to the sea, it improved, but by now only a quarter of the land was able to sustain life as it once had.

However, thanks to Auranos, what fertile soil was left was now used to plant vineyards so they could sell wine cheaply to their southern neighbor and drink themselves into a stupor rather than plant crops that could feed those who lived here. To Jonas, wine had become a symbol of the oppression of Paelsians. A symbol of the *stupidity* of Paelsians. And instead of refusing to accept this and beginning a search for a solution, they lived day to day with a weary sense of acceptance.

Many believed that their leader, Chief Basilius, would eventually summon the magic to save them all. The most devoted of his subjects believed him to be a sorcerer, and they worshipped him like a god bound to this world by flesh and blood. He took three-quarters of the wine profits as a tax. His people gave it over freely, solid in their belief that he would soon summon his magic to save them all.

Naive, Jonas thought, enraged. *So unforgivably naive.*

Tomas, on the other hand, hadn't believed in such nonsense as magic. While he'd respected the chief's position as leader, he believed only in the cold, hard facts of life. He had no problem regularly poaching from Auranos. He would have been more than happy to poach from Limeros as well, but the rocky terrains, wide moors, and frigid temperatures their northern neighbors had to offer weren't as conducive to wildlife as the temperate climate and grassy valleys of Auranos.

Jonas had been amazed when Tomas first snuck him across the border into Auranos. A white-tailed deer had practically walked right up and presented its throat to the boys' blades as if welcoming them into the prosperous kingdom. When the boys disappeared for a week at a time and returned laden with food, their father, unquestioning then as now, assumed they'd found a secret bounty of hunting in Paelsia, and they never told him otherwise. While the old man preferred them to work long hours in the vineyards, he allowed them their frequent journeys without argument.

"One day," Tomas had said to him while they stood in this very spot just before they crossed the border, *"everybody in Paelsia will get to experience the beauty and abundance Auranians get every day of their spoiled lives. We'll take it for ourselves."*

Jonas's eyes burned at the memory. Grief clawed at his throat. It had barely let go for a moment since the murder.

I wish you were here right now, Tomas. So much.

His hand brushed against the hilt of the knife used by Lord Aron to stab his brother in the throat. All while a cold, beautiful princess watched on with amusement.

That princess had quickly become Jonas's obsession—his hatred for her burned brighter with each day that passed. After he finished with Lord Aron, Jonas fully planned to use the very same blade to slowly kill her as well.

"This was meant to be," his father had said as the funeral flames for Tomas lit up the dark sky.

"It was not," Jonas gritted out through clenched teeth.

"There's no other way to see it. To bear it. It was his destiny."

"A crime was committed, Father. A murder at the hands of the same royals you would still sell your wine to in a heartbeat. And no one will pay for this. Tomas died in vain and all you can talk about is destiny?"

With the heart-wrenching image of his beloved brother's spiritless shell branded forever into his memory, Jonas moved away from the crowd who'd gathered to be a part of the funeral ritual. He met his sister's glassy eyes as they passed.

"You know what you have to do," Felicia whispered fiercely. *"Avenge him."*

And so here he was. A predator prepared to hunt an entirely different kind of prey.

"You look very serious." A voice spoke to him from the shadows.

Every muscle in his body tensed. He turned to his right, but before he could reach for his weapon, he was met with a fist slamming into his gut. He staggered back, gasping for breath. A body slammed into his and took him down hard to the damp, mossy ground.

A sharp blade pressed against his throat before he could summon the energy to get back to his feet. He stopped breathing and stared up into a pair of dark eyes.

A mouth twisted with amusement. "Dead. Just like that. See how easy it would be?"

"Get off me," Jonas gritted out.

The blade lifted from his throat. He shoved at the figure on top of him, which finally shifted back with a low rumble of laughter.

"Idiot. You think you could just disappear and nobody would notice you're gone?"

Jonas glared at his best friend. Brion Radenos. "I didn't invite you to come along."

Brion ran a hand through his messy black hair. His teeth flashed white. "I took the liberty of tracking you. You leave a substantial trail. Made it easy."

"I'm surprised I didn't notice you." Jonas brushed off his shirt, now ripped and dirtier than it had been to begin with. "You stink like a bastard pig."

"You were never the best when it came to insults. Personally, I take that as a compliment." Brion sniffed the air. "You aren't exactly the freshest flower in the valley right now either. Any border guard would be able to smell you when you got within fifty feet of him. Same goes for any hungry beastie looking for its next meal."

Jonas glowered. "Mind your own business, Brion."

"My friend running off to get himself slaughtered is my business."

"No, it isn't."

"You can argue with me all day and night if it'll keep you from entering this kingdom."

"Wouldn't be the first time I've entered this kingdom."

"But it would be the last. You think I don't know what you're planning?" He shook his head. "I'll say it again. Idiot."

"I'm not an idiot."

"You want to march into the Auranian palace and kill two royals. To me, that's the plan of an idiot."

"Both of them deserve to die," he growled.

"Not like this."

"You weren't there. You didn't see what happened to Tomas."

"No, but I've heard enough stories. I've seen your grief." Brion exhaled slowly, studying his friend. "I know how you think, Jonas. How you feel. I lost my own brother, remember?"

"Your brother slipped off a cliff when he was drunk and fell to his death. It's not nearly the same thing."

Brion flinched at the reminder of his brother's shortcomings, and Jonas had the grace to wince that he'd been low enough to bring up such a sore subject. "The loss of a brother is painful, no matter how he meets his end," Brion said after a moment. "And so is the loss of a friend."

"I can't let this stand, Brion. Any of it. I can't make peace with it." Jonas gazed across the open field beyond the thick, wild forest separating the two lands. By foot, the palace was still a full day's journey from here. He was an excellent climber. He planned to scale the palace walls. He'd never seen the palace itself, but he'd heard many tales about it. During the last war between the lands, nearly a century ago, the Auranian king of the day had built a glittering marble wall around the entire royal grounds, which contained the castle and the villas of important Auranian citizens. Some said an entire square mile was contained within these walls—a city unto itself. Part of such a large wall would be unguarded, especially since it had been so long since there was any substantial threat to worry about.

"You think you can kill the lord?" Brion asked.

"Easily."

"And the princess too? You think slitting a girl's throat will be that easy for you?"

Jonas met his gaze in the darkness. "She's a symbol of the rich scum that laugh at us and shove our noses in our poverty and dying land. Her assassination will be a message to King Corvin that this is unacceptable. Tomas always wanted a revolution between our kingdoms. Maybe this'll do the trick."

Brion shook his head. "You might be a hunter, but you're not a murderer, Jonas."

He turned away from Brion when his eyes began to sting. He wouldn't let himself cry in front of his friend. He wouldn't show weakness like that to anyone ever again. That alone would be the ultimate defeat.

"Something must be done."

"I agree. But there's another way. You need to think with your head, not only your heart."

He couldn't help but snort softly at that. "You think I'm using my heart right now?"

Brion rolled his eyes. "Yes. And in case there's any doubt, your heart is an idiot just like the rest of you. Would Tomas want you to run off to Auranos and stick daggers in royals even if he was a budding revolutionary?"

"Maybe."

Brion cocked his head. "Really?"

Jonas frowned and an image of his brother flickered in his mind. "No," he admitted finally. "He wouldn't. He'd think I was being a suicidal jackass."

"Not much better than getting drunk to forget your many woes and falling off a cliff, is it?"

Jonas let out a long, shaky breath. "He was so arrogant. *Lord Aron Lagaris.* Told us his name as if we should sink to our knees before him, like the meaningless peasants we are, and kiss his ring."

"I'm not saying the bastard shouldn't pay with blood. Just not with *your* blood." A muscle in Brion's cheek twitched at the mention of this.

While he was being incredibly levelheaded, apart from the takedown a minute ago, Brion wasn't typically the wisest of Jonas's friends nor the one expected to give advice. He was usually the first to jump into a fight that left at least one bone broken—either his or his opponent's. A scar bisected his right eyebrow as a mild reminder of one of these battles. Unlike most of his compatriots, Brion wasn't one to lie down and accept a "destiny" of oppression and starvation.

"Do you remember Tomas's plan?" Jonas said after silence fell between them.

"Which one? He had lots of plans."

That made Jonas smile for a moment. "He did. But one of them was to seek audience with Chief Basilius."

Brion's eyebrows went up. "Are you serious? Nobody sees the chief. The chief sees you."

"I know." Chief Basilius had been in seclusion for several years, unseen by any but his family and his innermost circle of advisors and bodyguards. Some said he spent his days on a spiritual journey to find the Kindred—four legendary objects containing endless magic that had been lost for a thousand years.

Jonas, however, like Tomas, reserved his belief for more practical answers. Thinking of Tomas now, he came to a decision and shifted his plans.

"I need to see him," Jonas murmured. "I need to do what Tomas wanted to do. Things need to change."

Brion looked at him with surprise. "So in two minutes you've gone from single-minded vengeance to potentially seeking audience with the chief."

"You could put it that way." Killing the royals, Jonas was realizing soberly, would have been a glorious moment of vengeance—a blaze of glory. But it would do nothing to help his people chart a new course for a brighter future. *That* was what Tomas would have wanted above all else.

Jonas didn't believe that Basilius was a sorcerer, but he had no doubt the chief was powerful and influential enough to make a change, to help take the people of Paelsia in a new direction and away from the growing poverty and desperation that had crippled them in recent years. *If* he chose to do so.

Since he lived apart from the community as a whole, maybe he was unaware of how dire Paelsian life had become. He had to be told the truth by someone who wouldn't be afraid to speak it.

"You suddenly look very determined," Brion said uneasily. "Should that make me nervous?"

Jonas grabbed his arm and flashed the first full grin he'd been able to summon since Tomas had died. "I am determined. Things are going to change, my friend."

"Now?"

"Yes, now. When better?"

"So, no more storming the palace and sticking daggers into royals?"

"Not today." Jonas could practically see Tomas at the corner of his mind, laughing at his younger brother and his constantly changing priorities. But this felt right. This felt more right than anything else in his life ever had. "Will you come with me to meet with Chief Basilius?"

"And miss witnessing his order for your head to be removed and placed on a spike for trying to incite a revolution in your brother's name?" Brion laughed. "Not for all the gold in Auranos."

CHAPTER 7

AURANOS

Tomas reached out to Cleo as if begging her to help him. He tried to speak, but he couldn't—the blade was lodged too deeply in his throat. He would never speak another word. The blood that gushed unstoppably from his mouth grew deep around them and swiftly formed a bottomless crimson lake.

Cleo was drowning in blood. It washed over her, coating her skin, choking her.

"Please, help! Help!" She struggled to reach up into the freezing air above the thick, hot blood.

A hand grasped hold of hers tightly to pull her above the surface.

"Thank you!"

"Don't thank me, princess. Beg me not to kill you."

Her eyes widened as she looked up into the face of the murdered boy's brother. Jonas Agallon's features were deeply etched with grief and hatred. Dark brows drew together over mahogany-colored eyes.

"Beg me," he said again, digging his fingers painfully into her flesh, hard enough to bruise.

"Please don't kill me! I—I'm sorry—I didn't want your brother to die. Please don't hurt me!"

"But I want to hurt you. I want you to suffer for what you've done." He shoved her back down. She shrieked as the murdered boy himself took hold of her ankle and began pulling her deeper into this ocean of death.

Cleo sat up in her bed screaming. She was twisted in her silk sheets, her body damp with sweat, her heart pounding loud in her ears. She looked frantically around the room from her canopied bed.

She was alone. She had only been dreaming.

The same nightmare had plagued her every night for a month. Ever since Tomas Agallon's murder. So vivid. So real. But just a dream fueled by endless guilt. She let out a long, shaky sigh and fell back against her silk pillows.

"This is madness," she whispered. "It's done. It's over. There's no going back to change it."

If there was a chance for that, she would have told Theon to step in and stop Aron's bartering. His posturing. His arrogance. She would have put an end to it before it escalated in such a horrible, deadly way.

She'd avoided Aron ever since they returned to Auranos. If he showed up at a social gathering, she would leave. If he moved closer to talk, she would shift her attention to a different group of friends. He hadn't protested yet, but she knew it was only a matter of time.

Aron liked to be included in her circle whenever possible. And if he threatened to expose her secret because of any perceived slight . . .

She squeezed her eyes shut and tried not to panic at the thought.

After a full month of avoidance, Cleo knew she had to talk to Aron. She found she needed to know if he too had nightmares about what happened. If he felt the same guilt. If she was to become engaged to this boy at her father's insistence, she needed to know that he wasn't a monster who'd cold-bloodedly kill someone and not give a single care for the pain he'd caused.

If Aron was wracked with guilt, it might change things for her. Perhaps he, like she, was deeply pained over his actions and attempting to hide his true feelings from the world. They would have this in common. If nothing else, it would be a start. She resolved to speak with him in private as soon as possible.

Yet she still spent the remainder of the night tossing and turning.

In the morning, Cleo rose, dressed, and breakfasted on fruit, soft cheese, and bread delivered to her chambers by a palace maid. Then she took a deep breath and opened her door.

"Good morning, princess," Theon said. He typically waited down the hall from her room in the mornings, ready to do his bodyguard duties—which included lurking about all day long in her peripheral vision.

"Morning," she replied as casually as possible.

She'd need to give her shadow the slip if she wanted to talk to Aron privately. Luckily, she knew this wasn't impossible. In the weeks since Theon's new placement she'd tested him a few times to see if she could successfully hide from him. It became a bit of a game that she often won. Theon, however, didn't think it was very amusing.

"I need to see my sister," she said firmly.

Theon nodded. "By all means. Don't let me stop you."

She moved through the hall, surprised when she turned the next corner to see Mira heading her way. Her friend looked upset and distracted. There was no immediate smile on Mira's round, pretty face at the sight of the princess like there normally was.

"What's wrong?" Cleo asked, clasping the girl's arm.

"Nothing, I'm sure. But I'm off to get a healer to attend Emilia."

Cleo frowned. "Is she still sick?"

"Her headaches and dizziness seem to worsen every day. She insists all she needs is more sleep, but I think it's for the best that someone looks at her."

Concern swelled in Cleo's chest. "Of course. Thank you, Mira."

Mira nodded, and with a glance at Theon standing nearby she continued down the hall.

"My sister," Cleo said under her breath. "Never one to accept help unless it's forced upon her. Duty above all. Just like a proper princess should be. My father would be so proud."

"She sounds very brave," Theon responded.

"Perhaps. But they call me the stubborn one. If I was feeling dizzy all the time, I'd want a dozen healers called to my bedside to make it stop." She paused at the door to Emilia's chambers. "Please let me speak privately to my sister."

"Of course. I'll wait right here."

She entered Emilia's bedchamber and closed the door behind her. Her sister stood on her open balcony, looking down at the gardens below. The morning sun brushed against her high cheek-bones and picked up glints of gold in her hair, which was a few shades darker than Cleo's since Emilia wasn't so given to spending time outdoors. She glanced over her shoulder.

"Good morning, Cleo."

"I hear you're unwell."

Emilia sighed, but a smile touched her lips. "I assure you I'm fine."

"Mira is worried."

"Mira is always worried."

"You might have a point." Mira did tend to exaggerate things, Cleo remembered, like the time she'd hysterically insisted there was a viper in her bedroom and it turned out to be a harmless garden snake. Cleo relaxed slightly. Besides, Emilia *looked* perfectly healthy.

Emilia studied her sister's face as she glanced toward the door. "You look rather conspiratorial this morning. Are you up to some sort of mischief?"

Cleo couldn't help but smile. "Maybe a little."

"Of what sort?"

"Escape." She glanced out the window. "Using your trellis like we used to."

"Really. May I ask why?" Emilia didn't seem surprised by this admission at all. She'd been the one who'd taught Cleo how to climb down to the gardens when they'd been much younger— back before Emilia had started shifting into a much more poised and perfect princess. Back when she didn't mind getting dirty or her knees skinned with her younger sister. Now Cleo was the only one who would consider such a feat. A proper future queen like Emilia would never do such a dangerous thing and risk hurting herself.

"I need to see Aron. Alone."

Emilia raised an eyebrow, disapproving. "Our father hasn't even announced your engagement yet. And you're sneaking off for some illicit romance before it's all official?"

Cleo's stomach lurched. "That's not why I want to see him."

"He'll make you a fine husband, you know."

"Sure, he will," Cleo said, sarcasm dripping from her voice. "Just like Darius made *you* a fine husband."

Emilia's gaze grew harsh. "Sharp tongue, Cleo. You should watch where you point it or you might hurt someone."

Cleo blushed, abashed. She'd just trod on some extremely unpleasant territory. Lord Darius Larides was the man to whom Emilia had been engaged a year ago at eighteen. However, the closer they got to the wedding day, the deeper Emilia sank into a depression at the thought of marrying him—even though all agreed he was a fine pick: tall, handsome, charismatic. No one knew why, but Cleo guessed her sister had fallen in love with someone else. If it was true, though, she never found out who. Emilia had never so much as cast a flirtatious glance at any of the men in the palace, and for that matter she'd seemed rather sad over the past few weeks. Embarrassed, Cleo changed the subject.

"I need to go while I have the chance," Cleo whispered, eyeing the balcony. The trellis outside was as good and strong as any ladder.

"You're that intent on escaping from your new bodyguard? And leaving him—I would assume—lurking outside my chambers?"

Cleo smiled pleadingly. "I'll be back as soon as I can. He'll never even know I was gone."

"And what do you suggest I tell him if he decides to check in on us?"

"That I suddenly discovered I had air magic or something and made myself disappear." She squeezed her sister's hands as she brushed past her at the window, intent on her plan. She would be gone no more than a quarter of an hour, then she'd be back.

"You've always had a taste for adventure," Emilia said, relenting. "Well, romance or not . . . good luck."

"Thank you. I might need it."

Cleo swung her legs over the side of the balcony and climbed easily down the trellis, landing softly on the grass below. Without looking back up at the window, she quickly made her way across the palace grounds, beyond the main castle, to the neighborhood of luxury villas, still within the castle walls. Only the most important of nobles got to live here, protected from any outside threat.

The palace grounds were a city unto themselves, with open-air cafés and taverns, businesses, shops, crisscrossing cobblestone streets, and beautifully kept flower gardens, including one with an expansive labyrinth of tall hedges where Cleo and Emilia had hosted a party a few months ago. More than two thousand people lived here happily and prosperously. Some rarely bothered to leave the compound at all.

The Lagaris's city villa was one of the more impressive homes, only a five-minute stroll away from the castle, and built from the same golden mix of materials as the castle itself. Aron sat outside, smoking a cigarillo, and he watched Cleo's approach with a lazy smile on his face.

"Princess Cleiona," he drawled, exhaling a long line of smoke. "What a delightful surprise."

She eyed the cigarillo with distaste. She'd never understood the interest some people had in sucking in fiery smoke from crushed peach-tree leaves and other herbs and exhaling it. Unlike wine, cigarillos were nasty, their smell not sweet and fragrant like peaches at all.

"I want to talk to you," she said.

"I was just sitting here watching the morning go by, thinking that I was so incredibly bored I might have to do something about it." There was a familiar slur to his words, but not too pronounced. Many would think nothing of it, but Cleo knew very well it was a sign that Aron had already started drinking. It wasn't even midday.

"And what were you going to do about it?" she asked.

"Hadn't decided yet." His grin widened. "But now I don't have to. You're here."

"Is that a good thing?"

"Of course. It's always a pleasure to see you." He looked at her pale blue silk skirt, which was wrinkled and dirty from her descent from Emilia's room. "Somersaulting through flower beds on the way over here?"

She absently wiped at the stains. "Something like that."

"I'm honored you'd make the effort. You could have simply sent word to me to come to you."

"I wanted to talk to you in private."

He looked at her curiously. "You want to talk about what happened in Paelsia, don't you?"

She felt herself pale. "Let's go inside, Aron. I don't want anyone else to hear us."

"As you wish."

He pushed open the heavy door and let her in ahead of him. She entered the opulent foyer with its high domed ceiling and marble floors, tiled in the pattern of a colorful sunburst. On the wall was a large portrait of Aron as a young, pale-skinned boy and his stern-looking but attractive parents. He stayed by the door, keeping it open a crack so the smoke wouldn't leave a lingering odor behind. His parents didn't approve of smoking inside the house. Aron might be arrogant and confident, but he was still seventeen and had to abide by his parents' rules until his next birthday—unless he wanted to move out ahead of schedule. And Cleo knew without a doubt that he didn't want that sort of responsibility, financial or otherwise.

"Well, Cleo?" he prompted when she didn't say anything for a full minute.

She summoned her courage and turned to face him. She desperately hoped that speaking with him would quell her guilt over the murder and help bring an end to her nightmares. She wanted him to justify his actions—to have them make more sense to her than they did right now.

"I can't stop thinking about what happened with the wine seller's son." She blinked, shocked to find that her eyes suddenly brimmed with tears. "Can you?"

His gaze hardened. "Of course I can't."

"How do you . . . feel?" She held her breath.

His cheeks tensed. He threw the half-smoked cigarillo out through the front door, waving his hand at the smoke left behind.

"I feel conflicted."

Already, she felt a large measure of relief. If she was to be engaged to Aron, she needed to know that they felt the same way about most things. "I've had nightmares. Every night."

"About the brother's threat?" he asked.

She nodded. It felt as if Jonas Agallon's eyes still bore into her. Nobody had ever looked at her with that much unbridled hate. "You shouldn't have killed that boy."

"He was coming at me. You saw it yourself."

"He didn't have a weapon!"

"He had fists. He had rage. He could have strangled me right where I stood."

"Theon wouldn't have let that happen."

"Theon?" He frowned. "Oh, the guard? Listen, Cleo. I know that it upset you—but it happened and there's no going back. Put it out of your mind."

"I wish I could, but I can't." She exhaled shakily. "I don't like death."

He laughed and she gave him a sharp look. He sobered immediately. "Apologies, but of course you don't like death. Who does? It's messy and it's unpleasant, but it happens. Often."

"Do you wish it hadn't happened?"

"What? The wine seller's son's death?"

"His name was Tomas Agallon," she said quietly. "He had a name. He had a life and a family. He was happy and laughing when he came to the stall. He was going to go to his sister's wedding— did you see the look on her face? She was destroyed. The argument never should have happened in the first place. If you liked the wine so much, you should have paid Silas Agallon a fair price for it."

Aron leaned his shoulder against the wall next to the door. "Oh, Cleo, don't tell me you really care about such things."

She frowned. "Of course I do."

He rolled his eyes. "Please. A wine seller's livelihood in Paelsia? Since when do you concern yourself with such unimportant matters? You're a princess of Auranos. You can have absolutely anything you desire, whenever you desire it. All you need to do is ask and it's yours."

Cleo wasn't sure how this had anything to do with a wine seller's asking price. "Is that really how you see me?"

"I see you for exactly what you are. A beautiful princess. And I am sorry I can't be as brokenhearted over all of this as you want me to be. I did what I had to do at the time, and I don't regret it." A hard edge went through his gaze. "I acted on instinct alone. I've hunted many times before, but this was different. To take the life of another . . . I've never felt so powerful in my entire life."

A shiver of revulsion went through her. "How can you sound so calm about this?"

He fixed her with a steady look. "Would you rather I lie and say I have nightmares too? Would that ease your own guilt?"

She deflated. That had been exactly what she'd wanted. "I want the truth."

"And that's what I've given you. You should be grateful, Cleo. There aren't too many people who speak the truth around here, even when they're asked for it."

Aron was handsome. He was from a noble family. He had a wry wit and a keen mind. And she'd never disliked anyone as much as she did him.

She couldn't marry him. There was simply no way.

A steely resolve flowed through her. Before visiting Paelsia, she'd been willing to yield—to a point—and allow her father to make an important decision like this for her. After all, he was the king.

"Have you heard of my father's plans?" she asked him.

Aron cocked his head, his gaze steady on her face. "Changing subjects so soon?"

"Perhaps."

"I am sorry you're upset about what happened in Paelsia."

He said it without any emotion, not even a flicker. He might be vaguely sorry that she was upset, but he wasn't filled with remorse that it happened, nor was he haunted by the echoes of the grieving brother's death threat.

"Thank you," she said.

"Now—have I heard of your father's plans?" He crossed his

arms over his chest and walked a slow circle around her. She suddenly felt like a fawn being observed by a hungry wolf. "Your father is the king. He has many plans."

"The plan involving the two of us," she said simply, turning as he turned so they could maintain eye contact.

"Our engagement."

She stiffened. "That's the one."

"When do you think he'll announce it?"

A cold trickle of perspiration slid down her spine. "I don't know."

He nodded. "This came as a shock to you."

She let out another shaky sigh. "I'm only sixteen."

"It's young for an announcement like this, I agree."

"My father likes you."

"The feeling is entirely mutual." He cocked his head to the other side. "I like you too, Cleo, in case you've forgotten. Don't doubt that, if that's what this is all about."

"It's not."

"This shouldn't have been a huge surprise for you. There's been talk for some time that we'd eventually be matched."

"So you're fine with this?"

He shrugged a shoulder, his gaze sweeping the length of her in a predatory manner. "Yes, I'm fine with it."

Say it, Cleo. Don't let this go on a moment longer.

She cleared her throat. "I don't know if it's such a good idea."

He stopped circling. "Excuse me?"

"This—this match. It doesn't feel right. Not right now, anyway. I mean, we're friends. Of course we are. But we're not . . ." Her mouth was dry. For a fleeting moment, she wished for some wine—any wine—to help the world seem golden and wonderful again.

"In love?" Aron finished for her.

She blinked and nodded, casting her eyes to the ornately tiled marble floor. "I don't know what to say."

She waited for Aron to say something, to take the pressure off and ease her anxiety, but he stayed quiet. Finally she braved a glance at him.

He studied her, his brow furrowed. "You want to ask your father not to make the announcement, don't you?"

She swallowed hard. "If we're both in agreement, then it'll be simpler to convince him that this isn't the right time."

"This has to do with what happened in Paelsia, doesn't it?"

She flicked her gaze to his. "I don't know."

"Of course you do. You're upset about what happened to someone of no consequence to your life. Do you cry over felled deer as well? Do you sob into your plate every night when you're served dinner from a hunt?"

Her cheeks flushed. "It's hardly the same thing, Aron."

"Oh, I don't know. Killing a deer, killing that boy—felt as if it had about as much significance to me, one or the other. I think you simply lack the right perspective. You're too young."

She bristled. "You're only a year older than me."

"It's enough for me to be able to see the world a bit more clearly." He closed the distance between them and grasped her chin. His skin smelled of smoke. "I won't agree to tell the king I don't want this. Because I do want this."

"You want to marry me?"

"Of course I do."

"Are you in love with me?"

Aron's lips curved. "Oh, Cleo. You're lucky you're beautiful. It absolves you of many shortcomings."

She glared at him and pushed back, but he just dug his fingers in harder—almost, but not quite, hard enough to hurt. His intentions were clear—he didn't want her to move.

"I remember that night, Cleo. It's crystal clear in my mind."

She gasped. "Don't speak of it."

"We're alone. Nobody's here to listen in." His gaze fell on her lips. "You wanted that to happen between us. Don't try to deny it."

Her cheeks flamed. "I'd had too much wine. I wasn't thinking straight. I regret it."

"So you say. But it happened. You and me, Cleo. We were meant to be together. That was only a taste." He raised an eyebrow. "Had your father picked anyone but me as your betrothed, I might have had to say something. I know you wouldn't have liked that. You don't want the king to know that his perfect princess had tarnished herself in the bed of someone who was not to become her husband."

She barely remembered that night six months ago, only that there was wine—too much of it. And lips that tasted like smoke. A fumbling of hands, of clothes, of lies whispered in the darkness.

A proper girl—a princess—was meant to remain pure and untouched until her wedding night—her virginity a gift to her husband. That Cleo had made such a mistake with someone like Aron, whom she could barely tolerate while sober, shamed her like nothing else. No one could ever know about this.

She pushed his hand away, her cheeks flaming. "I must go."

"Not yet." Aron closed the distance between them and pulled her tight against his chest, digging his hand into her long hair to free it from its loose twist so it hung to her waist. "I've missed you, Cleo. And I am glad you came to see me in private this morning. I think about you often."

"Let me leave," she whispered. "And say nothing about this."

He caressed the side of her throat, his gaze darkening. "Once we're engaged, I'll ensure moments of privacy like this will be much more frequent. I look forward to that."

Cleo tried to push against his chest, but he was strong. Stronger than he looked. She'd only succeeded in reminding him of the night she'd shamed herself and her family. He seemed to relish this secret they shared while she would rather purge it from her mind forever.

And, goddess, his breath smelled like he'd been drinking and smoking since sunrise.

There was a sharp knock on the partially open door. Aron's fingers dug into her sides, and he cast a dark look over his shoulder as the door creaked open.

"There you are, princess," Theon said casually.

Aron let her go so abruptly that she had to struggle to keep her balance and not go sprawling to the floor.

Theon looked from her to Aron and his eyes narrowed. "Is everything well here?"

"Well. It's well," she replied, throat full. "Very well. Thank you."

His fierce expression showed that he didn't find any humor in the thought that she'd snuck off behind his back. In fact, his gaze was hot enough to burn.

Still, she was more than happy to leave with her angry bodyguard than stay here a moment longer with Aron.

"I want to go back to the palace," she said firmly.

"Whenever you're ready."

"I'm ready now." She straightened her shoulders and glanced at Aron.

He looked bored. On the surface, anyway. Deep in his eyes was an unpleasant flicker—an unspoken promise that the drunken night she wanted to forget would only be the first of many between them. She shuddered.

She *had* to convince her father to end this nonsense. The king hadn't made Emilia marry her fiancé. This shouldn't be any different.

If Aron ever told her secret after that, she would . . . simply deny it. She could do that. She was the princess. Her father would believe her over Aron, even if she spoke lies out of necessity. That night would not ruin her. It could not. She refused to allow Aron to have that kind of power over her a day longer than he already had.

"See you soon, Cleo," Aron said, stepping outside when they did. He lit another cigarillo as he watched them leave.

Cleo didn't speak, intent on walking away from the villa as quickly as she could.

The heat of Theon's glare seared into the back of her neck. Finally, when they were nearly back at the castle, she spun around to face him.

"Need to say something?" she demanded, trying her best to hide that she was on the verge of tears. Nausea churned in the pit of her stomach.

If Theon hadn't intervened . . .

She was glad that he had, but she was still upset. And taking out her frustrations and anger on the nearest person was the only way she knew to cope.

Theon's fierce expression was not one of respect for a member of royalty, but the annoyance of someone forced to deal with a headstrong child. "You need to stop trying to run away from me."

"I didn't run away. I needed to see Aron alone."

"Yes, I saw that." He glanced over his shoulder in the direction of the golden villa down the road lined with green trees and well-tended flower beds. "Apologies for interrupting your romantic rendezvous. Looked like the two of you—"

"Were doing nothing at all," she cut him off, her voice catching on the words. While she didn't feel she should be overly concerned about her new bodyguard's opinion, she'd prefer he didn't guess that her chastity was but a memory. "That was not what you thought it was."

"Really."

"Yes, really. It was a conversation."

"Looked like an interesting conversation."

She furiously wiped at her eyes with the long sleeves of her dress. "It was not."

In a split second, Theon's expression shifted from anger to concern. "Are you certain that everything's all right?"

"What do you care? All I am to you is an assignment handed down from the king."

A muscle in his cheek twitched, as if she'd slapped him. "Excuse me for asking." Clarity dawned on his face a moment later. "Wait. You went there to confront Lord Aron about what happened in Paelsia. You feel bad about it."

Her chest ached. His words could apply to many things she felt bad about. "Let us go back to the castle."

"Princess, you were blameless. You need to know that."

Blameless? She wished he was right. She'd stood by and watched helplessly as the boy was killed. And months earlier, she'd allowed Aron to have his way with her, blaming the wine even as it was happening, not her own decisions. He hadn't forced himself on her. At the time, in her intoxicated haze, she had welcomed the amorous attentions of a handsome lord sought after by many of her friends.

She shook her head, her throat tight. It hurt too much to swallow. "The death of that boy haunts me."

He grasped her shoulders and drew her closer to him. "It's done. It's over. Put it out of your mind. If you're afraid of the boy's brother coming after you to get revenge, I will protect you. I swear I will. You don't have to worry. That's one of the reasons I'm guarding you." His expression darkened again. "That is, if you'd stop running away from me."

"I'm not running away from you. Well, not specifically," she said, suddenly finding words difficult to come by again. "I—I'm running away from . . ." She sighed. "Oh, I don't know anymore. I'm just trying to make sense of everything and finding that nothing at all makes sense."

"I heard your father talking to someone." Theon absently scrubbed his hand through his short, bronze-colored hair. "About your upcoming engagement to Lord Aron."

She had a difficult time finding enough air to breathe. "And how did he sound?"

"Pleased."

"That makes one of us," she grumbled darkly under her breath, her eyes on a horse-drawn cart that rolled down the road next to where they stood.

"You're not happy about the engagement?" His tone had regained its hard edge.

"Not happy about being forced into doing something that I have absolutely no say about? No, I can't say that I am."

"I'm sorry."

"Are you?"

Theon shrugged. "I don't think anyone should have to do what they don't want to do."

"Like being assigned a job you weren't interested in?"

His lips thinned. "It's different."

Cleo considered this. "You and me—it's kind of like a strange marriage. You're forced to be near me. I can't escape you. And we're going to be together a lot now and in the future."

Theon raised an eyebrow. "So you're finally accepting this arrangement?"

She chewed her bottom lip as she thought through her questionable decisions today. "I know I shouldn't have left the palace without telling you. I apologize if I caused you any trouble."

"Your sister was more than happy to let me know where you'd run off to."

Cleo gasped. "That traitor."

He laughed. "Wouldn't have mattered if she hadn't. Even though this is an arrangement neither one of us might have chosen, it's something I take very seriously. You're not just any girl; you're the princess. It's my sole duty now to protect you. So wherever you run off to, you can be certain of one very important thing."

She waited, her breath catching at the intense way the handsome young guard watched her. "And what's that?"

When he smiled, the look was equally menacing and enticing. "I will find you."

CHAPTER 8

LIMEROS

L

"I'm told Father's up to something downstairs."

Magnus's voice cut through Lucia's concentration, startling her. She quickly blew out the candle in front of her, closed her book, and turned to face him with what she knew was a guilty expression.

"Excuse me?" she said as calmly as she could.

Her brother cast an amused glance at her across the shadows of her chambers, with the sleeping area, a curtained bed with stiff linen sheets and a fur-lined blanket, on one side and the seating area on the other. "Am I interrupting something?"

She placed her hand casually on her hip. "No, of course not."

He drew closer to her lounge next to the window, which looked down to the expansive palace gardens. They were currently covered in frost as they were for all but a precious couple of warmer months. "What are you reading?"

"Nothing of any importance."

"Mmm." He raised a brow and held his hand out to her patiently.

Sometimes Lucia didn't like how well her older brother knew her.

Finally, accepting defeat, she placed the small leather-bound book in his hand. He glanced at the cover, then quickly flipped through it. "Poetry about the goddess Cleiona?"

She shrugged. "Comparative studies, that's all."

"Naughty girl."

She ignored the flush that immediately heated her cheeks. She wasn't being naughty; she was being inquisitive. There was a difference. Even so, she knew many, including her mother, would be displeased about her current reading material. Luckily, Magnus wasn't one of them.

Cleiona was the rival goddess to Valoria. One was thought of as good; one was believed to be evil. But this difference depended entirely upon in which kingdom one stood. In Limeros, Cleiona was considered the evil one and Valoria pure and good, representing strength, faith, and wisdom. They were the three attributes that Limerians put before all else. Every coat of arms stitched to adorn the walls of the great hall or anywhere else, every parchment that her father signed, every portrait of the king himself held these three words.

Strength. Faith. Wisdom.

Limeros devoted two full days a week to prayer and silence. Anyone in the many villages and cities right up to the forbidden mountains who broke this law was fined. If they couldn't pay the fine, they were reprimanded in a harsher manner. King Gaius had the common areas patrolled to make sure everyone stayed the course, paid their taxes, and strictly followed the command of their king.

Most didn't protest or cause a problem. And Valoria, Lucia was sure, would approve of her father's stern measures—as harsh as they sometimes seemed.

Limeros was a land of cliffs, vast moors, and rocky ground; a frozen place for most of the year, covered in a sparkling layer of ice and snow before it gave way to greenery and blossoms for that precious glimpse of summer. So beautiful—sometimes the beauty of this kingdom brought tears to Lucia's eyes. The window in her chambers looked out past the gardens to the seemingly endless Silver Sea, leading to faraway lands, and the sheer drop from the black granite castle walls to the dark waters crashing upon the rocky shore below.

Breathtaking, even when the winter had closed in and it was near impossible to go outside without being fully wrapped in furs and leathers to keep out the biting cold.

Lucia didn't mind. She loved this kingdom, even with the expectations and difficulties that inevitably came from being a Damora. And she loved her books and her classes, absorbing knowledge like a sponge. She read everything she could get her hands on. Happily, the castle library was second to none. Information was a valuable gift to her—more precious than any gold or jewels, such as those given to her by some of her more ardent suitors.

That is, if those suitors could get past her overprotective brother to give her those gifts. Magnus didn't think that any boy who had shown interest in Lucia thus far was worthy of the princess's attentions. Magnus had always been equal parts frustrating and wonderful to her. Lately, however, she wasn't so sure how to gauge his ever-shifting moods.

Lucia looked up into his familiar face as he cast her book to the side carelessly. The thirst for knowledge didn't spread evenly between the siblings. Magnus's time was taken up by his own classes, mostly horsemanship, swordsmanship, and archery—which he claimed to despise. All of which the king insisted upon, whether Magnus displayed a keen interest or not.

"Cleiona's also the name of the youngest Auranian princess," Magnus mused. "Never really thought about it before. Same age as you are, right? Nearly to the day?"

Lucia nodded, picking the book up off the lounge where it had fallen and tucking it under a pile of her less controversial books. "I'd like to meet her."

"Unlikely. Father hates Auranos and wishes for its ultimate demise. Ever since . . . well, you know."

Oh, she did. Her father despised King Corvin Bellos and wasn't afraid of expressing his opinion over meals in a fearsome burst of anger whenever the mood struck. Lucia believed the animosity had much to do with a banquet at the Auranos palace more than ten years ago. The two kings had come nearly to blows due to a mysterious injury Magnus had received during the visit. King Gaius hadn't returned since. Nor had he been invited.

The reminder of this trip made Magnus absently touch his scar—one that stretched from the top of his right ear to the corner of his mouth.

"After all this time, you still don't remember how you got that?" She'd always been very curious about it.

His fingers stilled as if he too had been caught doing something he shouldn't be doing. "Ten years is a long time. I was only a boy."

"Father demanded whoever cut you should pay with his life."

"He wanted the culprit's head delivered on a silver platter, actually. Seeing a crying, bleeding child troubled our father. Even when that child was me." His dark brows drew together. "Honestly,

I don't remember anything. I only recall wandering off, then feeling the hot trickle of blood on my face and the sting of the wound. I didn't get upset until Mother got upset. Perhaps I stumbled down a set of stairs or whacked myself on the edge of a sharp door. You know how clumsy I am."

"Hardly." Her brother moved with the grace of a panther—sleek, quiet. Many might think him deadly, given that he was the son of the iron-fisted King Gaius. "I'm the clumsy one in this family."

"I beg to disagree with that." His lips curved to the side. "One of grace and beauty, my sister, with a multitude of suitors at her beck and call. Forced to be siblings with a scarred monster like me."

"As if that scar makes you a monster." The thought was laughable. "You can't be blind to how girls look at you—I even see maids here in the castle wistfully watch you pass, even if you never notice them. They all think you're devastatingly handsome. And your scar only makes you more . . ." She took a moment to think of the right word. "Intriguing."

"You really think so?" His chocolate-brown eyes glinted with amusement.

"I do." She brushed his dark hair, long overdue for a trim, off his cheek to inspect the faded scar closer. She slid her index finger over it. "Besides, it's barely noticeable anymore. At least, I don't see it."

"If you say so." His voice sounded strangled now and his expression had shifted to one of distress. He roughly pushed her hand away.

She frowned. "Is something wrong?"

Magnus stepped back a few feet from her. "Nothing. I—I came

up here to . . ." He ran a hand through his hair. "Never mind. You probably wouldn't be interested. There's some impromptu political meeting downstairs Father has called. I'll leave you to your studies."

Lucia watched with surprise as he swiftly left her room without another word.

Something was troubling her brother. She'd noticed it lately, each day worse than the last. He seemed distracted and deeply distressed by something, and she wished she knew what it was. She hated to see him so upset and not know how to help ease his pain.

And she also wished very much that she could share her own secret, the one she'd been hiding for nearly a month—the one no one knew. No one at all.

Pushing aside her fear and uncertainty, she prayed to the goddess for enough strength, faith, and wisdom to weather the dark storm she feared was drawing closer.

Magnus followed the noise downstairs toward the castle's great hall. He pushed past several recognizable faces—boys of his age who considered him their friend. He offered them stiff smiles and received the same in return.

They weren't his true friends—not one of them. They were the sons of his father's royal council, who were basically required to be acquainted with the Limerian prince whether they liked it or not. And a few, as Magnus had overheard in passing, didn't like him at all.

Irrelevant.

He assumed every one of these boys—and their sisters, who would be more than eager if Magnus chose one of them as his future bride—was ready to use him whenever the occasion called for it. He was happy to do the same when it served his purposes.

He trusted not a single one of them. Only Lucia. She was different. She was the only one with whom he could ever be truly himself without putting on any act. She was his closest confidant and ally. They'd shared so many secrets over the years, trusting each other to keep silence.

And he'd just escaped from her chambers as if they'd been set on fire.

The secret of his growing desire for Lucia would have to be kept silent from everyone. Especially her. Forever. He would keep it buried deep in his chest until the fiery pain left only ash where his heart once was. He was already half there to begin with. Maybe when his heart had finally been burned away, everything would be easier.

It had been more than a month since the banquet, and he hadn't learned anything of interest that would elucidate the enigmatic conversation he'd heard between his father and Sabina. He'd asked Amia to pay special attention as she eavesdropped throughout the castle. If she ever heard Lucia's name, she was to report immediately back to him. The young maid had eagerly agreed to this, much as she eagerly agreed to anything Magnus had ever required of her.

In the hall, his father's voice was raised as he addressed the crowd of three hundred men. Those in attendance appeared to hang on his every word, their gazes fixed solely upon the king. Behind the king on the wall was one of the few pieces of artwork that the hall still held on its cold, flat walls—a large tapestry of the king himself perched upon his favorite black stallion, sword in hand, looking strong and stern and royal.

Magnus cast up his eyes. His father loved being the center of attention.

"A murder." The king's voice boomed through the hall. "Right in the middle of the Paelsian market a month and a half ago. It was a cool but beautiful day when Paelsians were out enjoying the sunshine, marketing their wares, trying to make a decent living for themselves and their families. But this was disrupted by a few wicked Auranian royals in their midst."

Murmuring surrounded Magnus. News had already reached some about the murder of the wine seller's son, but for others this was the first time they'd heard of it. Magnus was surprised that anyone actually cared.

He was surprised that his *father* seemed to care. When it had been mentioned to Magnus at Lucia's birthday banquet, he hadn't thought much of it. Later, when his father learned of it, the king had simply shrugged a shoulder.

Seemed as if he'd changed his mind. Perhaps it was due to the influence of the young, dark-haired man who stood next to the king. The one who had recently returned from a trip across the sea.

Magnus's cheek began to twitch.

His name was Tobias Argynos. He'd been brought to the castle to become the king's valet a year ago and soon thereafter was taken fully into his confidence. If the king needed something, Tobias would get it. The king considered him an asset and treated him as a favorite son.

If whispered rumors held any weight, then Tobias *was* a favorite son—the king's bastard born twenty years ago to a beautiful courtesan in Auranos.

Magnus had never taken to believing in idle gossip. But he would never completely ignore it, either. Whispered stories could turn to shouted truths as quick as day became night. Even so, it wouldn't jeopardize Magnus's position in the kingdom. He was the rightful heir today, tomorrow, and always. Still, the way the king had warmed to Tobias when he'd only been cold to Magnus all his life troubled him more than he'd ever admit out loud. The rightful prince received a scar on his face while the bastard stood next to the king as he gave speeches to a rapt audience.

Then again, fairness or kindness had never been King Gaius's goals. Strength, faith, and wisdom above all.

"Paelsians have suffered," the king continued. "I've watched this and my heart has bled for our poor neighbors. Auranians, on the other hand, flaunt their riches for all to see. They are shamefully vain. They have even begun to deny religion and prayer and instead raise up their own images as idols as evidence of their hedonism and excess. It was a selfish young lord—Lord Aron Lagaris—who killed the impoverished wine seller's son. The murdered boy was a fine and handsome young lad, one who could have grown up to help lead his people out of the squalor they have faced for generations. But he was cut down as a spoiled lord tried to show off in front of a princess—Princess Cleiona. Yes, named for the evil goddess herself, she who murdered our own beloved of beloveds, Valoria, goddess of earth and water. The two watched Tomas Agallon's young life bleed from him in front of his own family. They didn't feel sorry for the pain they caused that family and all Paelsians."

More mumbled conversation as the crowd listened to the king's tale.

"This isn't just a murder. This is an insult. And I, for one, am deeply outraged on behalf of all Paelsians, our neighbors who share a border with us all the way east to the Forbidden Mountains. The time is coming for a reckoning—one a thousand years in the making."

The mumbling grew louder and, Magnus could tell, it was in agreement with what the king was saying.

Tales spread about the opulence in Auranos. Streets paved in gold. Precious jewels woven into noblewomen's hair, discarded at the end of the day. Riches wasted on lavish parties that lasted for weeks. And, most distasteful of all, the fading interest in hard work and devout religion—the building blocks of Limerian society.

"What are you doing, Father?" Magnus said under his breath, bemused.

A strong hand clutched Magnus's shoulder and he turned with alarm to face a man whose name escaped him: a large, hulking member of the king's council, whose gray beard covered most of his face. Small, beady eyes flashed with excitement.

"Your father is the finest king Limeros has ever known," the man exclaimed. "You should be very proud to be his son."

Proud was one word Magnus would never use to describe how he felt toward his father, today or any other day. A fake smile stretched his cheeks. "Of course. And never prouder than I am at this very moment."

It was a week after the king's speech. Magnus's muscles were burning—he had just finished another swordplay lesson. Now, after cleaning up and changing into fresh clothes, he moved through the castle trying his best to resemble a shadow. It was a game he liked to play to challenge himself, to see how far he could get before anyone took notice of him. In the black clothing he favored, he could usually get quite far.

Today he'd avoided Lucia after seeing her briefly over breakfast. All afternoon, she'd stayed in her room studying.

Good. Out of sight, out of mind.

The lie slid smoothly.

Moving silently, he came across a boy waiting in the huge, high-ceilinged downstairs foyer with its winding staircase cut precisely into the stone walls. A son of local nobles, he knew. Again, Magnus was terrible with names. It wasn't a memory issue, it was a *lack of caring* issue. He remembered the names of people who interested him or who served a purpose in his life. This boy didn't interest him at all. Although the boy's interest in Lucia was another thing altogether.

At previous gatherings Magnus had observed in the boy's watchful eyes that he was one of many who had a crush on Lucia and that he was waiting for the opportunity to spend time with her and solidify their . . . friendship.

As Magnus did with many such suitors, he circled the boy like a sea monster, eyeing him with acute displeasure until beads of perspiration formed on the boy's pale forehead.

Lucia had called Magnus handsome, but he knew many found his appearance—dark hair, dark eyes, dark clothes, and, of course, the scar—to be intimidating and menacing. That he was King Gaius's son and heir to the Limeros throne only solidified this impression. Some kings earned their people's respect through love—as his grandfather had done. His father, however, preferred to earn their respect through fear and bloodshed. Different process. Same result.

Magnus could use the perception that he was just like his father. He had before; he would again. One should use every weapon available when there was the need. Right now, there was the need.

"You shouldn't be here," Magnus told him thinly.

The boy nervously dug the toe of his leather shoe into the gray marble floor. "I—I'm just . . . I'm not here to stay long. My parents thought it would be nice if I took Princess Lucia for a stroll around the palace grounds. It's not too cold today."

"Yes, how nice." The words were acid on his tongue as jealousy flashed through him like a bolt of lightning. "But she isn't interested in walks around the palace grounds. Not with, well . . . not with *you*."

The boy's eyes widened. "What do you mean?"

Magnus forced a tense look on his face as if he'd said too much and now felt guilty. "It's really none of my business."

"No, please. If you have any advice for me, I'd welcome it. I know you and Lucia are very close."

Magnus took hold of the boy's shoulder. "It's just that she's mentioned you to me." This would be an excellent time to know the boy's name—Mark, Markus, Mikah, something like that. "And she made it clear that if you ever stopped by, you should not be encouraged any further. She means no offense, of course. But . . . her interests in a potential suitor lie elsewhere."

"Elsewhere?"

"Yes. So that is where I suggest you go. Elsewhere."

"Oh." The boy's voice was weak and reedy. Already defeated.

Magnus had no patience for anyone who would be manipulated so easily. If the boy was truly interested in Lucia, he should be able to stand up to any adversity, including an overprotective older brother.

Weak things were so very easy to break.

If the boy had a tail, it would have been tucked between his legs as he scurried away from the castle and back to his parents' villa. And that was the end of Mikey. Or whatever his name was.

With a victorious smile on his face, Magnus returned to

slowly prowling the castle hallways. It didn't take him long before he came across something a bit more pleasant than one of his sister's admirers.

Amia smiled at him as they passed in the hall and then curled her finger, beckoning him to follow as she disappeared behind the corner up ahead. She led him into a small room used as the servants' chapel and closed the door behind them. They were alone. The girl bit her bottom lip, but her cheeks were flushed with excitement. "I feel as if I haven't seen you in ages, my prince."

"It's only been a day or two."

"An eternity." She placed her hands against his abdomen and slid them slowly up over his shoulders.

He let her. He craved someone's touch today to help quell the ache in his chest. If he closed his eyes, he could imagine that she was someone else. She shivered as he pressed her up against the stone wall and brought his mouth down to hers in a deep kiss. He threaded his fingers through her soft brown hair and imagined it flowed down to her waist and was the color of richest ebony. That her eyes were the color of the sky in summer, not a pale and wintry gray.

"Have you learned anything?" he asked, finally pushing away the fantasy. Amia smelled of the fish she'd been helping to prepare for dinner rather than of roses and jasmine. He could only fool himself so much.

"About your sister?"

His throat tightened. "Yes."

"Not yet." She gazed up at him as if entranced. "However, there's something else interesting happening as we speak. The king and Tobias are in a secret meeting with visitors."

Tobias, he thought with distaste. *Always lurking about.* "What visitors?"

"Chief Basilius arrived with an entourage an hour ago."

He stared at her, momentarily rendered speechless. "You can't be serious."

She grinned. "I was looking for you to let you know. If the Paelsian chieftain, one who never makes public appearances, has traveled to Limeros to speak with the king, something very interesting must be happening, don't you think?"

"Indeed."

Chief Basilius was rumored to be a powerful sorcerer feared and respected by his people. He stayed apart from other Paelsians in a private compound, devoting his days to meditation and, supposedly, magic.

Magnus didn't believe in such ridiculous notions. However, his father did, to an extent. King Gaius believed in the power of *elementia*. Magic that had been gone from the world since the days of the goddesses.

"Did you hear anything else?" he asked. "Do you know why the chief is here?"

"I tried to listen for as long as I could, but I was afraid I'd get caught."

"Amia, you don't want to ever be caught. My father would not take well to eavesdroppers."

"Even if I was eavesdropping on behalf of his son?"

"I wouldn't hesitate to say you were lying." He took her arm in his and squeezed it until she flinched. A flicker of fear went through her pale eyes. "Who do you think the king would believe? His son and heir? Or a kitchen maid?"

Amia swallowed hard. "I apologize, my prince. I would never say such a thing."

"Smart girl."

She took a moment to compose herself, shaking off the momentary unpleasantness between them. "As far as what I heard, it seems as if it's related to the murder in the Paelsian village last month and the meeting King Gaius called last week."

He eased his grip on the girl. "I think I'll join them. I have a right to be a part of such a political meeting as much as Tobias does."

"I agree completely."

The girl was nothing if not agreeable. He looked down at her. "Thank you for this information, Amia. I do appreciate it."

Her face lit up. "Will you need anything else from me?"

He considered this for a moment before stepping back from her. "Yes. Visit me in my chambers after I retire tonight."

Her cheeks reddened and she smiled demurely. "Of course, my prince."

Magnus left the chapel and headed toward his father's private meeting hall, which was situated on the main floor next to the great hall. He didn't bother to attempt to overhear anything; he simply walked straight in. There were a dozen men in the room and their gazes all shot to him immediately.

"Oh, I'm very sorry," he said. "Am I interrupting something?"

While he enjoyed acting the part of a shadow much of the time, there were other occasions that called for a more illuminated approach. Tobias's ongoing presence at the castle had raised his hackles more than he'd even realized before today. He felt the sudden and driving need to assert his position as prince and the rightful heir to his father's throne.

"This," King Gaius said from his seat upon the dais, always a step above everyone else, "is my son, Prince Magnus Lukas Damora."

Instead of an expression of outrage at the interruption, there was a small bemused smile on the king's lips at Magnus's unannounced entrance. Tobias simply glared at him, as if enraged on behalf of the king by Magnus's extreme rudeness.

"It's a great honor to meet the prince," a man's deep voice sounded out, and Magnus moved his gaze to his left. "I am Chief Hugo Basilius of Paelsia."

"The honor is ours, Chief Basilius," Magnus said evenly. "Welcome to Limeros."

"Join us, my son," the king said.

Magnus restrained himself from making a cutting remark about missing the invitation earlier and sat down across the table from the chief and four of his men.

The chief was a grander-looking man than Magnus would have expected, given the peasant status of his people. In Paelsia, there was no upper or middle class, only varying degrees of lower, especially in recent generations as their land had begun to fade away.

Even seated, it was obvious that Basilius was no peasant. He was tall, his shoulders broad. His long, dark hair was streaked with gray. His tanned face was lined, and there was a keen sharpness in his dark eyes. His clothes were finely made, stitched from soft leathers and silver fox fur. He looked more like a king than Magnus expected. He would have to guess that Basilius did not suffer the same lifestyle in his compound as the commoners of Paelsia.

"Shall we fill your son in on what we've discussed so far?" Basilius asked.

"Of course." King Gaius's attention hadn't left his son since he'd entered the room. Even without looking, Magnus felt his father's gaze like a burning sensation along the length of his scar. A cool line of perspiration slid down his spine, even though he tried his best to look completely at ease.

King Gaius had a quick temper, and Magnus knew firsthand what it was like to be punished if he pushed too far. After all, he had the scar to prove it.

A scar he remembered far too well how he'd acquired.

Ten years ago, the king had taken Magnus with him and Queen Althea on the royal visit to Auranos. They hadn't been very long at all in the opulent and richly decorated palace, a sharp contrast to the utilitarian and sparse Limeros castle, before Magnus had given in to his childhood curiosity. He'd wandered off during a banquet to explore the castle alone. He'd come across a display case of jeweled daggers and felt the overwhelming urge to steal a golden one encrusted with sapphires and emeralds. In Limeros, weapons were not as beautiful and ornate as this. They were practical and useful, forged from steel or iron. He wanted it more than he'd ever wanted anything else in his seven years of life.

His father caught him as he drew the dagger from its case. The king had been so enraged that his son would steal, potentially damaging his family name in the process, that he'd lashed out. Magnus's punishment came via the blade itself.

His father ripped it out of his son's hands and slashed its sharp edge across Magnus's face.

Immediately, he'd regretted his violent turn. But instead of helping Magnus and bandaging the wound, he'd knelt down before his son and spoken in a low, dangerous tone while blood dripped from the little boy's cheek and onto the shiny marble floor of the Auranian palace. He'd coldly threatened Magnus's life, his mother's life, and his little sister's life. Magnus was not to ever tell anyone how he'd received this injury.

To this day, he never had. He was reminded of this threat and his father's mindless rage every time he looked in the mirror.

But he was not a seven-year-old boy anymore. He was seventeen, almost eighteen. Just as tall as his father was. And just as strong. He didn't want to be afraid any longer.

"I sent word to Chief Basilius," the king said, "that I wanted to meet with him personally about the problems in his land, punctuated by the murder of Tomas Agallon at the hands of an Auranian lord. He agreed to come here and discuss a possible alliance."

"An alliance?" Magnus repeated with surprise.

"A joining of two lands for one purpose," Tobias spoke up.

Magnus sent a withering look at the king's bastard. "I know what an alliance *is*."

"I believe it may be the omen I've been waiting for," Chief Basilius said. "Long have I searched for a solution to aid my dying land."

"And what solution will aligning with Limeros bring forth?" Magnus asked.

His father and the chief shared a look of understanding, and then King Gaius met his son's gaze. "I have proposed that we combine our strengths and take Auranos from a greedy and selfish king who would let his people believe they can do whatever they please to whomever they please without a single thought to consequence."

"Take Auranos," Magnus said, not quite believing his own ears. "You mean to conquer it. Together."

The king's smile stretched. "What do you make of that, my son?"

That was a loaded question. It was clear to Magnus that this discussion had been going on for some time before he arrived. No one seemed the least bit shocked by the suggestion of war after generations of peace.

And now that Magnus had a chance to catch his breath, he wasn't all that surprised either. His father had publicly hated Corvin Bellos for a decade, and Limerian disapproval toward a kingdom devoted to hedonism and frivolous excess had been a hotly debated issue over royal council meetings and banquets for twice that time. No, reflecting rapidly, Magnus was surprised only that it had taken this long for his father to want action.

Chief Basilius's land sat directly between Limeros and Auranos. It was a stretch of a hundred and fifty miles that any army would have to cross to reach the Auranian border by land. A newly forged, friendly alliance would certainly make that a much smoother journey.

"I can tell you what *I* think of it," Tobias said. "I think it's a brilliant plan, your grace."

Magnus eyed the king's valet with distaste. Dark hair, brown eyes, same height and build as himself. Tobias's features were slightly softer than Magnus's. Otherwise, there was little doubt that they shared a father. It was disturbing, really, how much Tobias looked as if he could legitimately be Magnus's older brother. If the king ever admitted the boy's parentage and claimed him as a true son, it would put Tobias before Magnus in line for the throne. There was no Limerian law that stated that pure royal blood was necessary for the position. Even the son of a whore could become king.

"I think whatever my opinion is on the subject, my father will do as he pleases," Magnus finally said. "As he has always done."

The chief laughed out loud at this. "I think your son knows you too well."

"Quite," King Gaius said with amusement. "So, Chief Basilius, what say you? Do you agree to my plan? Auranos has grown lazy and fat over many years of peace and won't be able to withstand an unexpected attack. They will fall, and together we will pick up the pieces left behind."

"And these pieces we'll pick up," Basilius mused. "Are we to then share them evenly?"

"We are."

The chief leaned back in his seat and surveyed all those in the meeting room slowly. The four men standing at his back had curved daggers at their belts and were dressed from head to toe in leathers. They looked ready to head into battle today if given such an order.

"Are you aware of the rumors about me?" the chief asked. It took a moment for Magnus to realize he was speaking to him directly.

"Rumors?" Magnus repeated.

"Why I am the chosen one to lead my people."

"I have heard stories that you are the latest in a line of sorcerers once touched with *elementia*. That your ancestors were among the Watchers themselves, those who were guardians to the Kindred."

"You've heard correctly. This is why I am the chieftain of my people and why they trust me beyond all others. We do not have a god or goddess to worship such as you do. My people have me. When they pray, they pray to me."

"And do you hear these prayers?"

"In spirit, I hear all of them. But when they want something badly enough, they will offer a blood sacrifice to show honor to me."

Blood sacrifice? How deeply savage. No wonder they were a dying people, reliant on a handful of vineyards to keep their economy from stagnating completely.

"How interesting," Magnus said instead.

"The greatest sacrifice must be something that one truly values. To sacrifice something of no value is meaningless."

"Agreed."

"Is that what you're asking of me right now?" King Gaius asked. "A blood sacrifice to show honor to you?"

Basilius spread his hands and turned toward the king. "As there are legends about me, there are also many stories about you. It is difficult to separate truth from fiction."

"What have you heard?"

"That you are a king who accepts no less than perfection from all those who surround you. That you tax your people until they can barely feed themselves. Your army polices the villages of Limeros, and anyone who strays outside the rules you've set forth will pay dearly for their error, often with their lives. That you will torture and execute anyone accused of witchcraft found in your land. That you have ruled your kingdom with violence and intimidation and that your people fear you even as they bow at your feet. That they call you the King of Blood."

If Magnus had been required to speak after that little speech, he was certain that nothing would have emerged from his mouth. These were the rumors about King Gaius?

How incredibly . . . accurate.

He watched his father closely for his reaction, fully expecting him to lash out with threats and anger, throwing the chief and his entourage out of his kingdom immediately.

Instead, King Gaius began to laugh. It was a dark sound edged in danger and it made a chill run up Magnus's back as it echoed through the cavernous hall.

"Such stories," he said. "Magnified for entertainment value, of course. Are you offended by such possibilities?"

"Quite the opposite," Chief Basilius replied. "A man like that is one who would not sit back and let others fight his battles. He would fight them himself. He would kill and take what he needed, when he needed it. Are you that man?"

King Gaius leaned forward, all amusement fading from his face. "I am that *king*."

"You want Auranos, but I can't believe it is merely due to outrage over a murder committed in my land. Tell me why you're so driven to align with Paelsia to take it."

King Gaius didn't speak for a moment, as if assessing the man before him. "I want to watch the ruler of that land suffer as he sees his kingdom slip away from him and into the hands of someone he hates. This is my opportunity to have that."

Chief Basilius seemed satisfied by the answer. "Good. Then there is only the matter of you proving yourself to me in a way more tangible than words. Do this and I pledge to give this matter deep thought and have my final answer to you soon."

"Prove myself through blood sacrifice."

The chief nodded. "I want you to sacrifice something you care about very much, something over which you will mourn the loss."

The king's gaze flicked to Magnus. Magnus's grip tightened on the edge of the table. His palms were damp.

His father couldn't possibly agree to something so savage, not at the mere whim of this Paelsian peasant king.

"Tobias," King Gaius said. "Give me your dagger."

"Certainly." Tobias slipped his plain, steel-bladed dagger from the sheath at his hip and handed it to the king hilt first. "If you need a suggestion, your majesty, there are several thieves in the dungeon currently awaiting trial."

"Would that be acceptable to you, Chief Basilius?" The king rose from his throne on the dais. "Thievery is not a crime with a death sentence here. At the most, they would have had their hands severed. The unnecessary loss of any Limerian subject's life would also be a loss to my kingdom, to my economy—and therefore to me."

Basilius also rose. Magnus stayed right where he was, watching all this with a mix of interest and distaste.

"I am underwhelmed by this choice," the chief said. "There are those among my people who would sacrifice their own children for me."

"And you're fine with such a crime?" the king asked, his expression tense. "Family, to me, is the one thing I value more than anything else in the world. And children are our legacy, more precious than gold."

"We're finished here. I'll think through what you've proposed to me today." The chief moved toward the door. His tone no longer held the same enthusiasm at the prospect of an alliance as it had earlier.

"Tobias," the king said evenly.

"Yes, your majesty?"

"I do regret the necessity of this."

The king swiftly moved behind the boy, pulled his head back, and slashed the blade across his throat.

Tobias's eyes went wide and his hands came up automatically to his neck. Blood squirted out from between his fingers. He collapsed to the ground.

King Gaius looked grimly down at him as the boy's body went still.

Magnus fought with every ounce of his strength not to allow the storm of emotions inside him to show on his face. He commanded himself to wear only the mask of impassivity he'd worked hard to build over the years.

Basilius had paused at the doorway, casting a glance back at the king and the dead valet. His brows drew together. His guards had their hands placed over their own weapons as if ready to defend the chief, but Basilius waved them off.

"He was your valet, was he not?" the chief asked.

The king's face was tight. "He was."

"More than that, if the rumors hold true."

King Gaius did not reply to this.

Finally, the Paelsia chieftain nodded. "Thank you for paying me such a great honor. Your sacrifice won't be forgotten. I will be in touch with you very soon with my final decision."

The chief and his entourage left.

"Clear away the body," the king barked at a few guards standing by. Together they removed Tobias's body from where it lay. Only a pool of blood remained as evidence to what had happened. Magnus forced himself not to look directly at it.

He made no move to leave, nor did he speak a word. He waited.

It took several minutes before the king moved to stand behind his chair. Every muscle in Magnus's body tensed. While Tobias hadn't expected his death to come at the hands of his own father, Magnus would never underestimate the king in this regard.

He nearly jumped right out of his skin when the king clasped his shoulder.

"Difficult times require difficult decisions," the king said.

"You did the only thing you could," Magnus replied as evenly as possible.

"So be it, then. I regret nothing. I never have and I never will. Stand up, my son."

Magnus pushed back from the table and got to his feet to face the king.

His father swept his gaze over him, from head to foot, nodding. "I always knew there was something special in you, Magnus. Your behavior today only solidifies that for me. You handled yourself very well just now."

"Thank you."

"I've been watching you very closely of late. After a difficult childhood, I believe you have grown into a fine young man—one ready for true responsibility rather than merely the continued leisure of a young prince. I grow prouder to call you my son with every passing day."

That his father could ever be proud of him was a shocking revelation.

"I am pleased to hear that," he managed to say evenly.

"I want you to be a part of this. To learn all you can so one day you'll be able to take over my throne stronger for every lesson learned. I wasn't lying in what I said before. Family is the most important thing to me, above all else. I want you by my side. Will you agree to that?"

Had this been a developing decision for his father or was the removal of Tobias, and the means by which he was removed, enough to trigger this sudden parental attachment?

Did it really matter?

"Of course, I agree," Magnus said. "Anything you need."

As he said the words, he realized he actually meant them.

The king nodded. "Good."

"Is there anything you require of me right now? Or are we to wait until the chief sends message to you of his decision?"

The king glanced at the two guards who remained in the room.

A flick of his chin toward them sent them out of the room so he could speak with Magnus privately.

"There is something, although it's not directly related to my plans for Auranos."

"What then?"

"It's about your sister."

Magnus froze. "What about her?"

"I know she's close to you. Closer than she is to either me or her mother. I want you to keep an eye on her. If you notice anything about her that strikes you as unusual, you must tell me immediately. If you fail to do this, she could be in grave danger. Do you understand?"

His breath caught. "What kind of danger?"

"I can tell you no more than that for now." His expression shadowed. "Will you do as I ask without further question? It's important, Magnus. Will you watch over Lucia and let me know if you notice anything at all?"

The world felt uneven and jagged beneath Magnus's feet. He hadn't cared about Tobias, but the bastard's death had deeply shaken him.

Lucia, however, he did care about. Whatever his father was asking for was directly related to the conversation Magnus had overheard between the king and Sabina on the night of her birthday. One of magic and mystery. And if it put Lucia's well-being in danger in any way, he knew there was no answer for him to give but one.

He nodded. "Of course I will, Father."

CHAPTER 9

AURANOS

"I'm very pleased to announce to you all"—King Corvin spoke at the front of the great hall, upon the dais, to a large crowd of friends and nobles gathered for the celebration banquet—"that my youngest daughter, Princess Cleiona Aurora Bellos, shall be united in wedlock to Lord Aron Lagaris, son of Sebastien Lagaris of Elder's Pitch. I hope that you can join with me in celebrating this happy and joyous union. To Princess Cleo and Lord Aron!"

The crowd cheered. Cleo tried to hold back her tears as she stood at her father's side. She couldn't see faces anymore, only blurry shapes. But she would *not* cry.

"Smile, Cleo." Aron clinked his wineglass against hers as she sat down again behind the table filled to overflowing with the royal feast. The chiming sound made her spine stiffen. "You'll make everyone think you aren't thrilled about this announcement."

"I'm not, and you know it," she said through clenched teeth.

"You'll get used to it," he assured her, but he didn't sound like he cared much one way or the other. "And before you know it, it'll be our wedding night."

It sounded more like a threat than a promise.

It was official. She was betrothed.

After her unpleasant chat with Aron at his villa three weeks ago, she'd broached the subject with her father, hoping that he would allow her to dissolve the engagement before it was even publicly announced. Instead, he'd told her that it was for the best and that she needed to have faith in his ability to choose a suitable husband for his cherished daughter.

Her father, Cleo thought with growing dismay, was more in love with the idea of Aron as a son-in-law—a lord who'd allegedly jumped into battle to defend the helpless princess from a savage Paelsian peasant—than she could ever be.

Since that "talk," the king had been too busy to speak privately with Cleo. However, happily, he'd also been too busy to make any announcement. Every day that passed without it was a gift. A chance for her to figure out a solution.

But she hadn't. Not in time.

And here we are, she thought dismally.

She couldn't eat anything. Her stomach felt too sick to hold down a single mouthful of the veal, stag, stuffed chicken, fruits, or sweet pastries—to name only a fraction of the lavish five-course feast. And she refused to take even a single gulp of wine.

The first moment she could, she made her escape from the crowded banquet, avoiding Theon's eyes and slipping past the hoards of well-wishers who seemed excited at the prospect of a royal wedding.

"How wonderful this is," she heard one woman say as she passed, "to have such joyful news to celebrate. I hope it will be a spring wedding. How delightful. It's unfortunate about Princess Emilia, though. So, so sad she isn't well enough to attend."

Cleo's heart clenched at the words. Every time she grew so selfish as to be concerned only with her own problems, she had to kick herself. There was something much more important going on beyond the issues with Aron.

Emilia's dizziness and headaches had only grown worse. She'd taken to her bed, too weak to come to a meal any longer. No healer who'd been summoned to the palace could figure out what was wrong with her. They advised Emilia to get plenty of rest and wait it out. And hopefully, like a fever, her recent health problems would eventually break.

Hopefully.

Cleo didn't like "hopefullys." She liked certainties. She liked knowing that tomorrow would be pleasant and sunny and filled with fun activities. She liked knowing that her family and friends were healthy and happy. Anything else was unacceptable.

Emilia would be fine because she had to be fine. If Cleo wanted something badly enough, it would happen. Why wouldn't it? It always had before. Resolutely, she pushed her engagement to Aron out of her head.

From the great hall, Cleo headed directly for her sister's chambers. Emilia was propped up behind the gauzy drapes of her canopied bed on a multitude of colorful silk pillows, reading by candlelight. In the corner on an easel stood Emilia's most recently finished painting, a study of the night sky. She glanced over, her eyes somewhat glazed, her face pale and drawn, as Cleo entered the room.

"Cleo . . ." she began.

Cleo started to cry, hating every tear that spilled—for herself, for Emilia. Tears were worthless. All they did was make her feel weak and helpless against this current sweeping them all along in its wake.

Emilia put down the book, pushed aside the canopy draping, and held out her hand to her sister. Cleo staggered forward, dropping down onto the bed beside her.

"I hate to see you so unwell," she sobbed.

"I know you do. But that's not the only reason for these tears, is it? Father has made the announcement?"

Cleo just nodded, her throat too tight to speak.

Emilia squeezed her hand and looked at her very seriously. "He's not doing this to cause you pain. He honestly thinks Aron will make a good husband for you."

No, he wouldn't. He would make a horrible husband. Why could no one see this but her? "Why now? Why couldn't he wait two years?"

"Many, even those who live here, saw what happened in Paelsia as a direct insult to our neighbors. With the engagement of you to Aron, the king is stating that he accepts Aron and finds him to be a noble and worthy match for his precious daughter. The rumors that Aron acted out of protection over the girl he loves are solidified. Crisis averted."

"It's so unfair." That this was solely a political choice sounded so cold, so analytical. Ideally, to Cleo at least, marriage should be about love, not royal agendas.

"Our father is the king. Everything he does, says, chooses to have done is in service to his kingdom. To strengthen where it might become weak."

Cleo drew in a ragged breath. "But I don't want to marry Aron."

"I know."

"So what should I do?"

Emilia smiled. "Perhaps you should elope with Nic, like you told me he suggested."

Cleo almost laughed at that. "Don't be ridiculous."

"You do know that boy is madly in love with you, right?"

Cleo frowned and pulled back to give her sister a quizzical look. "He isn't. I'd know something like that."

Emilia shrugged. "Some truths aren't so easily seen."

Nic was most certainly *not* in love with her. They were good friends—nothing more than that. Out of the corner of her eye she saw Theon move past the open door to Emilia's room, making his presence known. He'd followed her from the banquet and up the winding staircase to her sister's chambers. She felt an odd rush of pleasure that he refused to let her evade him.

She took her gaze away from him standing silently at the doorway and returned her attention to her sister. Her breath caught. Blood trickled from Emilia's nose.

At Cleo's look of horror, Emilia grabbed a cream-colored handkerchief already stained crimson and wiped the blood away as if this was not unexpected.

The sight had made Cleo's own blood run cold. "Emilia—"

"I know you're upset about the betrothal," Emilia interrupted softly, not acknowledging the disturbing sight. "So I need to tell you something, Cleo, about my broken engagement. Maybe it will help you."

Cleo hesitated, surprised. She never thought she'd learn the truth about this. "Tell me."

"I was happy to be engaged at the time. I felt it was my duty. Lord Darius was not horrible. I liked him; I really did. I was prepared to marry him. Then again, Father had waited until I was eighteen to pick someone for me. There was no rush as there is now."

Eighteen seemed like a small eternity away. If only Cleo could have been given so much time to come to terms with all of this. "What happened?"

"I fell in love with someone else."

"I knew it!" Cleo clutched her sister's hand. "Who was it?"

Emilia moistened her pale lips with the tip of her tongue and seemed hesitant to speak. "A guard."

Cleo's eyes nearly fell from her head. It was the last reply she'd expected. "You can't be serious."

"I am. I've never felt such love as I felt for him. It overwhelmed me. He was so handsome and exciting, and he made me feel more alive than I'd ever felt before. I knew it was wrong, that a match like this would never be allowed, but when our hearts go on such a journey, all we can do is try to hold on tight. I told Father I couldn't marry Lord Darius. I begged him not to make me. I told him that if he did, I'd—that I'd kill myself."

A shiver went through Cleo as she remembered her sister's deep depression at the time of her engagement to Lord Darius. "Please don't say something like that."

"It was true at the time. And Father believed that I'd do it. He ended the engagement immediately, holding the life of the future queen of Auranos above an arranged royal wedding. Now I feel bad for scaring him, but at the time I couldn't think straight."

"Where is he now?" Cleo whispered. "This guard?"

Emilia's eyes filled with tears, which splashed onto her pale cheeks. "Gone."

The single word held so much pain that it was palpable. Her sister had her favorite book clenched in her hand, a devotional to the goddess Cleiona.

"I take my strength from reading about her strength," Emilia said quietly, gazing down at the gold-embossed cover. "She did what had to be done to protect Auranos, risking her own existence to keep this kingdom safe from outside harm. My faith is all I have to get me through this dark time. I know your faith leans in more practical directions."

Despite being named for the goddess, Cleo wasn't invested in religion; nor was she alone in that. Many in the kingdom had drifted away from what was previously considered an important part of Auranian life. Years ago, the king had relaxed the rule that there be a day dedicated to prayer. All days were equal here, and his subjects could use their time however they pleased.

Cleo shrugged. "I guess I have a hard time believing in things I can't see."

"I wish you'd give it a chance and learn more than you already know. Cleiona was so brave and strong. That's why Mother insisted that you be named for her. She'd lost the baby previous to you, and she was told she wouldn't be able to have another. You were a miracle. All she did was pray for your small and precious life when you came into being. She wanted so badly for you to survive. She insisted that you be named for the goddess, hopefully to give you the strength to survive. It was her last request."

"I wish both of us could have survived." Cleo's voice broke. For all King Corvin's riches, his beloved queen had still died in child-birth, and there had been nothing he could do to prevent it.

"Well, I do too, but I'm so glad that you are here."

"You know I'd do anything for you, right?" Cleo's voice caught on the words. "I love you more than anything else in the world."

"I know. And I love you too." More blood trickled from Emilia's nose before she wiped it away.

"What can I do to help you?"

"Nothing." Emilia blinked, her expression bleak. "I'm dying, Cleo."

"Emilia! Don't say that." A sob welled in Cleo's chest. This was her greatest fear spoken aloud for the first time.

Emilia squeezed her hand. "It's true. You need to prepare yourself for what's to come. You must weather the storm and come out the other side stronger than before."

"Stop it." Cleo's voice quavered. "Don't say these things. You're *not* dying."

"I am. I know I am. When the man I love died two months ago, I prayed to Cleiona to take me as well so I could be with him again. My prayers are being answered."

Emilia's face crumpled with grief and tears streamed down her cheeks. The tears were tinged with red. More blood.

Cleo gasped. Her sister had been in love with a guard who'd died two months ago. "It was Theon's father, wasn't it?"

Emilia's breath caught and she stared at Cleo with surprise before she began to sob harder.

Cleo had guessed correctly. Her sister had been in love with the king's bodyguard who'd been thrown from his horse to his death. A tragedy. Cleo's heart had bled for Theon's loss. She'd had no idea that it was a loss also felt by her sister.

"I'm so, so sorry." She hugged Emilia as her sister's blood-tinged tears soaked into the shoulder of her gown. It was unusual for her sister to be so emotional. She normally hid her tears, even from Cleo. Emilia had always been poised and perfect, smart and sophisticated, while Cleo struggled with being on her best behavior. Emilia was always the rock—comforting Cleo when she was upset over some idle gossip or a petty argument with a friend. Or the loss of her innocence to Aron.

"You're the same as you were yesterday and the day before," she'd soothed. *"Nothing has changed. Not really. Forget what troubles you. Regret nothing, but learn from any mistakes you make. Tomorrow will be a brighter day, I promise."*

"I'm so sorry he's gone," Cleo murmured into her sister's hair. "I wish it could be different. But please don't say you prayed to die. You can't ever say something like that."

"When I first learned of his death I thought I'd die, too. It was as if I'd lost my husband, not only my lover." Emilia drew in a shaky breath. "While Simon and I could never dream of being married in reality, two weeks before he died, he rode with me out to the Lesturne Valley, a few hours past town. We spent the day together, pledging our love with the beauty of nature as our wit-ness. It was perfect, Cleo. For just a few hours, everything was so perfect. We watched the sunset together and counted the stars as they appeared. He said we'd become stars when we died, watching over the ones we love. Now I watch the sky every night hoping to find him there. I miss him so much I know it's the cause of this illness. My grief has burrowed into me like a dark thing that eats away at my life."

"You mustn't allow it to." Cleo's throat was so tight, but her words held anger. "You can't. You're to be the queen one day. If you die, that means it'll be me. Trust me, Emilia, that would be a very bad thing. I would make a terrible queen. As horrible as all this has been for you and as much as my heart breaks for this secret you've kept locked tight inside you, I refuse to accept that you're dying from grief. You're sick, that's all. And sick people get well again."

"The healers I've seen don't understand what's wrong with me. They have no answers or medicine other than the ones that make me want to sleep all day." Emilia snorted softly. "Although, one suggested I seek help in Paelsia. That it was my only hope for survival."

"From whom in Paelsia?" Cleo asked immediately.

Emilia waved a hand. "It's a legend, that's all."

"*What* legend?"

Emilia's smile widened. "Suddenly, my sister, who only believes in things she can see, is interested in stories and legends."

"If you don't tell me, I swear I'll scream."

"Goodness, wouldn't want that." Emilia's pale face looked tired and she leaned her head back on her pillow. "The healer told me of a woman in Paelsia who acts as guardian to the original grape seeds that were infused with earth magic. They're the ones that helped the vineyards to begin to produce such incredible wine. She tends to these vineyards with her own earth magic that she shields from the rest of the world."

"Magic," Cleo said skeptically.

"I know you don't believe, which is why I didn't want to tell you."

"So this woman has magic seeds and is responsible for the vineyards growing so wonderfully in Paelsia. Why doesn't she use this magic to help Paelsia out of its poverty?"

"Perhaps her magic cannot reach that far. But legend has it that the seeds she possesses have the ability to heal even the more dire illnesses."

"And who is this woman that she'd have such magic at her disposal?"

Emilia looked reluctant to say anything else.

"Well?" Cleo persisted.

"An exiled Watcher. One who left the Sanctuary many years ago."

"A *Watcher*," Cleo said with disbelief.

"That's right. So you're right. Fantasy, that's all. Watchers don't really exist. There's no one out there spying on us through the eyes of hawks, hoping for clues of where to find the Kindred."

"I've never believed in such nonsense."

"Which is why I hesitated in telling you any of this." She wiped a fresh trickle of blood from beneath her nose. Cleo's heart, which had all but recovered itself, began to hurt again.

"Emilia . . ." Her eyes filled with tears. "I don't know what to do."

Emilia's expression held deep distress. "I—I never should have told you any of this. My story got away from me. I only meant to say that if you really don't want to marry Aron, tell Father. Make him understand that you'll die if you do. And if you fall in love with someone else, you need to spend as much time with him as possible because you never know when he might be taken from you. Follow your heart wherever it leads. Appreciate life, Cleo. It's a gift that can be stolen at any time. No matter what happens to me now with this illness, I don't regret a moment I spent with Simon."

Cleo gritted her teeth. "You *won't* die. I simply won't allow it."

Emilia exhaled shakily. "My head hurts very badly. I need to sleep. I can barely keep my eyes open any longer because of the ridiculous elixirs the healers had me drink. Good night, dear sister. Tomorrow will be better."

Cleo held on to Emilia's hand until she was certain that she had drifted off to sleep. After kissing her sister's forehead, she left the room and entered the hallway on unsteady legs. Theon stood next to the door, grimness etched into his handsome features.

With the door open, Theon easily would have heard every

word spoken between her and Emilia even if he hadn't been trying to listen.

"Thought you might try to escape via your sister's balcony again," he said quietly.

"Not tonight." She looked up into his strained face. "Did you know?"

He shook his head. "I knew my father cared about someone, but he wouldn't say who it was. I figured he was involved with a married woman. Now I know."

She hugged her arms around herself as she walked. The wall-set lanterns cast a flickering glow of light and shadow along the hall. "Do you believe any of what she said about exiled Watchers and magic seeds that can heal illnesses?"

"I don't know."

Cleo stopped walking and turned to face him. "You don't? You mean, you think it could be possible?"

"My father believed in magic, in long-lost legends of the Watchers of the Kindred. He told me that those who exile themselves to the mortal world will have children that can also be touched by magic. Witches."

"I've never believed real witches exist. Or Watchers."

His expression darkened. "I never did either, and I'm not sure you should start now."

"I wonder if those in the Paelsian villages themselves would know how to find this woman," she said under her breath after a moment. "If I could get a name, a location, I could find her and I could speak with her."

Theon was silent for a moment. "You aren't really considering chasing after this, are you? It was only a story your sister told you."

"If there's someone who can help Emilia, then I need to find her."

Theon looked concerned by the sudden determination on her face. "After what happened with Lord Aron, it's not a good idea for anyone from Auranos to set foot inside Paelsia's borders until this all blows over."

She looked at him with alarm. "Do you think it will?"

He nodded. "It's one of the reasons your father chose to act now in announcing your engagement. It's a distraction."

Her shoulders sank. "My future misery is being used as a distraction. How wonderful."

"Like your sister said, you don't have to marry him. Not unless you want to."

"You make it sound like I have a choice."

"Princess Emilia was able to stop her engagement because she loved someone else."

"So you think I should fall in love with someone else?"

He didn't respond to this right away. She realized that he was watching her carefully.

"Maybe you should," he finally said.

Her heart skipped a beat. Then her gaze moved to his lips, as if she couldn't help herself, before she looked away.

"I want to help Emilia," she whispered. "I can't lose her."

"I know."

"I need to go to Paelsia and try to find more information about this exiled Watcher."

Theon's expression hardened. "Forget this, princess. Besides, you don't believe in magic."

"I haven't believed in magic because I don't believe in anything that I haven't seen with my own eyes. Therefore, I must go to Paelsia as soon as I can and learn the truth for myself."

He studied her patiently, and a very small sliver of respect moved through his gaze. "You're determined to save your sister."

"She's dying. I—I feel it, Theon. I'm going to lose her if I don't do something immediately." She swallowed hard and looked up at him. "Would you go with me?"

Theon was silent for a moment. "If you get your father's permission for this trip, then of course I'll go with you."

This could be the answer she needed—that Emilia needed to restore her health. And if there was a little unrest in Paelsia, Cleo would make sure to avoid it. With Theon at her side, nothing could stop her. A swell of motivation and optimism filled her.

"Then I'll get my father's permission."

CHAPTER 10

LIMEROS

L

"She's just a girl. Nothing more. But you believe?"

Alexius could communicate with others of his kind mentally while in the mortal world, even in hawk's form. He turned his sharp eyes from the dark-haired princess who had emerged from the tall and ominous stone castle to his right to see his friend Phaedra, perched on the branch next to him.

"I believe."

"And what does it mean if she is?" Phaedra asked.

"Everything."

It meant that the Sanctuary could be saved, that they would finally have a chance to reclaim the Kindred for themselves before it fell into someone else's hands.

The Sanctuary would continue on well after the mortal world faded completely, but it wouldn't last forever. What had become their prison would soon become their grave.

Without *elementia*, everything eventually faded away. Especially that which was created from magic itself.

"And what if she isn't?" his friend persisted.

"Then all is lost."

Sixteen years ago, Alexius had seen the signs. Even the stars themselves aligned in celebration of this beautiful girl's birth. He'd watched as she was stolen from her cradle, the witches—descendants of one exiled from the Sanctuary itself—snatching her from her birth mother's protection.

It was true that the mother had no idea what she'd given to the world, but the common witches were not right to take the child and hide her away, spilling so much blood in the process. One witch—the one with goodness in her heart—had perished at the hands of her darker sister.

That sister still lived, watching over this girl as Alexius watched over them both.

Patience was one gift a Watcher prized above all. But even Alexius felt a flutter of nervousness in his chest. He believed, he'd watched, and he waited for a sign that he was right. That she was the one. He hated to say that his belief had begun to wane and that his patience was drying up.

Within him was now an unfamiliar stirring of anger that this wisp of a girl could become a disappointment to him, nothing more than a regular mortal—at best, another common witch. Being in this world too long was a danger to a Watcher. This growing anger was a sign that he needed to return to the Sanctuary soon to cleanse himself of such burgeoning and unhelpful emotion.

Perhaps he was wrong. Perhaps he'd wasted all his time studying this girl whenever she came outside. Whenever she stood on her balcony, gazing down into the frozen garden beneath her chambers. Watching her lips as she read to herself out loud, as she prayed to a false goddess who did not deserve such deep devotion.

Alexius wanted to turn away, to spend his precious hours in the mortal world on other pursuits, but he couldn't leave her.

Perhaps soon. But not yet.

He pushed off from the branch and flapped his wings, soaring high into the sky. From the ground, the beautiful dark-haired princess glanced up at him. For the briefest of moments, their eyes met.

All she would see when she looked at him was a golden hawk.

For some reason, this realization pained him.

CHAPTER 11

LIMEROS

$\mathcal{L}$

Lucia stood outside, her breath forming frozen clouds in the cold air with each exhale, watching the hawk fly high up into the bright blue sky. She could have sworn that it looked directly at her.

She brushed aside the thought and scanned the grounds, searching for any sign of her brother's return. After weeks of keeping her horrible secret hidden deep inside, she was ready to unburden herself, come what may.

Of course, the one time she desperately wanted to find Magnus was the one time he was nowhere to be found. She'd searched the halls of the castle for an hour only to learn from a kitchen maid that he was accompanying their father on a hunt but was expected to return soon.

It was strange, though. Magnus had never shown much interest in hunting with their father before. Magnus had never shown much interest in hunting at all. She wondered uncomfortably if the recent death of Tobias, who she knew (though she wasn't supposed to) was her half brother, had anything to do with this change. He'd been buried quickly and quietly, with no explanation given for his sudden demise.

To clear her head of her swirling thoughts, Lucia had gone outside and into the cold air and sunshine, determined to go for a brisk walk around the palace grounds and ready herself for her afternoon classes—art, geography, and, unfortunately, embroidery. She could rarely get through an entire class of needlework without stabbing herself. Magnus didn't seem to think she was clumsy, but her sore fingertips would claim otherwise.

To her far left, she caught a glimpse of a boy she knew—Michol Trichas. She raised her hand to wave at him, but he didn't seem to notice and turned away.

She picked up her pace to catch up to him, drawing her furlined cloak closer to block out the icy chill.

"Michol!" She greeted him with a smile, the frozen ground crunching under the leather soles of her shoes. They'd taken an art class together here at the palace a few months ago. Her father had wanted to abolish the subject entirely, but Lucia had begged him to reconsider, promising that the study of art was not simply a frivolous pursuit of aesthetic beauty, but one of history and heritage.

Michol was the son of local nobles who were also friends of the king. She liked him very much—had enjoyed talking to him about sculpture. They'd spent an hour discussing a sketch of a mysterious carved stone wheel located in the northernmost frozen reaches of Limeros, an area that never thawed. It was said to be originally from the Sanctuary itself—a legendary place of magic hidden in the Forbidden Mountains from which eternal mystical beings watched over the mortal world. Some more obscure texts that Lucia had read said that to encounter such a wheel was to discover a location marked by Watchers as a clue to find the lost Kindred—which could be a blessing or a curse, depending on the myths one believed.

Michol had attended her birthday banquet, and he'd promised to come back so they might go for a walk together and do some exploring of the palace grounds. He'd never returned, and she didn't understand why. Now he turned to face her with a sheepish expression. He raked a hand through his messy hair. "Princess Lucia, a pleasure to see you again."

She pushed away her nervousness and decided to be as straightforward as possible with the boy. "I haven't seen you in ages!"

"No."

"Are you trying to hide from me?" She tried to smile, but the thought that she was right was disturbing. Still, she was curious to know the truth. "Did I say something to offend you?"

He made a strange snorting sound, which might have been a nervous laugh. "Hardly."

"I've been waiting for us to go on that walk."

Michol stared at her as if perplexed. "Then I—I don't understand."

Lucia tucked her hands into the sleeves of her cloak to keep them warm. "That makes two of us."

"Your brother told me that you wanted nothing to do with me."

She blinked. "Excuse me?"

"I was here before to call on you and he made sure I knew that my presence was unwelcome. That you said I wasn't to be encouraged. That you, well . . . that you were interested in taking walks with *other* boys, but not with me."

Confusion gave way to clarity and a hot surge of anger. "Did he?"

"He did."

She struggled to breathe normally and not let her emotions get the better of her. Lately, strange things tended to happen when they did . . . things that she had to keep secret in case anyone found out.

She let out a long, steady breath and looked directly at Michol. "He shouldn't have told you that."

"Really?" His expression turned hopeful.

"And you never should have believed him without speaking with me. My brother does not control whom I see and when I see them. *I* do."

He blanched. "I didn't know."

"This isn't the first time this has happened."

Magnus had developed a bit of a habit of deciding who was deserving of his younger sister's attention. But she didn't need his opinion or his help in weeding out the unworthy. She was quite capable of doing that herself.

"Honestly," she muttered. "How dare he interfere in my life like this?"

"Does this mean we can have that walk after all?"

Lucia turned her gaze on the boy, studying him closely for the first time. At first glance he was handsome enough, a few inches taller than she, his skin pale and perfect.

It was too bad that he'd been born missing a backbone.

She forced a smile to her lips, one that brought a light of optimism back to the boy's eyes.

"Perhaps another time. Good day, Michol."

She returned to the castle without a backward glance, anger

toward her brother swelling with every beat of her heart as she quickly made her way through the shadowy halls. Magnus was interfering, overprotective, deeply annoying, and *incredibly* vexing. She turned the next corner.

"Lucia," Queen Althea said, with no warmth in her voice. Lucia froze in place at the sight of her mother.

"Yes, Mother?"

The queen's dark hair had turned gray in streaks. Her face was pale and drawn, and she seemed to peer down her nose at her daughter even though they were the exact same height. "What mischief are you up to this afternoon? And why are your cheeks so red?"

"No mischief. I was outside. It . . . it's cold."

"It's the dead of winter. Of course it's cold. Why were you outside?"

It always seemed to be the dead of winter in Limeros. Lucia cleared her throat, immediately on guard under her mother's close scrutiny. "I'm looking for Magnus. Do you know when he'll be returning from the hunt with Father?"

"Soon, I'm sure." Her lips compressed, and her eyes scanned the length of her daughter with distaste. "Your hair is a mess. You really shouldn't leave your chambers looking so slovenly. Someone might see you."

Lucia grimaced and touched her tangled hair. "I didn't think I looked that bad."

"Well, you do. I'll have a maid sent to your room immediately to help you look decent again."

Her cheeks felt tight, her insides turning hot as lava. "That's . . . so kind of you, Mother."

"Think nothing of it."

It was never a question of telling the queen her secret. While her mother had given Lucia life, she'd never given her a moment's kindness since. Lucia wondered if the woman was capable of showing love to anyone. She'd never seen evidence of it, apart from a few moments of motherly preening in front of company. Lucia had learned at an early age to seek approval elsewhere since it would never come from the queen herself. So she'd turned to books and learning. Any praise she received had been from her tutors. From Magnus. And, occasionally, from her father. She didn't go out of her way to seek her mother's approval, nor would she ever.

"Go back to your room, daughter," the queen said, her voice clipped. "Don't delay. We can't have anyone seeing the Limerian princess looking like you do."

"Very well." Despite her disinterest in her mother's opinion, Lucia had rarely felt as ugly in her entire life as she did at that very moment. She turned away from the queen and began to head toward her room, dreading the visit from the maid to help with her appearance. If her mother sent the usual one, she would be rough and pull her hair, leaving Lucia with a headache for the rest of the day.

In pain, but looking presentable. *Just as the queen wishes.* After her frustrating conversations with both Michol and her mother, she felt utterly annoyed. And tangled. And, admittedly, a bit frizzy.

"Lucia," a voice greeted her before she reached her destination. "Darling, is there something wrong?"

Sabina Mallius stood in her way, blocking her path to her room. *And now this,* Lucia thought.

"Nothing's wrong," Lucia said evenly. "But thank you for your concern." While she bore no strong love for her mother, she'd never speak ill of the queen to her father's mistress.

"Let me guess." Sabina gave her a pinched but sympathetic look. "You just spoke to Althea."

"My hair is messy," Lucia explained. Sabina was beautiful from morning until night, as if it took no effort at all to look that way.

"Your hair looks gorgeous to me—wild and free, not trapped and severe," Sabina said with a wave of her hand. "Don't let anyone ever tell you differently. Even your mother."

While her words were delivered flippantly, there was an edge to them.

"Are you angry with me?" Lucia asked on a hunch.

Sabina's eyebrows went up. "With you? Whatever for?"

"Never mind, I suppose. I apologize; I'm sure I'm imagining things."

Despite the queen's unpleasantness and lack of visible emotion toward her daughter, she had a great deal of influence over Lucia. She'd drummed it into her daughter's head that being dutiful, being polite, and looking neat and polished were the main qualities a true princess should cultivate.

Also, that Sabina Mallius was evil incarnate.

Queen Althea was threatened by the king's mistress living side by side with the rest of them all these years, even if she would rather cut out her own tongue than admit such a thing.

"Are you certain that everything's all right, my dear?" Sabina asked. "You look terribly upset."

"Do I?" Lucia had to work harder on her mask of indifference. Her brother had his perfectly formed, but her emotions still played on her face more than they should. Emotions could be used against her.

Emotions could trigger the strange . . . *happenings* that had been swirling around her lately like the beginnings of an ice storm.

"I'm searching for Magnus," Lucia said. "I want to talk to him when he returns from the hunt."

Although she was no longer sure she would tell him her secret quite yet. First she wanted to discuss the matter of him running off any boy who showed romantic interest in her.

"They're back," Sabina replied. "I saw them from my window approaching the castle only minutes ago. What do you want to talk to Magnus about?"

Lucia tensed. "Nothing that would interest you."

Sabina looked closely at her. "I want you to know something, dear. And I mean it from the very bottom of my heart."

"What's that?"

"If you feel like there's no one you can confide in, know that you can come to me." Sabina studied her face as if searching for some hidden answer. "Anything, Lucia. Anything at all. You're a young woman now, and the changes you're experiencing must be very difficult for you. I can help. Even if those changes might seem unusual or . . . frightening."

Lucia inhaled sharply. It was as if Sabina knew her secret without ever being told. "I don't know what you mean."

Sabina's eyes narrowed a fraction. "The worst thing is to have a horrible secret that you fear could be dangerous but no one to share it with. No one to trust. Do you understand?"

Lucia stared at her, mouth dry, unspeaking.

Sabina pulled her closer and lowered her voice to a whisper. "Because some of us share the same dangerous secret, Lucia. And I assure you it's nothing to fear. I can help you when you need me. And you will need me."

The same secret.

This was an opportunity right here to tell this woman everything. To unburden her soul of her strange discoveries. Of her strange new abilities.

But the words would not form on her tongue. She was not so stupid as to blurt out the truth to just anyone, no matter what they might say to coax it from her. "If there's anything I need to share, I promise to seek you out."

A muscle under Sabina's right eye twitched, almost imperceptibly. But then she nodded. "Very well, then. I'll see you at dinner, dear."

Lucia began to walk away from Sabina, forcing herself not to speed her steps. Likely, she mistook Sabina's meaning. The woman couldn't possibly know what was wrong with her. And the thought that Sabina might have the same strange abilities that had surfaced for her . . .

Impossible. There would have been some indication before this that Sabina was different.

No, Lucia had held her tongue and would continue to do so.

Sabina was right about one thing. Her father and Magnus had returned from the hunt. They were taking off their muddy boots in the foyer, a cylindrical room that had a ceiling as high as the entire castle itself. The smooth stone staircase cut into the cold stone wall, spiraling down to the main floor from the upper levels. Lucia quietly descended these stairs, keeping her brother directly in her sights. Despite the distractions she'd had since entering the castle, her anger toward Magnus hadn't decreased even a fraction.

A messenger approached her father and handed him a letter. The king sliced the envelope open and quickly read it.

His brow raised. "Excellent," Lucia heard him say.

"What is it?" Magnus asked.

"Chief Basilius has officially agreed to join forces with Limeros.

He likes my plan." His jaw tensed. "And he was deeply honored by my sacrifice."

"Should I offer congratulations now or wait until after you conquer Auranos?" Magnus asked drily after a moment.

Lucia stopped moving and inhaled sharply. Conquer Auranos?

"Before, during, after. It's all good." The king let out a humorless laugh. "This is all good news, my son. This is an important day that will live in infamy. And all of this one day will be yours. Every last piece of it. It's my legacy to you."

Magnus shifted his gaze as if he sensed Lucia's presence. Their eyes met. There was a hint of something in his expression that Lucia hadn't remembered seeing there before.

Greed.

It was like looking at a complete stranger. A chill went through her, freezing her in place. But it was only for a split second before his brown eyes regained their normal warmth and humor. She let out the breath she hadn't realized she'd been holding as she finally reached the bottom of the stairs.

"Lucia," he said with a smile.

She chose to pretend that she hadn't heard anything they'd been discussing. Her father despised eavesdroppers. "We must talk, brother."

"Oh?"

"I spoke with Michol earlier."

His dark brows drew together. "Michol?"

"Fine boy," the king said with a nod. "I believe he's smitten with you, daughter."

Clarity shone in Magnus's eyes. "He visited you, did he?"

"He told me of the talk you had together." Her words were clipped. "Care to elaborate?"

A smile twitched at his lips. "Not really."

She glared at him. How dare he find this even slightly amusing?

His smile grew. "I brought something back for you from the hunt."

Her expression turned to distaste. "Something you killed?"

"Come and see."

Lucia reluctantly approached, guarded as to what it might be. Despite his proficiency in archery, Magnus had never developed a taste for ending an animal's life simply for the sport of it. Other boys had mocked him behind his back for this, but he didn't care. He'd once told her that he'd have no problem hunting if it was to put food on the table, but to kill for the simple sport of it would never appeal to him. Lucia was dismayed to think that had changed. The whirlwind of emotions that had been building swirled inside her.

Suddenly, the tall, heavy iron doors behind her father and brother slammed shut.

The king looked over his shoulder with confusion. Then he cast a quizzical look at Lucia.

She averted her gaze, her heart pounding.

Up ahead, Magnus pulled something from a basket. It was small, furry, and had long, floppy ears.

Its nose twitched.

"It's a rabbit," Lucia said with surprise. "A baby."

"A pet. For you." He handed the animal to her. It nestled into the crook of her neck. She felt its rapid heartbeat beneath her fingertips and her own heart swelled. She'd always wanted a pet, especially when she was just a child, but apart from horses and a few wolfhounds owned by the king, her mother had never allowed it.

"You didn't kill it."

MORGAN RHODES

Magnus looked at her curiously. "Of course not. A dead rabbit wouldn't make a very good pet, would it?"

Its fur was so soft. She stroked it, trying to ease the animal's fear. She looked up at Magnus, her throat tightening. "So you think this excuses you for scaring off Michol—and who knows who else?"

He gave her a wary look. "Does it help a little?"

She hissed out a breath but couldn't keep the smile from appearing on her lips. "Maybe a little."

Magnus was challenging, annoying, opinionated, and relied on his masks to hide his true feelings from the world far too much. But she still loved him and knew without a doubt that she would do anything for him, even when he tested her patience.

And she would tell him her secret the next time she had the opportunity. Maybe then he'd tell her what had been troubling him lately. Even now as he gazed down at her holding his gift, there was a deep and bottomless sadness in his eyes.

CHAPTER 12

AURANOS

Cleo waited until her father was alone in his study and launched into a nonstop explanation about everything—although she didn't touch on the topic of Emilia being romantically involved with Theon's father.

The king didn't interrupt. He let Cleo speak for as long as she required.

Finally, she summed things up as simply as she could.

"No healer seems able to help her, and she's only getting worse. I know I can find this exiled Watcher. She holds the magic to save Emilia. But I have to leave soon, before it's too late. Theon can go with me for protection. I don't think we'll be gone very long at all." She wrung her hands. "I know this is the answer, Father. I *know* it. I can save Emilia's life."

The king regarded his youngest daughter for an entire minute of silence with a bemused expression.

"An exiled Watcher," he said. "Who possesses magic healing seeds."

She nodded. "Someone in one of the villages must know where to find her. If I must search every village in Paelsia, then that's exactly what I'll have to do."

He templed his fingers and watched her through hooded eyes. "The Watchers are only a legend, Cleo."

For the first time since she'd entered the king's meeting room, she felt a twinge of doubt about the outcome of their talk. "Well, that's what I thought too, but if there's a chance . . . I mean, you don't know that for sure."

"That there are those who watch us through the eyes of hawks, searching for their precious Kindred is a story that helps keep children in line and fearful enough to behave themselves lest they be witnessed acting naughty."

Her gaze flicked to the royal coat of arms on the wall, which bore two hawks, one golden, one black, beneath a single golden crown. It was as familiar to her as her own name and she knew it had to mean something. It was a sign she was right. "Just because you haven't seen something doesn't mean it isn't true. I've been wrong to take that stance until now."

He didn't look angry, just weary. His face was etched in more lines than Cleo remembered. "Cleo, I know how much you love your sister—"

"More than anything!"

"Of course. I love her too. But she is not dying. She is simply ill. And this illness, while severe, will pass if she gets enough rest. She will recover."

Frustration twisted in her chest. "You don't know that for sure. You have to let me go."

"I have to do no such thing." The king's expression only grew more tense. "It's unwise for you to even consider visiting that place again for any reason. Troubles have increased, not decreased, in the time that has passed since the Agallon boy's death."

"What kind of trouble?"

He sighed. "The kind that you need not concern yourself with, Cleo. I'll deal with it."

She squeezed her hands into fists. "If there's trouble *growing*, then I need to leave soon or I might not get the chance later."

"Cleo." There was a warning growl to her father's words now. He'd tolerated her up until now, but she knew he was tired and in no mood for anything he considered a waste of time.

But saving her sister's life wasn't a waste of time.

She crossed her arms over her chest and began pacing the grand room. "I mean, if I'm wrong, then I'm wrong. But I have to try. Why can't you see that?"

The king's lips tightened. "All I see is my sixteen-year-old daughter making up far-fetched stories so she can escape from her new fiancé's attentions."

She sent a look of horror at him. "You think that's what this is about?"

"I know it'll take a while for you to get used to this. By the time the wedding is planned, all will seem better. By then, Emilia will be well again and she can help you prepare."

That wasn't at all what this was about. But since he'd brought it up . . .

"You didn't make *Emilia* marry someone she didn't love."

He hissed out a long breath. "That was different."

"Why was that different? Because she threatened to kill herself? Maybe I'll do the exact same thing!"

The king just looked at her patiently, seemingly undisturbed by the threat. "You'd never do that."

"I wouldn't? I—I could do it tonight. I could throw myself down the stairs. I could stop eating. I could . . . well, there are many, many ways I could end my life if I wanted to!"

He shook his head. "You wouldn't, because you don't really want to die. You don't just live, Cleo. Life itself sings from your existence." The smallest smile appeared on his lips. "I know one day when you've finally outgrown this tendency to be overly dramatic to gain attention, your true self will come forth. And that Cleo will be a remarkable woman—one who deserves to bear the name of a goddess."

She glowered at him. "You don't even believe in the goddess!"

His expression shuttered. He'd been patient with her up until now, but she'd gone too far.

Ever since her mother had died in childbirth, the king had turned his back on any kind of prayer or worship, and his subjects soon followed suit. Emilia was the only religious one left in the Bellos family.

"I'm sorry," she whispered.

"You're young and you speak before you think. That's how it's always been with you, Cleo. I expect no better."

She ran a hand under her nose. "I didn't mean to hurt you."

"Don't worry about me. Worry about yourself. I do. I worry about you constantly when compared to your sister. You'll get yourself in trouble one day, Cleo, and I just hope that you'll be all right. It's one of the reasons I think a marriage to Aron, even at your young age, is a good idea. The duties of a wife will give you some well-needed maturity." When she flinched, his gaze softened. "I'm trying to help you."

"How is this helping? By reminding me that I have no control over my own destiny?"

He reached down to take her hand in his. "You need to trust me, Cleo. Trust me to make the right decisions for you, for our family."

"Family is the most important thing to me. That's exactly why I need to go to Paelsia," she said softly. "Please say yes."

His cheeks tightened. "No, Cleo."

Her eyes burned. "So instead you'll sit back and watch Emilia die? How is that making the right decisions for your family? You don't care about her. You don't care about me. All you care about is this hateful kingdom."

He sighed wearily as he sat down at the table and turned his attention to the papers in front of him. "It's time you left, Cleo. I have work to do. This conversation is over."

Cleo's heart slammed against her rib cage. "Father! Please, don't be like this. You can't be so cruel and uncaring that you'd deny me this!"

When he shot a look at her of barely bridled rage, she staggered back a step.

"Go to your chambers. And stay there until dinner. Theon!" Theon stepped into the room a moment later. He'd been waiting just outside. "See that my daughter returns to her chambers and please ensure that she makes no foolish attempt to travel to Paelsia in the coming days."

Theon bowed. "Yes, your majesty."

There was nothing left to say. There was more that Cleo wanted to say, but even she knew when to hold her tongue. All that could be gained from more arguing was to summon her father's anger even more. He might move up her wedding to Aron to a week from now as a punishment. Or even tomorrow.

The king didn't believe that Emilia was dying. But Cleo believed more than she had before. She felt the truth of it deep in her heart. Only something magical could save her.

"I'm sorry, princess," Theon said under his breath as they left the king's presence.

Cleo's cheeks were hot and her feet thudded against the floor as she unconsciously made her way through the labyrinthine halls and back to her chambers. She thought she'd been out of tears before, but there were buckets left. She cried them all when Theon left her, closing the door behind him.

But when her tears finally dried, their departure brought a slow and steely resolve.

The whole world—including her father—could repeatedly tell her no. In the end, it made no difference to her.

Cleo would fix this. No matter what it took or where she had to go, she would save her sister's life before it was too late.

After dinner, Cleo gathered her two closest confidants together—Nic and Mira. "I'm going," she said after she explained everything to them.

Nic blinked. "To Paelsia."

"Yes."

"To find an exiled Watcher to beg for some magical grape seeds."

She knew it sounded absolutely preposterous, but it didn't matter. "Yes, exactly."

A grin broke across his face. "That sounds fantastic."

"Are you joking?" Mira exclaimed. "Cleo, what are you thinking? Do you know how dangerous traveling there again could be?"

She shrugged defiantly. "I must do this. There's no other choice."

Her father would be furious to find that she'd gone against his wishes; she knew that. But she wouldn't be gone for very long. If she got the right lead, asked the right questions of the right people in the right village, then it would be a no bigger deal than her trip to Paelsia to help Aron buy wine.

She grimaced at the memory. Perhaps that wasn't the best example of a successful trip.

"The thing is, you can't tell anyone," she said. "I'm just telling you so you don't worry about me while I'm gone."

"Oh, no." Mira cast up her eyes. "Why would we worry? Oh, Cleo, I love both you and Emilia dearly, but you're making my brain hurt with all of this ridiculousness."

Nic crossed his arms. "I don't understand how the seeds work. They grow vineyards that create amazing wine . . . and they also cure diseases?"

"It's earth magic."

"Ah, I see. Perhaps you can ask this Watcher where the Kindred's been hidden for a thousand years. That would be very useful information, wouldn't it?"

She glared at him. "You're looking at me like I've gone completely crazy."

His smile stretched. "You *are* crazy. But in the best way possible. However, you going alone? Now, that's really crazy."

She shook her head. "I'm not going alone. Theon is coming with me."

"No, I'm not," Theon said quietly.

He'd been standing a bit behind her so he hadn't been in her direct line of sight as she spoke to her friends.

She spun around to face him. "Of course you're going with me."

He looked at her sternly. "Your sister never should have told you any of this. It put ideas in your head."

"And now that the ideas are there, I have to find out if they're true. Don't you see? This is the answer. This is what's going to save Emilia. If I don't go—if *we* don't go—she's going to die. I know it."

His face was tense. "Your father didn't give his permission for this trip."

"I don't care what my father said!" Her cheeks blazed with anger. "You heard him yourself. He doesn't understand. He doesn't believe. But I do. He'll be angry, but when he sees that this works, then he'll be grateful that we went against his wishes."

"He only wants to keep you safe."

"I will be safe. Besides, you'll be there to protect me."

"You might be ready to ignore your father's wishes, but I can't. He's the king. His word is my command. For me, for everyone in this kingdom. Do you know the penalty for going against a direct order from the king? It's death, your highness."

Cleo's heart pounded. "I wouldn't let anything happen to you. I swear it. You don't have to be afraid."

He bristled. "I'm not afraid. You're just being stubborn. Do you always get what you want?"

"Yes," Nic said at the same time that Mira said, "Actually, she does."

Cleo turned to Theon. "If I have to order you to come with me, I will. Don't make me."

"You can order me all you like, but the answer will still be no," he growled, giving her a dangerous look. "I answer to the king, not to you. He said no, so I must also say no. We're not going. Please, princess, try your best to accept this. Anything else will only make everything more difficult for you."

Her eyes burned, but no tears spilled this time. She was all out of tears. Now she just had boiling-hot anger to fuel her.

She turned to Nic. "What do you think?"

"That's a good question," Nic replied. "While I'm not sure it's the wisest idea I've ever heard, I know your heart's in the right place."

"Enough of this," Theon said sharply. "The discussion is over. There will be no trip to Paelsia today."

"I wasn't even planning to leave for two more days." She let out a slow, shaky breath. "Maybe by then you'll have changed your mind."

"Two days," Theon repeated, his hard gaze finally softening. "A lot can change in two days."

"I know."

"The same goes for you, princess. Think about this for two days. I hope that your commitment to this foolhardy plan will ease by then. Do you think that's possible? Will the idea of Watchers and magic seeds seem a little less ideal when some time has passed?"

"Maybe," she admitted with reluctance.

He nodded, seemingly satisfied by the answer. "I'll escort you back to your chambers now."

Cleo said good night to the Cassians and followed him, not speaking another word until she reached the door to her room.

"I am sorry," Theon said. "I know how much you love your sister. But I can't go against your father's wishes."

She let out a shaky sigh. "I don't blame you. Despite any harsh words thrown between us, I know your heart is true. You only want to do what's right."

His jaw stiffened and he averted his gaze. "I believe the same to be true about you."

That surprised her. "Don't lie. I know you think I'm a spoiled brat who only wants things her way."

"I never said that. And I don't think that. You are stubborn, but . . . well, let's just say that being stubborn isn't always a bad thing when it's for the right reason."

"My father said that I act overly dramatic to gain attention." She bit her bottom lip, doubting herself. Was that really how the king had always viewed her? No wonder when she'd asked for something so important he'd found it easy to turn her down.

"I must respectfully disagree with the king on this." Theon shook his head and drew his gaze to her again. "You're a girl who views the world in a certain way. You want what you want. And if obstacles are presented to you, you try to find a way around them. Or *through* them."

She looked up at him with gratitude. Considering what a short time they'd known each other, he saw her as she would like to be seen. She could only hope it was the truth. "Thank you for trying to protect me, even if occasionally it means that I can't have what I want."

"It's my honor to protect you, your highness. Sleep well." With a last searching look, Theon turned from her and moved down the hall.

Cleo went into her room, prepared for bed, and went to sleep.

And then, an hour before sunrise, she rose, dressed, and slipped out of her room, past the sleeping maid who was stationed by her door, waiting for her to awaken.

She'd knowingly lied to Theon when she said she planned to leave in two days. Emilia didn't have that kind of time. Cleo had made her decision to go right away, even if it had to be by herself. She had some money with her. She would hire someone else to be her guide. Once she was past the palace walls, she'd plan her next step.

"Morning, princess."

She froze.

For a split second she was certain it was Theon who'd discovered her ruse. But he didn't know her quite well enough to know when she was lying.

However, somebody else did.

Nic leaned against the wall around the corner next to a portrait of Cleo and Emilia's great-grandfather.

"Going somewhere?" he asked, his arms folded over his chest. His red hair stuck up in every direction as if he'd just rolled out of bed without a care to how he looked. He probably had.

"I—I'm hungry. I'm going to the kitchen."

"Oh, please. You can't lie to me, Cleo."

She straightened, forcing herself not to feel guilty. "All right, fine. I'm leaving. I'm going to Paelsia and I don't care what anyone says. Are you going to try to stop me?"

Nic studied her for a moment, his expression neutral. "No. But I'll tell you what I am going to do."

"What?"

He grinned. "I'm going with you."

CHAPTER 13

PAELSIA

It had taken well over a month of trying, but Jonas had finally been granted audience with Chief Basilius.

"Color me impressed," Brion said under his breath as they were led along the dirt path leading to the chief's gated, guarded compound. "You need to give me a few lessons from the Jonas Agallon school of charisma."

"It's easy."

"Says you." Brion glanced at the gorgeous girl who had her arm around Jonas's waist. The one who'd finally promised the two of them that they could meet the chief. Also known as her father.

Jonas had quickly realized that the only way he would ever get a chance to see the reclusive Paelsian leader was through his family. And Laelia Basilius was more than willing to help Jonas when he'd casually approached her at a tavern. She'd been performing there. The chief's daughter was a dancer.

And what a dancer she was . . .

"Snakes," Brion had said to him with surprise as they'd watched her perform to a crowd of over a hundred a week ago. "She's dancing with *snakes*."

She was. She really was.

"I never liked snakes before," Jonas replied. "But I'm starting to see the appeal."

Laelia was a stunningly beautiful girl—a couple years older than he was. And she danced with two snakes, a white and a black python that writhed and slid over her shapely body. He felt mesmerized watching her, her hips swaying, her long black hair—to her knees—flowing with the movements of her tanned body.

But he wasn't really seeing her.

All he could see was a beautiful golden princess with eyes the color of the sea standing over the body of his dead brother and next to his murderer.

Even though Jonas had been diverted from his original plan to sneak into the palace in Auranos to kill both Lord Aron and Princess Cleo, he remained fixated with the memory of her. He hated the royals and everything they stood for with every fiber of his being. But he had to focus. He had no choice. He tried to plaster a smile on his face as he and Brion drew closer to the Paelsian chief's daughter.

Before, when Jonas and Tomas had gone to taverns and made conversation with pretty girls—performers or otherwise—after a backbreaking day of work in the vineyards that added calluses to both their hands and spirits, Tomas had been the more popular one. Older, maybe a *fraction* better-looking. He was a born flirt. Jonas received plenty of attention to brighten his nights after difficult days, but he couldn't help but think the girls had preferred his brother.

With Tomas gone, that had definitely changed.

When he'd finally caught Laelia's eye that first night, her gaze slid over him with appreciation. After the music stopped, she slipped a sheer, gauzy wrap over her curves and waited coyly for his approach.

"Nice snakes," he said, offering her a wicked grin.

The grin didn't fail him.

She was his.

Laelia Basilius had no calluses on her hands or sunburnt face like the girls he was used to spending time with. When she laughed, it was from pure amusement and not edged in weariness from a hard day of manual labor. She liked Jonas. A lot. And a week later, she wanted to introduce him to her father.

"Come closer," the chief beckoned as they came into view. He sat before a large bonfire. Several topless girls danced for him until he waved his hand at them dismissively. They moved off to the other side of the campfire.

Sparks from the fire danced in the air. Stars speckled the black velvet sky. The carcass of a goat sat on top of the fire on a spit, roasting for a late dinner. The smell of scorched flesh hung in the cool night air. Laelia tugged at Jonas's hand. He kept his expression neutral, but he was found he was intimidated. He'd never met the chief before. He'd never known anyone who had. Basilius had been in seclusion for years. So this was the ultimate honor a Paelsian could have and he felt deeply honored to be here, no matter what steps he'd had to take to make this possible.

One thing that had deeply surprised him within the compound was its opulence. While the rest of Paelsia worked endlessly in the vineyards and struggled to find scraps to eat, it seemed that on the other side of the chief's compound's walls there were no difficulties at all. Part of him believed dutifully that the chief should be held to a different standard than a common Paelsian—and he was more than entitled to use part of his steep wine tax to make a private home for himself as leader. The other part felt an uneasy ache form in the pit of his stomach over this revelation.

He sank to his knees next to Brion and they both lowered their heads in deference to their leader.

"Rise." The chief smiled, the darkly tanned skin at the corners of his gray eyes fanning out in dozens of wrinkles. He wore his hair long and some of it near his face in *texos*, thin braids, which was the traditional hairstyle for men in Paelsia. Jonas had cut his hair when he turned thirteen. Short hair was easier to manage. Brion's hair was longer but not quite long enough to braid. Since the land had begun to fade, many traditions had started to fade as well.

"Papa," Laelia purred, running her hand over Jonas's chest. "Isn't he pretty? Can I keep him?"

The chief's lips curved to the side. "Laelia, my beauty. Please give us a chance to talk. I want to get to better know this boy you're so taken by."

Her shoulders slumped and she pouted. The chief waved his hand at her in dismissal until she finally retreated to join the other girls at the far side of the fire.

Jonas and Brion exchanged a mutually wary glance.

They were in. Now what?

"Chief, it's an honor—" Jonas began.

"Are you in love with my daughter?" the chief asked. "Have you come here to ask to be bound to her?"

Someone brought him a plate of food, turkey legs and venison and roasted yams, piled higher than any plate Jonas had ever seen in his life. His family frequently went hungry, and he'd been driven to illegally hunt in another land to keep his loved ones alive, but there was enough food in the chief's compound to feed his village for months.

A part of him deep down inside turned frosty and brittle at the realization.

Brion jabbed his elbow into Jonas's arm when he didn't answer right away.

"Am I in love with your daughter?" Jonas repeated, unsure how to answer this.

"Yes," Brion hissed under his breath. "Say yes, you idiot."

But that would be a lie. Jonas couldn't lie about matters of the heart. He'd tried before and failed miserably. There was a great difference between lust and love.

"I think Laelia is a beautiful girl," he said instead. "I've been very lucky she gives me any attention."

The chief studied him. "She doesn't bring many boys here to meet me. You're only the second."

"What happened to the first one?" Brion asked.

"He didn't survive," the chief said.

Brion's face fell.

The chief laughed loudly. "I jest. He's fine. My daughter grew weary of his attentions; that was all. I'm sure he still lives. Somewhere."

Or maybe Laelia fed him to her snakes, Jonas thought morbidly.

But none of this was why they were here. He wanted to get to the point immediately.

"Chief Basilius, I'm very honored to meet you tonight," Jonas said. "Because I need to talk to you about something very important."

"Oh?" He raised a bushy eyebrow. "And you choose my celebration feast to do so?"

"What are you celebrating?"

"A union with an ally. A partnership that will help create a much more prosperous Paelsia in the future."

This wasn't expected at all, but was an excellent thing to hear. Jonas's discomfort at witnessing the expanse of the chief's comfort eased a little. "I'm glad to hear it. Because that's exactly what I wanted to talk to you about."

Basilius nodded, his eyes glinting with curiosity. "Please, say what you came here to say."

"My brother was killed recently by an Auranian lord. His name was Tomas Agallon." Jonas's throat tightened. "It was a sign to me that things have to change. That Paelsia's current difficulties are not acceptable. I believe Auranos is an evil land filled with devious people. Years ago they tricked us into planting only grapes, so that today they can pay us a pittance for our wine while charging the moon for their crops. Yet they have so many resources, all of which are closed off to us. If we even tread a foot past the border, we risk our very lives. It's not acceptable." He took a breath and let it out slowly, gathering his courage. "I'm here to propose an uprising against them, to take what's theirs and make it ours. It's time we stopped waiting for things to change on their own."

The chief studied him for a long, silent moment. "I completely agree with you."

Jonas blinked. "You do?"

"And I'm very sorry for what happened to your brother. It was a tragedy to lose one of our own in such a senseless way. I had no idea that you were related to the murdered boy until now, and I'm so glad you have come here tonight. And you're right. Auranos must pay for its ignorance and narcissism—for what happened to your brother and for its citizens' complete disregard for my land and my people."

Jonas couldn't believe this was so easy. "You agree that we should rise up against them."

"Much more than that, Jonas. There will be war."

Jonas felt cold all of a sudden. "War?"

"Yes." The chief leaned closer, studying Jonas's face, Brion's face. "You two are valuable to me. You see what others do not. I want you to help me in what is to come."

"You sound like this isn't a crazy idea we're suggesting," Brion said with confusion. "Wait. Your celebration feast . . . this is something you're already planning, isn't it? Even without us saying anything?"

The chief nodded. "I have joined with the king of Limeros in a mutual goal to take Auranos for ourselves. Both Paelsia and Limeros will prosper greatly when Auranos falls."

Jonas stared at the chief in stunned silence. This went far beyond anything he ever could have dreamed possible.

"What happened in the market the day your brother was murdered triggered all of this," the chief continued. "Your family's sacrifice—the loss of your brother—was a tragedy. But it is one that will result in true change."

"You're really going to try to conquer Auranos," Jonas said with shock.

"Not try. Succeed. And I want you to join up with my forces. I have scouts going throughout Paelsia right now, gathering eligible men to join with the trained and ready Limeros army. King Gaius is a very smart man. Very smart. King Corvin, however, is clueless. No war in a hundred years. Peace for all that time. He has grown fat and lazy. Victory will inevitably be ours. And the people of Paelsia will look forward to a brighter future."

This was truly too good to be true. Jonas had to be dreaming.

"I need you to be ready to fight at my side to ensure a better future for your fellow Paelsians. Both of you."

Jonas and Brion looked at each other.

"Of course," Jonas said firmly. "Anything you need, Chief Basilius. Anything at all."

The chief considered both of them for a moment. "In the meantime, I want you to travel to the villages. Keep an eye open for anything unusual. If King Corvin gets word of our plans, he might send his own spies here to gather more information."

Jonas nodded. "Yes, Chief."

The chief nodded and smiled. "Now, please enjoy yourselves. Take part in my feast and celebrations. And Jonas, try to remember one thing that's more important than anything else . . . beyond war, beyond even death itself."

"Yes, sir?"

The chief's smile held. "Be careful with my daughter. She doesn't take disappointment very well."

CHAPTER 14

LIMEROS

$\mathcal{L}$

More than a week had passed since his private conversation with the king and Magnus still didn't know what troubled Lucia. The thought was a constant distraction to him.

Distractions weren't recommended in the midst of his swordsmanship class. He winced as a blunt wooden practice sword landed a painful blow to his chest.

"What's wrong, Prince Magnus?" his opponent asked with mockery edging his words. "Would you really let me win as easily as this?"

Magnus gave him a withering look. "I won't let you win at all."

Andreas Psellos was his complete opposite in looks despite their similar tall statures and leanly muscled builds. Where Magnus was dark, Andreas was light with fair hair and pale blue eyes. Where Magnus could never be described as "cheery," Andreas had an easy manner and a constant smile on his handsome face that rarely held malice—

Unless he was talking to Magnus.

They'd moved away from the rest of the class, consisting of four teams of two and an absentminded tutor who tended to wander off in the middle of their sessions, leaving them to practice without supervision.

"The years haven't changed you a bit," Andreas said. "I still remember that set of painted wooden blocks we battled over when we were only five years old. I believe you threw them out of a window so I couldn't get the chance to play with them."

"I've never enjoyed sharing my toys."

"Not with anyone but your sister."

"She's an exception."

"Indeed she is. A beautiful exception." Andreas cast a wistful look toward the black granite castle that stretched high into the blue sky. "Do you think Princess Lucia will be coming out to watch us spar like she did last time?"

"Unlikely."

Magnus's dark mood intensified. Not only had Andreas shown romantic interest in Lucia, but he was also the one boy who'd been mentioned several times by Queen Althea herself as a potential match. The Psellos family was rich, Andreas's father one of the king's royal council members, and their expansive villa, which sat only a few miles from the palace, was the finest on the western coast of Limeros.

The thought that Lucia could become betrothed to this golden boy with his easy smiles sent a rush of icy poison flowing through Magnus's veins.

Andreas snorted. "Come on, then. I won't hold back if you don't."

"Fair enough."

As their wooden swords clashed, Magnus now paid very close attention to the swordplay, trying hard not to let his mind wander again.

"I heard that you ran Michol Trichas off when he showed interest in your sister."

"Did you?" Magnus said with disinterest. "Are you offended on his behalf?"

"Just the opposite. He wasn't right for her. He's insipid and cowardly, hiding behind his mother's skirts when any opposition presents itself. He's not worthy of spending time with Princess Lucia."

"We finally agree on something. How delightful."

"However, you'll find that I'm not quite so easily dissuaded as he was." Their swords met and held, and Andreas's gaze turned icy. Magnus's muscles burned with the effort of taking the point and not allowing his rival to win. "You don't intimidate me."

"Not trying to."

"You chase off all of Lucia's suitors as if no one in Limeros is worthy of the princess's precious time and attention."

Magnus's gaze snapped to Andreas's. "No one is."

"Apart from you, of course." Andreas's eyes narrowed. "I think the attention you lavish on your sister compared to any other girl is . . . unusual."

Magnus went cold inside. "You're imagining things."

"Perhaps I am. But know this, Prince Magnus, when I want something, I get it. No matter what obstacle might present itself."

Magnus glanced toward the castle. "It looks like I was wrong. Lucia is coming out to watch us after all."

When Andreas's attention moved away from Magnus, he struck. He knocked the wooden sword out of Andreas's grip and then slammed the boy to the ground, where he lay on his back looking up, temporarily stunned.

Magnus pressed the blunt tip of his practice sword to Andreas's throat hard enough to bruise. "Actually, Lucia's in her embroidery class right now and won't be able to talk with you again until . . . well, I'm sure it'll be quite some time. I'll give her your regards."

Lesson over, he threw his sword to the side and turned from the boy still sprawled on the ground to return to the castle.

Some victories didn't taste quite as sweet as they should.

The idea that anyone, especially someone like Andreas, could guess that Magnus might have forbidden feelings for his younger sister had put a sick feeling into the pit of his stomach. He resolved to force himself to spend more time in the company of other girls to help stave off any future rumors.

And not girls like the one who approached him along the hallway with a smile stretching her rosy cheeks.

"My prince," Amia greeted him cheerily.

He cast a look around to check if anyone was watching. Speaking openly with a servant—especially such a low-ranking one as Amia—was frowned upon by his father. To imagine King Gaius's outraged reaction to his son doing more than talking with her was almost as humorous as it was foreboding.

"What is it?" he asked, his words clipped.

"You wanted me to keep an eye on your sister."

With this, he grabbed hold of her arm and pulled her around a corner and into a shadowed alcove. "Speak."

Amia twisted a piece of nut-brown hair around her finger. Her brows drew together. "It's the strangest thing. I was sent with a tray of food up to her room for a late lunch when she returned from her class just now. Her door was ajar. I should have knocked, but since my hands were full, I didn't. And I swear I saw . . ."

"What? What did you see?"

"Your sister stood before three candles and I watched as each was lit."

Magnus stared at the girl. "That's all? You watched my sister light some candles and you thought it worthy of mention to me? There's nothing unusual about that."

"No, my prince. It's just that—I swear, I . . ." She shook her head, her expression one of deep confusion. "I swear that Princess Lucia didn't light them. They lit all by themselves as she looked at them, each in turn. I was startled by this but cleared my throat to let her know I was there. She seemed disturbed that I might have been watching her, but I didn't give her any indication of what I saw. Possessing such an ability to summon fire could mean that she's a—" Her words cut off immediately at Magnus's sharp look. She bit her bottom lip.

Magnus grasped the girl's chin and looked down into her eyes. "Thank you, Amia. I want you to continue to tell me anything at all, no matter how seemingly insignificant. But know this—my sister is no witch. This was only your imagination."

"Yes, my prince," she whispered before he slipped away from her and began moving toward Lucia's chambers on the third floor of the castle without another word.

Lighting candles seemed like such a common practice, but not so common if the wicks caught flame all by themselves. Once at Lucia's door, he took a deep breath and then twisted the handle. It wasn't locked. He slowly pushed the door open.

Lucia sat on her plush lounge, her legs folded under her, holding the head of a daisy on the palm of her hand. The frivolous gift of flowers had been sent the previous day by another random Limerian boy interested in the princess. Her concentration on the flower was so complete that she hadn't heard the soft creak of the door.

Suddenly, the bright pink bloom rose from her hand and floated in the air as if suspended by invisible strings.

Magnus gasped out loud.

The flower dropped to the ground and Lucia's startled gaze snapped to where he stood at the open doorway.

"Magnus." She stood up, brushing off the front of her skirt. Her expression was tense. She beckoned to him. "Please come in."

Hesitating only a moment longer, he pushed the door open all the way and entered her chambers.

"Close it," she instructed. He did as she asked.

She took a deep breath and let it out slowly. "You saw what I just did?"

He nodded, his throat tight.

Lucia wrung her hands, pacing to her window to look outside just as a hawk flew away from its temporary perch on the edge of her balcony, its large golden wings flapping against the bright blue sky. He continued to wait, afraid to give voice to his racing thoughts.

This must be what he'd heard his father and Sabina talk about the night of her birthday banquet—of prophesies and *elementia* and signs held by the stars themselves. This was what he'd been asked to watch for.

"Lucia is now sixteen," Sabina had said. *"The time is drawing closer for her awakening, I know it is."*

The awakening of her magic.

It couldn't be true.

Finally Lucia turned to him, her gaze as fierce as when she'd confronted him about what he'd said to Michol. Still hopelessly confused, Magnus opened his mouth to demand answers from her, but she walked directly to him and threw her arms around him.

"I haven't been able to tell anyone this secret for fear of what it could mean. I've wanted to tell you for ages, but there's never been the right opportunity."

"I'm not sure what I saw." He pressed a hand to her back to hold her close while his heart hammered in his chest. A sudden and fierce need to protect her any way he could rose to the surface. It helped to push away his own uncertainty. "You can tell me this secret, Lucia. I promise not to tell a soul."

She let out a long, shaky breath and stepped back from his arms to look up into his face. "It started shortly before my birthday. I found that I could do things. Strange things."

"Magic," he said simply. The word felt foreign on his tongue.

She stared at him for a moment, her fiery and guarded expression turning bleak. Then she nodded.

"Elementia," he clarified.

"I believe so." Lucia drew in a shuddery breath. "I don't know why. Or how. But I can. And it feels as if it's been inside me my entire life waiting for the right time to emerge. I can do what I did with the flower. I can move things without touching them. I can light candles . . . without a match."

Magnus took this all in and tried to sort through it in his head. "You're a witch."

He regretted saying it as soon as the words left his mouth. She looked devastated by this possibility. Witches were persecuted in Limeros—even if only *suspected* of witchcraft. It was a dangerous thing to even suggest of someone. Here witchcraft was associated with the goddess Cleiona—an evil act committed in the name of an evil deity.

"Magnus," she whispered. "What am I to do?"

The king would want to know this. He'd wanted Magnus to keep an eye on Lucia—and to report back anything unusual he witnessed.

This was definitely unusual.

He paced the length of the room, his mind working and reworking what he'd seen. If Lucia was anyone else, he wouldn't have hesitated in letting his father know the truth. Whatever happened then would be none of his concern.

"Show me again," he said quietly.

After a slight hesitation, Lucia took the flower and placed it on her palm again. She looked at him and he nodded, trying to put her mind at ease.

"It's all right," he told her. "Don't be afraid."

"I'm not afraid." She said it so firmly that it made him smile. Despite her pretty dresses and the manners of a princess, his sister had a heart forged of steel. His own steely heart pounded harder.

Lucia turned her attention to the flower. With a small crease between her eyebrows, she focused on the bloom. Slowly it rose from her hand as Magnus watched in stunned silence. It revolved slowly in the air.

"Incredible," he breathed.

"What does this mean?" Her troubled gaze shot to his, and for the first time, he noticed the sheen in her eyes. She might say that she wasn't afraid, but she was. And she should be.

"I don't know." He studied her face, fighting the strong urge to take her into his arms again and hold her tight. His gaze brushed over her features—her small, straight nose, her high cheekbones, her full red lips. His mother's eyes were a bluish-gray color, his father's dark brown like his own. But Lucia's eyes stood out like sapphires—like precious jewels.

She was so incredibly beautiful it took his breath away.

"What is it?" she asked. "Do you see something on my face that shows I'm touched by this evil?"

The king had taken him farther north several years ago to witness the execution of one who was accused of witchcraft. The woman had slaughtered several animals and used their blood to try to summon dark magic. The king spoke with her briefly in private and then made the final judgment on her fate. Magnus was required to watch the execution so he would learn from it. He still remembered the witch's screams of pain and terror piercing the cold air as she was lit ablaze.

His father had turned to him and put a hand on the trembling boy's shoulder. "Remember this, Magnus. One day you too will have to decide the fate of those accused of such darkness."

A shudder of fear and revulsion quaked through him. He pushed back from Lucia and went to the door to check if anyone lurked outside. Then he closed the door and locked it.

"It is *elementia*," she said, a catch to her voice. "Specifically air magic, I think—the ability to move things. And fire, too. Cleiona was the goddess of fire and air. And she was evil!"

Magnus didn't speak for a full minute, his eyes cast downward at the marble floor. Slowly, he raised his gaze to his sister's. "Can you lift anything heavier than a flower?"

"I don't know. Please, Magnus, tell me what to do. Don't hate me for keeping this secret for so long. You can't turn your back on me now."

He frowned. "You think I'd do that?"

"If this magic is evil—"

"It's not," he said firmly.

She frowned. "Witches have been tortured and executed for what I can do."

"If a witch could really do what you can, she would never let herself be executed." As he said it, the certainty of his words rang true to him. "If anyone burned or beheaded had been capable of true magic, they would've been able to use that magic to save themselves."

"You don't think witches are evil?" Her blue eyes held deep uncertainty—and hope. She'd been tormented by this secret she had held inside her for so long without anyone to help her.

Magnus moved closer to her and cupped her face in his hands. "All I know is that you aren't evil. You are wonderful in every possible way. And don't you ever believe anything different from that or I'll be very angry with you."

She touched his hand, leaning into his touch. A sliver of relief slid through her blue eyes. "You mean it?"

"With all my heart." He raised an eyebrow. "Would I give such a fine gift as that fluffy bunny to anyone I thought might be evil?"

She laughed softly, and the sound lightened his heart. "I named her Hana."

"Lovely name. For a fluffy bunny."

"What am I to do, Magnus?"

He moved away from her and toward her stack of books. He picked a few, placing them down on her table next to the vase of flowers.

"Lift these books."

Lucia's eyes widened and she looked down at the heavy stack. "I've never attempted anything more substantial than a flower."

His jaw tightened. "You need to strengthen your skills. The stronger you are, the less I'll have to worry about you. If you master what you can do, then you'll be safe no matter what happens. And I'll help you practice."

He held his breath waiting for her answer. If Lucia really was a witch, with newly awakened *elementia*, there was no other choice. She *had* to practice. She had to strengthen her abilities. Because if anyone ever found out about this, especially the king, her very life would be in danger.

Magnus would never allow his sister to be executed for this. Lucia wasn't evil. He had trouble believing in the religion that was forced upon all Limerians, but he didn't have trouble believing in her.

Lucia's brows drew together. "I don't know if I can."

"Then don't do it for yourself. Do it for me."

Her gaze snapped to his. "If I do agree to try this, will you do something for me?"

"What?"

"Tell me why Father would join forces with Chief Basilius to conquer Auranos. Will there be war?"

He'd seen Lucia on the stairway when the king had received the message from the Paelsian leader. It was dangerous information for a sixteen-year-old girl to know, but before long she would have learned anyway. It seemed as if Amia was not the only girl in this castle skilled at eavesdropping.

"Will there be war?" Magnus repeated. "That's what Father wants. We'll have to wait and see where all his planning and scheming with Chief Basilius will ultimately lead. But you don't have to worry about that." He stroked the long, silky dark hair off her face. "Let's practice your magic now. You must master it so I know you'll be safe."

"Thank you, brother." Lucia went up on her tiptoes and brushed her lips softly against his before she gave him another fierce hug. "What would I ever do without you?"

Magnus's lips burned from her kiss and his heart felt as if it had been set ablaze—just like the witch once had been. "I hope we'll never have to find out."

CHAPTER 15

AURANOS

Theon Ranus had experienced anger, grief, sadness, and desire many times. But not fear.

Not until today.

"The princess isn't in her room. She's nowhere to be found!" The maid's cry quickened his steps as he made his way down the hall, the maid who was supposed to be stationed outside Princess Cleo's room during the hours that Theon slept and couldn't keep watch over her.

Cold fear crashed over him.

He knew immediately where she'd gone. She'd done exactly what she'd threatened. The princess had escaped the palace to go on her journey to Paelsia. Even after he'd refused to accompany her, she'd lied to him about her intentions to wait for two days and gone anyway.

Then, close on the heels of his fear for her safety came a hot line of anger that she'd do this, blatantly ignoring his warnings.

Foolish girl. Strong-willed, foolish girl.

The king had to be told. And Theon knew he had to be the one to deliver the news that Cleo and Nic had disappeared from the palace.

That was when he began to feel another glimmer of fear. This time for himself.

"How could you let this happen?" the king raged, his face bright red with anger.

Theon had no worthy answer. He knew Cleo wanted to do this. He knew she was stubborn and single-minded when it came to her sister's fading health. He should have anticipated this.

"I'll go to Paelsia myself and search for her."

"Damn right you will." There were dark shadows beneath the king's eyes as if he hadn't slept well. He looked much older than his forty-odd years today. "Of all the things I need to concern myself with, this only troubles me more. You were supposed to keep her safe. You failed me."

Theon could argue that he couldn't be by Cleo's side all the hours of the day or night apart from sleeping in the princess's bed with her, but he held his tongue and studied the floor obediently. King Corvin was not a cruel king, but he doled out punishment when necessary. Failing an assignment to keep the princess safe was not something that could go unanswered.

Why would she ever do something so foolhardy as this?

Even he didn't have to think too far on the subject. She did it because she was absolutely convinced that she could save her sister's life by chasing after the legend of an exiled Watcher. Breaking every rule to save Princess Emilia was both idiotic . . . and brave. Pure-hearted and courageous.

"I'll leave immediately," he said, his eyes still lowered. "With your permission I'll take a few more men."

"No more than two. We don't want to draw attention to this embarrassing situation."

"Yes, your majesty."

When the king didn't say anything else, Theon looked up to see that his face was now more pale and haunted than angry.

"Sometimes I feel as if I'm cursed," he said softly. "A slow, hungry curse that has worked its way across my entire life, stripping me of everything I love." He paused, his brow furrowing. "I met a witch once . . . in my youth. She was very beautiful."

Theon was surprised at the seeming non sequitur. "A witch? A real one?"

The king nodded with a sharp jerk of his head. "I hadn't believed in magic until I met her. She had her sights set on becoming my queen, but I . . . well, I met Elena, and that was it for me. The witch was but a momentary dalliance of a youth who enjoyed the attentions of pretty girls before his wedding to the woman who would become the true love of his life." He let out a slow exhale. "When I ended things with this witch, she was furious. I believe she cursed me. I lost my beloved Elena moments after she'd given my younger daughter life. Now Emilia is so unwell. I fear Cleo was right when she said she's dying. And Cleo herself—" His voice broke. "She has a mind of her own, one that will get her into trouble. More than she even realizes. You *must* find her."

"I will, your majesty. I swear I will."

"See that you do." The king raised a dark gaze to Theon's and a chill went down his spine. "Fail me again and you'll pay with your life. I'll kill you myself with my bare hands. Do you understand me?"

Theon nodded. He expected no less. He left the meeting room, his steps rushed, his heart beating hard.

He should have said he'd go with the princess. She was stubborn enough to go by herself—with only Nicolo Cassian to protect her. But he was no more than the king's squire, with no training, no strength, no carefully honed survival instincts. It wasn't nearly enough. Theon was the one who should be by Princess Cleo's side no matter what was to come. Today and always.

The king would kill him if he failed. And if something happened to Cleo . . . he'd *want* to die. The thought of her bright eyes extinguished, her light-hearted laugh silenced . . . he broke into a cold sweat and had to lean his forehead against the marble wall of the hallway.

I'm falling in love with her.

The realization hit him like a sword plunged through his chest.

There could be no real future for them. He wasn't royal—not even a knight. And she was already betrothed to another.

But . . . he was certain he'd seen something in her eyes—a joyful alertness when they argued. A catch to her breath. A flush to her cheeks. He'd come to enjoy spending time with her more than he ever would have believed or been willing to admit, even to himself. He wanted to be by her side and not only as her bodyguard.

He wanted *her*.

But he couldn't give in to these feelings. Even admitting them to himself was dangerous. For now, all Theon knew for sure was that he would find her and bring her back safely to Auranos. The future was uncertain, but this much was crystal clear. He would not fail.

CHAPTER 16

LIMEROS

L

The king had summoned Magnus to his throne room.

Goddess forbid that his father actually visited his son's chambers. No, instead he had to be summoned quite officially like a servant.

Irrelevant.

He took his time to arrive. He would obey, of course. He had no other choice, but even with the king's seemingly newfound appreciation for his son's existence, Magnus wouldn't rush to do so.

He had spent two days with Lucia, coaching her on a variety of exercises to help hone her control and skill. A lot of it seemed to depend on his sister's fluctuating emotions. When they argued—especially about the subject of her suitors that Magnus tried to discourage—her rising temper helped bring forth her magic. When her confidence wavered, it faded.

Therefore, he'd made sure that they argued frequently. It didn't take very much at all to bring a flush to her cheeks.

It would still take her a while to open herself up to her magic completely. Even if she wouldn't readily admit this, she feared it. That which one fears, one typically won't embrace with open arms.

Magnus felt similarly toward his father.

"You summoned me?" he said drily when he was finally in front of the king in his throne room.

King Gaius raised his gaze from the papers he studied and honed in on Magnus like an eagle spotting mildly interesting prey. "It took you long enough to get here."

"I came as quickly as I could."

The lie slid smoothly.

"What have you been up to, Magnus? You've been keeping to yourself a great deal the last few days. You missed an opportunity to go out hunting with me again just this morning."

"I've been reading."

The king smiled, but the warmth of it didn't reach his eyes. "I find that difficult to believe."

Magnus shrugged. "Did you just want to get an update on my hobbies or were we to discuss more important matters?"

The king leaned back in his iron-and-black-leather throne and regarded his son. "You remind me so very much of myself at your age. It's truly uncanny."

Magnus wasn't sure if this was meant to be taken as a compliment or an insult.

"How go your plans with Chief Basilius?" he asked, wanting to shift the focus off himself.

"Everything is lining up. Don't worry, my son, I'll keep you informed of every important step. And I'll be requiring your assistance in larger matters very soon."

Since the position of the king's valet was currently vacant due to the unexpected death of Tobias, Magnus was certain the king would need a new personal assistant to bridge such a gap. It sounded as if it would be him.

"As the king wishes, I obey." It was nearly impossible to say without noticeable sarcasm. Old habits died hard.

"I did call you here for a specific reason." The king studied him for a moment. "What of Lucia? Have you noticed anything unusual about her?"

Magnus knew this was coming, so he was prepared. He glanced briefly off to the side to see the Damora coat of arms, bearing the familiar words *Strength, Faith*, and *Wisdom*. "I've been watching her very closely, but she seems just as she's always been. If she appears distracted to you in some small way, maybe she just has a crush on some insipid boy."

"No, it wouldn't be something as meaningless as that."

"Well, I wouldn't know exactly what I should even be watching for, would I? You refuse to share any details with me."

So much for him being a part of the king's important future plans for this kingdom. Perhaps those were only words. The thought was oddly disappointing.

The king leaned forward from his plain but intimidating iron throne—the ornate golden, jeweled one Magnus's grandfather had ruled from had been permanently removed years ago. He pressed the tips of his fingers together. "I think you might be ready to learn the truth."

Magnus raised a brow, surprised. "So tell me."

"I keep forgetting that you're not only a boy anymore. You are very nearly a man and as such should be included in everything I do. Honestly"—the king stood up from his seat and walked a slow circle around Magnus, his gaze sweeping the length of his son with an odd mix of criticism and approval—"it's like looking into my past. Sabina mentioned this to me only the other day."

"Sabina mentioned what?"

"How very alike we are. You know, I met her when I was not much older than you."

Magnus's stomach soured. "How nice for you. Was she already married back then or did you wait until after her nuptials to bed her?"

The king gave him a thin smile. "Your tongue is tipped with spikes. But that's all right. A future king needs every weapon he can get at his disposal. Trust me, when you're on the throne, there will be very few you can trust."

"And yet you trust Sabina?"

"I do."

The only way to get answers from this impossible man was to ask questions directly—while not appearing to really care about the answers, of course. If he seemed too eager, he knew his father would continue to withhold the truth from him indefinitely.

"What prophecy is it that relates to Lucia? What are you waiting to see from her?"

The king didn't say anything for a long time. His eyes narrowed. "You know how I feel about those who listen in on my private conversations, Magnus."

He cringed internally. Sometimes even he knew not to speak so bluntly unless he wanted his father to lash out. It was difficult to remember sometimes. But he was on edge and having a difficult time controlling himself. His mask of indifference usually served him much better than this.

Learning that Lucia was a witch, however, had knocked his

world off balance. He'd found that the mask he'd depended on had shifted. It was difficult to set it back into its proper position without great effort.

Magnus was certain his father would not answer him. Perhaps he would send him away without any new information. That would be fine since he could go immediately to Lucia's chambers and continue with her practice.

Finally the king spoke. "If I admit something like this to you, Magnus, we're treading on very dangerous ground."

"The truth is only dangerous if it can inflict injury." He pretended to be more interested in a platter of apples and cheese on a nearby table than on every word his father uttered.

"Lies can make harsh truths less painful. But I believe pain is essential for growth." The king's gaze was unflinching. "Do you think you're ready for such honesty?"

Magnus looked his father right in his eyes, which were the exact same color as his own. As he studied his father's face, he couldn't help but see the coldness there. The king had reminded him of a serpent for as long as he could remember—just like the cobra that adorned the family crest. A slippery one with venom and fangs.

"I want to know about Lucia," Magnus said firmly. "And I want to know now."

The king stood up from his throne and paced to the other side of the room so he could look out a window down the sheer, frost-covered cliff side to the sea far below. "Many years ago, Sabina and her sister studied the stars looking for a sign of a special birth. A child to become one of legend and magic."

"Magic." The word itself was dangerous.

The king nodded slowly. "Sabina is a witch."

Magnus felt himself pale. He'd never cared for Sabina, but he'd never seen any indication that what his father claimed was true. "You took me to see a witch burn when I was twelve years old. It was a lesson on what happens to them should they try to work magic here in Limeros. And yet you say that your mistress is one? I didn't even know you believed in such things other than making examples out of those who might spread evil and lies."

The king spread his hands. "There are hard choices one must make as king. For a long time, I didn't believe. But it's true, Magnus. Magic is real."

"You would condemn one woman to death for being accused of witchcraft yet consider Sabina your closest advisor? One you also take to your bed?"

"I don't expect you to understand, only to accept that what I've done—what I've always done—has been for the benefit of my kingdom. Sabina is a rare exception for me."

His mind reeled. "What does this have to do with Lucia?"

"There was a prophecy of a child born who would one day possess the power not of a witch, but of a sorceress."

Magnus went very still. "And you believe it's your own daughter."

The king grabbed Magnus's shoulders and pulled him closer. "I have waited a very long time to learn if it's true. But there's been no sign that Lucia is anything as extraordinary as this. Sixteen years, Magnus. I grow frustrated."

His stomach clenched. "I don't know what to say."

"You've seen nothing. Nothing? Truly?"

Magnus chose his words wisely. "Truly. There is nothing for me to report. She is as any other sixteen-year-old girl might be. To think she could be a sorceress—" His throat tightened. "It's ludicrous."

Lies did soften the painful truth a great deal.

"I refuse to believe that," the king said through clenched teeth. There was a sheen of perspiration now on his father's brow. "She's the key, Magnus. She's essential to my plans. I need all the help I can get."

"What? You mean with Auranos?"

"Of course. Nothing else matters right now."

"Surely our army combined with Basilius's, though . . ."

"Basilius's? Ha. Untrained, underfed youths who've never held a sword before. Auranos, for all their lazy lifestyle, has an impressive military. No, we need a guarantee."

A chill went through Magnus. "What about Sabina? If she's a witch as you say she is, can't she use her magic to help you?"

The king's expression soured. "Whatever power she might have possessed as a younger woman has faded. She's useless to me in this regard. No, it must be Lucia. The prophecy said she'd have endless magic—drawn from all four elements."

All four. Magnus had only seen evidence of two so far—air and fire. But this meant that the other two, earth and water, might manifest later.

"With magic like that I could crush King Corvin and burn his world down all around him." The king's fists were clenched at his sides. "I could end him in a single day and take Auranos."

Magnus swallowed hard. "Maybe Sabina was wrong about Lucia."

The king cast a glare so sharp at him that Magnus's scar began to sting. "I refuse to believe that."

"Then I guess you'll have to be patient."

The anger faded from his father's gaze and he regarded his son again carefully. "You love your sister, don't you?"

Magnus crossed his arms over his chest. "Of course I do."

"She's a true beauty. She'll make some man an excellent wife one day."

His core turned hot as lava with immediate jealousy. "I'm sure she will."

The king's mouth twisted into a sinister smile. "Do you really think I don't notice how you look at her? I'm not blind, my son."

Bile rose in his throat, bitter and unexpected. "I don't know what you're talking about."

"Play innocent if it makes you feel better, but I see it. I'm a very smart man, Magnus. It doesn't take only courage to be king, but intelligence as well. I observe because then I can use what I see to my best advantage."

Magnus's jaw tensed. "How nice for you."

"And I see a brother who cares deeply—*very* deeply—for his beautiful younger sister."

Magnus eyed the door, seeking escape as soon as possible. "May I be excused, Father? Or do you wish to continue playing games with me?"

"No games, Magnus. I shall reserve my games for the battle-field or the chessboard. Do you honestly think I don't know why you haven't shown interest in any other girl who might one day become your bride?"

Magnus felt ill at the direction of this conversation. "Father, please."

"I *know*, Magnus. I see it in your eyes every time she enters a room. I see how you watch her."

Magnus felt the sudden need to run away, far away. A desperate urge to hide his face from the world. He hadn't shared this truth with anyone; he'd kept it buried deep, so deep inside that he'd barely glanced at it himself. He'd been appalled at the merest hint that Andreas might have some inkling of his darkest secret.

But now for the king to pull it out and flaunt it like some sort of prized animal he'd shot on a hunt, bloody and raw. Like it meant nothing.

"I need to go." Magnus turned to the door.

His father clamped his hand down on his shoulder. "Ease your mind. I'll tell no one of this. Your secret will remain safe from this day forward. But if you do everything I ask of you, I can promise you one thing. No man will ever touch her. If nothing else, you'll be able to take solace in that."

Magnus didn't say anything else. The moment his father let go of him, he burst from the room. He practically ran down the halls toward his chambers, where he sank down to the floor, his back pressed against the cold gray wall. He couldn't bear to face Lucia again tonight.

CHAPTER 17

PAELSIA

Stowing aboard a cargo ship carrying wine back and forth from Auranos to Paelsia wasn't as luxurious as being aboard her father's lavish yacht, but there was no way Cleo and Nic would ever willingly take on the many dangers of the Wildlands to cross the border by foot. Despite the unpleasantness of their journey, they'd successfully arrived—the first of many victories, Cleo hoped.

Cleo carried a bag of necessities, including a change of clothes—a dress equally as simple and unadorned as the one she presently wore; while she'd never look the part of a peasant, there was certainly no immediate indication of her being a royal princess—and a small sack of gold and silver coins, generic currency rather than recognizable Auranian centimos stamped with the face of the goddess, which might draw attention to their travels. She kept the hood of her cloak over her sun-kissed hair most of the time, but it was more to keep out the cold breeze than to remain incognito. There would only be a small handful in this goddess-forsaken land who'd have any idea who she really was.

And they walked. And walked.

And walked some more.

The journey to find Aron's wine the last time she'd been here felt as if it was an endless trip. It was but a glimpse of this.

Each village was a half day's journey from the next—at the very least. A couple times they'd managed to catch a ride on the back of a horse-drawn cart, but mostly they walked. Each village looked the same as the last. Small, poor, with a cluster of cottages, a tavern, an inn, and a market selling various modest wares, including small, sad-looking fruits and vegetables. These food items didn't grow so well in the cold soil as the grapes did. It was only more evidence that the vineyards and the grapes themselves were specifically touched by earth magic. This realization helped Cleo remain optimistic as the days dragged on.

Shortly after their arrival at Trader's Harbor, they wandered through the vineyards themselves, wide expanses of green vines planted in neat rows, the ground frosty, the pale green grapes cold to the touch but large and plump and sweet.

Before anyone could see them, catch them, they'd gathered as many bunches of grapes as they could and ran away. It wasn't a perfect meal served by servants in front of a blazing fire, but it filled their bellies—especially since Nic had proved useless at catching a quick-moving rabbit for dinner. They'd come upon an awkward and slow-moving turtle, but neither of them had had the heart to end its life. At the time, they hadn't been hungry enough for turtle meat. Instead, they ate the remainder of their dried fruit.

Beyond the west coast, where the harbor hugged the rocky shore and the vineyards grew, they traveled farther east along narrow and uneven dirt roads, stopping in each village to ask if anyone knew of the legends—and if there were any rumors of an exiled Watcher living amongst the peasants.

To anyone who asked, Cleo and Nic introduced themselves as a brother and sister from northern Limeros who were traveling together to research such stories. The thought was humorous to Cleo and she could barely keep the grin off her face whenever Nic told his tale—each time, it became more grand. Before long, they were the son and daughter of a famous Limerian poet who'd asked them with his dying breath to complete his life's work—a book about the Watchers of the Kindred.

Nic had an incredible imagination and an inviting way about him that set everyone's mind at ease. Paelsians were not open to visitors from other kingdoms, but they made an exception for the two once Nic got talking. He rarely failed to bring a smile to their weathered faces. Children especially loved Nic, gathering around him at a campfire beneath the stars for more stories that he made up on the spot. Before they left a couple of the villages, a few children followed them, begging Nic to stay just a little while longer so he could continue to entertain them.

Cleo had hoped to find the answers she sought quickly, but it was stretching into nearly a week since they'd arrived and she began to grow weary. Some days were better than others. They had gold that paid for rooms in village inns so they could get a semi-comfortable night's sleep on straw-packed beds. The meals served in the taverns weren't nearly the same as the ones in the Auranian palace but were far from horrible.

But tonight, after leaving such a tavern and beginning their walk to the inn to rent a room, they were cornered by a few large, rough boys who took her weighty sack of coins and left them with only a precious few found at the bottom of Nic's pockets.

Cleo cried for the first time since they'd arrived. It was a clear sign to her that their trip to Paelsia would get worse before it got better. Barely any money meant she'd soon have to return to Auranos, admitting failure and accepting punishment for running away from home to chase after myth and magic.

Not wanting to waste what little coin they had left, they slept in a dry, dusty riverbed, Nic's arms wrapped tightly around Cleo to stop her shivering. Her large, baggy cloak was drawn around the both of them for warmth.

"Don't cry," he whispered. "It'll be better tomorrow."

"You don't know that."

"You're right; I don't. But I can hope."

"We haven't found anything. Nobody believes there's a Watcher living here."

Maybe there wasn't.

She let out a long, shaky sigh and pressed her cheek against Nic's chest to listen to his heartbeat. The stars above them were bright in the black sky, the moon a shard of silver light. She'd never studied the sky for so long before, only looking up now and then in an absent kind of way. But she'd never seen it, not like this. So clear and vast and beautiful even in such a hopeless moment.

"Why would a Watcher be exiled from their home, anyway?" she asked.

"They say that some fall in love with mortals and they leave voluntarily. Once they leave, they can never return."

"To do such a thing for love. To leave paradise." She swallowed. "It seems like a waste."

"Depends who you're in love with."

This was true.

As Cleo looked up at the stars, she thought about Theon and wondered if he too might be looking up at the same moment. She knew he would have been furious to learn that she'd left and that she'd lied to him. At the time, she hadn't worried about it, thinking she'd return victorious before too much time had passed and all would be forgiven.

I'm sorry, Theon, she thought. *I wish you were here with me.*

As much as she adored Nic, the thought of instead having Theon's arms around her to keep her warm made her heart begin to race. She hoped that he understood why she'd had no choice but to come here. That he'd forgive her. Eventually.

"What do Watchers look like?" she whispered. "I never paid attention to the legends."

"Hardly anyone believes them anymore. The Watchers are all young and beautiful. Light shines from their golden skin. They spend their days in endless green meadows surrounded by splendor."

"But they're trapped in that paradise?"

"That's what the legends say. Since the Kindred was lost, they don't possess enough magic to leave. It's their punishment for losing what they were supposed to guard."

"But they can still watch us through the eyes of hawks." She said this as she spotted the outline of such a bird of prey flying far above them, silhouetted by the bright moon. The sight, while familiar, made her shiver.

"Not everyone, I'm sure. Some they'd find quite boring to watch. Aron, for instance. All they'd see is him drinking wine all day long and admiring himself in a mirror. How dull."

She laughed despite herself. "You might be right about that."

"I just had a thought."

"Uh-oh. What is it?" She looked up at his face.

"Imagine what Aron would say if he saw us like this. Sleeping in each other's arms. Would he be jealous?"

She grinned. "Insanely. Especially of the fact that we're broke and starving and freezing to death, with not a drop of wine between us."

He closed his eyes, his lips quirking at the edges. "For the chance to die in the arms of Princess Cleiona, it might just be worth it."

He constantly made silly comments like this. She normally brushed them off as only humor, but sometimes she wondered if her sister had been right—that Nic might be a little bit in love with her.

The worry drifted away as she fell asleep and dreamed instead of Theon.

"This is it," Nic said the next day when they resumed their search. "If we find nothing today, then we need to head back to the harbor and go home tomorrow. Agreed?"

Disappointment and weariness thudded with every step she took. "Agreed."

Nearly out of money and with no clues to give them hope, it was time for this adventure to end and for Cleo to accept defeat.

She squeezed her eyes shut as they walked and said a rare prayer to the goddess for assistance in their search.

Her stomach grumbled unhappily as if in reply. They'd found some dried-up fruit on some dried-up trees that morning, but it wasn't nearly enough to satisfy her.

"Yes, excellent," Nic said. "We'll follow your inner gurgle like a compass. I think it'll help."

She smacked his arm and tried not to grin since it was the last expression her face felt like making. "Don't tease. I know you're starving too."

"We'll have to choose between a tavern or an inn tonight. Can't have both."

It was so unfair. Just as Cleo had begun to look on Paelsians as kind and hardworking people, they'd been mugged, renewing her previous assumption that they were all desperate savages.

They're desperate because they have nothing. While I have everything.

It was a chilling thought. Perhaps Cleo too would become more savage if she had to live in this dying land for more than a week.

They entered the next village with its typical dusty streets and small stone cottages with thatched roofs. In the market, which was the busiest section of the village, they stopped a few people and asked them about the Watcher.

They received the same response they'd gotten everywhere else.

"Watchers? Don't know anything about that," one woman said, her lips peeling back from broken teeth. "Don't believe in such inane legends, dearie. If we had a Watcher among us with magic at her lovely, golden fingertips, do you think we'd have to sleep under broken roofs and eat frostbitten vegetables?"

"She's an exiled Watcher, so perhaps it's different for her."

The woman waved a dismissive hand. "It's bad enough that we put up with Chief Basilius, who uses our taxes for his luxurious compound working his so-called magic while the rest of us starve to death. Now he wants to steal our men for his foolish endeavors. Sickening."

"Quiet yourself," her gray-haired friend whispered harshly, grabbing her arm. "Don't speak ill of the chief. He'll hear you."

"He hears nothing but his own satisfied belches," the woman snarled back.

The woman's friend dragged her away before she said anything else.

"Broken roofs," Nic said, scanning the area. "She's right. Half the roofs around here have holes in them. How do these people manage to survive the bleakest days of winter?"

"Some don't." The voice came from a stall selling woven baskets. Cleo stopped and turned to see a small woman with gray hair and a deeply lined face regarding her with black, sparkling eyes. For a moment, Cleo recalled Silas Agallon, the wine seller, just before his sons arrived. What happened shortly afterward slid through her memory like rancid jam.

"Apologies, but what did you say?" Cleo asked.

"The winters are harsh here," the woman said. "Some aren't lucky enough to see the spring. That's just the way it is. You're not from around here, are you?"

"We're from Limeros," Nic said evenly. "Traveling through this land doing research on a book about the legend of the Watchers of the Kindred. Do you know anything about them?"

"I know some stories. My family used to tell them, and I know many tales passed down through the centuries, some that would have been lost otherwise."

Cleo's heart pounded. "Have you ever heard rumors a woman who lives here in Paelsia used to be a Watcher? She was exiled and now makes her home in a village in this land."

"An exiled Watcher around here?" The woman's brows went up. "How exciting. But no, I've never heard this rumor. I'm sorry."

Cleo's shoulders sank. "So am I."

The woman gathered her wares and rolled them up into a large piece of cloth, tucking them into a pack she swung over her shoulder. "You should find shelter. The storm is nearly upon us."

"Storm?" Nic repeated just as a crack of lightning forked through the darkening sky followed by a boom of thunder.

The woman gazed upward. "Storms in Paelsia are infrequent, but always sudden and severe. Our land is still touched by magic, even as it fades before our eyes."

Cleo's breath caught. "You believe in magic."

"Sometimes I do. Lately, though, it's not often enough." She cocked her head. "Are you sure you're from Limeros? You hold the slightest accent that makes me think of our southern neighbors."

"Of course we're sure," Nic said without hesitation. "Cleo and I have traveled extensively across Mytica as well as overseas, so we've managed to pick up many things along the way. Accents, habits, friends. Hopefully we can count you among the latter. My name's Nicolo, but please call me Nic."

"Eirene." A smile helped fan the wrinkles out around her eyes. "A pleasure, young man. And you"—she turned to Cleo—"that's an unusual name you have. Is it short for Cleiona?"

Her gaze snapped to Nic's. He'd used her name in conversation without thinking.

She forced her gaze to remain steady. "I blame my father for my name. He had a special interest in mythology. He didn't discriminate among the goddesses as many Limerians would. He considered them both as equals."

"Smart man. Now I strongly suggest you find a room for the night."

They exchanged a look just as the cold rain began to fall. Cleo pulled the hood of her cloak over her hair, but it only took a few moments before she was soaked.

"We'll have to find shelter, but we can't afford an inn," Nic said. "We need food more and have not enough coin for both."

Eirene studied them before she nodded. "Then you'll come home with me. I can feed you and give you a dry place to sleep for the night."

Cleo looked at her with shock. "Why would you do such a thing for complete strangers?"

"Because I would hope a stranger would do the same for me. Come."

Eirene led them to her home five minutes away from the market. By then they were drenched through to their skin—and everything in Cleo's bag was wet. As Nic helped Eirene build a fire in the hearth, the stone chimney rising up through the thatched roof, Cleo glanced around. The floors were tightly packed dirt, almost as hard as marble. It was otherwise very clean, but sparse. Wooden table, wooden chairs, straw mattresses at the far side of the room. While it was nothing compared to even the most modest villa in Auranos, it was certainly livable enough.

They were given worn wool blankets to warm themselves and a clean change of clothes while their own clothes dried out by the fire. Nic changed into the simple shirt and trousers, while Cleo wore a plain woven dress that made even the unadorned dress she'd been wearing beneath her cloak look incredibly elegant in comparison.

She leaned toward him while Eirene worked in the kitchen. "This itches."

"This too."

"I suppose it's better than being nude until our clothes dry out."

"Oh, absolutely." He gave her a mischievous grin. "How horrible that would be."

While Eirene prepared dinner, she asked them questions about their trip to Paelsia. Cleo sat back and let Nic work his special magic, weaving his tale about their research trip like a master storyteller.

"So you seek this exiled Watcher to interview her?" she asked.

"Partly," Cleo said, exchanging a glance with Nic. "But I—*we*—also have another sibling. An older sister who's gravely ill. We heard a rumor that this Watcher might hold the means to cure her."

"Grape seeds." Eirene nodded. "Infused with earth magic. Correct?"

Cleo's eyes widened. "So you have heard the legend."

"I have. But I'm sorry to tell you that's all it is. There had to be some explanation for the vineyards' success, so some believe this is the reason. However, most believe that Chief Basilius himself is responsible for whatever magic makes such wine possible so his people can use that wine in rituals to honor him."

"What's the truth?"

She gave a small shrug. "It's not for me to say."

Cleo leaned back in her chair, frowning. "But you did say that you believed in magic."

Eirene nodded. "I do, although I would never say such a thing in Limeros. While I'm no witch, I wouldn't want such a dangerous light shone in my direction for what I believe."

"Do you know of any witches who live around here?" While the thought that the Watcher was only a legend pained Cleo, perhaps she could find a witch instead. Any connection to magic was an important path to follow.

"For a Limerian to ask about witches with interest, you must be very determined to save your sister. This is the real reason you've come to Paelsia on this search, not merely for your book. Isn't it?"

Cleo's eyes suddenly burned with tears. "My sister's the most important and precious person in my entire life. If she dies from this horrible disease, I don't know what I'll do. I need to help her."

The door opened and a pretty dark-haired girl ran inside, soaking wet from the cold rain that fell in sheets outside. Her eyes fell instantly on Cleo and Nic.

"Who're you?" she demanded.

Eirene grimaced. "Sera, please. Be polite. These are my guests. They'll be staying with us for dinner and overnight."

The girl's expression didn't become any friendlier with this announcement. "Why?"

"Because I say so, that's why. This is my granddaughter, Sera. Sera, this is Cleo and Nicolo. They're visiting from Limeros."

"Cleo," the girl repeated, turning the name over on her tongue.

Cleo's heart beat harder at the fear that the girl might recognize her for who she really was. She willed herself to remain calm. "It's a pleasure to meet you, Sera."

Sera stared at her a moment longer before she flicked a glance to her grandmother. "Should I set the table?"

"Please."

They sat down for dinner at the small, rickety wooden table. Cleo was so hungry she couldn't help but enjoy every mouthful of the hearty barley stew served in a small wooden bowl—something she would have turned up her nose at if she were still at the palace, but for which she was very grateful tonight. And, of course, there was wine. If there was one thing Paelsians didn't scrimp on in their difficult, laborious lives, it was wine.

Cleo had been about to decline the offer of a glass from Eirene's flacon, but she held her tongue. Wine had led to regrets and unpleasant memories in the past, but one glass wouldn't hurt. She still nursed her first by the time Nic was on his third. It helped to loosen his already loose tongue.

"You seem like you know a lot about witches and Watchers," he said to Eirene. "Is there anything you are willing to share that might help our research?"

She leaned back in her chair until it squeaked. "I have stories. But stories are not facts."

"I like stories. Love them, actually. Most of the time they're better than facts."

"What about stories involving goddesses?"

Sera groaned. "Not this again. Grandmother loves to be controversial and tell this story. But no one believes the goddesses were Watchers."

Cleo nearly choked on a mouthful of wine. "Do you mean Cleiona and Valoria?"

Eirene smiled wickedly. "Are you willing to hear such a scandalous possibility? Or are you too devout in your worship, as most Limerians are?"

Limerians believed that Valoria was an ethereal being who embodied earth and water magic. Cleiona embodied fire and air. They were equally strong, but their violent rivalry caused them to destroy each other, at which time nearly all *elementia* was shut off from the mortal world. Limerians believed Cleiona was the instigator of this final battle—that she'd attempted to steal Valoria's power, leading to their beloved goddess's demise. They viewed Cleiona as evil for this reason, the dark to Valoria's light.

Auranians—when they were more religious as a whole—believed just the opposite.

"I'm open," Cleo said, eager to learn anything about the Watchers that might help her. "Tell your tales. We're grateful for anything you're willing to share."

Sera cleared the empty plates from the table. "Tell them about Eva."

"I will. Patience, dear."

"She was the last sorceress," Sera said. "She could command all four elements all by herself. No one and nothing else was that powerful except the Kindred itself."

For a girl who'd seemed reluctant to hear her grandmother's stories again, she now seemed eager to tell them herself. Cleo repressed a smile. "So a sorceress is a very powerful witch?"

"More than that," Eirene said. "Eva was one of the Watchers, the beings that live beyond this world in a protected enclave called the Sanctuary. Watchers, as you may have heard in the old legends, were the protectors of the Kindred, four crystals that held the truest, purest essence of *elementia*. Obsidian for earth, amber for fire, aquamarine for water, and moonstone for air. The magic could be seen inside the crystals, swirling around if you were to look closely.

"The sorceress wore a ring that enabled her to touch the crystals without becoming corrupted by their infinite magic. For as beautiful as they were, they were also very dangerous. The Watchers guarded them to keep the Kindred safe. But also to keep the mortal world safe from the Kindred.

"A millennium ago, Mytica, which is now divided into three lands, was united as one, and everyone lived prosperously and in harmony. Back then, the existence of magic was as accepted as life itself. Harmony in the Sanctuary translated to harmony here."

Cleo remembered reading in her history books, when her tutor insisted she pay attention, that Limeros, Paelsia, and Auranos were once one large land with no borders. It had been very hard for her to believe. The people from the different kingdoms were so different now, but once they had been united.

"So what happened?" Nic asked. "I know they say the Kindred has been lost for a thousand years."

"It wasn't lost, precisely," Eirene replied. "It was stolen. While the Sanctuary seemed harmonious and the Watchers devoted to guarding the Kindred—which gifted them with eternal youth, beauty, and magic—there were a few among their ranks who aspired for more."

"More than eternal youth, beauty, and magic?" Cleo asked. "What's left?"

"Power. It has always been a strong motivator for some. A quest for power—for ultimate power—is the reason behind most evils the world has witnessed. There were two Watchers in particular driven to take more power for themselves. But I'm getting ahead of myself."

"I like the part about Eva and the hunter," Sera said. "It's my favorite."

"My granddaughter is a romantic." Eirene laughed and got up from the table to pour them all more wine. "While Eva was a powerful sorceress the other Watchers respected as their leader, she was also quite young compared to some of the elders. Some might say she was naive. She often ventured beyond the veil of the Sanctuary and into the mortal world. It wasn't locked then as it is now. In the Sanctuary there is no wildlife, so her favorite thing to do was bird-watch. One day, she came across a hunter who had been mortally injured by a mountain lion. He'd traveled too far into the Forbidden Mountains and lost his way. As he lay dying, she appeared to him.

"Some say it was love at first sight. She then did what was not allowed—she used her powerful earth magic to heal the hunter's wounds and save his life. Over the next few weeks, she left the Sanctuary to meet with him again and again. Their love only grew stronger. The hunter begged her to leave the Watchers and stay with him in the world of mortals, but she knew she couldn't leave her responsibilities behind so easily. However, one day she found that she was pregnant, and she began to wonder if it could be different. If she could live two lives or if she'd have to sacrifice one forever—either the mortal man she loved or the other immortals who shared her magic.

"Eva had two older sisters, who learned of her secret, and it gave them more reason to be jealous of her. While they, as Watchers, were also powerful, their skills paled in comparison to their younger sister's magic.

"When she gave birth to the hunter's daughter, the sisters emerged from the Sanctuary and kidnapped the child. They threatened the baby's life if Eva didn't bring them the Kindred past the veil into the mortal world. Remember, within the Sanctuary, only Eva had the ability to touch the Kindred.

"It was then that Eva made her choice. The thought of losing her baby was too much for her to bear. She took the Kindred from the four corners of the Sanctuary and brought them to the sisters in the mortal world. Each took two for themselves, and the moment they touched the stones, they were corrupted by the magic. It changed them forever."

"It turned them into goddesses," Cleo said, barely breathing. "The sisters were Valoria and Cleiona."

Eirene nodded gravely. "The Kindred were absorbed into the sisters' very skin. They became fire and air, earth and water. But now that the Kindred had been taken from the Sanctuary, the two were unable to return. They were trapped in the mortal world. And while they had the power of goddesses, they had the bodies of mortals.

"Eva knew this and hadn't warned them. Their fury combined was enough to destroy her. The child was lost. Some say she died, others that she was left on the doorstep of a peasant's cottage as a last act of kindness of the goddesses for their dead sister.

"The hunter found the body of his love in the forest but no sign of where his daughter was. He took the ring from Eva's finger to remember her by . . . and to lie in wait for his moment.

"The goddesses remained apart until the final battle, when each wanted to take the other's power—realizing after many years that possessing all four of the Kindred would give one ultimate power and immortality even in the mortal world. They destroyed each other.

"The hunter had been spying on them all this time. As the goddesses were destroyed, the Kindred reappeared in their crystal form. He had Eva's ring, so he could touch the crystals without being corrupted. He hid the crystals where no one could see them or find them. And then, having achieved this last task in his life, he died."

"Great. A story with a happy ending," Nic said, stunned.

"Depends how you look at it, really." Eirene smiled. "More wine?"

Nic pushed his glass forward. "Please."

"So the Kindred were never found," Cleo said.

"Not to this day. Although many believe that they're only a myth. That the Watchers are merely legend—stories told through the years with no basis in fact."

"You said you believe in magic. But do you believe in these stories?" she asked.

Eirene poured more wine for Nic and herself. "With all my heart."

Cleo's head swam from everything she'd been told. "The Watchers search for the Kindred. Isn't it said that they see through the eyes of hawks?"

Eirene nodded. "They seek to find the Kindred and return it to the Sanctuary. If they ever leave other than in their bird form, in these spirit journeys, they cannot return. The Sanctuary is closed off from the rest of the world. It exists on a different plane from this one. And all except a trace of magic has stayed with them— but it's said to be dying off. The longer they go without having the Kindred in their possession, the more their world fades. Just as this one does."

"Do you think it's related?" Nic asked.

Eirene's expression was grim. "Most definitely."

"I just like the love story part," Sera said. "The rest is kind of hard to believe, if you ask me. Grandmother, I promised a couple friends that I would meet them at the tavern. Do you mind if I go out?"

"No, go ahead."

After bidding them farewell, Sera grabbed a cloak and walked out of the cottage, leaving the three of them alone.

"I must admit, I'm surprised that you're not more outraged at the suggestion that your beloved goddess Valoria from Limeros is a corrupted Watcher," Eirene said.

Cleo and Nic exchanged a look.

"We have very open minds," Nic replied. "Although it's a surprise that she could be as evil as you say she was."

"I never said she was evil. Nor was she good. Even in the darkest and most cruel person, there is still a kernel of good. And within the most perfect champion, there is also darkness. The question is, will one give in to the dark or the light? It's something we decide with every choice we make, every day that we exist. What might not be evil to you could be evil to someone else. Knowing this makes us powerful even without magic."

"Other Watchers leave the Sanctuary." Cleo slid her index finger around the edge of her empty glass. "They can never return. But it's happened."

"So the rumors go."

"Do they keep their magic? Could a Watcher who holds healing seeds infused with earth magic really exist?"

"You have such hope for this that I would hate to say no." Eirene smiled and reached across the table to squeeze Cleo's hand. "You must continue to believe with all your heart. Sometimes belief is all it takes to make something real."

"I believe I would like to go to sleep very soon," Nic said.

Her smile widened. "An excellent suggestion, young man."

With the story and the meal over, Eirene prepared beds on the floor by the hearth for both Nic and Cleo. She snuffed out the candles, pulled the canvas covering across the window for privacy, and bid them good night.

Cleo settled down onto the thin straw mattress and stared up at the dark ceiling.

And though her thoughts first turned unbidden to Theon and what he might be doing, when she fell asleep, she dreamed of sorceresses and goddesses and magic seeds.

CHAPTER 18

PAELSIA

"I had to escape," Sera said later at the tavern. With its dirt floors and smudged glasses, it wasn't much and wasn't large enough to accommodate more than a couple dozen people, but it served its purpose. It was a place for the work weary to find a cheap drink and some company.

"Really. Why's that?"

A smile played on the lips that half the boys in a ten-mile radius were well acquainted with. "My grandmother's taken in a couple of strays for the night. Had to suffer through her stories again. Immediately thought of you when they were introduced to me. The girl's name is Cleo—just like that hateful princess. I've never known anyone else with that name."

Jonas stared with shock at the girl seated next to him at the small wooden table in a darkened corner of the tavern. He'd never heard of anyone else with that name either. "What did she look like?"

"Looked like a princess, if you ask me. Blue eyes. Fair hair.

Around my age. Pretty thing, I suppose." Sera twisted a piece of dark hair between her fingers.

"You said her name was Cleo."

"That's right."

Blondes weren't that common in Paelsia. They weren't common anywhere, really, but there were still a few, more often from northern Limeros. Jonas remembered Cleo's hair, bright as the sun, long and flowing down her slim body.

He'd dreamed of tearing that hair out a piece at a time while she begged for mercy.

Jonas cast a glance to the other side of the tavern to see Brion sitting by the warmth of the fire, his eyes already closing. They'd been busy for days scouting and had stopped for a nightcap before spending the night at the home of his sister Felicia and her husband, a short distance outside of the village. Chief Basilius's men were way ahead of them. All eligible men—and boys—on the west coast had been signed up to join the Paelsian army. In their travels, they'd found no sign of any troublemakers or spies. Unless this girl that Sera, whom Jonas knew casually from his visits to Felicia and Paulo, spoke of was the Auranian princess herself.

"Maybe I'll tell you more later." Sera boldly scooted her chair closer so she could slide her hand down Jonas's chest and over his abdomen. He grabbed her wrist and she flinched.

"Tell me *now*."

"You're hurting me."

"No, I'm not. Don't exaggerate."

She bit her bottom lip and looked coyly at him, her feigned distress forgotten. "Maybe we should go somewhere a bit more private where we can discuss anything you like."

"Not tonight." He wasn't the least bit interested in going

anywhere private with her tonight or any other night. No, he was only supposed to have private time these days with Laelia, a girl he was already tired of spending time with. But until everything worked out with the chief and Jonas's hope for a successful rebellion against Auranos, he thought it best not to end things between him and the snake dancer. It might backfire on both himself and Brion if they offended Chief Basilius's daughter. Being kicked out of the chief's trusted circle would be the least of their worries then.

"You said this Cleo girl is at your grandmother's cottage?" Jonas said very quietly and very firmly.

"That's what I said," she replied, now sullen. "She and her friend are staying there overnight."

"This is impossible." He let go of her completely. "She wouldn't be stupid enough to show her face around here."

"You don't think it's actually the princess, do you? She didn't act much like a princess."

If the blonde was Cleo—and he had a sickly gut feeling that it was—then she had a specific reason for being here. But what was it? Was she a spy for her father? He'd seen intelligence and cunning in her eyes that fateful day at the market, an ugly maliciousness that betrayed her outward beauty. He wouldn't underestimate her. "Who is she with?"

"Some boy named Nicolo. He seemed harmless."

He relaxed by a fraction. If Sera had said that she was here with Lord Aron, he wouldn't have been able to control his rage a moment longer.

Jonas's jaw was so tight that it made it difficult to speak. He pushed back from the table and got to his feet. "Thank you for telling me this, Sera."

"You're leaving? So soon? Just because this girl might really be Princess Cleo?"

Jonas flinched as if his brother's death had happened only minutes ago rather than more than two months. His grief was as raw and bloody as it had been that very first day.

Revenge. That's what he'd wanted. But now with his newfound association with Chief Basilius, he wasn't sure that was the best course of action. He needed to talk to the chief and find out what to do next. By horse, the chief's compound was only a two-hour ride away.

He glanced over at Brion. His one hard-earned mug of dark ale sat untouched while he slept, his face lit by the crackling fire.

Jonas would let him have his rest. He'd go and see the chief alone. Only then would he decide what the princess's ultimate fate would be.

CHAPTER 19

LIMEROS

L

Magnus stood on the balcony of his chambers, staring off into the darkness. He'd stayed in his room tonight, opting to take dinner there instead of trying to deal with his family downstairs. He still didn't think he could look his father in the eye after their private conversation earlier that week.

There was a knock at his door and he moved off the balcony toward it, certain it would be Amia come to pay him a visit. He wasn't sure if he was in the mood to appreciate the maid's particular talents tonight, no matter how enthusiastic she might be.

But it wasn't Amia.

"Magnus." Sabina leaned against the edge of the doorway when he opened it. "Good evening."

"Good evening," he said without any feeling. This was a surprise. Sabina had never knocked on his door before. After what he'd learned about her from his father, he watched her warily, but with interest.

Everyone had secrets.

"Everything all right?" she asked. "I was worried when you didn't come down for dinner tonight."

"I'm fine. Thank you for your concern."

"I wondered if I might speak with you."

"About what?"

"A private matter."

He tensed. Sabina and the king were such close confidants that he worried what this might entail. However, he didn't think he could refuse. He was certain she wouldn't be deterred if he simply tried to ignore her.

"Of course." He opened the door wider. "Please come in."

She did, her silky red dress hugging her body. He'd have to be blind not to notice her beauty. While his mother, the queen, was quite plain and showed her age with every passing year, Sabina looked the same as he ever remembered. Tall, willowy, with long dark hair and amber-colored eyes. Her lips were always turned up in a smile that never looked entirely friendly.

"Close the door," she said.

With only the slightest hesitation, he did as requested.

She moved toward the window, trailing her fingertips over each piece of furniture she passed, including the wooden posts at the foot of his bed, each carved to resemble a serpent. "Goodness, it's cold in here. You should close your window and have someone light a fire."

"Perhaps later. What do you want to talk about?" If he could move this along, he'd be happy. If Amia wasn't going to stop by tonight, he'd rather spend the rest of the evening alone.

Sabina slowly turned to look at him. "The king told me about the conversation you had together."

He couldn't find his breath for a moment before he managed

to shift his invisible mask of indifference back into place. "Is that so?"

"Yes."

"He's very sharing."

"He can be when he's in the right mood." She smiled at him. "So you know."

Magnus weighed his words before speaking. "Can you be more specific? I know lots of things."

"Not that many. Just enough to cause trouble. But I think we can trust you, can't we?"

"With what?"

"Don't be coy, Magnus. It doesn't suit you. With the secret about Lucia, of course. Of the prophecy of her being a sorceress. Of the magic that I'm sure she's already shown to her trusted brother."

He looked at her sharply. "You're mistaken. She's shown me nothing of the sort."

She laughed. "Oh, Magnus, you do amuse me. Sometimes I find it hard to believe that you're Gaius's son. The resemblance is uncanny, of course, but you have a much softer heart. Especially when it comes to your sister."

He knew she meant this not as an asset, but as a fault. "It's not nearly as soft as you might think."

"Isn't it? But perhaps a heart takes experience and time to harden. When you will not flinch to learn shocking truths. I hope to be here when that happens. I think you have the potential for greatness, even if you don't believe it yourself."

He'd rarely noticed before how much he utterly disliked this woman.

"Thank you for your opinion, Sabina. Now, what exactly was it you wanted to see me about? Or was it just to rehash part of my conversation with Father that, really, is none of your business?"

"I thought I'd come for a visit. We so rarely get to spend any time alone together."

"Ah," he said blandly. "And I so enjoy your company."

She watched him with that predatory look he'd noticed her give other people when they weren't watching. She was the most intimidating woman he'd ever known. Her dead husband, on the other hand, had been the kindest man who had ever set foot inside the palace. But he'd always had a look on his face as if he constantly expected someone to strike him. Perhaps his wife.

Magnus hoped very much that he didn't share the same look. Those who appeared to be victims were always the easiest to victimize.

"You know, without that scar, you'd be a flawlessly handsome young man." Sabina cast a leisurely glance over him. "Even with it, you're still very attractive."

He absently brushed his fingertips against his scar. "I appreciate the compliment," he lied.

"Aren't you going to compliment me in return?"

"I grow weary of games, Sabina. Either get to the point or leave." He gave her a piercing look. "Unless you want to demonstrate your magic. My father said you're a witch, but I've never met a real witch before and I must say I'm curious."

"A real witch would never blatantly use her powers in the open for anyone to see. That would be risking exposure to those who might mean her harm."

"I suppose you're right."

"You'd best tell Lucia the same thing."

His chest tightened. "My father believes she's a sorceress, but I've seen no evidence of anything unusual."

"Are you sure?" Sabina eyed him with open amusement. "I think you're lying."

"I'm not. What I am sure about is that I'd like you to leave my chambers." He forced a smile. "If you please."

"Am I making you uncomfortable?"

"Not at all. But I'm tired and I wish to sleep."

That annoyingly amused look remained on her face. It was as if nothing he said had any effect on her. "I like you, Magnus."

"I'm deeply honored," he said drily.

She moved closer to him, sweeping her gaze over his tall frame from head to toe and then slowly back up again. "Your father has become obsessed with this drive to conquer Auranos. He hasn't had much time for me lately, except to seek guidance on certain decisions. He's spent today organizing a meeting in Auranos with Chief Basilius and King Corvin himself to discuss matters before they escalate."

"He's a busy man."

"I grow lonely." Again she walked slowly around him. Her gaze felt weighted and uncomfortable. "And I know that you're also lonely. You haven't yet chosen a future bride, even though you're only weeks from turning eighteen. And you spend so very much time all by yourself. Whatever do you do with your days and nights, Magnus?"

"Nothing that would interest you."

"I know you enjoy the attentions of a pretty kitchen maid, don't you? But she's the only one I'm aware of. I don't believe for one moment that you're interested in such a girl as anything more than a short and meaningless distraction."

He hated that she knew so much about him. "It might be meaningless, but it's not always short."

He tensed when he felt her hand brush over his back, trailing across to his shoulders as she circled him. "You are very nearly a man. And a very fine man at that. A bit soft around the edges still, but I think the right handling would help sharpen your edge. You could become a fine weapon in many ways."

Magnus stared at her, unclear about her meaning. But not all *that* unclear. "What are you suggesting?"

"The same thing that I suggested to your father when he was not much older than you. I'm offering myself to you as a lover."

"Is that so?" His words were measured, quiet.

"Yes."

"You're old enough to be my mother."

This finally helped her smile to slip at the edges. "Age can be an asset, Magnus. With age comes experience. You are young, and apart from that maid and perhaps a handful of other meaningless girls, you have no experience."

"You have no idea how much experience I have."

"Not nearly enough. It's clear in every move you make. You want to feel wanted. Needed. Desired." She trailed her fingertips over his chest. "I can make you feel those things."

Magnus couldn't believe this was actually happening.

"And what does my father have to say about this offer of yours?"

"Gaius doesn't know, of course. Nor does he need to know."

"Sharing a mistress with my father doesn't sound like a very good way to help strengthen our father-son bond."

"As if you've ever cared about any father-son bond."

He shrugged noncommittally. "Maybe I do now."

"This is why I came to see you tonight. To offer you this. To offer you myself. I can stay with you tonight if you'd like. Gaius won't know where I've gone. And I promise I can make you forget any problem that you might think you have." She went up on her tiptoes and pressed her lips against his.

She kissed him until she realized that he wasn't kissing her in return. She stepped back and looked up at him with confusion. "Is there a problem?"

The taste of her lips was more poisonous than pleasurable. The thought that the same mouth had kissed his father filled him with disgust. "I think you should leave."

Her amber eyes widened a fraction. "Are you denying me?"

"I'd say that's a good guess. Apologies, Sabina, but this is not something I want. I'm sure you'll have no trouble finding someone else to warm your bed while my father's otherwise occupied. But it won't be me."

Something unpleasant flashed across her beautiful face. "Don't make a hasty decision before you've given yourself time to think about it."

"Fair enough." He cocked his head. "There. I've thought about it. I'm still not interested."

Sabina's expression hardened. "I suppose for someone already lusting after his own sister, I'm not all that surprised."

The words were like a slap to his face and Magnus flinched. His father's closest confidant would be told every secret. Or perhaps she'd guessed all on her own.

The cold smile returned to her lips. "I am curious how long you've felt such an unnatural and shameful desire for her. A year? More than that? Since she was only a child?"

"Shut your mouth." He gritted the words out, his fists clenching at his sides.

"Such delicious pain I see on your face." She grasped his chin before he pushed her away. "Does this torment you, Magnus? You wear such a sullen expression usually, so cold and uninvolved—like a wall of ice. I've found your true weakness."

"You've found nothing of the sort."

She laughed at this. "Haven't I? Oh, Magnus, I know so much more than you do. Shall I tell you another secret about your beloved sister that your father keeps hidden from you?"

A storm of emotions swept through Magnus. He wanted to push the woman out of his room and slam the door in her face. But he couldn't. If there was something else he needed to know about Lucia . . .

"Tell me," he growled.

"Ask me nicely."

He trembled from the effort it took not to reach out and crush the woman's throat. "Please tell me."

"So polite," she hissed. "So not like your father in that way. He only says what he needs to when he needs to. That he didn't tell you this makes me curious why he'd keep such a secret, knowing how tortured you are over this."

"And now you want to tell me. It shall be your revenge against him for not paying you enough attention lately. He deserves it. So go ahead."

She was silent for so long he thought she might have changed her mind. "My younger sister Jana was gifted with sight—a rare thing for a common witch. Within herself, she held the ability to read the tales the stars can tell. She believed in the prophecy, passed down from generation to generation, that one day a child would be born who would hold *elementia* within her greater than anyone since the original sorceress, Eva—she whom my kind worship as you worship your goddess." Her expression shadowed with the memories of long ago. "Sixteen years ago, Jana saw the birth heralded in the stars. Lucia's birth. Together, my sister and I combined our magic to increase its power tenfold in order to locate her, knowing she would need our guidance one day when her magic finally awakened within her. My sister perished in the quest, but I brought Lucia here to Limeros to be raised as a princess . . . and as your sister."

Magnus stared at her. He could barely breathe. "You speak nonsense."

Her eyes sparkled. She took delight in his confusion. "Of course, you were never told anything about this. No one was, at Gaius's insistence. After being unable to carry another child after you, Althea, too, agreed wholeheartedly to keep this secret. All for the chance to claim a beautiful child as her own daughter—even if that princess was delivered to her by someone she's always loathed."

"What you're saying is impossible."

"Not impossible." Sabina grasped the back of his neck and brought their faces closer together so she could whisper. "Lucia is not your sister by blood, Magnus. Does this revelation fuel your passion, or does the thought that your heart's desire is no longer forbidden make it less exciting?"

"You lie." He grabbed the front of her dress. "You're trying to play with my mind."

"I'm not lying. She's not your sister." Her eyes narrowed. "However, she was raised as your sister and knows you only as a brother. She doesn't feel the same toward you as you do toward her. So tragic."

He let go of her and stared at her with shock and confusion. His entire world was in tumult, spinning.

"Maybe I'll have a little talk with Lucia." Sabina's smile was unpleasant as she stroked away the crease he'd created in the front of her crimson dress. "Would you like her to learn your dark little secret and see what her reaction is? I'd be happy to tell her myself."

"Secret?" The door squeaked open to reveal Lucia standing beneath its arch. Magnus froze. "What secret?"

When Magnus hadn't joined the family for yet another dinner, Lucia had begun to worry. After studying for most of the evening, she was ready to do some more practicing. Magnus had served as an excellent tutor. Tonight she wanted to focus on her fire magic.

She left her room and wandered the halls until she came to her brother's room. The door was mostly shut, but she heard raised voices inside.

And her name, and something about a secret.

She pushed the door open and was surprised to see Sabina standing only a foot away from Magnus. Both of their faces were flushed and they cast angry glares toward her as she entered.

Perhaps she should have knocked first. "What's wrong?" she asked.

"Such a sweet girl," Sabina purred. "Isn't she, Magnus? So very sweet, your sister. Like honey melting on your tongue."

"Leave her alone," he growled back. Lucia was surprised to hear the catch in his voice.

"I've left her alone for sixteen years," Sabina said, her words clipped. "Both my time and patience grow short."

"She's innocent in all of this."

"Or perhaps waiting under the surface is something harder and less breakable, just like I sensed with you." Sabina turned a smile on Lucia, one that made a chill run down her spine. "If you don't wish to experience my personal tutoring, Magnus, maybe she would. Less fun than the sessions I had planned for you, of course, but still very necessary."

"Magnus?" Lucia asked, frowning. His face was as tense as she'd ever seen it.

"You should go," he said.

"Why?" Sabina asked. "This is an excellent opportunity for the three of us to get to know each other better. Lucia, dear, how are you?"

Lucia tightened her lips. She didn't trust this woman. "Fine, thank you."

"Really? You haven't been feeling strange lately?"

Lucia watched her warily. "I don't know what you mean."

"Magnus told me how powerful your magic is."

It was as if she'd just been punched in the stomach. It took effort not to stagger back from the blow. "What?"

"I said no such thing," Magnus snarled.

"Perhaps not." Sabina gave each of them a thin smile. "But now I know everything I needed to know. It's true. Your powers have awakened."

Cold fear washed over Lucia that this woman knew anything about her. This was the continuation of their last confusing conversation in the halls about dangerous secrets. Sabina *knew*.

"Don't be worried," Magnus said calmly. The anger had left his voice and expression, but it still burned in his eyes. "Your secret is safe with Sabina. For I know a secret about her—she's a witch."

Lucia's mouth dropped open at this revelation.

"Now that we have all of this out in the open," Sabina said, gazing at her curiously, "perhaps you can tell me what you're able to do."

It took a moment for her to find her voice. She raised her chin and looked directly in the older woman's eyes. "Not much at all."

A look of frustration crossed Sabina's face. "Can you be more specific?"

"No, she can't." Magnus came to stand next to Lucia and put his arm around her shoulders. His proximity comforted her immediately. "It's late. This is not a discussion we should be having right now."

"Is that why you came to Magnus's room?" Lucia demanded. "To question him about me?"

"That was one of the reasons," Sabina said with a twisting smile. "Shall I tell you about the others?"

Magnus shot the woman a dark look. What secrets did he have that he'd chosen to tell Sabina, but not her?

"Do you know how powerful you are, Lucia?" Sabina asked.

She shook her head. "I don't understand any of this."

"Your father would be unhappy if I told you everything without him being here. Believe me, I've already revealed enough to ensure his anger. But know this . . . it was foretold. Your birth was foretold. Your ability to access *elementia* as no one has in a thousand years was foretold. You're not a witch, Lucia, darling. You're a sorceress."

Her anxiety swelled to a fever pitch. "You're wrong. I might be able to do a little bit of magic, but it's nothing that vast."

"Perhaps you've only dabbled up until now, but if it's already begun to awaken, that means it's yours—a pool of magic waiting for you to fully plunge into. All four elements for you to wield at will."

"You could still be wrong," Magnus said firmly.

"I'm not wrong!" This was shouted, as if Sabina had been on the very edge of her temper and had finally stepped beyond. "I'm right, as I've been from the very beginning. I would never have sacrificed all I have if I'd had any doubt. I know if you reach into your abilities as deeply as you can, you will awaken the rest of it."

Lucia felt an overwhelming urge to flee this room and this woman—this *witch*—who'd always intimidated and frightened her. She looked to Magnus, but he didn't say a word. His brow was furrowed.

"Magnus, are you all right?" she asked again. His expression wasn't impassive as it usually was but tormented.

"I didn't want this," he said. "Any of it. I wanted you to be safe."

"Oh, Magnus," Sabina drawled. "Stop playing at being a saint to your little sister. It doesn't fool me. You're just like your father, but you keep denying it."

He turned his fierce gaze on her. "I'm nothing like my father. I *hate* him and everything he stands for."

"Hate is a strong emotion. Much more powerful than indifference. But those who burn with hate can also love just as intensely. Can't they?" She smiled at him, as if they shared a private joke about this. "When you hate—or *love*—do you do so with all your heart? So much that it feels as if you might die from it?"

"Shut up," he growled.

"I gave you a chance, but you didn't take it. I could have helped you in so many ways."

"You help no one but yourself. It's always been that way. I can't believe I never guessed that underneath it all you were an evil witch who should be burned at the stake like the others my father put to death."

Sabina backhanded him hard across the scarred side of his face. "Watch your mouth, boy."

"Or what?" He touched the corner of his mouth and came away with blood on his fingertips. He cast a dark look at her.

"Don't you dare touch him!" Lucia snarled. Seeing Magnus struck by this nasty woman had summoned a wave of anger from deep inside her, anger unlike anything she'd felt before.

No—that was wrong. She'd felt it before. One time, three years ago, when she'd hidden behind a corner while Magnus had been reprimanded by their father for talking back to him in public. Magnus had tried to rise up and hit his father back, but he'd been beaten down. Her brother had finally run from the room and gone straight to his chambers. Lucia had followed him and found Magnus curled up in the corner, a frozen look of pain on his bloodied face that went much deeper than physical. She'd sat down next to him and put her head on his shoulder. Hadn't said a word, just sat with him and listened to his quiet sobs until they finally faded away to nothing.

She'd wanted Magnus to kill their father for hurting him.

No, that was wrong too. She had wanted to kill him herself.

"I dare," Sabina said. "With the full permission of your father, the king. I can strike your brother whenever I want. I can *do* whatever I want. Just watch me, little girl."

She lashed out and hit Magnus again. He snarled at her; his fist was so tight that Lucia was certain he would strike back. If Sabina was not a woman, she was certain he wouldn't have hesitated.

Lucia had no such problems with gallantry. She lashed her hand through the air in a flicking motion. Sabina's head moved as if she'd been slapped, even though she stood six paces away. The witch pressed her palm to her reddened cheek, her eyes wide but glowing with excitement.

"My darling girl," she exclaimed. "Very good! Yes, just like that. So it's anger that helps you grasp hold of your magic, is it? Perhaps it will be anger that can fully awaken it."

"Stop this," Magnus hissed. "I don't want this."

"Nobody asked you." Sabina grinned, even though a trickle of blood slid down the corner of her mouth. She drew out a dagger from beneath her skirts, from a leather sheath strapped to her thigh. Then she moved so fast that Lucia could barely follow her.

Suddenly, Sabina was behind Magnus, digging the tip of her dagger under his chin so sharply that blood slid down his throat.

"Magnus!" Lucia shrieked.

"I . . . can't . . . move . . ." Magnus managed with effort.

"The *elementia* a common witch like me can summon takes great effort or sacrifice," Sabina said calmly. Blood now trickled from her nose. "But I can do a little when necessary. Air can bind. Air can suffocate."

"Don't hurt him!" Lucia's stomach clenched. She was both furious and deeply frightened—two opposite emotions that raged against each other.

"I wish to test your earth magic tonight," Sabina said. "When I slit your brother's throat, you'll have just enough time to summon the magic required to heal him and save his life. Delving into your powers that deeply will help awaken all of them. Gaius will understand that I had to use extreme measures. I'm saving him precious time."

Healing? Earth magic? Lucia had never even attempted anything like that before.

Sabina wasn't bluffing. The witch was going to slit Magnus's throat. Blood already streaked down his skin. With despair, she watched the tip of the knife sink deeper into her brother's skin. Pain flashed across his expression.

Fury exploded from within her.

Lucia didn't think. She simply acted, now blind with rage and fear.

She screamed and thrust both hands toward Sabina, forcing the magic that slept deep inside to the surface.

Sabina flew backward and slammed against the stone wall of Magnus's chambers. There was a sickening *crack* as the back of her skull shattered against the hard surface. Lucia kept her arms thrust outward. It was enough to hold the woman in place. Sabina's feet now dangled above the ground.

Blood gushed from the witch's mouth and she made a sickly gurgling noise.

"Good," she managed. "Your . . . air magic . . . it's even stronger than I thought. But untrained. You can heal me. You—you need me."

"I don't need you! I hate you!" Lucia's rage only blazed hotter. As if to match her rampant emotions, flames burst from Sabina's chest. The witch looked down at herself, panic finally showing in her wild, pained gaze.

"Enough! No . . . Lucia, it's enough! You've proved yourself—"

But before she could utter another word, a raging inferno lit up the dark room, consuming Sabina completely. Lucia's long, wild hair was swept back from her face from the blast of the heat wave. Sabina's scream of agony was cut short as her blackened corpse fell heavily to the ground and the flames disappeared.

Lucia shook from head to toe as Sabina dropped to the floor, her eyes wide with horror at what she'd done. She'd hated Sabina enough to want her to burn.

And she'd burned.

Magnus was at her side the next moment. He sank to his knees next to her and pulled her against his chest, holding her tight to stop her from trembling.

"It's all right," Magnus soothed.

"She was going to kill you." Her words came in tight bursts.

"And you saved my life. Thank you for that." He wiped her tears away with his thumbs.

"You don't hate me for what I've done?"

"I could never hate you, Lucia. Ever. You hear me?"

She crushed her face against his chest, taking comfort from her brother's strength. "What will Father do to me when he learns of this?"

Magnus tensed and she pulled back from him to look up into his face. Her brother's attention was on the door—now fully open. Standing there was her father.

He was staring at the charred remains of Sabina Mallius. Then his gaze slowly tracked to his children.

"You did this, didn't you, daughter?" His voice was soft, but never before had it sounded so dangerous.

"No, it was me," Magnus said, raising his chin higher. "I killed her."

"Liar. It was Lucia." The king moved toward them and gripped Lucia's arm, lurching her up to her feet and away from Magnus. "You killed Sabina, didn't you? Answer me!"

She opened her mouth, but nothing came out for a moment. Her throat was nearly too tight to speak. "I'm so sorry."

Magnus sprang to his feet. "Sabina was going to kill me."

"And you saved him with your magic." The king shook Lucia. "Didn't you?"

All Lucia could do was nod, her gaze moving to the floor, hot tears streaking down her cheeks.

The king grasped her chin and forced her to look into his face. His grim expression was now mixed with something else.

Victory.

A hawk took flight from its perch on the edge of the balcony as the king said, "I couldn't be more proud of you than I am right now."

CHAPTER 20

THE SANCTUARY

Alexius transformed back into his body once he returned to the Sanctuary and opened his eyes, staring up at the constant blue sky that never shifted to night.

"I was right," he whispered.

He'd watched over the dark-haired princess for years, waiting for a sign. In recent months he'd despaired that he was wrong and had been following a girl who held no magic within her.

But he hadn't been.

A sorceress had finally been born to lead them back to their former glory. The magic that he'd witnessed pour from the girl's very being tonight held no equal in the mortal world—nor in the immortal one.

"You were right about what?" someone asked.

Alexius tensed and sat up to find that even Watchers were watched. It was another elder, Danaus. While all Watchers held the same eternal youth, the same level of beauty, Alexius had always felt that there was something slightly dark and sinister about Danaus lurking just beneath the surface.

Danaus had never done anything that went beyond the unspoken rules of the Sanctuary. But there was still ... something. Something that Alexius didn't trust.

"I was right that spring is soon to come," he said. "I sensed it even in frozen Limeros."

"Spring comes every year in the mortal world."

"Yet it's always a miracle."

Danaus's lips thinned. "A true miracle will be to find the answers we seek after so many centuries."

"Impatient, are we?"

"If I was still capable of taking flight in the mortal world, I think we'd already know where the Kindred is."

"Then it's truly a shame that you can't." Only the younger Watchers were able to transform into hawks or—much more rarely—visit the dreams of mortals. Once Watchers moved beyond a certain age, they lost these abilities forever. "You could always physically leave this realm."

"And never return?" Danaus smiled coolly. "Would that please you, Alexius?"

"Of course not. But I'm saying it's an option if you grow weary of waiting for the rest of us to find the answers."

Danaus picked up a leaf that had fallen from an oak tree. The leaf was not green with life but brown. It was a small but disturbing sign that the Sanctuary was fading. There was no autumn here, when leaves would naturally die. Only summer. Only daylight. Eternally.

At least, until the Kindred was lost. The fade had taken many centuries to begin, but it finally had.

"You would tell me if you'd seen something of importance,"

Danaus said. It was not a question. "Anything that could return the Kindred to its rightful place."

It seemed ludicrous to think something dark about an elder, but Alexius was not that young and not that naive. He remembered when two of his kind had turned their backs on the Sanctuary, killing the last sorceress and stealing what was so priceless and essential to their existence. They had given in to their greed. To their lust for power. Ultimately, it had destroyed them. And now their actions, so many years ago, had the potential to destroy everything.

Who was to say that they were the only ones who could not be trusted?

"Of course, Danaus." Alexius nodded. "I will tell you anything I learn, no matter how small it might seem."

It was not in a Watcher's nature to lie, but he felt he had no choice.

What he'd discovered had to be protected. At any cost.

CHAPTER 21

PAELSIA

It had been a long night, and Jonas knew he wouldn't be getting a wink of sleep.

First, he'd gone to Sera's grandmother's home and looked in the window, through a small opening in the worn canvas covering, to prove to himself that it couldn't possibly be Princess Cleiona that Sera spoke of. Ever since he'd left the tavern, he'd doubted his own instincts.

The golden-haired girl slept upon a straw mattress by the fireplace, her eyes closed, her face peaceful.

It was her.

Fury burned inside him. It took every ounce of strength he possessed not to barge into the cottage, wrap his hands around her royal throat, and squeeze until he witnessed the life slowly fade from her eyes. Maybe then he could rest. Maybe then he could feel that his brother's murder had been avenged in some small way.

Such a moment of pure vengeance would taste so sweet. But it would be over too soon. Instead, he rode hard to the chief's camp and told him about Princess Cleo's unexpected presence in Paelsia.

The chief hadn't seemed to care. "What difference does it make if some rich and spoiled child decides to explore my land?"

"But she's the Auranian princess," Jonas argued. "She could have been sent here by her father as a spy."

"A sixteen-year-old spy? Who's also a princess? Please. She's harmless."

"I strongly disagree."

The chief eyed him curiously. "Then what do *you* suggest?"

An excellent question. And one he'd considered since confirming Cleo's identity. How bold and disrespectful she was—this princess who saw no harm in coming to the same place where she'd caused such pain and suffering.

He took a deep breath before he spoke, trying his best to remain calm. "I suggest we look at this as an opportunity to capture her. I'm certain her father would go to extremes to ensure her safe return. We could send him a message."

"I'm to travel to Auranos with King Gaius for a meeting with King Corvin in four days. We hope to negotiate his surrender. You and your friend Brion will be joining me. If we were to deliver such a message, we'd do it ourselves."

To see King Corvin's face when they told him that Cleo was in their grasp . . .

It would be a small serving of revenge on behalf of all Paelsians to a selfish, self-involved king who had no vision beyond his own glittering kingdom.

"What better than to have the king's own daughter if the negotiations go awry?" Jonas said.

Any battle, no matter how well organized, would result in the loss of Paelsian life—especially with the untrained citizens who were being recruited to fight side by side with the armored Limerian knights and soldiers. A surrender from King Corvin without the necessity of war would be an ideal outcome. The chief pursed his lips, fiddling with the high mound of food on the plate before him, even now after midnight. Jonas ignored the girls who danced behind him by the campfire as Basilius's late night entertainment.

It still troubled him to see a glimpse of the same excess and decadence here in the compound as what he wished to rebel against in Auranos. Many in the villages told stories of the luxuries Chief Basilius was allowed as their leader—paid for by the excessive wine tax. None had a problem with it. They held him to a different standard; he represented their hope. Many worshipped the chief as a god, believing that he held powerful magic within him. Perhaps such magic could only be coaxed out with dancing girls and slabs of roasted goat meat.

Finally the chief nodded. "It's an excellent plan. I officially give you the task of detaining the girl. King Gaius begins his journey from Limeros to my compound tomorrow—from here we will go to Auranos united. I'll let him know the news of King Corvin's daughter when he arrives."

Jonas grimaced. He hated that the Limerian king—the leader of a land who'd treated Paelsia no better than Auranos had over the years—was such a close confidant of the chief now. He would have liked to argue that this wasn't necessary, but knew he'd be soundly ignored—or worse, banished from the compound and the chief's confidence—if he did.

So be it.

"Go," the chief ordered. "Find this girl and lock her up somewhere nice and tight." He gave Jonas a thin smile. "And try your best to treat her with respect. She is royalty." The chief was well aware of Jonas's personal issues with the princess, as was everyone within twenty miles of his village.

"Of course." Jonas bowed and turned to leave.

"Once we've secured King Corvin's surrender, however, you have my permission to do whatever you wish with her." With Jonas dismissed, the chief resumed his large meal and his attention shifted to the dancing girls.

Jonas couldn't guarantee that he'd be able to treat the princess with respect. His obsessive hate for her was palpable, bitter, and growing by the day. His blood boiled. Part of him wished he hadn't come to see the chief. He could have killed Cleo in the unprotected cottage and nobody would ever have had to know but himself. Waiting until after they'd seen the Auranian king might prove a challenge.

But even he recognized that a permanent change for his people was more important than revenge. The princess was worth more alive than dead.

For now.

CHAPTER 22

PAELSIA

Cleo's optimism had fully returned by the time she and Nic were ready to depart from Eirene's cottage before dawn the next morning. She clutched the old woman's hands and looked into her wise old eyes. "Much gratitude for your generosity. You were too kind to us."

"You have a good heart, Cleo." Eirene smiled. "And I can see that you love your older sister with every piece of that heart. I hope that you find the answers you seek to save her."

So did Cleo. "Tell me the best way I can contact you. Does this village have a central place where messages can be sent—perhaps the inn? I want to send you something when I return home to repay you for your kindness." She would make sure that the old woman was sent money and gifts for coming to their aid last night. Eirene and Sera would live very comfortably for years to come.

"That's not necessary."

"I insist!"

Eirene's brows drew together. "Very well. I am good friends with the owner of the tavern. I suppose he could accept a message for me. I'll write down his name for you."

She went into her cottage and returned a few moments later with a small ragged envelope that she pressed into Cleo's hand.

"Thank you." Cleo smiled as she tucked it into the pocket of her skirt.

"Magic will find those with pure hearts, even when all seems lost. And love is the greatest magic of all. I know this to be true." She kissed Cleo's cheeks and then did the same with Nic. After a last farewell, Cleo and Nic began walking away from the cottage. The sun had still not risen.

Eirene's story last night about the goddesses and the Watchers didn't work as a deterrent to Cleo's quest. It only solidified her growing belief that the magic she sought did exist. Emilia's life would be saved. Cleo focused on nothing else but that. And when she set her mind to something, it happened. No matter how she had to go about achieving it.

Unfortunately, she seemed to be in the minority this morning.

"You're going home," Nic told her firmly.

"Excuse me?" She stopped walking to face him. They were only a few cottages away from Eirene's.

"You heard me," Nic said. "Home. You're going there. Without delay."

"I can't go! Not yet."

"I thought we already agreed on this." He sighed and raked a hand through his messy red hair. "It's been a week and we've found nothing but stories. I don't think it's safe for you to remain here traipsing about with me. Perhaps it was wrong for me to allow you to come here in the first place."

"You *allowed* me?" She raised her voice. "I do what I want when I want."

"Which might be part of the problem. You're so used to getting your own way that you fail to be cautious when the situation calls for it."

She just glared at him.

"No argument?" he said, nodding. "Excellent. So you agree it's time for you to go back to Auranos."

"I'm not finished with my search. There are still villages to visit."

"I'll stay for a while. And I'll do whatever I can to find information on this Watcher you're convinced is hiding out somewhere in this land. But first I'm going to see you onto a ship back to Auranos so I know you're safe—and so, more importantly, the king knows you're safe. We've been gone long enough."

One side of her wanted to fight this with every fiber of her being. The other side couldn't help but see Nic's logic. Her heart swelled with gratitude toward him. "You'd really stay here for me?"

"Of course I would."

She threw her arms around him and squeezed tightly. "You are truly my best friend in the entire world, do you know that?"

"I'm glad to hear it. Besides, I'm in no hurry to go back to the palace and face the wrath of the king for running off with his daughter."

He was undoubtedly right, but she'd hoped not to think of that for a while longer. Both her father and Theon would be livid with her—and Nic. It was one thing if she returned victorious with the solution she'd sought in the palm of her hand and another if she scurried back defeated with her tail between her legs.

So they'd be angry. Fine. It wouldn't be the first time, nor would it be the last. She'd deal with any repercussions when the time came.

"I want to stay and help you," she said softly.

"Accept it, Cleo. You can't always have everything you want."

She snorted against the softness of his tunic. "Very well. Have it your way. You can be the hero."

"It's always been my dream."

"Back to the harbor, then."

"The harbor." He nodded and presented his hand to her. She took it.

As they started walking, Cleo had the oddest sensation that they were being watched. She turned her head to look, but no one was there. A mile west of the village, they turned onto a dusty road and she felt it again. Like cold fingers trailing down her spine.

"Ouch. You do have quite a grip on you, Cleo."

"Shh," she whispered. "Somebody's watching us."

He frowned. "What?"

They turned to see in the gathering light a tall, dark-haired boy moving toward them along the road. Cleo froze in place as he swiftly caught up to them. Her breath caught as she realized it was the very same boy who haunted her dreams.

Jonas Agallon.

"What are you—" she began.

He gave her an unfriendly grin. "Morning, princess. Such an honor to see you again."

And then he slammed his fist into Nic's face, dropping the boy to the ground. Nic scrambled back up to his feet immediately, his nose gushing blood.

Cleo screamed. "What are you doing?"

"Relieving you of your protection." Jonas swung Nic around until he faced Cleo and pressed a dagger—the very same jeweled dagger that Aron had used to kill Tomas!—to Nic's throat.

"Don't!" she shrieked. "Please, no! Don't hurt him!"

This was all happening too fast. How did he even know she was here?

"Don't hurt him?" Jonas eyed her. Nic fought against him, but Jonas was much taller and more muscular. He was able to keep the skinny boy easily under control. "Are you saying that you care for him? That his death might cause you pain?"

"Let him go right now!"

"Why should I?" His dark-eyed gaze swept over her. She shivered under the coldness of his glare.

"Run, Cleo!" Nic shouted.

But she didn't run. She would never abandon him like this.

"What do you want from me?" she demanded.

"That's a dangerous question. I want lots of things, none of which would probably set your pretty mind at ease. For now, I want to kill your friend and watch you grieve his loss."

"No, please!" She staggered forward with an immediate urge to grab his arm and wrench the knife away from Nic's throat. But she knew she wasn't nearly powerful enough to do that. This was a very strong boy, one who hated her for what happened to his brother. One who had threatened in public to kill her. She had to think. She had to remain calm so she could negotiate with this heathen.

"I can give you plenty of money if you spare his life."

His expression turned to ice. "Money? How about fourteen Auranian centimos for each case of wine? Sounds fair, doesn't it?"

Cleo swallowed and tried not to sound as if she was begging. "Don't kill him. I know you hate me for what Aron did—"

His eyes flashed. "*Hate* is such a small word for what I feel for you."

"Your gripe is with me, then. Not with Nic. Let him go!"

"Sorry. I don't follow orders very well."

"You mean to kill me to avenge your brother's death." Her throat thickened with fear.

His expression tightened. "No. My goal today doesn't include such a pleasure as that. Your friend here, on the other hand, might find that today is his last."

"Cleo, are you deaf?" Nic snarled. "I told you to run!"

"I'm not leaving you!" Her voice broke and tears burned in her eyes.

Jonas frowned at her. "Isn't that sweet? You should do as your friend suggests and try to run. You won't get far, but you can try. It would be a moment of bravery for such a cowardly girl."

She glared at him. "If you think I'm cowardly, you know nothing about me."

"I know enough."

"No, you don't. What happened to your brother was a tragedy. I don't defend what Aron did because he was wrong. And I was wrong not to stop it when I had the chance. I was horrified about what happened that day. So you can hate me all you want, but I swear to the goddess that if you harm Nic, I will kill you myself."

In that moment, she meant every word. Every weak, meaningless, and laughable word. Still, Jonas stared at her as if he'd never expected her to say such a thing.

"Shocking," he said. "Maybe there's more to you than beauty and a shallow personality."

"Don't you dare insult her," Nic snapped.

Jonas rolled his eyes. "Looks like you have at least one admirer among us. This one would give his life for you, wouldn't he? Wouldn't you, Nic? Would you die for the princess?"

Nic swallowed hard, but his eyes held steadily on Cleo's face. "I would."

Oh, goddess, this was all too much. She couldn't stand by and watch Nic die at the hands of this disgusting boy. "And I'd die for him too," she said firmly. "So take that ridiculous dagger and point it in my direction instead."

Jonas turned his narrowed gaze fully on her. "I can make you a deal to spare your dearly devoted friend's life. Are you willing to bargain with me?"

She glared at this boy, one she both feared and loathed. There was only one answer that could give Nic the chance to get away. "Yes."

"The deal is this: you will come with me of your own free will. You won't try to escape. You won't give me any problems." He cocked his head. "And I let your boyfriend here run away with his head still attached to his skinny body."

"No, Cleo," Nic snarled. "Don't do this."

She kept her chin raised and didn't look away from Jonas's searing glare. "You want me to trust that you won't kill me? To agree to go with you even though I don't know where you'll take me? I've heard what happens to girls who are kidnapped by savages."

He laughed. "Is that really what you think of me? A savage? How Auranian of you. I could just kill him, you know. I'm bargaining with you *because* I'm no savage."

If she went with Jonas, she was putting her fate in the hands of a boy who hated her and blamed her for his brother's death. But if she said no or tried to run away, she had no doubt this heathen would kill Nic. She couldn't live with herself if she let that happen.

"Fine. I'll go with you," she finally said. "Now take that blade away from his throat or you'll be very, very sorry, you scum-sucking son of a pig."

It was a meaningless threat at best. However, if she got the chance to get that dagger away from him, she wouldn't hesitate to thrust it deeply into his throat.

"Understood, princess." He eased the blade away from Nic's neck.

"Cleo, what are you doing?" Nic's words were panicked. "You can't agree to this."

What she despaired about wasn't that she'd fallen into the clutches of a savage boy who was willing to kill without a second thought. It was that her search for her sister's cure was now at a dead end.

"Keep searching for the Watcher," she urged. "Don't worry about me."

"Don't worry about you? For this moment forward all I'll do is worry about you."

"Jonas said he wouldn't kill me."

"And you believed him?" Nic's expression twisted with agony. Normally Nic was the one with a smile and a joke and very rarely serious. But he was now.

She had to believe him. She had no choice. "Go. And don't try to follow us."

Jonas took her by her upper arm and yanked her with him along the dirt road, back in the direction they'd taken from the village, still muddy from last night's rainstorm. He cast a dark look over his shoulder toward Nic. "Follow us and the deal's off. I'll keep the princess and I'll kill you. Now run along home where it's safe."

Nic stood there in silent fury, his fists clenched at his sides as Jonas dragged Cleo away. His face was now as red as his hair. She looked back over her shoulder at him as long as she could until he was only a speck in the distance.

"Where are you taking me?" she demanded.

"Shut up."

She hissed out a breath. "Nic's not around for you to threaten anymore."

"So now you're going to give me a hard time? I don't suggest it, princess. You won't like the result."

"I'm surprised you'd even bother to use my royal title. It's obvious you don't respect it."

"What would you prefer I call you? Cleo?"

She looked at him with disgust. "Only my friends call me that."

He scowled at her. "Then I'll definitely never call you that. No, I like *princess*. Or, maybe, *your highness*. It reminds me how high and mighty you consider yourself when faced with a lowly savage like me."

"That term seemed to bother you. Why? Are you afraid it's true? Or do you consider yourself more refined that that?"

"How about you shut up like I asked you to earlier? Or I can gag you if you'd prefer."

She was quiet for a moment. "Where are you taking me?"

He groaned. "And it begins again. The princess has a big mouth."

Her thoughts raced. "You're going to use me to extort money from my father. Aren't you?"

"Not exactly. A war is brewing, princess. Did you know that?"

She gasped. "War?"

"Between Limeros, Paelsia, and your precious, glittering Auranos. Two against one, which are odds I can support. I believe it's
possible your delicate presence in my land will help end things
quickly and without bloodshed."

Cleo reeled from this possibility. She'd known there was unrest—
but war? "As if you'd care about something like that. I'd think
someone like you would relish any chance to spill blood."

"I don't really care what you think."

"You would use me against my father? Hold me hostage? You
make me sick."

His grip on her tightened painfully. "Your silence is worth any
price to me right now. So be quiet or I'd be happy to cut out your
tongue, your highness."

Cleo stopped talking. She went quiet and still, as docile as she
was capable of being, and he continued to lead her along the road.
Past the village, it turned into a smaller muddy path. A brown
rabbit darted in front of them and into a meadow with tall grass—
surprisingly green for this otherwise faded, dreary landscape. She
didn't ask any more questions. She knew he wouldn't answer them.
And she didn't want to risk losing her tongue.

Finally, fooled by her suddenly calm demeanor, Jonas let go
of her arm long enough to wipe the back of his hand across his
forehead.

Without a moment's hesitation, she bolted away from him, feet
quick as the rabbit's as she left the path and burst into wide, grassy
meadow. If she could reach the forest on the other side, she might
be able to hide until nightfall. Then she'd find her way back to the
harbor. And escape.

But before she made it to the tree line, Jonas caught up to her.
He grabbed hold of the back of her dress, pulling her to a rough

stop in the tall grass. It was abrupt enough that she stumbled, fell, and slammed her head against a chunk of stone protruding from the earth.

Darkness fell all around her.

Princesses, in Jonas's opinion, should be meek, polite, and easy to manage. So far, Princess Cleiona Bellos had been none of the above. Even the chief's daughter Laelia, who spent much of her time either dancing erotically or playing with her snakes, was the more sweet and gentle by far.

This girl *was* a snake. And he wouldn't underestimate her again.

Jonas twisted his ankle on the uneven ground as he raced after her. Pain and fury stormed through him. If she'd just knocked out her brains so they oozed onto the stone, a weathered sculpture that he now saw was in the shape of a wheel, he would be happy to stand here and rejoice. Instead, he waited and tested his bad ankle. At least it wasn't broken.

As he stared down at her, impatience turned his entire body tense and jittery. "Wake up."

She stayed still.

He studied her face. He couldn't deny that she was lovely . . . maybe even the most beautiful girl he'd ever seen. But the most beautiful girl could still be deceptive and evil.

"Wake up," he demanded. "Now."

He nudged her with the tip of his boot but received no response.

Jonas swore loudly and crouched down at her side, jabbing the dagger blade-side down into the dirt next to her so he could have both hands free. Then he felt at her throat for a pulse.

There was one.

"Too bad," he breathed, although part of him was deeply re-lieved. He studied her face, pushing the silky hair back from it. She was tiny, a foot shorter than him and at least seventy pounds lighter. Her dress wasn't as fancy as the one she'd worn that day in the market, but it was still made from silk. She wore tiny blue sapphires in her pierced ears, but that was the sum total of her jewelry. Smart, since any flashier jewelry would have undoubtedly made her more of a target for thieves. Her face was free of the paint Laelia wore, but her cheeks were still bright and sun-kissed and her lips the color of roses. Unconscious, she didn't seem nearly the cold, manipulative, rich bitch he'd fully decided she was.

Finally her eyelashes fluttered open.

"It's about time, your highness. Did you have a nice nap?"

Then Jonas jerked back, startled, as the sharp tip of his dagger pressed up against his chin.

"Get away from me," the princess snarled.

He didn't need to be told twice. He carefully shifted back from her, surprised that she'd managed to pull the weapon out of the ground without him noticing. Just as he'd begun to think she was harmless and vulnerable, the beautiful snake had managed to sharpen her fangs. She got up awkwardly, keeping the dagger trained on him, and retreated to the other side of the stone wheel that she'd fallen over.

He eyed her warily. "So now you have my dagger."

"I have Aron's dagger."

"Finders keepers. He left it stuck in my brother's throat."

The hardness in her eyes softened and they grew shiny with tears.

He scoffed. "You can't think I honestly believe you feel bad about that."

"Of course I do!" Her voice broke.

"Your Lord Aron killed him without a second thought. Despite this, you've still agreed to marry him, haven't you?"

When she laughed, it was a sound removed from humor. "I *loathe* Aron. Our engagement was not my choice."

"Interesting."

The hardness returned to her gaze. "Is it?"

"You have to marry someone you loathe. That makes me happy."

"So glad my misfortune could help brighten your day." She glared at him. "In any case, I have the knife now. If you come anywhere near me, I'll be sure it finds your heart."

He nodded gravely. "You do have my weapon. Very dangerous now, aren't you? I suppose I should be frightened."

She glared at him crouched six feet away from her, the knife clutched tightly between her fingers. "Tell me more about this war against Auranos you mentioned. What is your goal?"

"To take your precious land and split it evenly between Paelsia and Limeros. You have too much and we have nothing, and it's all because of policies your greedy country enacted a century ago. So we'll take what you have and make it ours."

"It won't happen. My father will never back down."

"Which is why it's excellent to have his sparkling jewel of a daughter as a bargaining chip. I'm going with Chief Basilius myself for a meeting with your father. We'll see what he has to say. But perhaps the king doesn't mind losing one daughter when he already has another who is his official heir. Princess Emilia could have been a better choice—but she's not in Paelsia. I'm still curious, your highness. Why are you here?"

"None of your business," the princess hissed.

His brows drew together. "Did I hear you ask your friend to

continue searching for a Watcher? What kind of nonsense was that?"

Something dark and unpleasant flashed across her beautiful face. "None of your business," she said again, then added, "savage."

Jonas ignored his frustration and held out his hand to her. "Give that dagger to me before you cut yourself."

She jabbed the weapon in his direction. "I'm not planning to cut myself. But I'm planning to cut you if you come any closer."

The girl's tongue was a thousand times more dangerous than any weapon in her possession. He'd be surprised if she'd ever held one before. Still, he watched her carefully. As much as he despised her, the view was quite lovely.

"Enough of this," he said aloud.

He pounced on her, grabbing her wrists and easily knocking the dagger away. He pushed her back, stretching her arms up over her head, keeping a tight hold of her wrists. He pressed his body down firmly on hers, pinning her in place against the wheel. She looked up at him with both alarm and fury.

"Get off me, you beast! You're hurting me!"

"If you're trying to appeal to my compassionate side, you'll find that I don't have one when it comes to you." He adjusted so he had her wrists secured in one hand. The other came down to press against her throat. He stared into her eyes and finally saw a satisfying edge of fear there. She thought he would kill her, despite his earlier promises.

He increased the pressure on her throat and stared down into the face of the girl who'd stood by her fiancé's side as his brother bled to death.

"Why are you in Paelsia?" he demanded. "Are you here to spy for your father?"

She looked up at him with wide eyes. "Spy? Are you mad?"

"That's not an answer."

"No, I'm not here to spy, you fool. That's ridiculous."

"Then why? What did you mean when you told your friend to search for a Watcher? Talk," he growled, bringing his face down only an inch away from her own. Her quickening breath was hot and sweet against his skin. "Or you'll be very sorry."

"I'm here for my sister," she finally said, not breaking eye contact. He couldn't tell for sure if she was lying.

"Your sister," he repeated.

"There's a legend of an exiled Watcher in Paelsia who possesses grape seeds infused with earth magic that have healing powers."

He rolled his eyes. "You want me to believe you're literally searching for a Watcher. Do you chase after rainbows as well?"

His mocking earned him a withering look. "If I have to. My sister is horribly ill. She's dying and no one can help her. So I came against the judgment of my father to find that Watcher and beg for her help."

Jonas processed this ludicrous story, but one thing rang out above all else. "The heir to the Auranian throne is dying."

"I'm sure you're thrilled to hear it."

"You think so, do you?"

"My pain is your glory. You hold me responsible for your brother's death, and now you know my sister lies dying in the palace and I'm helpless to save her." Tears leaked from the corners of her eyes.

He watched her carefully, waiting for a sign of deception.

"You don't believe me," she said, despair edging her words. "All you see when you look at me is something evil. But I'm not evil." She drew in a ragged breath. "I'm not!"

At first glance, she appeared so small and fragile—but the princess possessed a fierce and fiery core that could burn anyone who got too close. Even Jonas felt its heat. It surprised him. *She'd* surprised him.

"Are you going to say something or are you just going to keep staring at me?" she asked, looking up at him with those wide blue-green eyes.

He got to his feet so fast he nearly retwisted his ankle. Then he yanked her up with him and he didn't try to be gentle about it. She swayed on her feet, seemingly unable to find her balance for a moment. She was lucky she was only dealing with a bit of dizziness after knocking herself out. It could have been much worse.

Without a word, he grabbed the dagger, shoved it into the leather sheath on his belt. He began to drag the princess back out to the road.

"Where are you taking me?" she demanded, bringing their conversation around full circle.

"Somewhere quiet where I'll make sure you don't cause any more trouble. You know, you really should have used that knife on me when you had the chance, your highness. You won't be getting away from me again."

Cleo glared at him, the fire back in her eyes. "I won't hesitate to kill you next time."

He gave her a cold smile. "We'll see about that."

As soon as he got Cleo to the storm shed at the edge of Felicia and her husband's property, he bound her hands in front of her and attached a chain to her ankle—a long one, for range of motion—to ensure she wouldn't be able to leave. She cursed at him, fighting him every step of the way. It didn't slow him down very much.

"I know you hate me." Tears glistened in her eyes. She was fueled by anger now, so the fear came and went.

"Hate you?" he asked. "Don't you think I have that right?"

"I hate myself for what happened to your brother. I'm truly sorry for what Aron did. Tomas didn't deserve to die."

"You're only saying this to try to save yourself."

"Not only," she admitted.

He couldn't help but laugh at her honesty. "You think I'm going to hurt you."

"You already have."

"Compared to your normal lifestyle, anything would be a hardship, your highness. But you'll be safe here."

"For how long?"

"A few days. A week at the most."

She looked around the shed's interior with horror. "Here?"

"My sister and her husband have already agreed to watch over you. His friends will guard the door in case you think about trying to escape. You'll be brought food and water daily." He thrust his chin to her left. "There's a freshly dug hole over there for her majesty to use when she requires. It's not a golden bejeweled chamber pot, but it'll suffice. These would be considered luxurious accommodations for a Paelsian, princess. You have no idea."

"You are a horrible savage for keeping me here. My father will have your head for this."

Jonas took hold of her throat again and pressed her up against the wall.

"I'm not a savage," he snarled. "And I'm not a heathen."

"And I'm not an evil bitch who rejoices in the deaths of others."

"A few days of adversity won't break you. They might even do you some good."

Her aquamarine eyes flashed. "I hope you're torn apart by wolves on your trip to Auranos."

Jonas would expect no other reaction from her. Anything less would be a disappointment.

As he moved toward the door, he looked over his shoulder at her. "I'll see you again soon, your highness. Try not to miss me too much."

CHAPTER 23

LIMEROS

$\mathcal{L}$

M agnus needed answers. And he needed them now.

He'd waited for his father to rage about the witch's death after he'd swept Lucia out of Magnus's chambers. Instead, all had been eerily calm. Sabina's scorched body had been quietly taken away and discarded. No funeral was planned. No one, not even the servants, seemed to be gossiping.

It was as if the king's mistress had never existed in the first place.

But Magnus didn't give a damn about Sabina Mallius, alive or dead. Only what she'd told him about Lucia's origins. He needed to know if it was the truth.

The next morning he sought his father out to demand answers but learned that the king had already left on a journey to Auranos with Chief Basilius. He wasn't expected back for two weeks.

Sabina's words echoed in Magnus's mind, but he didn't know what to believe. The witch had been a deceptive, manipulative woman—which had been proved without a doubt on the night of her death. As Magnus had watched the woman burn, he hadn't felt a single ounce of pity. She deserved exactly what she received.

But now there were so many questions.

The king had already arranged for a special tutor to be at the ready to help Lucia with her *elementia* once it awakened. It was an old, withered woman who knew much of the legends and the prophecy. His sister spent nearly all of her waking hours now with this woman, on direct orders from the king.

His sister.

The question that burned brightest inside him was if what Sabina told him was true—that Lucia was born to a different family and brought to the castle as a baby to be raised as a full-blooded Damora. Since he was not yet two years old when the queen allegedly had given birth to her, he had no memory of this.

The second day after Sabina's death, Magnus couldn't hold any of this in a moment longer. He needed answers. And staring at his sister's face across the table at dinner last night without being able to speak to her about this possibility had proved too much for him to bear. With his father absent there was only one other person in the castle who'd be able to tell him the truth.

"Magnus," Queen Althea greeted him outside after his archery class. With war looming, his lessons had increased at the king's request in number and intensity, but he'd been able to keep up. He was ready for a fight—and if it was one guaranteed to spill blood, it didn't bother him.

His mother enjoyed taking afternoon walks around the palace and through the icy gardens directly next to the cliffs. When he was a boy, she'd stare out at the seemingly endless Silver Sea and tell him tales of what was on the other side—realms filled with strange people and fantastical creatures.

His mother had long since stopped telling him such amusing stories. Along with Limeros's climate, her personality had steadily grown colder over the years. The warmer moments now were barely noticeable.

"Mother," he said, casting a glance at the swirling white-crested water crashing to the rocks far below.

"I was about to look for you. There's a message waiting for you from your father delivered earlier by falcon." Her long gray hair was loose and swept back by the cold wind from her aging face. She wore a full cloak and her normally pale cheeks were bright with color from the chill.

He got right to the point. "Did Sabina Mallius steal Lucia from her cradle in Paelsia and bring her here for you to raise as your daughter?" he asked.

Her gaze snapped to his. "What?"

"You heard me."

Her mouth worked, but no words emerged for several moments. "Why would you think such a thing?"

"Because Sabina told me so herself before Lucia set her on fire." He tried to enunciate his next words so there would be no misunderstandings. "Lucia is not my blood sister. Is this correct?"

"Magnus, my darling—"

"Don't Magnus, my darling me. The truth is all I seek from you today, Mother. If that's even possible. It's a simple answer—yes or no. Is Lucia my sister?"

The queen's expression filled with anxiety. "She is your sister in all ways but blood. As she is my daughter."

He had his answer. And it was as if the world quaked beneath his feet.

"But not from your womb."

She did not reply to this.

Magnus's heart pounded hard. "Why didn't you ever tell me?"

"Because it's not important. This is how your father wanted it to be. Perhaps he planned to tell you the truth eventually, but it was not my place to do so."

He laughed, a sound as sharp as the edge of a sword. "No, of course not. If he said for you to raise her as your own, that's what you must do. I wonder sometimes, Mother, if you also fear the king's wrath. Or if you were one of the few that managed to escape it."

"As king, your father only does what he must."

Magnus once loved his mother, but as she sat back and allowed the king to heap abuse upon him—both physical and verbal—this love had greatly faded.

"You can't tell her. Not yet." Her voice was heavy with worry. "She's a sensitive girl. She wouldn't understand."

"If that's what you think of Lucia, it only proves just how little you know her. No, the girl you raised as my sister may not share my blood, but she is a Damora. With that label, any sensitivity must be burned away as soon as possible if one wishes to survive. And Lucia now has the ability to burn many things away, should she choose to."

"I only did what I had to do."

"Of course." Magnus turned from her and began to walk away, leaving her standing at the edge of the cliff all alone. He had the answer he sought. The was no reason for further conversation. "As we all must."

He went into the castle to find the message delivered from the king. It was written by his father's own hand, which meant it was too confidential to trust to a servant. Magnus read the message twice through.

Princess Cleiona from Auranos had been captured while traveling through Paelsia and was being detained there. The king instructed Magnus to take two men with him to retrieve the princess and escort her back to Limeros. The king stressed it was an important assignment he was trusting his son with, one that could turn the negotiations with King Corvin to Limeros's favor.

While unwritten, it was clear to Magnus that his father meant to threaten the girl's life in pursuit of his own goals. It was to be expected from the King of Blood. This possibility didn't trouble him. In fact, he was surprised that King Gaius hadn't thought to send men directly into Auranos weeks ago to kidnap the girl from her own bed if it would mean an easier way for him to get his hands on King Corvin's land and gain more power for his kingdom.

His first inclination was to turn his back on this and sulk, waiting for his father to return so they could have it out about truths left unspoken.

But this was a test he couldn't ignore.

Magnus, no matter what, didn't want to lose his claim to the throne on the off chance the king claimed another bastard as his rightful son. The possibility that King Gaius might have eventually meant to do this with Tobias had never been spoken between them, but it hung in the air like the foul odor of a cesspit.

The trip to and from Paelsia, to the location noted at the bottom of the message, would take four days. Four days to prove his worth to his deceptive and manipulative father.

Unlike the answer he'd demanded from his mother, this question didn't have two possible answers. It only had one.

CHAPTER 24

AURANOS

King Corvin was nothing like Jonas expected him to be.

Paelsians widely believed him to be a devious and manipulative man who ignored their squalor while those in Auranos lived lavishly and opulently, with no heed to how much they spent or how much they wasted. Jonas had hated King Corvin before he ever laid eyes on him.

The king was a formidable-looking man. He was tall, with heavy muscle like a knight slightly past his prime. His light-brown hair, peppered with gray, hung to his shoulders; his beard was short and well groomed. His blue-green eyes were keen and sharp—and, Jonas couldn't help but note, the exact same color as the princess's. At first glance, and despite his glittering palace inlaid with actual gold, King Corvin didn't look like a man who encouraged hedonism and self-indulgence in his people.

Appearances could be deceiving, Jonas reminded himself.

At Chief Basilius's compound, they'd met King Gaius and his men and traveled together to Auranos to show that they were now allies.

King Gaius was also a strong-looking man. Short black hair, dark eyes, tight skin on his sharp cheekbones. A thin mouth. He looked stern and severe. But there was something in his eyes, a wickedness that betrayed the rest of his orderly appearance. Jonas wasn't sure if he appreciated that edge or if it made him even more distrustful of the man.

He'd heard many tales of how King Gaius ensured his subjects behaved themselves—by heavily policing them with a trained army ready to uphold the strict laws the king set forth. His was a reign painted in blood. Jonas would never underestimate someone like that, even if he wasn't sure how many rumors were true.

King Corvin did not turn them away. He invited them into his palace and into his great hall to meet with him. This was where Jonas and Brion now sat, on either side of the chief. King Gaius and his men sat at the other side of the large square table. Behind King Corvin positioned on the dais were two guards.

They all had even numbers present. But there would be no violence today. Today was for discussion only. And Jonas had been advised to let King Gaius do the talking on Paelsia's behalf. He was shocked and dismayed that the chief had agreed to this.

"Who are these boys?" King Corvin asked, referring to Jonas and Brion. He didn't ask the same of Gaius's men. Since they wore the dark red uniforms of Limerian palace guards, it was obvious to all that they were the king's bodyguards.

The chief nodded at each of them. "This is Jonas Agallon and Brion Radenos."

"They're your guards?"

"More than that. Jonas is soon to become my son-in-law."

Jonas felt Brion's surprised gaze land on him.

Son-in-law? A sick feeling churned in his gut. Perhaps it would be wise to end things with Laelia sooner than he'd planned. She obviously had the wrong impression about their future together. Jonas heard a sound. He thought it was a muffled snort of laughter coming from Brion's direction even though there was nothing remotely funny about this. He kept his eyes forward, not leaving King Corvin for a moment.

"Must we feign civil conversation?" the king of Auranos said tightly. "Say what you came here to say and be done with it."

"I consider you a very good friend, Corvin." King Gaius offered him a warm smile. "I know I should have made more of an effort to keep our ties strong."

"Were they ever strong?"

"We have so much in common. Two prosperous lands flanking that of Paelsia. Three lands that could be very strong together. Close friendships will make it even stronger."

"So you're offering me friendship today," the king said thinly and with distrust etched into his expression. "Is that it?"

King Gaius nodded gravely. "Friendship above all. Family above all. I know what it's like to have a young family. To hope for a brighter future for them. Paelsia, however, has fallen on much harder times than we have."

"And you wish to help them."

"With all my heart."

King Corvin glanced at Chief Basilius. "I know that Paelsia prides itself on being a sovereign state. You've not asked for any assistance, nor have we offered any. But I truly didn't realize how difficult times have been for you."

Jonas found this impossible to believe, but he swallowed back any poisonous comments that rose in his throat.

"We are a proud people," the chief said. "We tried to resolve our problems by ourselves."

King Gaius nodded. "I'm overwhelmed by how courageous the Paelsians have been through these lean years. My heart bleeds for their suffering. But the time has come to change all of that."

"What do you propose?" King Corvin asked, with a noticeable thread of distaste when speaking to the Limerian king. "Should we begin a charity for them? Collect money? Clothing? A food drive, perhaps? Allow more open travel between our lands? There's been a great deal of poaching here from Paelsians over the years. Is this something you think I should simply turn a blind eye to?"

"If our borders were fully open to each other, poaching would not occur. It would not be stealing then."

King Corvin templed his fingers and looked across the table at him steadily. "I'm certainly open to discussion on all matters."

"Yes, well, discussion would be lovely," King Gaius said, "if this were twenty years ago and my father still ruled. But times have changed."

King Corvin regarded him with barely veiled distaste. "Then what do you want?"

"Change," King Gaius said simply. "On a much grander scale."

"Such as?"

King Gaius leaned back in his chair. "Chief Basilius and I want to take Auranos and divide it evenly between us."

King Corvin was quiet for a moment, holding the other king's gaze. Finally his lips peeled back from straight white teeth and he laughed. "Oh, Gaius. I forgot how much you enjoy joking around."

King Gaius didn't crack a smile. "I'm not joking."

King Corvin's expression went cold as ice. "You want me to

believe that you've aligned with this chieftain to take my land and split it. You must think I'm very stupid. There's another reason. What's your real goal here? And why now, Gaius? After all this time?"

"When better?" was all King Gaius allowed.

King Corvin cast a pitying look at Chief Basilius. "You trust him with something this important?"

"Completely. He proved himself to me in ways that very few ever would dare to. He honored me with a true sacrifice. That is worth its weight in gold to me."

"Then you're an unforgivable fool." King Corvin pushed back from the table and got to his feet. "This meeting is over. I have more to worry about right now than listening to nonsense."

"We're giving you this one chance to agree to our terms," King Gaius said, undeterred. "You would be wise to accept. Your family would be treated well. You would be given a new home. An allowance. There doesn't need to be any blood shed because of this."

"Everything you touch becomes stained with blood, Gaius. That's why you haven't been welcome in my kingdom for ten years." He turned toward the door and a guard pushed it open.

"We have your daughter."

King Corvin's shoulders tensed and he slowly turned around. His annoyed expression had shifted to something much more dangerous. "I don't think I heard you right."

"Your daughter, Cleiona." Gaius enunciated the words perfectly. No room for misunderstanding. "Seems that she was found wandering through Paelsia without protection. Not very wise for a princess, is it?"

Jonas tried very hard to keep any expression off his face. This was what he'd waited for all this time and why he hadn't killed

Cleo himself. Instead, the promise of her continued life would be used to ensure a brighter future for his home and family.

"You really shouldn't let your youngest travel to other lands without proper protection," King Gaius said. "But don't worry. I'll personally ensure her safety."

"You dare to threaten me?" King Corvin's words were edged in poison.

King Gaius spread his hands. "It's very simple. Surrender your kingdom when we return with our combined army at our backs. And no one will have to suffer."

King Corvin's grip on the edge of the doorway was so tight that Jonas was sure he would tear off a strip of wood from it at any moment. "Harm my daughter and I will personally tear you apart."

King Gaius remained calm. "How could I wish harm to your youngest, Corvin? I know the love a father has for his children. My eldest, Magnus, for example, is proving his worth in so many ways. Even right at this moment. I'm very proud of him. As I'm sure you're proud of your daughters. You have two, do you not?" The Limerian king frowned. "The older one, I've heard, has fallen quite ill. Will she recover?"

"Emilia is fine."

King Corvin was lying. Jonas saw it in his eyes.

Cleo claimed to have journeyed into Paelsia chasing after the legend of an exiled Watcher who might be able to save her sister's life. She'd been telling him the truth. The truth when he'd only expected more lies.

"Think about what we've discussed here. Think very carefully." King Gaius rose from his chair. The others, including Jonas, took his lead and did the same. "When I return, I expect you to be out in front of your palace gates offering your immediate and absolute surrender."

King Corvin was quiet for a moment, his expression tense. "And if I don't?"

King Gaius swept his gaze around all those present for this meeting. "Then we'll take Auranos by force. And I'll personally witness your young daughter tortured for a long time before I finally allow her to die."

"And I will be sure to do the same to yours," King Corvin hissed.

King Gaius laughed at this. "I would dare you to try."

They left. Jonas felt King Corvin's strained gaze heavy on him as he moved toward the exit.

"It was your brother who was killed that day in the market," the king said to him as he passed. "I recognized your name."

Jonas nodded but didn't meet the other man's eyes.

"Whether you realize it or not, your grief and desire for vengeance has caused you to align yourself with scorpions," King Corvin said. "Be very careful that you don't get stung."

Jonas cast only a short glance at the man, fighting to keep his expression neutral, before he followed the others from the room.

CHAPTER 25

PAELSIA

The princess was proving to be more elusive than Theon had hoped. After arriving in Paelsia with two trusted guards, he'd searched far and wide, scouring the villages they came across for any clues.

One thing was certain—Cleo and Nic had been there, stopping long enough to make a lasting and mostly favorable impression on the locals before carrying on. Theon was surprised to learn they said they were traveling as sister and brother . . . from *Limeros*. Clever.

But then he'd hit a wall. Nothing new. No clues to where they might now be. And every day that passed deepened his desperation and fear that something horrible had befallen her. Finally he instructed the guards to split up so they could individually cover more ground, telling them that if they found nothing in seven days' time then they were to return to Auranos without him.

It had been his duty as Cleo's bodyguard—his *only* duty—to keep her safe. The king's promise to kill him if he failed was the farthest thing from his mind. He was more concerned with the princess's safety.

It wasn't until ten days after she'd left Auranos that he found a solid lead. In a village five miles southeast of Trader's Harbor, the neighboring village to the infamous one where Aron had killed Tomas Agallon, a woman told Theon she'd seen a fair-haired girl and a redheaded boy traveling together a week ago—and that the boy had returned alone the previous evening. Heart in throat, Theon spent the morning searching the village and the surrounding areas.

The woman had seen the boy, but not the girl.

And then, on a narrow, muddy road after yet another strange and unexpected thunderstorm, Theon finally spotted Nicolo Cassian. The boy was headed straight for him.

For the briefest of moments, Theon thought he was only seeing things. But it was true. He ran toward Nic and grabbed hold of the front of his tunic.

"Where is the princess? Answer me!"

Nic looked as grave and weary as Theon felt. "I knew you'd be here, somewhere, looking for us. You don't know how glad I am to finally find you."

"You won't be glad when I get you back to Auranos. You're going to pay dearly for taking the princess away from the safety of the palace."

Despite Theon's harsh words, Nic met his gaze with defiance. "You really think I forced her to come here? Cleo has a mind of her own, you know."

"Where is she?" he demanded.

"Taken by a Paelsian three days ago. He held a knife to my throat, threatened to separate my head from my body. Cleo bargained for my life by agreeing to go with him." He looked destroyed by this. "She shouldn't have. She should have run away. She should have let him kill me."

Theon's stomach lurched. "Do you know who it was?"

Nic nodded, his expression grim. "Jonas Agallon."

Theon finally let go of Nic's dusty tunic and found that his hands were now shaking. The name was as familiar as his own. Jonas. The boy who'd threatened her life. The one she'd had night-mares about. And Theon hadn't been here to protect her.

"She's going to die—or she's already dead. And it's my fault."

"I know where she is."

His attention snapped to Nic. "You do?"

"Ever since she was taken, I've been asking around, trying to learn more about Jonas and his family. I know where his sister lives. They have a storm shed on their land two hours' journey east from here, which is where I think she's being held."

His breath caught. "You think? Or do you *know*?"

"I don't know for sure since I haven't seen her, but it's being guarded. I found my way there yesterday to check for myself. A woman goes in once a day with a tray of food and water and comes out with an empty one. I only left because I knew I had to send a message to . . . well, to you. And here you are hunting me down like a stray dog. Thank the goddess." His breath hitched. "We need to save her, Theon. It's not too late."

The smallest piece of hope finally returned to Theon's heart. "Take me there immediately."

If Cleo had learned one thing in her three days of captivity it was this—Felicia Agallon hated her every bit as much as Jonas did. But despite this hate, the girl observed her brother's orders to bring Cleo food once a day—which consisted of stale rye bread and well water, made palatable only by the addition of honey. The first time, as Felicia scowled at her across the shadows of the small, cold, windowless shed with only a tiny, ragged hole in the roof to let in any light, Cleo looked down at the water with wariness.

"Is it poisoned?"

"Would you blame me if it was?"

Cleo was going to argue, but she held her tongue. "Not really."

Felicia studied her for a few moments of uncomfortable silence. "It's not poisoned. Jonas wants you to keep breathing, although I'm not sure why."

Still, Cleo waited as long as she could before she drank or ate anything. For much of her time, she tried to sleep on a pile of straw, sipped water, and nibbled at the hard pieces of bread. It was as far removed from luxury as she'd ever experienced.

She attempted to chew through the ropes binding her wrists, but that didn't work. Even if she succeeded, the chain around her ankle was another serious problem. Also, the shack was locked from the outside and guarded. She couldn't let herself think of her sister or her father or Nic. Or Theon. She was a mouse caught in a trap with no escape, waiting for the cat to return.

Waiting.

And waiting.

The last time she'd seen Felicia, only hours ago, the girl had given her a smug look as she handed over the tray of meager food and drink.

"Not long now," Felicia said. "I've received a message that he should be arriving very soon to take you away from here."

"Jonas?" Cleo whispered. "He's returned so soon?"

"No, not Jonas." She snorted. "Soon you won't be his problem anymore."

She left, closing the door to trap Cleo in the dark shed once again with only her racing thoughts and mounting worries to keep her company.

After what felt like an eternity of slowly passing time, she heard something. Shouts. Grunts. Slams.

Then there was a knock at the door.

Fear rendered her very quiet and still. There was another bang, louder this time. Then voices, muffled. She held her breath and tried to be brave enough to face whatever dark demon might burst through.

It occurred to her that whoever was outside wasn't trying to knock—they were trying to break down the door. As she had that thought, the door swung inward. Cleo shielded her eyes as painfully bright sunlight streamed into the darkness.

When Theon entered the shed, her mouth fell open with shock at the same time that her heart leapt in her chest.

"See?" Nic said with triumph. "I knew she was in here."

"Is anyone else here?" Theon demanded. It took her a moment before she realized he was speaking to her.

She tried to stop gaping at the two of them. "I . . . what? Here? No, nobody's here right now. Just me. But there are guards outside."

"I took care of them already."

Nic rushed to her side and grabbed her arms. "Cleo, are you all right? Did that savage touch you?"

The concern she saw on his face made tears fill her eyes. "I'm fine. He didn't hurt me."

Nic let out an audible sigh of relief and hugged her tightly against him. "I was so worried."

Theon didn't say anything, but he came toward her when Nic finally released her. His jaw was tight. She almost cringed away from him since he looked completely livid.

"Theon—"

He raised a hand. "I don't want to hear anything beyond you being fine right now."

"But—"

"Princess, please."

"You have a right to be angry with me."

"How I feel doesn't matter. I need to get you home. Now be still so I can free you before the guards I knocked out wake up."

She closed her mouth as he began to work on her bindings. He was more efficient than gentle with the ropes, and her wrists were more abraded by the time he finished than they'd been to begin with, but she didn't utter one word of complaint. Then Theon unsheathed his sword and hacked through the chain. He eyed the shackle still circling her ankle. "The rest of it will have to wait until we get to a blacksmith."

Theon clamped his hand on her wrist and guided her out of the shack and into the sunshine. Nothing had ever felt so good to her as the bright sun did on her face. Nic fished into her bag that he held, which she'd dropped when Jonas took her, and pulled out her cloak, putting it over her shoulders so she could stay warm. She looked at him with gratitude.

Then her gaze went to the three unconscious men who lay in awkward positions near the entrance to the shed. She hadn't seen their faces before, but knew they'd been stationed outside to prevent her from trying to escape.

"Theon!" Nic yelled. "Watch out!"

Theon turned sharply and caught Felicia's arm. The girl had

snuck up behind them, knife in hand, ready to stab Theon in his back. He disarmed her easily.

"You killed my husband!" she cried.

"I killed no one. These guards—your husband—were all unarmed. You, however . . ." His eyes flashed with anger. "You imprisoned Princess Cleiona of Auranos here."

Fear went through Felicia's gaze. "I did only what I was told. I was to keep her here until he arrives today to fetch her." Her expression hardened and she raised her chin. "He's close. I think I can hear horses approach. You'll have no chance against him."

"Who's close?"

An unpleasant smile appeared on her face. "Stay awhile longer and find out."

"You're bluffing."

"Am I?"

Theon let go of her so abruptly that she staggered back, nearly falling to the ground by her husband's side.

"Let's go, princess," Theon said, not taking his fierce gaze from the unpredictable Felicia. "And ignore her. You're safe now with me. All is well."

Immediately, they began swiftly walking away from her prison and back to the muddy road beyond. Cleo didn't say a word to the girl who'd kept her locked in the shed for three days on Jonas's orders. She wanted to hate her but found that emotion difficult to hold on to; it slipped through her fingers and disappeared completely.

She knew there was a village close by—the same village where she and Nic had met Eirene and stayed with her for the night.

"We can get a ship back," Nic said. "I already checked—there's one leaving tomorrow at sunrise. You'll be back in Auranos before you know it, Cleo, and all will be well."

Her stomach twisted. "All is not well. I never found the Watcher."

Theon nodded at Nic. "I need to speak with the princess alone. Would you give us some time?"

Nic looked at her. "Depends. Cleo?"

She nodded. "It's all right. I should let Theon have his say now. Then when I get home, I'll only have to be reprimanded by my father."

Reprimanded was likely putting her future punishment mildly. She wished she could say it was unfounded, but she was prepared to accept her fate.

"Then I'll head into the village and get something for us to eat," Nic said reluctantly.

"We'll meet you there," Theon said, his voice firm. "We can't tarry long, especially after the threat that girl made that someone is coming for you."

With a last glance at Cleo to confirm that she was all right with being left alone with Theon, Nic turned and took off at a fast clip. Cleo watched him leave, afraid to return her gaze to her angry bodyguard.

"Despite everything, I'm not sorry that I came here," she said when silence fell between them. "I did this to help my sister and I'm devastated that I failed. I know you despise me right now and I'm positive that my father was enraged when he learned I was gone." She drew in a tired breath. "But I had to do it."

When she finally turned to him, Theon's expression had changed. Where before it was fury and hardness, there was now something more raw in his expression.

"However, the pain and trouble I've caused you personally," she whispered. "I am deeply regretful for that."

He reached down to take her hands in his. "I was so worried about you."

Cleo was surprised that he'd drawn so close to her. "I know."

"You could have been killed."

"Theon, I wasn't thinking straight."

"Neither was I. And neither am I at this very moment."

She looked up at him just as he captured her mouth with his and kissed her deeply.

This was not a chaste kiss of friendship. This was a kiss of true passion, such as she'd only dreamed of before. Her heart leapt in her chest and she wrapped her arms around him to pull him closer. When it finally ended, he stepped back from her, his eyes steady on the ground, a deep frown creasing his brow.

"My humble apologies for that, princess."

She pressed her fingers against her lips. "Please, don't apologize."

"I shouldn't presume. I shouldn't think that you might feel . . ." He swallowed. "I'll ask your father to assign someone else as your bodyguard when we return. Not only did I fail to keep you safe, but I don't have the right objectivity anymore. You've come to mean more to me than the daughter of the king. Such a short time and . . . you've come to mean everything to me."

Cleo's breath caught. "Everything?"

Theon raised his gaze to lock with hers. "Everything."

Tears stung her eyes. "Well, actually, that makes things much easier."

He frowned. "I don't understand."

"It's obvious. I can't marry Aron or anyone else. I refuse, no matter what my father says." Her heart swelled to overflowing. "I—I was meant to be with you."

Theon's breath came quicker, but his expression only grew more grave. "But I'm only a guard."

"I don't care!"

"Your father will care. Quite a lot, I'm sure."

"My father will simply have to deal with it. Or I'll just run away again." A smile touched her lips. "With you."

Theon laughed, a deep rumble in his chest. "Wonderful. You'll tell your father that the guard he assigned to keep his daughter safe has coerced her to break off her engagement and that will make everything all right. I'm sure he'll just accept it and not throw me in the dungeon."

"Maybe he won't accept it. Not right away. But I'll make sure he knows there are no other answers."

He was quiet for a moment as he searched her expression. "So you do feel something for me."

"You saved me. And even before that . . . well, I just knew, without knowing." Her heart felt lighter with each word she spoke.

Theon shook his head. "I didn't save you. Nic figured out where you were. I just knocked out the guards and broke down the door."

Cleo's smile widened. "Well, I'm not in love with Nic, so I guess we'll just have to figure it out."

He pulled her into his arms again, more tentatively this time. "I'm still furious that you ran away and nearly got yourself killed. This is not the right place for you right now."

"There's no other place I could find the answer I need."

"The search will have to wait."

"But it can't wait." Her throat grew tight again.

He studied the ground for a moment before raising his gaze to hers. "We can't stay here. You must realize that, don't you?"

Cleo's heart beat hard enough to burst from her chest. She couldn't forget the real reason she'd come here. Yet she also couldn't deny that he was right. If there was a war against Auranos brewing, this was no place for its princess. Her throat thickened. "I wish there was another answer."

"Give it a week," Theon said. "And I'll return here myself. I'll find out if this legend you believe in so completely is true. Let me do that for you."

She looked up at him with gratitude before she nodded. "Thank you."

"I'll also find Jonas Agallon when I return." His expression darkened. "He needs to answer with blood for what he's done."

She shivered at the suggestion of violence. "He blames me for what Aron did to his brother. He still carries Aron's dagger."

Theon looked at her sharply. "Did he threaten you with that dagger?"

She nodded, then turned her face forward so she wouldn't see the flash of rage in his eyes.

"If I find him," Theon growled, "he won't have to worry about taking his vengeance on anyone for his brother's death. He'll be joining his brother in the everafter."

"He grieves for Tomas. It doesn't excuse him for his actions, but it gives meaning to them."

"I disagree."

Cleo couldn't help but give him an amused look.

"What?" he asked cautiously.

"We do disagree on a lot of things, don't we?"

Theon squeezed her hand. "Not everything."

Her smile grew. "No, not everything." She reached her arms around his neck and kissed him again, softly at first and then harder.

In that moment, her optimism fully returned. Theon would return here soon without her and he would certainly have an easier time in his search than she had. She would face the wrath of her father in Auranos. After he calmed down about her ill-advised journey, she would explain very simply that she had fallen in love with a guard and if the king wanted his youngest daughter to be happy—and *of course* he did—then he would end her betrothal to Aron and approve Theon as a suitor for her. There was no reason why Theon couldn't be knighted and given a higher position within the palace to help raise his social status and make him suitable in anyone's view to court a princess. It wasn't as if she was the eldest daughter and first in line for the throne.

It was then that she heard something that made a chill race down her spine.

Hoofbeats.

Theon tensed, pulling away from their embrace. Three figures on horseback were approaching from the same direction they themselves had come. They came upon Cleo and Theon swiftly and moved around them to block the road to the village up ahead.

"Ah, here you are. She was right, you haven't gotten very far." The one in the middle didn't look very old at all, eighteen or nineteen at the most. He had dark hair and dark eyes and was dressed all in black. The men on either side of him wore red uniforms that Cleo immediately recognized as Limerian.

She drew her cloak closer around her to stop herself from shivering.

"Whom do you address?" Cleo asked crisply.

"You are Princess Cleiona Bellos," the dark-haired boy said, staring down at her with a rather bored expression. "Correct?"

Theon tightened his grip on her wrist. She took this to mean that she wasn't to answer the question.

"Who wants to know?" Theon asked instead.

"I am Magnus Lukas Damora, prince of Limeros. It's an honor to meet the princess in person. She's every bit as lovely as I've been told."

She stared up at him in surprise. Prince Magnus. Of course she'd heard of him. But this was not their first meeting. He'd visited the palace with his parents when she was very young, only five or six years old. Her gaze moved to his cheek, where he had a scar that stretched from the corner of his mouth to his ear, and a sudden memory returned to her, one that she hadn't thought of since she was only a child.

A boy, crying, his cheek weeping blood. It dripped onto a colorful rug at the palace. His mother, the Limerian queen, handing him a cloth napkin to press against his face. She hadn't gotten down on her knees and hugged him to her chest. His father, the king, growled at the boy to stop making a mess.

This boy didn't look at all like one who would cry over a little blood. In fact, the cold way he studied her made her feel as if she'd been touched by ice. Some might find him very handsome, but she did not. There was a cruel and unpleasant edge to his appearance. He made her immediately uneasy.

But dealing with unpleasant people was part of her duty as the king's daughter.

"It's a great pleasure to make your acquaintance, Prince Magnus," Cleo said, keeping her voice polite and measured. "Perhaps we'll meet again sometime soon. We're about to meet our friend in the village up ahead before we return to Auranos."

"How nice for you," he replied. "And who is your friend who stands next to you?"

"This is Theon Ranus, a palace guard who has accompanied me here to Paelsia."

"What are you doing in Paelsia, might I ask?"

"Enjoying the scenery," she said pleasantly. "I like to explore."

"I'm sure." His horse stayed steady, and the prince's gaze remained fixed on Cleo's face. "But you're lying. I was informed that you were being kept in a locked shack nearby—one with a broken door and three unconscious guards with bruises to their temples, not to mention the half-hysterical peasant girl who feared I'd be unhappy you were no longer in her care. It took me a little longer to arrive here than I thought. I'm not all that familiar with the Paelsian landscape. I, unlike you, am not enjoying the scenery." He glanced around with distaste. "In fact, I'll be happy to leave as soon as possible."

"Don't let us stop you," Theon said under his breath.

Magnus looked down at him sharply. Instead of saying anything, a smile snaked across his face. Then his gaze flicked back to Cleo and she felt pinned in place by those emotionless eyes. "So you managed to escape your captors. Clever girl."

She fought not to look away from him, to show any weakness. "I can thank the goddess that I managed to get away. With Theon's help."

"Thank the goddess," Magnus repeated. "Which goddess is that? The evil one you're named for? The enemy to my people's goddess?"

Her patience had been stretched so thin it was ready to snap. "As much as I'm enjoying this conversation, Prince Magnus, it's time that we were on our way. Please convey my good wishes to your family when you return to Limeros."

Magnus nodded at his guards, who both slipped off their mounts. Cleo's racing heart picked up more speed.

"What do you mean by this?" Theon didn't wait another moment before unsheathing his sword and stepping in front of Cleo.

"This likely would have been much easier had the princess stayed where she was until I arrived," Magnus said. "I was asked to bring her back to Limeros."

Cleo inhaled sharply. "You will do no such thing."

"My father, King Gaius, requested it of me himself. And that's exactly what I'll do." His dark-eyed gaze moved to Theon. "I strongly suggest that you don't try to stop my men right now. There doesn't need to be any blood spilled here today."

Theon raised his sword. "And I strongly suggest that you turn around and leave the princess right where she is. She's not going anywhere with you."

"Back off, boy, and I will let you run back to your land while you're still breathing."

Theon actually laughed at that, and Magnus glared down at him.

"Honestly," Theon said. "I'm a little underwhelmed right now. You're the Limerian prince, the next in line for the throne. I'd always heard that you came from a line of great men."

"I do."

"If you say so. Maybe you're the exception to the rule."

"Amusing." Magnus flicked his hand. "Guards, take the princess. And deal with her protector. Now."

The guards moved closer to Theon.

"Theon . . ." Cleo's throat was almost too tight to speak.

"Stay behind me."

Panic forked through her. She thought they'd gotten away. She'd escaped from Jonas. All they had to do was meet Nic and travel the rest of the way to the harbor to find a ship to take them home. And all would be well again.

"What does your father want with me?" she demanded. "The same thing Jonas wanted? To use me against my father in your war?"

"Consider it an attempt to improve relations between lands. Take her," Magnus snapped at his men. "Now."

But to take Cleo, they first had to get through Theon. The two men—and they were men, not boys—unsheathed their weapons. Cleo was terrified for Theon. But she'd never seen him wield a sword before.

He was incredible.

Cleo staggered back from him as he clashed with the two, their swords clanging and sparking as they fought. The blond guard slashed Theon's arm and blood welled, streaking down the sleeve of his blue uniform. That he continued to use that arm gave her some relief that it was only a flesh wound. Then he thrust his sword through the blond guard's chest.

It was a killing blow. The Limerian guard fell to his knees with a grunt and then face forward onto the dirt.

Magnus swore loudly. Cleo looked up at him still on his horse. He seemed shocked by the guard's death, as if he'd been fully expecting that Theon would easily surrender and give custody of Cleo over to him without argument or resistance.

There was nothing easy about this. But Cleo was confident that Theon was going to win. He was her hero. He'd saved her once. He would save her again.

Theon fought harder against the second guard, who moved toward Cleo. This one was older and more experienced, and he handled his sword so easily it was as if it was another limb. Cleo had witnessed guards practicing together with wooden swords and then again matched in tournaments every summer with real ones made from iron and steel. But she'd never seen a fight like this.

Just as she feared Theon would be defeated, the other guard

lost his footing on the rocky ground. Theon didn't hesitate—he ran him through with his sword.

The guard's weapon clattered to the ground and he collapsed. A moment later, he choked on his own blood and fell limp. He was dead.

Cleo had also stopped breathing, but now she exhaled deeply and shakily as relief flooded through her. Theon had stopped them. He'd killed them to defend her, but she knew there had been no other choice. They would have taken her against her will and dragged her back to Limeros as a prisoner of war to use against her father.

Theon had just saved her life again.

Cleo looked toward him, gratitude welling in her heart, a smile ready to bloom on her face. His chest heaved with labored breath; his forehead was damp with sweat. Their eyes met and held.

Then a sword thrust through the center of Theon's chest from behind, the sharp, bloody tip impaling the front of his uniform. He looked down at it with shock as the sword pulled back and dark blood soaked the fabric.

Horror crashed all around her.

"Theon!" Cleo screamed.

Theon touched his chest and drew his hand away coated with blood. His pained gaze met hers again briefly before he collapsed heavily on his back, his eyes open and staring straight up at the sky.

Magnus stood behind Theon holding a bloody sword.

He frowned down at Theon's body, his brows drawn tightly together as he shook his head. "He killed my men. He would have killed me next."

Cleo trembled violently from head to toe and her feet moved without conscious effort. She collapsed at Theon's side, grabbing his arms, his shoulders, his face. She couldn't see past the tears in her eyes.

"Theon, you're all right. It's only a wound. Please, look at me!" Her hysterical sobs made her words impossible to understand.

He was fine. He had to be. She already had it all planned. He would take her back to Auranos and her father would be angry for a while. She would tell the king that she loved Theon and she didn't care that he was a guard. He was everything she'd ever wanted. And Cleo always got whatever she wanted—provided she wanted it badly enough.

"I regret that it had to come to this," Prince Magnus said. "If your guard had backed off when I told him to, this wouldn't have happened."

"He's not just a guard," she whispered. "Not to me."

When she felt the prince touch her arm as if to pull her up to her feet, she screamed and clawed at him.

"Get away from me! Don't touch me!"

His expression was stone. "You have to come with me now."

"Never!"

"Don't make this more difficult than it's already been."

She stared at him in shock, not seeing anything but a blur. This horrible creature before her was no better than the most evil beast. He'd done this to Theon. Theon had come here to rescue her, and now he was . . .

Now he was . . .

No, he wasn't. He would survive this. He had to.

Cleo pushed away from Magnus and clutched Theon's body, trying to hold him, trying to shield him from the prince who might try to hurt him again. His blood soaked into her dress, the one she'd tried not to dirty even while forced to wear it for days on end locked in the cold, dark shed. She didn't even look at the other bodies. They were dead. But Theon wasn't. He *wasn't*.

"Enough of this." Magnus grabbed Cleo's arm and wrenched her to her feet. "This has all gone very wrong and now I need to get you back all on my own. Don't try my patience another moment. Behave yourself."

"Let go of me!" She lashed out and scratched him across his face as deeply as she could. It was enough to draw blood on the same side as his scar. He snarled and pushed her back from him. She stumbled and fell hard to the rocky ground. All she could do was lie there, stunned and gasping for breath.

Magnus loomed over her. Blood streaked his face and hands. His face was flushed, but he now looked more upset than enraged. For a moment, he reminded her of the small boy he'd once been, crying, his face bleeding.

He reached for her.

Then something hurtled at him and struck the side of his head. He fell to the ground with a grunt and lost hold of his sword. Cleo scrambled to her feet as Nic ran up to them. He'd thrown the palm-size rock that hit Magnus.

The prince wasn't unconscious, but he was disoriented. He groaned.

Nic surveyed the deadly scene with horror. "Cleo! What happened here?"

She grabbed the prince's heavy sword and raised it up. She'd never been allowed to hold one before. But she summoned the strength now—strength she never knew she had—to hold it over Magnus's chest. She could barely see past her tears. Rage and pain was all that gave her the strength to press the tip of the bloody sword over the prince's heart.

Alarm showed through his disorientation. "Princess . . . no . . ."

"He was trying to save me. You made him bleed." She choked out the words. "Now I want to make you bleed."

Nic grasped her wrist. "No, Cleo. Don't do this."

Her arms ached from holding the heavy sword steady. "I need to stop him from hurting anyone else."

"He's stopped. Look at him. We've already hurt him. But if you kill him, then this will be even worse than it already is. We need to go home. Now."

"He wanted to take me back to Limeros as a prisoner. Theon stopped him."

Nic finally took the sword from her grasp. "He won't take you. I promise he won't."

Magnus looked up at Nic, his expression grim but relieved. "Thank you. I'll remember your assistance today."

Nic glared down at him. "I didn't do this for you, asshole."

He turned the sword around and bashed Magnus in the head with the hilt. It was enough to knock the prince out cold. Then Nic threw the sword to the side. His hands were now covered in Theon's blood.

Cleo staggered back to Theon and dropped down next to him. She stroked the bronze-colored hair off his forehead.

He stared straight up at the sky. He wasn't blinking. His eyes were such a beautiful shade of dark brown. She loved his eyes. His nose. His lips. Everything about him.

As she touched his lips, her fingers slid over the blood.

"Wake up, Theon," she said softly. "Please, find me again. I'm right here. I'm waiting for you to rescue me."

Nic touched her shoulder gently.

She shook her head. "He'll be fine. He just needs a moment."

"He's gone, Cleo. There's nothing you can do."

She pressed her hand to Theon's blood-soaked chest. There was no heartbeat. His eyes were glazed. His spirit had departed. This was nothing but a shell. And he wasn't going to find her ever again.

She couldn't control the sobs that wracked her entire body. There were no words for this pain. She'd lost Theon just when she'd realized how much he meant to her. If she hadn't come here, Theon wouldn't have had to follow. He'd loved her. He'd wanted her to be safe. Now he was dead and it was all her fault.

Cleo leaned over and kissed his lips—their third kiss.

Their last.

Then she let Nic lead her away from Theon's dead body and Magnus's unconscious one and toward the harbor.

CHAPTER 26

PAELSIA

By the time Magnus came to, all three horses had run off. He was alone, in the middle of Paelsia, surrounded by three corpses. A hawk circled in the sky high above. For a moment, he thought it might be a vulture.

He dragged himself to his feet and looked down at the fallen men. He swore under his breath, then cast a dark look in the direction of the village in the distance. There was no sign of Princess Cleo and whoever that was who'd knocked him out.

He tried very hard not to look at the Auranian guard whom he'd stabbed, but his gaze kept turning in that direction. The young guard's eyes were still open, staring up at the sky. Blood had caked on his lips and a pool of it soaked into the dirt next to his body.

Magnus realized he was trembling. This guard had taken out two of his men. As soon as he turned around, Magnus could have been killed too. He'd had to strike first. And so he'd chosen to stab the guard in the back. Like a coward.

He crouched down and looked very hard at the Auranian,

knowing he would never forget the face of the first person he'd slain. The boy wasn't much older than he was. Magnus reached over and closed his eyes.

Then he left the bodies there, went to the village, purchased a horse from a Paelsian who'd seemed fearful and intimidated by Magnus's very presence, and rode hard back to Limeros. He stopped only when he was so tired he nearly fell off his mount, sleeping a few hours before continuing on, numb, broken, and beaten.

The blood had dried on his cheek where the girl had clawed him. At least it had stopped stinging. He wondered briefly if it would leave new scars there. It would serve as a visible marking of his defeat and humiliation.

When he finally returned to the Limerian palace, he left the horse outside without calling for a groom to take it away and give it food and water. He could barely think. It was a monumental effort to even walk a straight line.

Magnus went directly to his room, closing the door behind him. Then he collapsed to his knees on the hard floor.

Some said that Magnus was just like his father in looks and temperament. He'd disagreed until today. He *was* his father's son. He was cruel. Manipulative. Deceptive. Violent. Stabbing the guard in the back to save his own life was something that King Gaius would have done. The only difference was that the king would not dwell on it afterward. He would never doubt his actions. He would celebrate them like he celebrated his daughter's newfound magic after it had turned his mistress into a pile of charred meat.

Magnus wasn't sure how long he knelt there in the darkness. But after a time, he knew he was no longer alone.

Lucia had entered his chambers. He didn't see her yet, but he felt her presence and smelled the light floral fragrance she always wore.

"Brother?" she whispered. "You've returned."

He didn't reply. His mouth was dry, parched. He wasn't even sure if he could move.

Lucia came to his side and gently touched his shoulder.

"Magnus!" She knelt down next to him and brushed the hair back from his cheek. "Your face. You're hurt!"

He swallowed. "It's nothing."

"Where have you been?"

"On a trip to Paelsia."

"You look . . . oh, Magnus." Concern coated her words. She didn't know what he'd done. What he'd been instructed to do.

Retrieve Princess Cleo and bring her back to Limeros.

Such a simple task. Magnus had no doubt that his father never would have given it to him if he hadn't been positive his son would succeed.

But he'd failed.

Lucia got up and returned a few moments later with a glass of water and a wet cloth. "Drink this," she told him firmly.

He drank. But the water only worked to wash away his numbness, making his pain that much more acute.

Lucia cleaned his wound gently with the cloth. "What scratched you?"

He didn't answer. Lucia wouldn't understand what he'd done.

"Tell me," she insisted. The steely edge to her tone earned her a direct look. "That's right. You need to tell me what happened. Right now."

"Will you make it all better?"

"I might."

As he drew in a ragged breath, her expression grew more grave. She stroked his hair back from his face. "Magnus, please. What can I do?"

He shook his head. "Nothing."

"Why did you go to Paelsia?"

"Father sent me there to bring something back for him. I failed. And . . . bad things happened. He's going to be very angry with me." He looked down at the floor, looked at his hands. He'd left his sword downstairs. He hadn't bothered to wipe the guard's blood off it.

"What bad things happened?"

"The guards who accompanied me—they were killed."

Her eyes widened. "They were killed? But—but you got away. You were hurt, but you got away." She touched his face softly. "Thank the goddess you survived."

He looked into her beautiful eyes, taking strength from the way she looked at him, as if he could never be capable of doing anything truly horrible. "I killed someone."

Lucia's lips parted in surprise. "My poor brother. You've experienced such horrors. I am so, so sorry."

"I'm a *murderer*, Lucia."

"No." She captured his face between her hands to force him to keep looking at her. "You're my brother. And you're wonderful. You could never do anything horrible. Do you hear me?"

She hugged him tight, so tight that he could almost forget what had happened. He held on to her. She was his anchor to keep him from being swept completely out to sea.

"Father won't be angry," she whispered. "Whatever he wanted you to do isn't as important as having you return safely home."

"He might disagree with that."

"No, he won't. I felt terrible about what happened with Sabina." Her voice caught. "But he assured me that I'm not bad and that my magic is nothing to fear. That what happened was meant to happen. It was fate."

"And you believed him?"

Lucia was quiet for a moment. "It took me a while, but I do believe him now. What I can do—I'm not afraid of it anymore. Let me show you what I've learned."

She pressed her hand against his injured cheek. Her skin grew warm against his and begin to glow with a soft white light. He stared into her blue eyes, willing himself not to pull back from her as the heat grew and sank into his skin. It hurt, but he forced himself not to flinch away from her. When she finally pulled back from him, he touched his cheek to find that it was smooth, apart from his previous scar, and that the new scratches had vanished. Lucia had healed him with earth magic.

"Incredible. You're incredible."

A small, confident smile played at her lips. "I was surprised how kind Father was to me after . . . well, after what I did. I love him for not making this worse for me."

Magnus hated that Lucia had been taken in by a few kind words from the king enough to forget the past. "Do you love him as much as you love me?"

She leaned against him and let out a soft laugh. "The truth?'

"Always."

"Then it shall be our secret," she whispered in his ear. "I love you more than any other."

He pulled back from her and looked into her eyes, holding her beautiful face between his hands. Could this be real?

"Does that make you feel better after your horrible ordeal?" she asked.

He nodded slowly. "It does."

And then, heart swelling, he crushed his mouth to hers, kissing her as deeply and passionately as he'd always dreamed. Her lips were so soft and sweet, and they filled him to overflowing with hope and love.

With a chill, he suddenly realized that her hands were pressed flat against his chest and she was trying to push him away. When he broke off the kiss, she skidded back from him, landing hard on her backside. She brought her hand up to cover her mouth, her eyes wide and appalled. And something else. Disgusted.

His lips tingled from the feel of her, the taste of her, but the reality of what had happened crashed over him like a bucket of ice-cold water.

She hadn't kissed him back.

"Why would you do such a thing?" Her voice was pitchy and muffled by her hand.

"I'm sorry." His heart hammered in his chest. Then he shook his head. "No, wait. I'm not sorry. I've wanted to kiss you like that for so long, but I was afraid."

Her hand trembled as she pulled it away from her mouth. "But you're my brother."

"You said that you loved me."

"Yes. I love you desperately . . . as my *brother*. But this . . ." She shook her head. "No, it's not right. You can't do something like this ever again."

"You're not really my sister." He wouldn't let himself feel shame for what he'd done. He'd given in to his love for her in a real way, and he refused to let it be turned into something vile. It wasn't vile; it was pure. The purest thing in his entire world. "Not by blood. You weren't born into this family. You were born in Paelsia. Sabina stole you from your cradle. You were raised here as my sister, but we're not related by blood. If we're together, it's not forbidden to us."

Her face had paled so much that she now resembled a ghost.

The fierceness had left her eyes, replaced by shock. "Why are you saying these horrible things to me?"

"Because they're the truth. The truth that you should have been told by the king himself. He wants to use your power for his own gain. That's why he had you brought here, why he's raised you as his daughter."

Lucia shook her head. "And you've known this all the time?"

"No, I learned of it only the other night from Sabina herself. But Mother confirmed that it's true."

"I don't understand." She staggered up from the floor to her feet. He followed suit, watching her warily. His disgrace in Paelsia was momentarily forgotten. He hadn't meant to tell Lucia like this, not so bluntly.

"Ease your mind," he soothed. "Please. The king still considers you his beloved daughter. I know he does. And we were raised together, side by side. This is all true. But to consider you only my sister now that I know the truth . . . I can't. You're so much more to me than that."

Lucia met his gaze. "Please don't say these things to me."

"You're the only one in the world who means anything to me." His voice broke. "I love you, Lucia. I love you to the very depths of my soul."

She just stared at him.

"You said that you loved me." He tried to keep his voice firm. "More than anyone else."

"As a brother. As my dear brother, I love you unconditionally."

It was as if his heart had stopped and the world crashed down all around him. "Only as a brother."

"You can't do that ever again. You can't touch me like that. It's wrong, Magnus."

He clenched his fists at his sides. "It's *not* wrong."

"I don't feel the same way toward you."

"But someday you might—"

"No." Tears shone in her eyes. "I will never feel that way. Please, let us never talk of this again." She ran a hand over her long dark hair, as if attempting to straighten it. She moved to the door, but he caught her wrist to stop her.

Magnus's eyes burned. "Please don't leave me."

"I have to. I can't be near you right now."

She pulled out of his grasp and left his room.

He stood there facing the door, unmoving, unthinking. Stunned by what had just happened.

She would turn her back on him and punish him for this. For showing her how he felt. For opening his heart in ways he'd never done before with anyone.

Magnus had always been a fool. A child. One who was easily beaten or abused by those who were larger or stronger or more powerful. All his life he'd endured so much pain and developed only a thin mask to cover his true feelings. But masks could easily be removed and smashed with only a few words.

As of today, he was no longer a child. He had killed. He had lost the one he loved more than any other—and she would never trust him as she had before. Nothing would be the same with Lucia from this day forward. He'd destroyed that forever. And for a moment, all alone in his chambers, he clenched his fists at his sides and let himself cry over the loss of his beautiful sister and best friend.

Then his heart, now broken into a thousand pieces, slowly began to turn to ice.

CHAPTER 27

AURANOS

Cleo could barely function as she returned to the palace. Sounds were muted, and all she could really hear was the rush of blood through her veins and the pounding of her heart.

Theon was dead.

"Try not to worry. Stay next to me," Nic whispered as they were brought immediately before the king. The guards hadn't given Cleo a chance to go to her room first. Frankly, they seemed surprised that she'd returned at all.

She didn't speak. She wasn't sure that she could speak.

The tall wood and iron doors swung inward, and there he was. The king. A guard had hurried ahead to inform him of Cleo's return.

His face was pale. He looked even older than she remembered.

"Cleo," he began. "Is this real? Have you truly returned, or are you only an illusion?"

They were ushered into the room and the doors shut heavily behind them. Cleo got a pitying look from one of the guards. He knew of the king's temper.

"I'm sorry," she managed, but could go no further before she started to cry.

The king swiftly moved toward her and gathered her into his arms. "My poor girl. I'm so relieved you're home."

This was a surprising reaction since the king had been stern with her for so long she'd practically forgotten his tender side. Finally he let go of her and helped her to a chair. His gaze flicked to Nic. "Explain."

Nic shifted his feet. "Where should I begin?"

"I am furious that the two of you went to Paelsia against my wishes, but I had no idea that the difficulties between the lands would result in conflict like this. I was visited by King Gaius, who told me that he had Cleo in his grasp."

Cleo shivered at the memory of the dark-haired boy with the cold, cruel eyes.

"He definitely tried," Nic said with a nod. "But we got away."

"Thank the goddess," the king breathed. "How?"

"Theon," Nic began, and his voice caught. Despite his previous smooth words, he also fought tears. "He fought Prince Magnus's men. Killed them so they wouldn't lay a hand on the princess. Then the prince killed Theon."

"What?" the king gasped.

"We had no choice but to leave his body on Paelsian soil. We had to flee immediately."

"I wanted to kill the prince," Cleo managed. "I had the chance to, but . . ."

"I wouldn't let her," Nic admitted. "If she'd killed Prince Magnus, I knew things would be even worse than they already are."

The king took this information in. "You were right to stop her. But I understand her desire for vengeance."

Vengeance. The word sounded so decisive. So final. It was what Jonas wanted when he'd taken her. She'd seen the fiery hate in his eyes for her role in his brother's death. If this was how he'd felt toward her, she was grateful that she was still alive.

His goal was to put her somewhere Prince Magnus could find her. They were working together to destroy her father. It was a miracle that she'd escaped. A miracle that came at too high a price.

"Cleo, you're so pale," the king said with concern.

Nic touched her arm. "She's still in shock."

"Do you now see why I didn't want you to go, daughter? I know you wanted to try to help your sister, but there's too much at risk right now."

"I failed." Her voice broke. "I didn't find anything to help Emilia. And Theon's dead because of me."

He cupped her face and kissed her gently on her forehead. "Go to your chambers and rest. Tomorrow will be better."

"I thought you'd be so angry with me."

"I *am* angry. But to see you alive and well and returned to me is the answer to my prayers. So my happiness that you're safe is more powerful than any anger. Love is stronger than anger. Love is stronger than hate—stronger than anything. Remember that."

Nic helped her to her chambers, and he too kissed her forehead before he left her there, tucked into her warm bed. He left her in the dark room and she tried to sleep, but she was plagued by nightmares. One after another, and each of them starring a different dark-haired boy. One Paelsian and savage, dragging her along a dusty road to lock her in a small, dirty shack. The other cruel and haughty, with a scar on his face and a bloody sword, laughing over the body of Theon.

She woke in the night, sobbing.

"There, there," a familiar voice soothed. A cool hand brushed her forehead.

"Emilia?" She sat up in her bed, realizing that her sister was with her. The shadows of the room weren't enough to cover how thin and pale her sister looked or the darkness under her eyes. "What are you doing here? You should be in bed."

"How could I stay away when I learned that my little sister had finally returned?" Emilia's face was grave. She climbed into the bed next to Cleo. "Father told me what happened. Cleo, I'm so sorry about Theon."

Cleo opened her mouth, but no words came for a long time. "It's my fault."

"You mustn't think that."

"If I hadn't run away, he wouldn't have had to come after me. He would still be alive."

"It was his job to protect you. And he did it. He protected you, Cleo."

"But he's gone." It was only a tiny gasp.

"I know." Emilia held her as she sobbed, tears that seemed to have no end. "And I know how you feel. When I lost Simon, I thought that it would be the end of me too."

"You really loved him."

"With all my heart." She stroked Cleo's hair. "So mourn Theon. Cherish his memory. Thank him for his sacrifice. One day, I promise this pain will fade."

"No, it won't."

"Right now it's still too fresh. It might seem as if this grief will never let go of the hold it has on your heart." Emilia's jaw tightened. "But you must be strong, Cleo. There are hard times ahead."

Cleo's chest hitched. "War."

Emilia nodded. "King Gaius wanted Father to turn Auranos over to him without a fight. He told Father he'd do horrible things to you if he put up any opposition."

Cleo trembled at the thought of it. Emilia leaned closer. "And just between you and me, I believe Father would have done exactly as King Gaius asked before it was too late to save you."

"He couldn't. There are so many people in Auranos, he couldn't just give it over to the Limerians."

"And the Paelsians. Paelsia and Limeros have partnered in their hatred against us."

"Why do they hate us so much?"

"Envy. They see that we have so much here. And they're right. We do."

Cleo exhaled shakily. Her actions had nearly brought about the ruin of her father's kingdom. "My trip was wrong in so many ways. But I still can't bring myself to fully regret it. I wanted to help you."

"I know." A small, sad smile touched her lips. "I know you did it for me. And I love you for that so much. But I don't think even a Watcher could have helped me anymore. I'm not sure I even believe they're anything more than legend."

"They're real."

"Did you meet one?"

Cleo faltered. "No. But a woman I met, Eirene, she told me tales I'd never heard before. About a sorceress and a hunter, about the Watchers. Did you know the goddesses were Watchers who stole the Kindred and exiled themselves? Now the Watchers wait to find the next sorceress, who can lead them to the hidden Kindred to restore their magic before it dies away completely. It's all so incredible."

Emilia's smile held. "Sounds like quite a tale."

"It's real," Cleo insisted. "The goddesses stole the Kindred and split it between them, but the power made them enemies. Before that, all of Mytica was one. We were all friends once upon a time."

"No longer. The Limerian king hates Father. He wants to destroy him. He's hungered for Father's land since before he was on the throne. His father was a kind and gentle king who only wanted peace. King Gaius will be happy to spill oceans of blood beyond his own borders if it will get him the power he desires."

Cleo's chest tightened. "His son is a vicious, evil creature. If I see him again, I'll kill him."

This didn't bring a look of concern to Emilia's face, rather one of admiration. "You have such boundless passion and determination. And strength."

Cleo stared at her. "Strength? I could barely lift a sword to try to save my own life."

"Not physical strength. Strength here." Emilia pressed her hand against Cleo's heart. Then she touched her forehead. "And here. Although up here is a part that you could probably work on a bit, so no more trips to dangerous lands will be in your immediate future."

"I'm not strong," Cleo insisted. "Neither heart nor mind."

"Sometimes you don't realize how strong you are until you're tested. As the youngest daughter in this family, you haven't been tested very much in your life, Cleo. Not like me." Emilia's face shadowed. "But I believe you will be. Very soon. And you must draw from that strength. You must increase it. And you must hold on to it because sometimes that small glimmer of inner strength is all that we have to help us press forward through the darkness."

Cleo clutched her sister's hands. "And you must also be strong. I will send a guard back to Paelsia to continue my search. And he will be successful."

Theon had promised he would go. Now she would have to find another to take his place. If Emilia had enough strength to leave her bed and come to Cleo's side in the middle of the night, there was still hope for her recovery.

"I'll try," Emilia said, a weary tone to her voice. She turned her head to look out the window. "I'll try very hard to be strong. For you."

"Good." The sisters were quiet for a moment. Emilia continued to gaze at the stars.

"You need to know that Limeros and Paelsia are gathering an army to enter Auranos in the coming weeks. They expect that Father will give up the moment they arrive."

Panic swelled in Cleo's chest. "He can't give up."

"If there isn't an immediate surrender, they'll fight to take the palace."

An anger burned inside Cleo's chest. "What will he do?"

Emilia's grip on her hands tightened. "Had you been in the Limerian's clutches, I think he would have done anything to save your life."

"And now that I'm back?"

"Now," Emilia said, gazing into her sister's eyes, "if King Gaius is looking for a war, a war is exactly what he'll get."

CHAPTER 28

LIMEROS

Magnus had expected his father to be furious over his failure in Paelsia. He'd been prepared to face his fate after waiting for over a week. He stood by the thick iron railing as King Gaius entered the downstairs foyer upon his return. The king didn't waste any time in getting to the point as he peeled off his riding gloves and a servant helped him remove his mud-encrusted cloak.

"Where is Princess Cleiona?"

Magnus looked at him unflinchingly. "I would assume she's in Auranos."

"You failed me?" the king roared.

"We were ambushed. My guards were killed. I had to kill the guard accompanying the princess in order to escape with my life."

The king's face reddened with fury and he stormed toward Magnus, raising his hand to strike him. Before he made contact, Magnus caught his wrist.

"Don't," he said, his voice dangerously low. "If you ever dare to hit me again, I'll kill you too."

"I asked you to do one simple thing, and you failed me."

"And I barely returned home alive. Yes, I failed to bring you King Corvin's daughter. But it's over. You'll just have to find another way to get what you want. Perhaps your own daughter will be all the assistance you need." His face tensed. "Even though she's not your daughter by blood."

The king's eyes widened a fraction—the only sign of any shock over Magnus's words. "How did you learn of this?"

"Your mistress told me before Lucia turned her to ash. Then I confirmed it with Mother." His lips twisted. "What do you have to say about that?"

King Gaius stayed locked in Magnus's grip for another moment before he yanked his arm away. "I was going to tell you when I returned."

"You'll forgive me if I find that difficult to believe."

"Believe what you must, Magnus. What Sabina and your mother told you is true. It changes nothing." Finally his rage lessened and he nodded slowly. "But I trust in fate. We'll have to go into this war without any guarantees."

No apologies for a lifetime of lies, but Magnus hadn't expected any. And so he would offer no apologies for his failure in Paelsia. "Were there guarantees even with Princess Cleiona in our grasp?"

"No. Only speculation." He studied his son's face. "You've learned from this failure and from recent truths offered from the lips of deceitful women. It's made you stronger." He nodded again and a grin stretched across his face. "All is well. Destiny smiles on us, Magnus. Wait and see. Auranos is ours."

Magnus kept his expression stony and unamused. "I feel the sudden need to crush others beneath my feet."

This only made the king's smile widen. "Got a taste for blood, did you? For the feel of a sword piercing flesh?"

"Maybe I did."

"Excellent. You'll get to experience a great deal more of it very soon, I promise."

The next day when his father summoned him, Magnus didn't delay in going to his side, leaving in the middle of his swordsmanship lesson. Andreas and the other boys watched him leave, attempting to guard their distaste.

"If you'll excuse me," Magnus said, throwing down the sword he'd used to break two of the boys' arms in the last week. They were lucky they didn't practice with sharpened steel or he would have taken the entire limb. "I have royal business to attend to."

Everything seemed so much simpler with his new outlook. He was the son of the King of Blood. And he would live up to that title in any way he could.

His father waited at the entrance to the eastern tower, where prisoners of special interest to the king were kept.

"Come with me," the king said before leading Magnus up the narrow spiral staircase. The black stone walls higher up were coated with frost. There were no fireplaces in the towers to bring any warmth to them.

Magnus wasn't sure what to expect when they reached the top. Perhaps a prisoner about to lose head or hands. He might be the one allowed to pass final judgment on a murderer or pickpocket. But when he saw who the prisoner was, his steps faltered.

Amia was chained in the small stone room, her arms raised

above her head. Two guards stood by obediently. The girl's face was bloody. Her gaze moved to him and widened before she bit her bottom lip and stared down at the floor.

"This," the king said, "is one of our kitchen maids. She was caught eavesdropping outside my meeting room. You know how I feel about spies."

"I'm not a spy," she whispered.

The king strode across the room. He grasped hold of her chin and forced her to look at him. "Anyone who listens to conversations while hidden is a spy. The only question is, for whom do you spy, Amia?"

Bile rose in Magnus's throat. The girl spied for *him*. She'd been an asset ever since he'd first taken notice of her. She'd told him many interesting pieces of information.

When she didn't reply, the king backhanded her. Blood bubbled from her mouth as she sobbed.

Magnus's heart thundered in his chest. "Seems as if she doesn't want to say."

"Perhaps she's protecting someone. Or perhaps she's simply stupid. The question is, and why I brought you up here, what do you think I should do with such a problem? Spies are usually tortured for information. While she hasn't been helpful yet, a few hours on the rack might loosen young Amia's tongue."

"I—I only listen because I'm curious is all." Her voice broke. "I mean no harm."

"But I do," the king said. "I mean a great deal of harm to stupid girls who become too curious. Now, let's see. One listens to private conversations with the ears. So perhaps I should slice yours from your head and have you wear them as a necklace as an example for everyone else." He held his hand out to a guard, who placed a dagger in it. She whimpered as he traced the edge of the blade along the side of her face. "But you see with your eyes. I can take those as well. Pluck them out of your head right now. I'm quite good at it. You'd barely feel a thing. I've found that those with bloody holes in their face tend to learn from their mistakes."

"Tell him," Magnus demanded, forcing the words out. "Tell him who you spy for."

Tell him it's me.

Amia's breath hitched and she cast a look at him. Tears streamed down her cheeks. "No one. I spy for no one. I'm just a stupid girl who eavesdrops for her own entertainment."

Magnus's chest tightened.

He didn't underestimate his father. The king took great plea-sure in playing with prisoners, male or female. He had a taste for blood that could never be sated. It had been born in him. Magnus's grandfather, who'd died when Magnus was only a small child, had been disappointed that his son and heir had such a wide sadistic streak. The former king of Limeros had been known to be kind and gentle. Though even the kindest and most gentle king had a torture chamber in their castle's dungeon.

"I grow bored." Magnus forced the words out. "I'm not sure why you made me stop sword practice for this meaningless matter. The girl is a fool, obviously, with a simple mind. But harmless. If this is her first offense, this should be enough to scare her. Should she be caught again, I'll cut out her eyes myself."

The king glanced at him, a smile curling the side of his mouth. "You'd do that? And could I watch?"

"I would insist that you do."

The king took the girl's face between his fingers, squeezing hard enough to bruise. "You're very lucky that I agree with my son. See that you behave. If you step out of line once, just once, whether it's eavesdropping or merely breaking a plate, I promise that you'll be back here. And your eyes will be the very least that you'll lose. Do you understand?"

She inhaled shakily. "Yes, your majesty."

He patted her cheek. "Good girl." Then he glanced at the guards. "Before you send her back to work, give her twenty lashes to ensure she doesn't forget."

Magnus left the tower with his father and forced himself not to cast a single glance back at the girl. Her sobs echoed off the stone walls all the way down to the ground floor.

"My son." The king put his arm around Magnus's shoulders. "Such a gentleman. Even to the lowliest kitchen whore."

When he laughed, Magnus made sure to join in.

The next day, when his father had gone out on a hunt, Magnus found Amia in the kitchen mashing the distasteful *kaana* for their dinner while the head cook butchered a half dozen chickens. The girl's face was bruised black and blue, her right eye swollen shut.

She tensed when she noticed Magnus standing there.

"I said nothing," she whispered. "You have no right to be angry with me."

"It was stupid of you to get caught."

She turned back to her work. Her shoulders shook with her sobs. How this girl had survived so long in the Limerian castle, he honestly didn't know. There was no steel inside her. No ice. No hardness at all. He was frankly surprised that a violent beating and twenty lashes hadn't killed such a weak, soft girl outright. That she was still standing was a shock to him.

"I didn't expect you to speak up for me," she said quietly.

"Good. Even if he'd taken that knife to your eyes, I wouldn't have tried to stop him. No one tells my father what he can and can't do. He does as he pleases. And anyone who gets in the way is trampled."

Amia didn't look directly at him. "I have much left to do for dinner. Please let me get back to work, your highness."

"No. You're finished here. Permanently."

He grabbed her wrist and roughly pulled her along with him out of the kitchen and along the halls of the castle. He listened to her sobs. She likely thought that he was taking her back to the tower for more abuse—at his hand this time. Even so, she didn't struggle.

Finally, when they'd emerged into the cold late afternoon air, he let her go. She staggered back from him and looked around, uncertain. Her gaze fell on the horse-drawn wagon waiting nearby.

"You're leaving," he said. "I've instructed the driver to take you east. There's a well-populated village fifty miles from here that will make a good home for you."

Her mouth gaped open. "I don't understand."

Magnus placed a sack of gold in her hands. "This should be enough to last you for a few years."

"You're sending me away?"

"I'm saving your life, Amia. My father will kill you. Soon enough, he'll find a reason, no matter how small, and I'll have to be a part of it. Watching you die doesn't interest me. So I want you to leave and never return."

She stared at the heavy sack she now held, her brows drawn together. Clarity entered her expression and her gaze snapped to his. "Come with me, my prince."

He had to admit, that response almost made him smile. "Impossible."

323

"I know you hate it here. I know you despise your father. He's an evil, cruel, heartless man." Her chin raised as if she'd said something she was proud of. "You're not like him. You'll *never* be like him. You try to hide it, but you have a good, kind heart. Come with me and we could start a new life together. I could make you happy."

He took her arm and led her to the wagon, picked her up by her waist, and placed her aboard.

"Be happy enough for both of us," he told her.

Then he turned away and walked back into the castle.

The queen of Limeros was smiling. How . . . bizarre. Lucia eyed her warily as they met in the hallway.

"Mother," she said, although she now knew that word wasn't exactly the most appropriate one. Her initial anxiety and fear had since been replaced by outrage that this important information had been kept from her for her entire life.

"Lucia, darling. How are you?"

She snorted, a very unladylike sound that raised the queen's eyebrows. "Apologies, but I don't remember the last time you inquired about my well-being."

The queen winced. "Have I really been so uncaring toward you?"

Lucia shrugged. "Now I know why. You're not really my mother. Why would you care?"

The queen glanced down the hallway to ensure that they were alone. She drew Lucia a few steps down, into a secluded alcove. Lucia expected her expression to harden, but it did just the opposite.

"You should have been told a long time ago. I wanted to tell you."

"You did?" Lucia gave her a look of sheer disbelief.

"Yes, of course. Something so important shouldn't have come as a shock to you. I apologize for that."

"You do?"

"I do. *Truly*. Even though I am queen here, I still must do as the king commands. He didn't want you to know. He was afraid you'd be upset when you learned the truth before it was the right time."

"I *am* upset! Where is my real mother? How can I find her?"

Again, the queen cast a glance down the hallway as if fearful that anyone was listening. This was a secret, after all. Goddess forbid that anyone learn that the Limerian princess was born in Paelsia.

"She's dead."

Lucia's breath caught. "How did she die?"

The queen looked grim. "Sabina killed her."

"Why would she do such a horrible thing?" Nausea rose inside her.

"Because Sabina Mallius was a vile, evil bitch who deserved her fate."

Lucia fought to breathe normally, uncertain what to believe. The world had been shaken all around her and would never settle completely again. "Why did Father keep Sabina around so long after she did this?"

The queen's expression soured further. "Other than her obvious charms? He also saw her as a wise advisor. One who could help him get what he most wants in life: power."

"That's why I was taken at the cost of my birth mother's life." Her throat closed. "Because he thought I could help him to become more powerful."

"Your birth was heralded in the stars. Somehow, some way, Sabina found out where you were. At the time, I was trying to have another child but failing. My body had been devastated by miscarriages. So to be presented with a lovely little girl that I could raise as my own and no one would know the difference . . . well, I didn't ask for details. I simply accepted everything."

Lucia felt faint, but she forced herself to appear as strong as possible. "If you were so happy to get the chance to raise me, why is it that you can barely look at me? Why have you never said a kind word to me?"

"Of course I have." But then her brows drew together as if she doubted her own words. "I don't know. I never realized that I was hurting you. My own mother was a cruel and . . . cold woman. Perhaps I took after her more than I . . . more than I realized. But it wasn't on purpose, Lucia. I love both you and your brother."

"He's not my brother," Lucia said quietly. She'd tried not to think about what happened in Magnus's chambers. The feel of his mouth on hers, demanding what she couldn't give in return. The devastated look on his face when she'd pushed him away . . .

"Family is the most important thing in the world," the queen said firmly. "It's what you have left when everything else falls apart. And you do have a family. Your father is so very proud of you."

"I don't know how he can be proud of me. I killed Sabina." Her gaze flicked to the queen. "Is that why you're being so kind to me today? Are you afraid of what I can do?"

The queen's pale bluish-gray eyes widened a fraction. "I could never fear you, daughter. I admire you. I see what a strong and beautiful woman you're growing up to be. And I am awed by what you're capable of now."

Lucia's stomach clenched. "I killed her, Mother. I crushed her against the wall and then I set her on fire."

Something slid behind the queen's gaze, something cold and

dark. "I'm glad she's dead. And I'm glad she suffered. I celebrate her death."

Her words chilled Lucia. "Death is not something to celebrate."

Queen Althea looked away and changed the subject.

"Your father wants to see you right now. I was on my way to your chambers to tell you. He has something very important to discuss with you. Go to him. Now."

The queen left the alcove and continued on down the hallway without a backward glance. Lucia watched her walk away.

Then she went directly to her father's meeting hall, where lately he spent most of his waking hours.

"Come in, Lucia," her father called as she pushed open the large doors. She entered to find that her father wasn't alone. Magnus was with him. Her chest tightened at the sight of him.

He wasn't looking at her. He stood by the wall, his gaze fixed on the king. Magnus had spent a great deal of time with their father since the king arrived back from Auranos. She had no idea how he'd reacted to Magnus's admitted failure during the trip leading to the deaths of two guards. She wished she knew the whole story. Magnus had been so upset when he returned.

"I know this has all been very difficult for you. Especially what Magnus told you about your birth."

She tried not to look at her brother. Nevertheless, she now felt the chill of his gaze on her. "I'm trying to accept everything as best I can."

"Know this: you are my daughter. I love you beyond any other I ever could have hoped to have. You are a part of this family today, tomorrow, and always. In every way. Do you believe me?"

His words felt solid and truthful. A small, tense piece of her finally relaxed. "I believe you."

The king sat down in a tall-backed chair. She braved a look at Magnus, but he'd averted his gaze again. He had yet to even acknowledge her presence. It had been that way since the night she came to his room and tried to comfort his pain more than a week ago. At every meal since, he'd flatly ignored her. When she'd crossed his path, he sidestepped her. She'd become like a shadow to him.

She'd wounded him deeply. But she'd had no choice. What he wanted from her, she couldn't give him.

"Do you know what my plans are when it comes to Auranos?" the king asked her.

She nodded. "You mean to conquer it alongside the chieftain of Paelsia."

"Very good. And do you think this is a wise plan?"

Lucia squeezed her hands together on her lap. "It sounds very dangerous."

"Yes, it will be dangerous. But it's meant to be," he said. "Magnus will be at my side. Together, we might have to give our lives in this siege to ensure the future strength and prosperity of Limeros."

She looked at him with alarm. "Please don't say that."

"You care about us, don't you, Lucia? Even now that you know of your true origins."

She was an orphan who'd been taken in by this family, no matter how that situation had come about. Without her adoptive family, she had nothing. Without the Damora name, she was a Paelsian peasant. "I do."

The king nodded. "I want you to come with us. Your magic was foreseen to be more powerful than anything the world has witnessed in a millennium. Your magic is the key to our success. Without you, there are no guarantees that we'll survive."

She swallowed hard. "You want me to use my magic to help you conquer Auranos."

"Only if absolutely necessary. But we will inform them that we have a very powerful weapon at the ready. Perhaps then they will back down without a fight."

"I'm not sure this is entirely wise," Magnus finally said. "The prophecy could still be wrong. Perhaps Lucia is just another witch."

Magnus's voice was so cold, so detached, it sent a chill racing down her spine. He made it sound like an insult. Like something easily discarded. She watched him, and his eyes flicked to her for a second before they moved away.

He hated her now.

"You're wrong. But, of course, the ultimate choice is up to Lucia," the king said. "I believe with all my heart that she's the key to our success or failure. To our life or death."

Lucia's love for Magnus would never die, no matter how cold he now tried to make himself appear. She would do anything to keep him safe. Even if he was cruel. Even if he hated her now until the day he died.

"I'll go with you," she said firmly after a long silence passed. "And I'll do everything in my power to help you defeat Auranos."

CHAPTER 29

AURANOS

The combined forces of Limerian and Paelsian foot soldiers marched across the border of Auranos.

A little less than three months ago, Jonas had stood at this very border planning to make a forbidden crossing so he could exact vengeance for his brother's death. The threat of Auranian border guards executing him on the spot was the same danger he'd faced when poaching with his brother.

But today, no mere border guards attempted to stop the invasion of five thousand strong. They had retreated to join the main Auranian force a few miles inland.

"Nice armor on the Limerians, huh?" Brion commented as he and Jonas marched side by side. They hadn't been given horses like many of their countrymen. Instead, the chief had given them the task to keep an eye out for any stragglers and to ensure that everyone continued to move forward toward their destination. Brion likened this to being dogs trained to keep sheep properly herded.

"Very shiny," Jonas agreed.

The Limerians were much better equipped than the Paelsians. He could spot most Paelsian recruits from fifty feet away. No helmet. No armor. And if a recruit held a sword, it was one that appeared rusty or blunt. Or, more likely, the Paelsians carried cruder weaponry carved from wood and studded with spikes. Still worked well enough to beat down an enemy, but it was far from perfect.

"Have you stopped obsessing about Princess Cleo yet?" Brion asked.

Jonas shot him a withering look. "I'm not obsessing."

"If you say so."

"I'm not."

"Didn't see her myself. Who knows? Maybe she was worth obsessing about. Gorgeous blonde, right?"

The mention of the princess had stripped any brightness from Jonas's current mood. "Close your mouth."

"Just remember, Laelia wants you back safe and sound, so try not to think too much of the princess. Got to get back to your betrothed as soon as possible."

Jonas grimaced. "I never agreed to any marriage."

"Good luck telling the chief. He's already picking out your wedding gift."

Jonas couldn't help but grin just a little, despite the subject matter not being remotely amusing to him. He had no intention of ever marrying Laelia Basilius.

But Brion was right about one thing. He had been obsessing about Princess Cleo ever since he returned home to find that she'd escaped from the shed only minutes before Prince Magnus arrived to claim her, her rescuers rendering Felicia's husband and two of his friends unconscious. They were lucky they hadn't been killed.

Felicia had been furious about the entire situation and swore she'd never forgive Jonas for getting her involved. It would take time for her to cool off.

By now, the princess was very likely back behind the Auranian palace walls, safe and sound. The golden-haired viper was full of surprises.

Jonas cast another glance over the men who surrounded him. Some from Paelsia were as young as twelve years old. Not men at all. And the numbers weren't nearly equitable. There were far more Limerians here. Probably three of them to every Paelsian.

Brion raked a hand through his messy hair. "Tomas would be proud his death has caused this kind of uprising. He would have liked to have been here to help us destroy these greedy Auranians."

"Right." But Jonas wasn't so sure. He'd been thinking way too much, ever since the meeting with King Corvin. The moment King Corvin had looked at King Gaius and questioned his motivation— questioned why he'd split Auranos with the chief. Something about that interaction rang true to him.

King Gaius wasn't to be trusted.

Jonas's hatred toward Auranian royals drove his desire to crush those who lived here, to take what was theirs so his land could prosper—and that was what the Limerian king offered. He focused on following orders and marching like everyone else, eyes forward on the path ahead.

But something still bothered him. Confusion wasn't a new development for him, but at a time like this, when he'd pledged his life to the defeat of another land, he'd like to fully believe in the core reasons for the battle. He wanted the pure clarity he'd had before.

The clarity that his people were dying, his land was fading, and while most—like his father—believed that it was fate, Jonas did not. The clarity that Auranos had everything and refused to give assistance or to return to the trade agreement that had gotten Paelsia into their grape-ridden mess in the first place. The clarity that, just like poaching from their land to feed the hungry bellies of his family, he could gladly poach their riches as well in the name of his brother.

Easy. With this army, Jonas believed they would succeed.

King Gaius had stepped in and offered his assistance and proved himself to the chief's satisfaction. He'd earned the chief's trust. But he'd never helped Paelsia in any other way before this. Only in this siege against Auranos did he suddenly appear with ideas and plans. With his ready army, trained for battle from oppressing his own people.

"What is it?" Brion asked. "You look like you've been chewing on the ass end of a goat."

Jonas looked at his friend, opened his mouth, but then closed it again. "Forget it. It's nothing."

He couldn't share his current thoughts with Brion, not when they were so dark and revolutionary. But still they rose to the surface and demanded his attention.

What if King Gaius changed his mind? What if he wanted *all* of Auranos to himself? If King Gaius played things the right way, he could conquer not one land . . . but *two*.

Everything would be his.

What if that had been his plan all along?

However, the question was, with the army that King Gaius commanded—Jonas looked around at it again, at the fierce men in their strong armor—why wouldn't he have simply taken Paelsia first if that was his plan? Why bother teaming up with a weaker land? Why work so hard to gain Chief Basilius's trust?

He sent a glance in the direction of King Gaius and Prince Magnus, riding their mounts, backs straight and tall in their saddles. Accompanying them was the Limerian princess, Lucia. At first glance, she appeared both beautiful and haughty to Jonas. He had no idea why they would bring her along on such a dangerous journey.

They looked so . . . royal.

Jonas hated royals—all of them. That much hadn't changed. And yet the chief had irrevocably aligned himself and Paelsia with these royals. From this day forward, their destinies were joined.

Despite the warmth of the Auranian air, something deep inside him went cold at the thought.

CHAPTER 30

AURANOS

Lost in her grief over Theon, Cleo had no clue how bad the conflict outside the palace walls was until she saw Aron in the halls of the castle pacing, his face strained with worry. Aron *never* looked worried unless he was worried about running out of wine.

She and Mira had been on their way to their afternoon art class. The tutor was an old man who hated being kept waiting, but Cleo grabbed Mira's arm to bring her to a stop.

"What are you doing here, Aron?" she asked.

Aron laughed, but the sound held no humor. "Is that any greeting for your future husband?"

Her face tightened. "It's so . . . wonderful to see you again, Aron," she forced out.

He honestly thought he had the upper hand with her. But she was confident that her future and his were not destined to intertwine.

"*I'm* glad to see you, Aron," Mira said sweetly. Cleo looked at her quizzically, but only for a moment. "But you're looking a bit blanched. Is something wrong?"

"Wrong?" Aron said. "Oh, no, I can't think of a thing. The palace is surrounded by savage enemies, but there's nothing to worry about. Only our impending deaths!"

His near hysteria couldn't breach the walls of Cleo's sadness, which had rendered her oddly serene. "They won't breach the walls."

Their enemies had set up camp a few miles from the palace walls, but to her knowledge they hadn't made any threatening move yet. Messages were being delivered back and forth between her father and the Limerian king and Paelsian chieftain. Their enemies demanded that the king surrender, but he refused. And *he* demanded that the Paelsians and Limerians turn around and go back to their homes.

Three days had passed since their arrival, and no one had budged an inch. Cleo was now forbidden to go anywhere outside the castle. She looked at Aron coolly. "Is that why you're here? Have you and your parents taken refuge at the castle in case there's a breach on the palace walls?"

Aron held his familiar gold flask to his lips. He took a long sip from it and then wiped his mouth off with the back of his hand. "Our villa isn't nearly as well protected as the castle itself."

"You think we're in that much trouble?" Mira asked, distressed.

Nic approached from down the hall. Cleo looked at him with open gratitude on her face. If it wasn't for Nic, she wouldn't be standing here right now.

"What's going on?" Nic asked. His gaze flicked to Cleo.

"Aron's moved into the castle," Mira informed him.

"Oh, don't sound so disappointed, Mira," Aron replied. "I know you like having me around. I'm the life of the party."

Mira blushed.

"Why would anyone be disappointed at your presence?" Nic said. "You're very welcome here, Aron. Anytime. My castle is your castle."

"This *isn't* your castle. Despite the king's affection for you and your sister, you're really nothing more than glorified servants." Aron took another gulp from his flask.

Nic gave him a withering glare. "Are you too drunk to even take a simple joke, you worthless bastard?"

Aron tucked his flask into his pocket and grabbed Nic by the front of his shirt. "Don't mess with me."

"Oh, I'll mess with you if I want to."

"When did you grow a pair? Did running off with my future bride give you some courage?"

"Your future bride hates you." Nic shoved the other boy back. "And by the way, your breath stinks like a horse's ass."

Aron's face reddened with anger.

"Enough," Cleo snapped, turning on her heel. She needed to see her father. Having Aron here was unacceptable, but if it was a sign that negotiations were going poorly, then she needed to know the truth. She left the others and went straight to her father's meeting hall. Inside, there were many men milling about and arguing loudly with each other. She finally found her father in the very middle of the chaos.

He glanced at her wearily as she approached. "Cleo, you shouldn't be in here."

"What's going on?"

"Nothing you need to concern yourself with."

She bristled. "I think if there's about to be an all-out attack on my home, then I need to concern myself. How can I help?"

The man standing next to her father snorted. "Sure you can help. Can you handle a sword, princess?"

She straightened her posture and gave him a sharp look. "If I have to."

"They're very heavy." The man rolled his eyes. "You should have had sons, Corvin. They would be more use to us right now than daughters."

"Hold your tongue," the king growled. "My daughters are more important to me than anything else in this kingdom."

"Then you should have sent them away before this escalated. Somewhere safe."

"The castle isn't safe?" Cleo asked with growing alarm.

"Cleo, go now," the king said. "Go to your classes. Don't worry about any of this. It's too overwhelming for you."

She looked at him steadily. "I'm not a child, Father."

The unpleasant man laughed at that. "How old are you? Sixteen? Do as your father suggests and go learn to paint. Or embroider. Or whatever it is that little girls do. Let us men deal with nasty things like this."

Cleo couldn't believe how this man dared to speak to her.

"Who are you?" she growled.

He seemed amused, as if a kitten had just shown him sharp claws. "Someone who is trying to help your father with a difficult situation."

"Cleo, forgive Lord Larides's rudeness; he—like all of us—is under a great deal of stress right now. But don't worry, they won't breach the entrance of the castle. Even if they get through the palace walls, you're safe here, Cleo. I swear it. Go to your friends. To your sister. Let me handle this."

She recognized the name—and now she recognized the man himself. He'd grown his beard longer since last she'd seen him. He was the father of Lord Darius, her sister's former fiancé. His family was in the king's trusted circle.

All these men saw when they looked at her was a little girl who'd run away on a whim to search for magic seeds. Who caused trouble. Who was utterly useless in every way except looking pretty. Maybe she was. And if that was true, then being here was only causing more problems for her father. Finally Cleo nodded and turned away. Her father caught her wrist and then kissed her quickly on the forehead.

"It will be all right," he said firmly, pulling her out of earshot of his council members. "I know it's been difficult, but we will survive this. No matter what happens. Be strong for me, Cleo. Do you promise me to do that?"

He looked so worried that all she could do was nod in agreement. The gesture seemed to help clear some of the darkness from his eyes.

"I promise."

"Whatever happens, remember that Auranos has been a powerful place of beauty and prosperity for a thousand years. It will continue to be so. No matter what happens."

"What *will* happen?" she asked quietly.

His expression remained tense. "When this is all over, things are going to change. I see now that I've been blind to troubles just outside my own kingdom's borders. If I'd paid more attention, this never would have happened. I won't repeat my past mistakes. Auranos will continue to be a strong and dominant force, but we will be kinder and more benevolent to our neighbors going forward."

His words didn't do much to assure her that all would be well. "Will the fighting start soon?"

He squeezed her hands.

"It's already begun."

CHAPTER 31

AURANOS

While he waited for the order to attack, Jonas stood shoulder to shoulder with the men who were about to become his battle brothers, Limerian and Paelsian alike. The sun beat down upon them. Sweat poured over his forehead and into his eyes, making them sting.

He'd believed the Auranian king would surrender without a fight. As he'd waited out the three long days that stretched between their arrival and this moment, as the rations quickly ran out for all but the most privileged, forcing them to individually pillage the forest for food, as the sun burned down upon them with little shelter for the common soldier apart from the thick line of forest two miles from the palace walls, he'd believed this would end without bloodshed. That King Corvin would be swayed by the legion of Limerian and Paelsian soldiers waiting for their call to battle.

But this was not to be. Blood would spill.

The troops gathered in formation on King Gaius's orders and

began the trek toward the walls. There was a river to cross, bisecting the green and grassy land of rolling hills and valleys. Beyond that the walled palace came into view—a spectacular golden sight that made Jonas's breath catch in his chest.

As did King Corvin's massive awaiting army, fully outfitted in sleek shining armor, burnished helmets atop their heads. The Auranian crest glinted golden on their shields.

They stayed like this for a full hour. Waiting. Watching. Jonas's heart pounded hard in his chest, a heavy sword gripped so tightly in his hand that it began to form blisters on his already rough skin.

"I hate them. And I'd kill them all for a chance at a life like theirs," he said under his breath to Brion, unable to keep his gaze away from the massive shining palace—so different from the modest cottages in Paelsia. And this land—so lush and green when his own was fading away and turning dry and brown. "They would take everything and let us suffer and die without even a thought."

A muscle in Brion's cheek twitched. "They deserve to suffer and die as well. Let grapes feed *their* nation."

Jonas was ready to die today to help his people have the chance at a better life tomorrow. Nothing was ever easy. And all living things eventually died. If this was to be his day, then so be it.

King Gaius rode his sleek black stallion along the line of waiting soldiers, tall in his saddle, a look of sheer determination on his face. Prince Magnus rode nearby, his cool gaze moving across the waiting troops. The cavalry would lead the charge. War flags were held high bearing the colors of Limeros and the words *Strength. Faith. Wisdom.*

Sounded very proper and studious. That the flags were red was the only indication of King Gaius's reputation as the King of Blood.

Chief Basilius and his flank of elite bodyguards were nowhere to be seen. Earlier, Jonas had walked through the city of tents set up on the other side of the forest. The chief had taken four tents to himself, needing the space for privacy, meditation, and rest to help summon his dormant magic to aid their efforts.

"The sorcerer will awaken," the rumor among the troops went. "His magic will crush our enemy to dust."

Chief Basilius would be their key to victory.

Jonas chose to believe this was true as well, despite his mounting doubts.

King Gaius addressed the troops. "Today is a day a thousand years in the making. A day when we take what has been kept just out of our reach. Out of *your* reach. What you see across this kingdom is yours for the taking—every one of you. No one can hold you down unless you refuse to get back up. Take this strength that I know you have—take it and help me crush those who would oppose us."

A chant began among the gathered soldiers, quiet at first but growing in strength and volume with each repetition.

"King of Blood! King of Blood! KING OF BLOOD!"

Before long, Jonas found that he was joining in—and in doing so, he became charged with the energy and bloodlust of the crowd. But a part of him knew that King Gaius wasn't his king. He had no king.

Yet he was following this King of Blood into battle and was willing to lay his life on the line in the process.

"Three months ago, an innocent Paelsian boy died at the hands of a selfish Auranian lord," the king roared. "Today we will gain vengeance for that. We will take the Auranian kingdom and strip the king of his power forever. Auranos is ours!"

The crowd cheered.

"Bring me King Corvin's head and I will give you treasure unlike anything you've ever seen," he promised. "Spare no one. Show me a river of blood! Take it all. Kill them all." He raised his sword above his head. "Attack!"

The troops charged forward, racing across the field. The ground thundered beneath their feet. At the river less than a mile from the palace walls, the Auranian force met them head-on in a violent slam of bodies and clash of sword and shield.

Men on both sides fell all around Jonas, taken down by steel-tipped arrow, by battleax, by sword before the fighting had barely begun. The coppery scent of blood filled the air.

Jonas slashed and fought his way through the thick mass of bodies, staying close to Brion, the two lifelong friends watching each other's backs.

The carcasses of horses fell heavily to the ground and in the river itself. Their riders, crawling off, met with the thrust of their enemy's swords through their chests. Pain-filled screams and cries filled the air as flesh met metal and hacked-off limbs scattered.

They fought to get closer to the walls. To take the palace by force. They were so close now, but the Auranian troops were equally vicious and brutal.

Jonas found himself knocked to the ground by the slam of a shield to the side of his head, and he lay there stunned, the metallic taste of blood flooding his mouth. A hawk soared in circles above the battle as if observing from a disinterested distance.

An Auranian knight appeared above Jonas, raising his sword to bring it down into Jonas's heart.

But another sword swung first, taking the Auranian down hard. A figure slipped off his mount and quickly rammed a smaller blade into the knight's neck, wrenching it to the side to rip out his throat in a spray of blood.

"Are you going to just lie there like a rock?" a voice snapped. "Get up. You're missing all the fun."

A gloved hand appeared before his face. Jonas shook his head and forced himself to sit up before Prince Magnus helped yank him to his feet.

"Make sure to leave a few for me." A glimmer of a grin played at the prince's lips. He got back on his horse and rode farther into the battle, bloody sword in hand.

The battle had progressed closer to the palace—but not yet close enough to take it. Fires burned in patches all over the expansive battlefield. The stench of death filled Jonas's nostrils. He forced himself to take stock and found that his sword was gone.

Jonas had been out cold and hadn't realized it. For how long had he lain there in the trampled grass surrounded by bodies? He swore loudly and worked his way through the bodies, searching for another weapon. Someone had been by—a scavenger for one side or the other who'd collected the weapons of the fallen. Finally he found an ax. It would do.

An enemy charged him—an enemy with his left arm already hanging off him after a brutal injury. But there was more fury than pain in the man's eyes.

"Paelsian scum," he snarled as raised his sword. "Die, you maggot!"

Jonas's muscles ached and burned as he swung his ax upward to meet flesh and bone. The spray of blood hit his face dead on.

Lit only by the torches stuck in the ground and the bright moon in the black sky, Jonas fought his way forward. He'd traded his battle-ax for a pair of short curved swords that looked as if they belonged to one of the chief's personal guards. They felt right in his hands and allowed him to slash through anything that opposed him.

Many had already fallen beneath his blade. He'd lost count of the lives he'd taken.

Jonas also showed the signs of a battle that had lasted twelve hours without relief. He bled from a wound on his shoulder. Another blade had found his abdomen, just beneath his ribs. He would live, but the injuries were starting to slow him down.

"Jonas," a voice called out to him from the tangle of bodies on the ground.

Jonas thrust a sword up into an Auranian's gut and watched the light leave the man's eyes before he glanced to his left.

A boy lay on the ground nearby, half-crushed by a fallen horse. Jonas fought to get to his side.

"Do I know you?" His gaze quickly moved over the boy's injuries. The horse that had crushed his legs wasn't the problem. It was the deep bloody wound to his stomach with the spill of glistening intestines showing beneath. A horse hadn't caused that. A sharp blade had.

"You're from my village. You're Jonas—Jonas Agallon. Tomas's younger brother."

Now he recognized the pale boy's face although he couldn't at first summon a name. "That's right. Leo, isn't it?"

Two soldiers clashed nearby, stumbling past them. One tripped over a body and the other—thankfully on Jonas's side—finished him off. To his left, a hail of burning arrows flew through the air from the archers stationed on top of the palace walls.

"Jonas," the boy Leo said, his voice almost too low to understand. "I'm scared."

"Don't be." Jonas forced himself to keep his attention on the boy. "It's only a shallow wound. You'll recover just fine."

He lied. Leo would not live to see the next sunrise.

"Good." The kid gave him a pained smile, but his eyes were glossy with tears. "Just give me a minute to rest and I'll get back out there."

"Rest for as long as you want." Despite his better judgment, he crouched down at the boy's side and took his hand. "How old are you?"

"Eleven. Just turned."

Eleven. Jonas felt the remnants of the half-cooked rabbit he'd eaten earlier churn in his gut. The whiz of an arrow pierced the air nearby and caught a soldier in the chest. Not a killing wound. It only made the soldier—a Limerian by the crest he wore on his sleeve—rip it out and let out a harsh cry of pain and rage.

Jonas turned his attention back to the dying boy. "You were very brave to volunteer for this."

"My older brother and I weren't given much choice. Had to come. If I could hold a sword, I would serve King Gaius."

Serve King Gaius.

Hot anger worked its way up Jonas's throat, thick enough to choke on. "Your family will be very proud of you."

"Auranos is so beautiful. So green and warm and . . . I've never been here before. If my mother could experience this, have a life like this, then it's all worth it."

The boy coughed up blood. Jonas wiped it away with his already bloody sleeve as he sent a searching glance around the area. Men fought close by—too close. He wanted to stay with this boy, but he couldn't afford to be here much longer. But if he could get this kid back to camp—find him a medic . . .

The boy's grip on his hand tightened. "C-can you do me a favor, Jonas?"

"Anything."

"Tell my mother I love her. And that I did this for her."

Jonas blinked hard. "I promise."

The boy smiled, but then the expression faded away and his eyes glazed over.

Jonas sat there a moment longer before getting to his feet. He let out a roar of anger into the skies above at the unfairness that a boy so young had to die tonight to help the King of Blood claim Auranos.

And the Paelsians—including himself!—were helping him every step of the way, baring their throats to their enemy's blade in the process—sacrificing their very futures.

The boy's death made it all unutterably clear to Jonas. There were no guarantees that King Gaius would hold true to any promises he'd made. He had the numbers. His army was vast and trained. Paelsia was there as nothing more than cannon fodder.

He needed to fall back and talk to the chief. Immediately. Clutching his blades, he turned from the boy—to be met with an arm covered by a spiked gauntlet slashing toward him. It missed his face by barely an inch as he spun out of the way. It was an Auranian who'd lost much of his armor apart from his breastplate. His ugly face was slashed, his hair matted with blood. Someone had attempted to slash his throat, but he'd gotten away before the blade had left more than an angry-looking scratch.

"Saying goodbye to your little brother?" The knight smirked. One of his front teeth had been knocked out. "That's what you get when you try to mess with us. You get my sword through your guts. And you're next, savage."

Fury burned inside Jonas. The knight attacked, slicing his sword through the air—clashing with Jonas's blades hard enough to rattle his teeth. The sound of a steel-tipped arrow ripped through the air inches away from his ear, catching a nearby Paelsian soldier in the back of the leg. He fell to the ground, screaming.

The Auranian knight had been trained for this, but he was already injured from hours of fighting. His fatigue was Jonas's only advantage.

"You're going to lose," the knight hissed. "And you're going to die. We should have put you out of your misery years ago— your entire goddess-forsaken land. You should be thanking us for stomping you out like the filthy cockroaches you are."

Jonas didn't care if he was called a cockroach. They were resilient, strong, and resourceful creatures. It beat being called a savage. But he really didn't like being told he was going to lose.

"You're wrong. Our misery is over. But yours has just begun."

Jonas threw all his body weight toward the knight, taking him down to the ground hard. Throwing his blades to the side, he wrenched the knight's sword out of his hands and pressed it against his throat.

"Surrender," Jonas growled.

"Never. I fight for my king and kingdom. I won't rest 'til every last one of you filthy savages is dead."

Suddenly, there was a knife in the knight's hand. Jonas felt the bite of pain as it pierced his side. Before it could burrow too deep, he rolled away, grabbing hold of the sword with both hands.

With every remaining piece of his strength, Jonas brought the sword down on the knight's unprotected throat. The head flew away from the rest of the body. He wiped the spray of blood from his eyes with his sleeve.

He staggered to his feet and, in pain, fought his way back across the field, across the river that now ran with blood under the night sky. Hot, thick blood ran down his own side from his wounds, but he kept moving forward. Or . . . backward.

Through the thick curtain of forest to the other side, where the city of tents had been created. Hundreds milled about in the medical area—injured, dying. Wails of pain and misery met his ears.

Jonas kept moving, his legs weak. Finally he reached his destination—the chief's tent. These tents—supplied by the Limerians— were larger than any Paelsian cottage he'd ever seen. This was where the elite rested and took their meals, which were lavishly prepared by dedicated cooks and servants.

While eleven-year-old boys fought and died in battle two miles away.

Basilius's guards recognized Jonas despite his covering of fresh blood—his own and that of those he'd killed—so they didn't protest when he pushed through the flap leading into the expansive, furnished tent. Bile rose in Jonas's throat to see such luxury after what he'd just experienced for the last half day.

"Jonas!" the chief exclaimed with enthusiasm. "Please, come in! Join me!"

Exhaustion and pain made him stumble as he walked. He feared his knees would give out completely. The chief's gaze went to his injured side and over his face, noting his wounds. "Medic!"

With only a word, a man approached and pulled at Jonas's shirt to inspect his wounds. A chair was suddenly behind him and he sat down hard. It was a good thing since he'd become very dizzy and disoriented. His skin was cold and clammy. The world suddenly appeared dim at the edges. He worked hard to breathe normally and regain his strength.

The medic worked on him, swiftly cleaning and bandaging the wounds.

"So tell me," the chief said with a big smile. "How goes the battle?"

"Haven't you been meditating all this time? I thought maybe you could see us through the eyes of birds." He wasn't sure why he said this. A child's story, he vaguely recalled. One his mother believed.

The chief nodded, his smile staying right where it was. "It's a gift I wish I had. Perhaps it's one I'll develop in the coming years."

"I wanted to talk to you personally," Jonas forced out. He worried about Brion now, feeling guilt about leaving the battlefield before the siege had been successful. He'd lost sight of his friend early in the battle. Brion could be out there dying, with no one to protect him in case an Auranian came by to finish him off. Or an errant arrow pierced his defenseless flesh.

With Tomas gone, Brion was as close to a brother as Jonas had.

His eye burned, but he chose to believe it was caused by the smoke from the chief's pipe. The scent of crushed peach leaves and something sweeter filled the air. Jonas recognized it as a rare herb found in the Forbidden Mountains that allowed pleasurable hallucinations.

"Please, speak freely." Dismissing the medic, the chief waved a hand and sat down behind a table that had previously held a feast. The bones of the slaughtered goat scattered across the surface along with a dozen empty bottles of wine.

"I have concerns," he began, his jaw tight. "About this war."

"War is something to be taken very seriously. Yes. And you strike me as a serious boy."

"Growing up in Paelsia, I didn't have much of a choice about that, did I?" He tried to keep the bitterness out of his words, but he didn't succeed. "I've worked in the vineyards since I was eight years old."

"You're a fine boy. Your work ethic is commendable." The chief nodded. "I'm so impressed that my Laelia found you."

More like the other way around. Jonas had found Laelia. He had spent time in her bed, listening to her gossip about her friends, to her stories about her hateful snakes, all in an attempt to gain the chief's confidence so that he might convince him to rise up against the Auranians and take what should have been theirs.

Even if Tomas had never been killed, Jonas would still want that for his country.

But *this*—this was wrong. He felt the truth of it deep inside him.

There was no time to play games. Boys were dying on that field, giving their lives to get a few feet closer to the palace walls. He had to say what he'd come here to say.

"I don't trust King Gaius."

The chief leaned back in his padded chair and regarded Jonas with curiosity. "Why not?"

"There are more Limerians here than Paelsians. The king's reputation precedes him—one of brutality and greed. What guarantee do we have that after we give our lives to help him take Auranos he won't turn around and kill us? Enslave us? All so he can keep everything for himself."

The chief pursed his lips and puffed on his pipe. "You really feel this way?"

Frustration coursed through Jonas. His heart pounded. "We need to pull back. Reassess before there are more casualties. A boy died in front of me, barely eleven years old. While I want to see Auranos fall, I don't want our victory to be painted with the blood of children."

The chief's expression turned grave. "I'm not one to start something and back away."

No, he was one to start something and wait in his luxurious tent for it to be over. "But—"

"I understand your concerns, but you need to put your faith in me, Jonas. I have searched deeply within myself to find the answers I seek. And the answer is, alas, war. This will not end until it's over. It's my destiny to align with King Gaius. I trust him. He paid me blood sacrifice unlike any I have ever witnessed before. Incredible." He nodded. "King Gaius is a good and honorable man who will hold true to every promise he's made to me. I have no doubt about this."

Jonas clenched his fists at his sides. "So if he's so good and honorable, where has he been while our land has been dying? While our people are dying? Where was his assistance then?"

Chief Basilius sighed. "The past is the past. All we can do is look toward the future and try our very best to do whatever it takes to make it a brighter one."

"Please, consider what I've said to you." The more he'd spoken, the more convinced Jonas was that they were headed down a very dark and bloody path. What he'd seen on the field of battle had only been the beginning of the misery to come.

"Of course. I'll consider everything. I value your opinion, Jonas."

"What about your magic? Do you think you can use any of it to help us?"

The chief spread his hands. "That won't be necessary. King

Gaius tells me that he has a very special secret weapon at the ready once we make it through the palace walls. This is not a battle that will continue for days and weeks—or months. It will be over tomorrow. I promise you that."

Jonas's mouth was so dry he wished there was still some wine in one of those bottles. "What secret weapon?"

The question was met with an enigmatic smile. "If I told you that, it wouldn't be a secret, would it?" The chief stood up and came around to Jonas's chair to slap him on the back. Jonas tensed from the pain from his freshly patched-up wounds. "Trust me, Jonas. When all of this is over and we're reaping the rewards of what we've earned here in Auranos, your wedding feast will be the grandest ever witnessed before in Paelsia."

Jonas left the tent with the sound of the chief's laughter echoing all around him. He might as well have spoken to a stone wall for all the good it did.

Bleakly, he looked up at the dark sky, speckled with bright stars and a heavy moon, and wondered why it didn't show a single sign of the coming storm.

CHAPTER 32

AURANOS

Emilia was now so ill that even lifting her head caused her pain and horrible nosebleeds. Cleo had taken over from Mira to read to her sister to take her mind off the battle raging outside the palace walls. The castle felt somber and gray and dismal. Cleo tried to find a ray of hope to cling to, but with each hour that passed since the siege began in full force, everything only seemed more bleak.

"Please, don't cry." Emilia's voice caught. "I told you, you must be strong."

Cleo wiped the tears from her cheeks and tried to concentrate on the writing of the small, worn book of poetry—one of Emilia's favorites. "Can't a strong person cry?"

"You mustn't waste any more tears on me. I know you've shed so many already for Theon."

Cleo had tried to make her peace with what had happened, but she felt as if the pain was still muffled, as though it was too new. Too raw and hadn't fully hit her yet. Losing someone she'd only just started to love was bad enough, but the thought of losing Emilia too . . .

Cleo held her sister's thin hand gently. "What can I do to help you?"

Emilia settled back on her multitude of colorful pillows. On her nightstand was a large bouquet of flowers Cleo had picked in the castle courtyard, the closest she could get to being outside. It was in the direct center of the castle, a large patch of walled greenery with apple and peach trees and a beautifully groomed flower garden. Both sisters liked to take classes out there when the tutors were agreeable.

"Be strong, that's all," Emilia said. "And try to spend more time with your friends in this strange and confusing time, not only with me. I don't mind being alone tonight."

Even in her current strife, the future queen of Auranos kept a stiff upper lip, just as she'd always been trained. It was very nearly amusing how unlike the two sisters were despite less than three years separating them in age—Emilia so mature and Cleo the opposite.

Cleo twisted her finger through a lock of her hair. "I've been trying to avoid them. Aron's now lurking in the shadows. I never know when he's going to jump out at me."

This made Emilia laugh. "You mean, he isn't out waving a sword around and trying to protect his future wife?"

Cleo gave her a squeamish look. "Don't even joke about something like that."

"I'm sorry. I know you find no humor in this situation."

"None at all." Cleo sighed shakily. "But enough about Aron. My foremost worry is your well-being, sister. And as soon as this battle is over, which I hope will be very soon, I'll send a guard to Paelsia as I promised I would."

"To search for this Watcher with healing seeds to help save my life."

"Yes, and don't say it with such skepticism. You're the one who gave me the idea in the first place. Before, I didn't even believe in magic."

"Now you do?"

"I do. With all my heart."

Emilia shook her head. "There's no magic that can save me now, Cleo. It would be best that you try to accept what's meant to be."

Cleo stiffened. "Never."

Emilia laughed again, although it was a weak sound in her chest. "So you believe that you can fight destiny and win."

"Without a doubt." As long as Emilia breathed, there was still hope for a way to cure her.

Emilia squeezed her hands. "Go, find Mira and Nic."

"Should I send Mira to you later?"

"No. Let her have a night off from attending to me. I'm sure she's having a difficult time worrying about the siege outside."

"At least it's a quiet siege. I think that must be a good sign." If she didn't already know something horrible was happening outside, she never would have guessed it. The sounds of battle did not penetrate the thick castle walls.

Emilia didn't smile at this. She just looked tired and sad. "I hope so."

"Tomorrow will be a better day." Cleo bent over and kissed her sister's cool forehead. "I love you, sister."

"I love you too."

Cleo slipped out of Emilia's chambers and padded along the hallway. It was eerily quiet in the castle. The windows had all been blocked with boards.

Being cooped up gave her far too much time to think about Theon. She missed him being around, shadowing her at the castle, giving her stern looks when she did or said something mischievous. The relief on his face when he'd found her unharmed in Paelsia. The heat in his gaze when he admitted that he cared deeply for her.

And then, the surprised pain when the Limerian prince impaled him with a sword and stole his life forever.

She pushed away her tears as she moved through the same hallways they'd walked together. His loss was a constant weight on her heart, and it only grew heavier with each day that passed.

She was so tired that she retired to her chambers rather than go in search of Mira and Nic. There, however, she found that she only stared at the ceiling, unable to sleep.

If she'd found the exiled Watcher, everything would be different. She would very possibly have the means now to return Emilia's health and vitality.

Perhaps it *was* only a legend. It pained her to even consider this.

All that had kept her optimism and belief going had been Eirene's stories. They'd been so alive, so real. Eirene had given Cleo hope.

She'd all but forgotten the old woman these past days. The envelope with the name of the local tavern owner, through whom Cleo had planned to send her gifts of gratitude, had gone untouched and unopened.

"Good fortune will find those with pure hearts, even when all seems lost."

They were Eirene's parting words to her. All certainly seemed lost right now. Trapped in a castle, with no idea when she'd be able to safely leave again. Her sister fading away before her very eyes.

Cleo swung her legs out of bed, determined to find the envelope. Even if she was unable to send anything yet, she could gather what she needed in her spare time. Lately, she had a great deal of spare time.

The small envelope sat on her dressing table, beneath a pile of unread books. She picked it up and broke the seal.

Instead of an address, she was surprised to find a note and two tiny brown pebbles inside.

The note read:

Princess, please accept my apologies that I couldn't tell you the truth about myself. It is a secret that I've held for many years that no one knows, apart from legend, not even my granddaughter. A pure heart is worth more to me than gold. Yours is such a heart. Use these precious seeds to heal your sister so she can help lead Auranos toward a brighter future. —Eirene

Cleo read the note three times before it began to make any sort of sense to her. But when it did, the note literally dropped from her hands.

Eirene had seen through her and Nic's lies about being from Limeros. She'd known Cleo was the Auranian princess.

Even more than that—Eirene was the exiled Watcher herself. While they had searched for her, she had found them instead.

And Cleo had no idea.

She looked down at the tiny pebbles and her eyes widened. These were the grape seeds infused with earth magic. They'd been in her possession the entire time.

Two seeds that were capable of healing someone near death.

If she'd known this, she could have saved Theon's life with one of them.

The hopeless thought wrenched her heart from her chest. She let out a loud cry of pain, then gave in to her grief and collapsed to the floor, drawing her knees tight to her chest.

Even while wracked with sobs, she knew she had no time for tears or regrets.

She had to get to Emilia.

Cleo forced herself up from the ground and ran for the door. She burst into the hallway, only to crash right into somebody. Nic staggered back a few feet away and gingerly rubbed his chest.

"Ouch. You do have a habit of frequently hurting me, Cleo." He studied her red, swollen eyes with concern. "I heard a cry from your chambers. I thought you were in distress."

Her heart fluttered like a hummingbird's wings. "I was. I am. I—I have the seeds. Eirene . . . she was the Watcher."

He stared at her blankly. "How much wine did you have tonight? I believe you might be even drunker than Aron."

"I'm not drunk. It's true." Her heavy heart lifted. "Come. We must go to Emilia's chambers immediately."

"You really believe in magic?" he asked.

"Yes!"

He nodded and a grin crept across his face. "Then let's go save your sister."

They hurried through the hallways toward Emilia's room, passing through a corridor where she caught part of a conversation between two guards.

"Their forces are relentless," one said. "The palace walls aren't impenetrable."

"They've breached the walls?" Nic asked sharply, drawing Cleo to a halt.

The guards looked sheepish, as if they hadn't meant to be overheard.

"I'm afraid so," one said, nodding gravely. "But they won't get into the castle."

"How can you sound so confident of that?" Cleo said, concern twisting inside her.

They exchanged a look. She might only be sixteen, but as princess they were obligated to answer her questions. "The doors of the castle are fortified by a witch's spell."

She looked at him with disbelief. "My father never told me this."

"The spell is renewed every year by the same witch to keep it strong. But she won't be much help to us anymore."

"Hush," his friend hissed.

"Why?" Nic asked. "Where's the witch now?"

The first guard's jaw tensed and his eyes shifted back and forth between his friend, Nic, and Cleo. "King Gaius sent her head to the king in a box three days ago. But it doesn't matter. Whatever that bastard king tries to do now, the spell will still hold. He will fail."

Cleo knew the king of Limeros had a horrible, bloodthirsty son, but it sounded as if the father might be even worse—just as the rumors she'd heard about him threatened. "Why wouldn't my father tell me any of this?"

"The king wants to protect you from the bad things that are happening."

"So why are *you* telling us?" Nic asked.

"Because you have a right to know that we're all in danger here." His expression hardened. "The king has put us all at risk by refusing to surrender."

Cleo inhaled sharply. "You think he should?"

"It would save a great many more deaths outside on the battlefield. Does he think that we can stay inside this castle forever, with or without a spell keeping the doors sealed? We're no better than a cornered rabbit waiting for the wolf to tear out its throat."

Cleo looked down her nose at this sniveling coward. "How dare you speak ill of my father? He's making the best choice he can to keep Auranos strong. Yet you'd prefer he surrender to the King of Blood? Do you think that the world would be better then? Do you think those who have already lost their lives would be saved?"

"What do you know?" the guard asked darkly. "You're only a girl."

"No," Cleo said firmly. "I am a princess of Auranos. And I support every one of my father's decisions. And unless you too would like to find your severed head in a box, you'd do best to respect your king."

There was now a cowed look to the guard's expression as he lowered his head in deference to her. "My apologies, your highness."

Cleo clutched the seeds so tightly in her hand they bit into her skin. "Get back to work," she said icily before continuing on along the hall.

"That was brilliant, Cleo," Nic said. "You defeated him with words."

She gave him a sidelong look, almost amused. But worry creased her brow. "It's not good out there, is it?"

He shook his head, his own amusement fading. "No. It isn't."

"Do you think we'll lose?"

"King Gaius and Chief Basilius have a lot of men ready and willing to die for their cause. No matter how long this takes."

"My father must never surrender."

"If he feels he has no choice, he'll have to."

Cleo remembered the coldness in Prince Magnus's eyes as he

murdered Theon. She couldn't bear to see him ever again. "No, he won't."

"Oh, no?"

She forced a confident smile, pushing away the dark memories. "Don't you see? We can't even think that we'll lose—because we won't. We'll be victorious and send those greedy pigs back where they came from. Then when all is calm again, we can focus on helping those in Paelsia who really deserve our help rather than those who would steal our land in its entirety."

"Put that way, I almost believe you're right."

"I am right." Cleo held out the seeds in the palm of her hand. "These are going to make all the difference. When Emilia is healed, the world will be a brighter place full of endless possibilities."

He nodded. "Then lead on, princess."

When they arrived at Emilia's door, Cleo didn't bother to knock; she simply let herself in. Nic lingered at the door, respectful to her sister, who was tucked into bed. Cleo rushed to Emilia's side, not able to keep from smiling. Emilia faced the window, too weak to even turn her head to see her sister enter her room.

Cleo could barely control her excitement.

"Emilia! You won't believe what I have here. The seeds! Don't ask me how it's possible, but it is. This will cure your illness, I know it will." Emilia didn't reply, but Cleo continued. "Watchers are real—I met one, even though I didn't realize it at the time. She seemed no different than you or me. And she wanted to help you."

Cleo glanced over her shoulder toward Nic, who'd taken a tentative step inside the room. He looked distressed, his brows drawn together.

"Cleo . . ." he began.

"I know it's been hard," Cleo continued, sitting gently on the bed. "First losing the one you love. We have that in common now, so I know how you feel. But we must go on and face what's ahead together. It won't be easy, but I'll be strong. Just like you told me to be."

Nic put his hand on her shoulder. "I'm so sorry."

She shrugged off his hand. "No, she'll wake up. She'll be fine. Better than ever." She stroked her sister's long honey-colored hair, splayed against the silk pillow. "Emilia, wake up. Please."

"She's gone, Cleo," Nic said softly.

"Don't say that." Cleo began to tremble. "Please don't say that."

"I'm sorry. I'm so sorry."

Emilia stared sightlessly out of the window at the star-studded sky. Her skin was cool to the touch. She could have been gone for hours—ever since Cleo left her earlier.

When Cleo tried to get up from the bed, her legs crumpled beneath her. Nic caught her before she hit the floor. The seeds dropped from her hand. The well inside her broke—the one she'd been hoping would keep holding. She began to sob, beating her fists against Nic's chest. It was too much sadness for her bear. She would die from this. She *wanted* to die.

The answer had been in her hand, the answer to save her sister's life. But it was too late. She had failed.

Emilia was gone.

"I'm sorry," Nic murmured, taking her blows without complaint. He tried to pull her against him to comfort her, but she kept fighting.

"The seeds!" she cried, and then fell to the ground, searching for the seeds she'd dropped. Finally she found them and grabbed hold of the side of the bed to pull herself back up.

Emilia's face was ghostly white. Even her eyes seemed to have paled to a colorless gray. Cleo touched her sister's face with trembling fingers, opening her bloodless lips and pushing both seeds inside. As they each touched Emilia's tongue, they shimmered with white light and disappeared.

Like magic.

"Please." The word was more of a soft cry. "Please work."

She waited for what felt like forever, but nothing happened. Nothing.

It was too late.

Cleo finally turned to face Nic. His eyes brimmed with tears as he saw the grief on her face. A coldness, like shards of ice, sank slowly into her.

"My sister is dead." She barely recognized her own voice. "She died alone looking at the stars."

Emilia and Simon had counted stars the romantic night they'd spent together. He told her they'd become stars when they died and would watch over those they loved. It was why Emilia's face had been turned to the window tonight. She'd been searching for him.

Nic stayed close but silent. She didn't expect him to say anything. There was nothing he could say to make this better.

"I was too late," she said. "I was too late. I could have saved her, but I was too late."

She clutched her sister's cold hand and sat on the side of the bed next to Emilia for so long that the sun began to rise. Nic stayed with her the whole time, sitting on the ground near the window, his legs crossed.

"We should close her eyes now," he finally said.

Cleo couldn't talk. All she could do was nod.

Nic came over and reached toward Emilia, closing her eyes

so Cleo could almost fool herself again that her sister was only sleeping.

"We need to tell your father," he said. "I'll do it. Don't worry. Don't worry about anything. It'll be all right."

She shook her head. "Nothing will be all right ever again."

"I know this isn't going to be easy for you to hear right now, but you have to be strong. Can you do that?" He cupped her face. "Can you be strong?"

In her last conversation with Emilia she'd asked Cleo to be strong. It was all she wanted. And Cleo said she would.

"I can try," she whispered.

Nic nodded. "Let's go."

He put his arm around her as they moved toward the door. Cleo glanced over her shoulder one more time at her sister. She looked so peaceful in her bed, as if she would wake up at any moment from a pleasant dream, ready for breakfast.

They began to walk down the hall toward her father's chambers, Nic's hand at Cleo's back to support her in case her legs gave out again.

A moment later, an explosion shook the entire castle.

CHAPTER 33

AURANOS

A sunrise was the most beautiful thing in the whole world, even during a time of war. Lucia has risen extra early and stood outside her tent as she waited for the sky to turn a vibrant mix of pink and orange beyond the city of tents. A hawk flew high above, its golden wings catching the first edge of morning light.

She hated being here. She'd been kept away from the worst of the battle, but she wasn't ignorant. Men were dying on all sides of this siege. And she wanted it over with.

Lucia had resolved to ask her father's permission to return to Paelsia, but the thought was swept away the moment her brother was helped into her tent by two of her father's guards. The king himself entered afterward, his expression grim. Magnus's face was bloody, his eyes half-closed.

"What happened?" she exclaimed.

A medic rushed in as the guards stepped back, and he cut through Magnus's jacket and shirt to remove them. His arm had been sliced all the way to the bone. A vicious, bloody wound on his abdomen showed he'd also been stabbed.

"I didn't even know he was still out there until he was brought back here to camp on a stretcher," the king said. "I hadn't wanted him to be so involved in the combat so soon, but he likes to go against my orders. Foolish boy."

Lucia reached for him but pulled her shaking hand back to press it against her mouth instead. "Magnus!"

"He's lost a great deal of blood. I wanted him brought here for privacy."

Anger lit up inside her. "Magnus, why would you do such a thing? Why would you be so irresponsible as to put yourself in this kind of danger?"

Magnus's pained face and half-glazed gaze tracked to where she stood only a few feet away. He didn't reply.

The medic suddenly looked afraid and Lucia's attention shot to him. "What are you doing? Help him! Save him!"

The man's face had paled a great deal as he'd examined the prince's injuries. "I'm afraid it's too late for that, your highness. He's close to death."

The king swore, drawing his sword and holding its tip to the medic's throat. "You are speaking about the heir to the throne of Limeros."

"I—I can't help him. His injuries are too severe." His voice trembled and he squeezed his eyes shut, as if expecting that his punishment for this announcement would be death.

"I can help my brother," Lucia said. "But tell the medic to leave first."

"Leave," the king snarled, nicking the medic's throat with his sword. Blood immediately gushed from the wound. "Attend your own injuries."

Holding his hand to his neck, the medic scrambled away from the king's sword and fled from the tent.

Lucia sank to her knees next to where her brother now lay. The floor of the tent was soaked with his blood. His breath came slower, but his gaze didn't leave hers. Even through the pain, he looked at her with anger. And wariness.

"I've heard what you've done to the boys from your swordsmanship classes," she said softly. "I don't like who you're trying to become. My brother is better than that."

His eyes narrowed, his brows drawing together.

"You wish to go out into the thick of the battle so you can draw another's blood. Is it so you can sink steel into flesh believing it will make you feel like more of a man? How many did you kill today?" She didn't expect an answer. Even if he was currently capable of speech, they hadn't spoken since the night he'd arrived home from Paelsia.

"If you were anyone but my brother, I would let you die. But no matter how many men you kill, no matter how much of an ass you insist on being, no matter how much you despise me—I still love you. You hear me?"

Pain slid through his gaze, and Magnus turned his attention to the wall of the tent as if he couldn't bear the sight of her face anymore.

Her heart ached, but it didn't matter anymore. Nothing mattered except her magic.

Luckily, she was feeling extremely angry at the moment. It would help.

She didn't know how her magic worked, only that it did. She'd been practicing, alone and with the tutor her father had provided— the old woman who claimed to also be a witch, despite not being able to demonstrate any real magic of her own.

Air, water, fire, earth.

She shot her father a look as she pressed her hands against Magnus's arm. Bone was easily visible beneath the blood and muscle. Her stomach lurched.

"I asked to help with other injuries, Father. I could have practiced before this. I might fail." The king had denied her the chance to help others who were hurt, leaving the medics to the insurmountable task of dealing with the injured.

"You won't fail," her father said firmly, sheathing his sword. "Do it, Lucia. Heal him."

She already knew she could heal a few scratches from practicing on herself. But a deeper wound from a knife or a sword like this . . . she wasn't sure.

The only thing she knew for certain was that she couldn't lose him.

Lucia concentrated all her energy on healing his wound. As the warmth of her earth magic left her hands and entered his arm with a pale glow of white light, he arched his back up off the ground as if in agony.

It almost made her stop, but she didn't dare. She wasn't sure if she could channel this level of magic again. Using any of her magic to its extreme—such as what she'd done with Sabina—weakened her. Her tutor believed it was because such magic was still new, and it needed time and practice to grow stronger.

Instead of pulling back for fear of hurting him more, she forced more magic through her hands and into his wound. He writhed in pain beneath her touch as her hands glowed bright white. The wound began to knit together—flesh joining, smoothing, becoming whole again.

She didn't stop. She shifted her hands to his mangled stomach and poured her magic into the wound.

This time a harsh cry of pain escaped his throat.

She steeled herself against the sound until he was healed. After his arm, she moved her hands over his bloody face, healing the bruises and cuts there until finally he batted her hands away.

"Enough," he snarled.

That didn't sound like eternal gratitude for saving his life. "Did it hurt?"

He let out a snort, which could have been a pained laugh. "It burned into my bones like lava."

"Good. Perhaps through pain you can learn a lesson not to be so reckless."

Her sharp tone earned the full weight of his gaze. "I'll try my best, sister. Though I'll offer you no guarantees."

Her eyes stung. It took her a moment to realize she was crying, which only made her angrier. "I will stab you myself if you are ever so foolish as to nearly get yourself killed again."

His fierce expression finally eased. Her tears—infrequent as they were—tended to affect him, even when they were quarreling. "Don't cry, Lucia. Not over me."

"I'm not crying over you. I'm crying over this stupid war. I want it over."

The king inspected Magnus's bare arm and stomach, using a cloth to wipe the blood away. The wounds were completely gone. Pride unlike anything she'd ever seen before shone in his eyes. "Incredible. Just incredible. Your brother owes you his life."

She gave Magnus a look. "My payment need only be his gratitude."

Magnus swallowed hard, and something vulnerable slid behind his brown eyes before he looked away. "Thank you for saving my life, sister."

The king helped Lucia to her feet. "You say you want this war over."

"More than anything."

"We're at a standstill. We've breached the palace walls, but we can't get any farther. King Corvin and everyone who stands in the way of this war ending quickly and easily are barricaded inside the castle and they refuse to surrender."

"So break down the door," Magnus said, pushing himself up from the bloody ground. His face was pale and there were dark circles under his eyes. While she'd healed his wounds, it would still take him a while to recover completely.

"We would if we could. But the door is infused with a protection spell. It can't be broken . . . not by normal means."

"A protection spell," Lucia said with surprise. "From a witch?"

"Yes."

Anger toward the king's mounting deceptions sparked within her. "So *this* is why you brought me here. Because you already knew about this. Why didn't you tell me until now?"

"Because I wasn't sure if what I'd been told was true until we had access to the door itself. The witch said to have cast the spell was brought before me to answer questions. She wasn't very much help."

"Where is she now?" Magnus asked.

"Gone."

"You let her go?" Magnus said, disbelief coating his words. "Or did you kill her?"

The king gave him a thin smile. "She was one who conspired with my enemy. She could help him now. She would not switch allegiances. Her death was swifter than she deserved."

A shiver went down Lucia's arms. The king returned his attention to Lucia, his harsh expression shifting to one of caring and concern. He took her hands gently in his. "I need your magic to break through that spell."

She glanced toward her brother for some sort of guidance. It was an old habit.

Magnus caught her worried look. "It sounds dangerous."

"Not for my daughter," the king said. "She isn't just a witch; she's a sorceress with an endless supply of powerful magic at her fingertips."

"Are you absolutely certain of that?" Magnus said, his words clipped. "If you're wrong—"

"I'm not wrong," the king said firmly.

"Of course I'll help you, Father," Lucia said. "For Limeros."

Seeing Magnus nearly killed in this battle made her want it to be over, no matter what it took to make that happen. All she wanted was to go home again as soon as possible. The king squeezed her hands and smiled at her. "Thank you. Thank you, my beautiful daughter."

Without delay, and with the protection of twenty Limerian guards, they guided her across the battlefield, scattered with bodies. She tried not to see the faces of the dead. All this senseless pain and destruction could have been prevented if Auranos had surrendered. She had grown to hate them as much as her father did for letting this escalate.

"You must stop if it becomes too much for you," Magnus said when they arrived at the castle's entrance, only loud enough for her to hear. "Promise me."

"I promise." She nodded, then turned her attention to the tall wooden doors before her. There was no mistaking that there most definitely was a spell on these doors. A very powerful one. "Can you see it?"

"What?"

"The spell. It shimmers on the door. I—I think it's created from all four elements combined."

Magnus shook his head. "I see nothing but a door. A big one."

The door wasn't the problem. The spell was. And it was cast by a very powerful witch—one who had delved deeply into magic to create something like this.

Blood magic helped with this spell, Lucia thought suddenly. Someone—or many someones—had been sacrificed to create such protection.

That the Auranians were willing to allow such a thing only strengthened her resolve. There was blood on their hands as much—or more so—than anyone else's.

It would take a great deal of Lucia's magic to break through this wall of protection. She couldn't doubt herself. Her power was strongest when it came from a deep, emotional place inside. She remembered how she'd felt when she saw Magnus at the edge of death and summoned her newfound magic.

It rose up to the surface to greet her. The strength of air, the grit of earth, the endurance of water, and the scorch of fire.

Magnus and the others watched as she thrust her hands out toward the doors, toward the spell, and unleashed it all.

As Lucia's magic met the other witch's blood magic, they combusted. The protection spell rose up like a fiery dragon in an attempt to fight her—but her father was right. Her magic was more powerful. It compensated. It changed. It grew right before her eyes.

The doors exploded in a ball of fire, shaking the ground beneath their feet. The shock wave hit everyone within a hundred-foot radius, knocking them backward. Lucia hit the ground hard and pain crashed over her.

Screams of terror filled her ears. People were dying, on fire, some with their throats slashed from sharp wooden shards hitting them; some victims lay in pieces, limbs scattered. Rivers of blood soaked into the earth.

The last thing Lucia saw before she passed out was the force of her father's army storming through the broken, burning doorway and into the Auranian castle.

CHAPTER 34

AURANOS

After the explosion that blasted open the front doors, chaos descended. Cleo couldn't give in to her grief, couldn't fall to her knees and sob over her sister's death. She had no choice but to keep moving. Their enemies had breached the castle.

Screams of fear and the violent clang of swords met her ears as she and Nic ran through the halls. She clung to his arm. "What can we do?"

There was sweat on his brow as he kept his attention on their path. "I have to find Mira. We need to . . . I don't know. I want to help. I want to fight, but I know your father would want me to keep you and my sister safe."

"How? How can we be safe now?"

Nic shook his head, his expression grim. "We'll have to hide. Then try to escape when we have the chance."

"I need to find my father."

He nodded, then swore under his breath. Storming down the dark hallway toward them was Aron. He grabbed hold of Nic's shirt.

"They're everywhere," Aron cried. "Goddess help us. They managed to blast their way in!"

"Are you all right?" Cleo asked despite herself. The boy bled from a cut under his left eye.

"Someone grabbed me. I fought him, got away. Took this for protection." He had a bloody dagger clutched in his right hand. A flash of Tomas Agallon's murder tore through her mind and her throat closed. She forced the memory away.

As Aron drew closer, she could smell the wine on his breath. "You're drunk!"

He shrugged. "Maybe a little."

Her lip curled with disgust. "It's barely daybreak and you're already drunk."

He ignored her. "So what are we supposed to do now?"

"Nic wants to find Mira and then for us to hide."

"I think that's an excellent idea. What about your sister?"

"Emilia—she . . . she's dead." Her throat tightened and Nic pulled her closer to his side.

Aron's bleary face went pale with shock. "Cleo, no. I can't believe it."

Cleo drew in a ragged breath. "There's no time. Say nothing more about it. She's gone and there's nothing I can do to help her now. We need to survive. And I need to find my father." She looked at Nic. "Go find Mira. Meet us in the corridor by the stairs to the upper level in fifteen minutes. If we're not there, continue on and hide where you can. There are plenty of rooms up there. Find one and be as quiet as you can. This is a very large castle, and this siege can't last forever."

"It'll be all right?" Nic gestured at Aron. "With him as your only protector?"

"It'll have to be."

Nic nodded. "I'll see you soon. Be safe, Cleo." He quickly kissed her cheek before he turned and ran off down the hall.

"Maybe we should go with him," Aron suggested. "There's safety in numbers."

"Not necessarily. Larger numbers could draw more attention."

Cleo tried to push past her fear and grief to find an answer. She only had one. Find the king and then they all had to hide until this was over. If Auranos was unsuccessful in its attempts to fight off this enemy, they would have to find a way to escape from the palace and go into exile until they could make this right again. She hoped that her father had a better plan in mind. For now, survival was the only goal.

Aron didn't argue any further, instead running alongside her in silence as they made their way through the labyrinthine hallways. When they turned the next corner, Cleo skidded to a stop.

She couldn't speak. She just stared at the familiar person who now stood facing them holding a sword.

"Well, well," Prince Magnus said. "Just the princess I've been looking for."

A wall of fear descended upon Cleo. All she could see was Magnus thrusting his sword through Theon's chest.

"Who are you?" Aron demanded.

"Me?" Magnus cocked his head. "I am Magnus Lukas Damora, crown prince and heir to the throne of Limeros. And who are you?"

Aron blinked, surprised at being faced with such a formidable member of royalty, even though he was their enemy. "I am Lord Aron Lagaris."

This earned a thin smile from the prince. "Yes, I've heard about you. You're rather famous, Lord Aron. You killed the wine seller's son and started this whole ball rolling, didn't you?"

"It was self-defense," Aron said nervously.

"Of course it was. I have no doubt." Magnus's unpleasant smile stretched wider. "And you're also, if I'm not mistaken, currently engaged to Princess Cleiona. Is that right?"

Aron straightened his back. "It is indeed."

"How wonderfully romantic." His gaze flicked to Cleo, who did everything she could not to recoil from the very sight of him. "As you can probably already tell, we've arrived. And we're not going anywhere. Surrender."

"To you?" Cleo's words burst forth without any forethought. *"Never."*

His expression tightened. "Oh, come now. I know we've had some unpleasantness between us in the not-so-distant past, but there's no reason why you can't be nice."

"I can think of about a million reasons why I would never want to be nice to you."

"Princess, you must not be rude to those who are now guests in your land. I'm offering you my hand in friendship right now."

Her cheeks burned. "You dare invade my home, and now you treat me like an ignorant child?"

"My sincere apologies if you've taken it that way. My father will be pleased to finally make your acquaintance. Don't make this more difficult than it has to be. I've failed to bring you before him once. I don't intend on that happening again."

Cleo clutched Aron's arm, waiting for him to do something, to say something. To show that underneath the drunken, selfish exterior was a true hero she could forgive for anything horrible he'd done in the past.

"The prince is right," Aron replied, his expression grim. "If we want to live through this, we need to do as he says. We need to surrender."

She gave him a cold and enraged glare. "You are so incredibly pathetic, you make me want to vomit."

"Uh-oh, don't tell me there's trouble between you and the boy you love, even before your wedding day." Magnus's dry words twisted with amusement. "Don't make me give up on my romantic ideals of true love."

Cleo turned to face this monster. "No, actually you killed the boy I loved right in front of me."

He looked at her with confusion before clarity slid through his dark eyes. Then his brows drew together. "I told him to stand down."

"He was protecting me." Her bottom lip trembled. "And you killed him."

That small frown that contradicted his usual icy expression grew a fraction deeper.

"Wait," Aron said. "Who are we talking about?"

She ignored him and forced herself to keep her expression neutral. "Prince Magnus . . ."

"Yes, Princess Cleiona?"

"I want you to give your father a message from me."

"You can certainly deliver it yourself, but all right. What is it?"

"Tell him that his son has failed again."

Cleo turned and began running away as fast as she could. She knew the halls of this castle better than anyone. The prince's roar of anger echoed against the stone walls as he lost sight of her.

Another time, another place, she might have smiled at this

small victory. And while she felt a twinge of regret at leaving Aron behind, it was only a twinge. If he wanted to surrender to the Limerians so easily, he still had every chance to do so—without her at his side.

Angry shouts and the clash of metal on metal came from up ahead and she froze, pressing up against the wall. *Can't go that way.* She'd have to find another path. She couldn't give up on finding her father.

As she turned the next corner, someone grabbed her by her hair, wrenching her so hard that it felt as if it would be pulled out by its roots. She screamed and tried to kick and claw at whoever it was. A Limerian soldier eyed her curiously.

"What do we have here?" he asked. Her gaze shot to his sword, which dripped blood to the marble floor. "Pretty little thing, aren't you?"

"Let go of me," she snarled. "Or you're dead."

He laughed. "You have spirit. I like that. Won't last long, but I like it."

Then, astonishingly, he let go of her and staggered forward. Out of the corner of her eye, Cleo watched his companion fall to the ground, collapsing at the same time as her attacker. Both bled out onto the floor.

King Corvin stood there, his face a mask of fury, his sword covered in blood to its hilt.

"Father!" she gasped.

"It's not safe here." He grabbed her arm and half-dragged her down the hall.

"I was looking for you. Those men . . ."

"I know. This shouldn't have happened." He swore under his breath. "I don't know how they got through the doors."

"I was told they were protected by a witch's spell. Is that true?"

He eyed her. Her heart lurched to see that he'd been hurt. There was a vicious cut on his temple and blood dripped steadily down his cheek. "They were."

All her life, Cleo had never realized her father believed in witches or magic. He'd turned his back on the goddess after her mother had died, so she'd never asked. She wished she'd known the truth. He pulled her into a small room at the end of the hallway. He closed the door and pressed his back against it. A small window let in just enough light to see.

"Thank the goddess I found you," she said, finally allowing herself a measure of relief. "We need to get to Nic and Mira. We need to keep hidden until we can find a chance to escape."

"I can't leave, Cleo." He shook his head. "And we can't leave Emilia here by herself."

And just like that, the tears that hadn't spilled since she'd left her sister's room began to flow like an endless river. "She's gone. Emilia's gone. I found her earlier in her chambers." She struggled to find her breath as she sobbed. Her chest hitched. "She—she's dead."

Grief flashed across the king's expression as well as something darker and more bleak. "I was wrong, Cleo. I'm sorry. I should have sent my men to find this exiled Watcher you told me about in Paelsia. I should have believed what you claimed was possible. I could have helped save her life."

She had no response to that. She wished he'd done so too. So much. "It's too late now."

He reached out and clutched her arm so tightly that she yelped in pain. It was as effective as a slap to bring her to her senses and stop her tears.

"You need to be strong, Cleo." His voice caught. "You are now the heir to my throne."

Her stomach lurched. She hadn't even thought of that. "I'm trying, Father!"

"There's no choice anymore for you, my darling girl. You *must* be strong. For me, for Auranos, for everything you hold dear."

Panic tightened her chest. "We need to go right now."

There was deep pain on the king's face. His eyes shone with tears. "This isn't right. I've been a fool. Such a blind fool. I could have prevented this, but it's too late now."

"No, it's not too late. Don't say that!"

He shook his head. "They're going to win, Cleo. They're going to take it all. But you must find a way to take it back."

She looked at him with confusion. "What are you talking about?"

Sweat dripped from his brow. He felt at his neck, pulling a long gold chain from underneath his shirt. He tugged to break it. On the end was a gold ring with a purple stone that he pressed into her hand. "Take this."

"What is it?"

"It belonged to your mother. She always believed it had the power to help find the Kindred."

"The Kindred," Cleo breathed. She remembered Eirene's words. Four crystals that held the essence of *elementia*. It was what had been stolen by the two goddesses and split between them. Fire and air, earth and water. "But why would my mother have something like this?"

"It was passed down through her family line from a man who was said to have been involved with a sorceress. It was so many years ago that it became legend. Your mother still believed it was true. I was going to give it to Emilia on her wedding day." His voice broke. "But since that never came to be, I held on to it. You must take it. If you can find the Kindred, you'll be powerful enough to take back this kingdom from those who seek to destroy us all."

She looked up into his face, clutching the ring tightly. "I never knew you believed in magic."

"I believe, Cleo. Even when I didn't believe, I believed in your mother's faith in it." He gave her a pained smile. "But please be careful. Whatever weapon King Gaius used to breach the protection spell must be powerful and dangerous."

"Come on, we need to move," Cleo urged. "We'll find the Kindred together. We'll take back this kingdom together."

He pressed his hand against her cheek, his expression one of aching sadness. "I wish that were possible."

"What are you—" Cleo's words cut off. There was something in the way he was standing, pressed up against the wall. His other hand was now tight against his side. Her gaze moved to the floor, where she finally saw the pool of blood that had formed there.

Her eyes shot back to her father's face. "No!"

"I killed the one who did this to me." He shook his head. "Small comfort."

"You need help. You need a medic. A healer!"

"It's too late for that."

Cleo pressed her shaking hand against his side to find it soaked with blood. Pain crashed down upon her. "No, Father, please. You can't leave me. Not like this."

He slipped a few more inches and she grabbed hold of him to help him stay on his feet. "I know you'll be a wonderful queen."

Tears streamed down her face so much that she could barely see. "No, please. Please don't leave me."

"I love you." Her father's voice had grown strained, as if it took great effort now for him to speak. "I'll always love you. Be smarter than me. Be a better leader than me. Help bring Auranos back to its former glory. And believe in magic . . . always. I know it's out there waiting for you to find it."

"No, please no," she whispered. "Don't go. I need you."

He finally slipped out of her grasp to the floor. His grip on her hand tightened painfully, then eased off completely.

Her father was dead.

Cleo had to clamp her hand over her mouth to keep from screaming. She collapsed to the floor and hugged her knees to her chest, rocking herself back and forth. A cry of anguish locked in her throat, threatening to choke her. Then she clutched onto her father, not wanting to let him go even though she knew he was gone. "I love you. I love you so much."

He hadn't surrendered to the Limerians. If he had, this all could have been avoided.

But even as she thought it, she knew it wasn't the truth. This king of Limeros, King Gaius, was a tyrant. A dictator. An evil man who would kill anyone who got in his way. If her father had stepped aside to prevent violence and bloodshed, she was positive he would have been killed anyway so he wouldn't be a threat in the future.

Cleo kept her head against her father's shoulder, the same as when she was little and needing comfort from some silly thing—hurt feelings, a skinned knee. He'd always drawn her to his side and told her it would be all right. The pain would ease. She would heal.

But she would never heal from this. She'd experienced so much loss that it felt as if a part of her heart had been gored out of her chest, leaving a bloody wound behind. She would stay here and let Prince Magnus find her. Let him drive a sword through her as well so she could find peace and quiet after all this chaos and pain.

The hopeless thought only lasted a few minutes before she could hear her sister's voice in her head, urging her to be strong. But how was she supposed to be strong when everything had been taken from her?

The ring caught her eye. She'd dropped it. The large amethyst glittered in the meager light of the room.

She was a descendant of the hunter—the man from Paelsia who'd loved the sorceress, Eva. Who'd hidden the Kindred after the goddesses destroyed each other out of greed and vengeance. If what her father had told her was true, this had been Eva's ring— the ring that allowed her to touch the Kindred without its infinite magic corrupting her.

Cleo grasped the ring and slipped it onto the middle finger of her left hand.

It fit perfectly.

If this ring had the power to help her find the Kindred, it also gave her the power to wield the Kindred's magic without becoming corrupted by it. She could use that magic to take back her kingdom from those who'd stolen it. The thought worked to dry her tears and give her clarity. She wouldn't surrender. Not today, not ever.

Cleo gazed upon her father's face one last time before leaning forward to kiss him.

"I'll be strong," she whispered. "I'll be strong for you. For Emilia. For Theon. For Auranos. I swear, I'll make them pay for what they've done."

CHAPTER 35

PAELSIA

Alexius watched the old woman as she put her laundry out to dry on a line stretched between two withered trees near her humble stone cottage. Her face was grim, and she glanced up in his direction every few moments.

"Be gone," she said harshly.

He didn't move from his perch.

"I know who you are. I know you've been here many times before." She put her hands on her hips. "It's you, isn't it, brother? None of the others would bother with me now."

His sister, Eirene, had left the Sanctuary more than fifty mortal years ago. Then she'd been beautiful and young and full of life and would have stayed that way eternally. But now, beyond the veil, she'd become wrinkled, hunched over, and gray from age and hard work.

She'd made her choice. Once one left the Sanctuary, one could never return.

"Are you aware of the war that rages right now?" she asked. Alexius wasn't certain if she really believed that he was her brother or if she was slightly mad—a woman who talked to birds. "It will end with blood and death as all wars do. The King of Blood searches for the same thing as you, I know it. Do you think you'll find it before he does?"

He couldn't reply to her, so he didn't bother trying.

"The girl was born. She lives, brother. I saw it in the stars years ago—but you likely know this already. She can find the Kindred. The elders will be pleased to have all restored to normal."

Eirene's expression soured. "Without the crystals, the Sanctuary will fade away. I see it in this land. It's all connected. Everything is connected, brother, even more than I ever believed it was." She laughed, but there was no humor to the sound. "Perhaps it's for the best. If I'm to die a mortal, why shouldn't the same fate be given to all, no matter how long they've lived or how important they think they are? All things must eventually come to an end."

Eirene had left the Sanctuary because she'd fallen in love with a mortal. She'd turned her back on immortality for the chance at love. She believed a handful of years that contained passion and life was better than an endless pristine existence. He'd been disgusted by her weakness then. For a Watcher, fifty years was only a breath of time.

"Beware of one thing, brother." She glanced over her shoulder at him as she was about to return to her small cottage. "Don't overestimate your ability to deal with mortals, especially the pretty ones. After two thousand years, it could finally be the death of you."

He still hadn't told Danaus, Timotheus, or even Phaedra about the beautiful dark-haired princess's magic. She was too important, and Alexius had begun to trust fewer of his kind in recent months. He had to continue to keep watch over her. He had to find the right time to communicate with her.

And, very soon, he would have to find a way to kill her.

CHAPTER 36

AURANOS

Victory was theirs. The king of Auranos had been killed. The eldest princess and heir to the throne was found dead in her chambers. But there was still a loose end. Princess Cleiona had escaped the palace.

For such a young and seemingly innocuous girl, she was very wily.

If Magnus ever came face-to-face with her again, she wouldn't slip through his fingers a third time. He didn't like being frustrated. He also didn't like the splinter of guilt that had worked its way under his skin over the relentless tragedy that had befallen the girl—both her father and sister's deaths, as well as the guard who'd protected her in Paelsia. The one she'd said she loved. The one Magnus had killed with his own sword.

Irrelevant. It was done. And there was nothing he could do to change it even if he wanted to.

Magnus hadn't told his father that he'd come close to capturing her again. He didn't think the second failure when it came to the princess would earn him any favor with the king. Besides, he didn't want to interrupt the king's celebrations. Magnus was the only other person invited to the private dinner with Chief Basilius in his father's heavily guarded tent. They toasted their mutual victory with the finest Paelsian wine.

Magnus abstained. He was too concerned with Lucia's health to be in the right frame of mind to celebrate. She still lay unconscious, hours after her magic broke through the front doors of the castle, ensuring their victory. The force of the explosion had also knocked him out, but when he came to minutes later, he was only shaken, not injured.

Lucia, however, was covered in blood. Out of his mind with panic, Magnus carried her to the medics. By the time he'd arrived, her cuts and abrasions had miraculously—or magically—faded away completely. But she remained unconscious.

The medics, baffled, told him that she needed rest and that she would wake eventually. While he waited, he'd prayed to the goddess Valoria to bring Lucia back. His sister believed in the goddess with all her heart. He didn't, but he was willing to give it a try.

At least two hundred people—from all three kingdoms—had been killed in the explosion. But Lucia lived. And for that Magnus was grateful.

She'd willingly healed him when he'd been moments from death, even after their many difficulties. He'd believed she hated him, but she helped him in his greatest time of need.

The injury was his own fault. He'd been distracted during battle when something caught his eye—golden hair streaked with bright red blood. The body of Andreas Psellos, his sister's suitor and Magnus's fiercest rival since childhood, lay in pieces on the battlefield. The sight had stolen Magnus's breath long enough for an Auranian to land not one but two deep blows with his sword before he too had been slain by a Paelsian soldier.

Andreas was dead and would no longer be a problem.

The victory felt much more shallow than Magnus ever would have expected. He'd despised the boy, it was true. But to see him defeated, broken, bloody . . .

It had bothered him.

But now he did his best to put it out of his mind. The battle was over and despite many casualties, they were the victors. Magnus lived, and Lucia now lay in a coma for doing the king's bidding. Over twelve hours now and he'd heard nothing new about her.

It was dinnertime and the king and the chief clinked their glasses, laughing over their victory and toasting to the bright future. Magnus sat with them at the table, his food untouched.

"Oh, my son," the king said, smiling. "Always so serious, even now."

"I'm worried about Lucia."

"My darling secret weapon." The king beamed. "Every bit as powerful as I always hoped she'd be. Impressive, yes?"

"Very," the chief agreed, downing his fourth glass of wine. "And a beautiful girl. If I had sons, I think we could make a fine match between our lands."

"Indeed."

"Speaking of . . ." The chief glanced at Magnus. "I do have a daughter who is yet unspoken for. She's only twelve, but she would make an excellent wife."

Magnus tried to keep the look of disgust off his face. The thought of a bride so young made him utterly nauseated.

"You never know what the future may bring," his father said, running his finger around the edge of his wineglass. "So I suppose we should give some thought to how to deal with the spoils of war. The coming days and weeks are going to be very interesting."

"We must appoint representatives to ensure that everything remains equal, as we discussed. Of course, I trust that Limeros will be honest in its dealings with us."

"Of course."

"So much here, so many riches. Gold, treasures, resources. Fresh water. Forests. Fields upon fields of crops. A land teeming with game. It's a paradise."

"Yes," the king said. "And, of course, there is the matter of the Kindred."

The chief raised a dark, bushy eyebrow. "You believe in the Kindred?"

"Don't you?"

The chief drained his next glass. "Of course. I have searched for signs of its location through years of meditation, sending my own magic out across the miles to try to sense where it could be."

"Have you had any luck?" the king asked.

The chief waved a hand. "I feel I am close to something."

"I believe they're here in Auranos," King Gaius said evenly.

"Do you? What gives you that impression?"

"Auranos flourishes, green and lush, like the legendary Sanctuary itself, while Paelsia wastes away and Limeros turns to ice. Simple deduction, really."

As the chief considered this, he swirled the remaining amber-colored wine around in his glass. "Others have considered the same thing. I'm not sure I necessarily believe that. I believe the carved stone wheels found in Limeros and Paelsia point to clues of its location."

"Perhaps," King Gaius allowed. "But to have taken this land

from King Corvin is to possess everything the land contains with unrestricted access to tear it apart in my search. To find even one crystal would mean endless magic—but to possess them all . . ."

The chief nodded, his eyes lighting with greed. "We could become gods. Yes, this is good. We will find them together, and we will split them down the middle—fifty-fifty."

"You like that plan?"

"I like it very much."

"You know, your people already consider you their god. Enough to pay you blood sacrifice and enough wine tax to support your comfortable lifestyle." King Gaius leaned back in his chair. "They believe you're a great sorcerer descended from the Watchers themselves who will soon rise up and deliver them all from squalor."

The chief spread his hands. "Without my people I am nothing."

"I have known you for some time now and I have yet to see a spark of this magic."

A glimmer of unfriendliness moved over the chief's face. "You haven't known me that long. Perhaps one day I will show you my true power."

Magnus watched his father carefully. There was something strange going on here that he wasn't quite understanding, but he knew better than to speak. When the king had asked him to be a part of this dinner meeting and celebration, he'd specifically told Magnus that he was only there to observe and to learn.

"When do we begin our search for the Kindred?" the chief asked. Both his plate and wineglass were now empty.

"I intend on beginning immediately," the king replied.

"And which two elements do you wish to possess?"

"Two? I wish to possess all four."

The chief frowned. "All four? How is that splitting things fifty-fifty?"

"It's not."

"I don't understand."

"I know. And that's just . . . sad, really." A smile stretched across the king's face.

The chief stared at him for a moment, a drunken glaze in his eyes, thanks to the two bottles of wine he'd drunk. Then he started to laugh. "You nearly had me. No, Gaius. I trust you to hold true to your word. We are like brothers after the blood sacrifice of your bastard. I don't forget."

"Neither do I." The king's smile held as he got to his feet and moved to the other side of the table. "Time for rest. Tomorrow is a bright new day. I've had enough of tents. We shall move into the castle. Much finer quarters there."

He offered his hand to Chief Basilius, who still chuckled over their amusing exchange. He took the king's hand and got to his feet, unsteadily. "A fine meal. Your cooks are to be commended."

King Gaius watched him. "Show me some magic. Just a little. I feel I've earned this."

The chief patted his belly. "Not tonight. I am too full for such displays."

"Very well." The king extended his hand again. "Good night, my friend."

"Good night." He clasped the king's hand and shook it.

King Gaius pulled him closer. "I believed the stories. The ones of you being a sorcerer. I've seen enough magic not to doubt such tales until I have enough evidence to disprove it. I must admit, there was some fear. While I am a man of action, I don't possess any magic of my own. Not yet."

The chief's brows drew together. "Are you calling me a liar?"

"Yes," King Gaius said. "That's exactly what I'm calling you."

Taking the dagger he'd concealed in his other hand, King Gaius slashed the chief's throat in one smooth, quick motion.

The chief's eyes bugged out with surprise and pain and he staggered back from the king.

"If you're really a sorcerer," the king said coolly, "heal yourself."

Magnus gripped the edge of the table but didn't make a move. Every muscle in his body had grown tense at the exchange.

Blood spurted from between the chief's fingers. His panicked gaze shot toward the tent's entrance, which was guarded only by King Gaius's men. His trust had allowed him to come in here with no bodyguards nearby.

"Oh, and that fifty-fifty deal of ours?" the king said with a thin smile. "It was for a limited time only. Auranos is mine. And now, so is Paelsia."

The chief looked completely shocked by this turn of events before he collapsed to the floor with a heavy thump. The king nudged his shoulder so the chief turned over onto his back, his eyes wide and glazed, blood oozing from the gaping wound at his throat.

Magnus fought against the urge to leap back. In a way, he couldn't say he was all that surprised. He'd been waiting for his father to turn the tables on the chief for a while now.

When the king flicked a look at his son as if to gauge his reaction to this, all he saw was a mildly bored expression on the prince's face.

"Come, now. You're not impressed at all?" He let out a sharp bark of a laugh. "Oh, Magnus, you've got to give me a little credit."

"I'm not sure if I should be impressed or concerned," Magnus said evenly. "For all I know, you might do the same thing to me."

"Don't be ridiculous. I'm doing all of this for you, Magnus. Together we will find the Kindred—it's been my life's goal from the time I was a boy and first heard the tales. To find all four will give us ultimate power. We can rule the universe itself."

A shiver moved down Magnus's spine at the maniacal look in his father's eyes. "I can't say that my father doesn't have scope."

"Clear and precise. Now"—the king moved toward the entrance to the large and luxurious tent—"let us inform the people of Auranos and Paelsia that their leaders are dead and they now must bow before me. Or die."

AURANOS

"Just once," Brion said under his breath, "I would have liked you to be wrong."

Jonas glanced at him. "I've been wrong lots of times."

"Not this time."

"No. Not this time."

They stood at the edge of the forest and watched as the chief's blood-covered body was strung up for all to see. The Limerian king flaunted the murder as a symbol of the chief's weakness. He was no sorcerer or god, as his people had always believed. He was only a man.

A dead man.

After his death last night, the Limerian army had turned their blades on the same Paelsians they'd previously fought with side by side. Those who refused to bow down before King Gaius immediately had their throats slashed or their heads severed completely and put on spikes. Most bowed and pledged allegiance to Limeros. Most were afraid to die.

With every moment he'd been forced to witness this atrocity, Jonas's heart grew darker. Not just Auranos but also Paelsia had fallen to these greedy and deceptive Limerian monsters led by their king of blood and death. It was everything he'd feared.

He'd grabbed Brion just in time. His friend had been faced with a Limerian's sword, and by the fierce and insolent look on Brion's face, he wasn't going to bow before King Gaius. As the knight raised his blade, ready to remove Brion's head, Jonas killed him, grabbed Brion, and fled.

He'd killed many since this war began. He'd considered himself a hunter before this, but of animals, not men. Now his blade had found the hearts of many men. What little inside him was still a boy of only seventeen years had hardened to compensate for this. Each time he killed, it became easier, and the faces of the men whose lives he took became less distinguishable from one another. But this was not the path he ever would have chosen for himself had he known where it would ultimately lead.

Together, Brion and Jonas had found other boys they recognized from their country, those who refused to surrender to this madness. There was now a group of six of them, all gathered in the protection of the forest.

"So what now?" Brion asked, his expression grim and haunted. "What can we do but watch and wait? If we go out there again, we'll be slaughtered."

Jonas thought of his brother. Since his murder, everything had changed. A life of hardship and squalor in Paelsia paled in comparison to the horrors that lay ahead. "We need to wait and see what happens next," Jonas finally said.

"So we're supposed to stand back like cowards?" Brion growled. "And let King Gaius destroy our land? Slaughter our people?"

The idea of it made Jonas's stomach clench. He hated feeling powerless. He wanted to act now, but he knew that would only get them all killed. "The chief made many mistakes. He's gone now. And, if you ask me, he was a lousy leader. We needed someone who was strong and capable, not one who would so easily be fooled by someone like King Gaius." Jonas's jaw was tight. "Basilius's defeat sickens me. Because of his greed and stupidity, the rest of us must suffer."

The other four boys gathered around grumbled about the unfairness of it all.

"But we've always survived despite the odds stacked against us." Jonas raised his voice to be heard above the others. "Paelsia has been dying for generations. But we still live."

"It's King Gaius's now," a boy named Tarus said. The kid wasn't much more than fourteen and was the older brother of the boy Jonas witnessed die on the battlefield. "He's destroyed us and now he owns us."

"Nobody owns us. You hear me? Nobody." Jonas remembered his brother's words all those years ago. "If you want something, you have to take it. Because nobody's ever going to give it to you. So we're going to take back what's been taken from us. And then we'll create a better future for Paelsia. A better future for us all."

"How?"

"He hasn't a clue," Brion said, actually smiling now for the first time in days. "But he's going to do it anyway."

Jonas couldn't help but grin back. His friend was right. He would figure out how to fix this. There was not a doubt in his mind.

Jonas cast a look toward the Auranian palace. While it glittered golden under the sun, part of it still burned from the explosion at dawn yesterday. A black cloud of smoke rose up above it.

He'd heard the reports. The king was dead. The eldest princess, Emilia, was also dead. However, Princess Cleo hadn't yet been found.

When he'd heard this news, he was surprised at the lifting of his heavy heart.

The girl whom he'd blamed for his brother's death, the one he'd fantasized about killing to gain vengeance, the one who'd cunningly managed to escape her own fate, her shackles, and a locked and guarded shed.

She was queen now. A queen in exile.

And he had to find her.

The future, both Paelsia's and Auranos's, now depended completely on her survival.

CHAPTER 38

AURANOS

Princess Cleo's bedchamber was now Lucia's. Magnus stood by while the medics and healers surrounded her, but they left when they could do nothing more to help. She lay there in the large canopied bed, her beautiful face pale, her midnight-black hair fanned across the silk pillows.

Magnus stood stonily by her bedside cursing the goddess who hadn't answered his prayers. One healer remained, wiping Lucia's forehead with a cool, damp cloth.

"Get out of here," he snapped.

The woman looked at him with fear before scurrying out of the room. He was getting that reaction a lot lately. With his actions on the battlefield, with the ease with which he took the lives of those in his path, and the fact that he had been present when Chief Basilius was murdered, his reputation as the Prince of Blood had grown to nearly match his father's reputation.

Only Lucia had ever been able to see the real him—even before his sword had tasted blood. But perhaps that Magnus had died the night when he'd shown her his true feelings. The mask he'd always worn had shattered, but a new one had grown, stronger and thicker than ever. He should be happy for this improvement. Instead, he felt nothing but grief for what had been lost.

"The love of a brother for his sister," the king said from behind him. Magnus's shoulders tensed, but he didn't tear his gaze from Lucia's face. "It's truly a beautiful thing."

"She's not improving."

"She will."

"How do you know for sure?" Magnus's words were as sharp as his sword.

"I have faith, my son. She is exactly as the prophecy said she'd be—a sorceress unlike any the world has seen in a thousand years."

He struggled to swallow. "Or she's merely a witch who's now destroyed herself to help you gain your victory over Auranos."

His father scoffed. "Magnus, you are such a pessimist. Just wait. Tomorrow I'll address my new subjects and set their minds at ease about their future. Everyone is now an honorary citizen of Limeros. They will celebrate my victory."

"And if they don't, you'll make sure they're punished."

"Can't have any dissenters. Wouldn't look very good, would it?"

"You don't think anyone will oppose you?"

"Perhaps a few. I'll be forced to make examples of them."

His father's calm demeanor about all this was infuriating.

"Just a few? We've swept in here and killed their king, the eldest princess, and taken over their land—as well as murdering the Paelsian leader. You think they'll all simply accept that?"

"We were not responsible for Princess Emilia's death. So

tragic that she was ill. I'd never kill an innocent girl. After all, her ongoing presence in the palace would have helped ease my way into the hearts of Auranos's citizens."

"And Princess Cleiona? What about her? She's queen now."

The king's expression tightened. It was the first sign of strain Magnus had seen. "She'd be smart to come to me and beg for my protection."

"Would you give it to her? Or slit her throat too?"

The king smiled—a cold smile—and put his arm around his son's stiff shoulders. "Honestly, Magnus. Slit the throat of a sixteen-year-old girl? What kind of monster do you take me for?"

Something caught Magnus's attention. Lucia's eyelids fluttered. His breath caught. But after he waited a few moments, nothing more happened. The king tightened his grip on Magnus's shoulder as if he guessed that he was now in great distress.

"It's all right, son. She'll recover in time. This is only temporary."

"How do you know that?" His voice was strangled.

"Because the magic is still within her, and I'm not through with it yet. I need it to find the Kindred." The king nodded with confidence, his expression very serious now. "Leave us, Magnus. I'll sit with her."

"But Father—"

"I said to go now." There was no mistaking his firm tone. This was a non-negotiable request.

Magnus moved from the side of the bed and sent his father a dark look. "I'll return."

"I have no doubt that you will."

He left the room and pressed his back up against the wall in the hallway outside. It was as if he'd been stabbed through his heart. If Lucia never awoke, then she was lost to him forever. Grief for the only person in the world he'd ever loved and who'd loved him in return buckled his knees.

He felt at his face, wondering what the hot dampness was. For a moment he thought he was bleeding.

Swearing under his breath, he pushed the tears away, vowing that they would be the last he ever shed. Strength, not weakness, was what he needed from this day forward.

CHAPTER 39

AURANOS

King Gaius stood on the castle balcony, looking down upon those gathered to hear him speak about his victory here in Auranos, a crowd of more than a thousand.

They were terrified of both him and his army that surrounded them, watching for any signs of trouble. Cleo drew the loose hood of her cloak closer to her face as she listened to this hateful man speak his lies and false promises with a smile on his face.

She was exhausted. All day and all night she'd stuck to the shadows of the walled palace city, now overrun by Limerian security. But no one paid much attention to a mere slip of a girl.

Whenever she began to lose faith, she touched the ring her father had given her for strength—her mother's ring. The sorceress Eva's ring.

Cleo's kingdom had been torn from her. Her family was dead. She was alone. But she wasn't ready to run yet. Nic and Mira hadn't made it out of the castle in time. King Gaius had obviously extended his "generous" hospitality to them. They also stood on the balcony with him as Auranian representatives, looking pale and distraught but as brave as possible given the situation.

To see proof that they lived gave her a glimmer of hope that she could free them. She needed her friends at her side if she was going to come up with a plan to right what had gone so horribly wrong. It was her father's last request.

Cleo refused to think she would fail.

Suddenly, she felt someone's gaze hot on the side of her face. When she glanced to her left, her breath caught. Jonas Agallon, also cloaked, stood not a dozen feet from her. She feared he was about to raise an alarm when he touched his index finger to his lips.

The boy who had kidnapped her, imprisoned her, and let Prince Magnus know of her location so he could attempt to drag her to Limeros as a prisoner of war was telling her to keep quiet. To stay calm.

Cleo froze in place as he slid through the crowd, moving closer until he stood directly behind her.

"I mean you no harm," he whispered.

She slowly turned to face him.

"I wish I could say the same." She pressed the sharp tip of her dagger against his abdomen.

Instead of looking alarmed, he had the nerve to give her a small grin. "Nicely done."

"You won't be saying that when you're bleeding to death."

"No, I don't suppose I will. You shouldn't be here, your highness. You need to leave immediately."

She glared at him and pressed her dagger closer to flesh to prove she wasn't fooling around. "Says who? A Paelsian savage who pledges allegiance to the man who's stolen my kingdom and destroyed my family?"

His jaw was tense. "No. A rebel who wants to bring an end to the King of Blood." Ignoring the danger the dagger presented, he leaned forward to brush his lips against her ear. "One day very soon, be ready."

She looked up at him with confusion as he slipped away from her. She immediately hid the dagger back under her cloak so no one would spot it. When she looked around again, Jonas was lost in the crowd.

"So you see"—King Gaius spoke loud and clear from his royal perch—"the future belongs to Limeros. And if you join me, it will belong to you as well."

The crowd murmured with displeasure, but the king's smile only grew wider.

"I know you're concerned for the safety of your princess Cleiona. Rumors abound that she was killed. I assure you, that's not the case. She's safe and well and shall soon be my guest at the palace. Consider this an act of generosity to show that I am benevolent toward all Auranians during this transition."

Cleo frowned with confusion. How could he say those things? She wasn't his guest.

"We really have to stop meeting like this," a hatefully familiar voice said. She looked to her right with alarm to see that Prince Magnus now stood next to her.

Before she could reach for her dagger again, two guards grabbed her arms and held her firmly in place. Prince Magnus drew closer and slid his hand under her cloak to locate her weapon. He eyed it with disinterest.

"Unhand me," she demanded.

"Didn't you hear my father?" Magnus asked with a glance up to the balcony before his brown eyes flicked to hers. "You're cordially invited to be our guest. My father doesn't take disappointment well, so I advise you to accept as gracefully as possible." His dark brows drew together as he studied her. "I know this must be a very difficult time for you."

She spat at him. "I will see you dead."

He wiped the spit away and then grasped her chin. His gaze turned to ice. "And I, princess, will see you at dinner." He nodded to the guards. "Bring her in."

Holding her arms tightly, the guards marched Cleo toward the palace. As much as she wanted to fight, to scream, Cleo kept her head haughtily high. She would be fierce. This particular fate could ultimately serve her well. Inside the palace, she would be reunited with Nic and Mira. Together they would find a way to escape. They would figure out how to use her mother's ring to locate the Kindred. With it, she would possess more than enough power to take back Auranos and vanquish their enemies forever.

Jonas had told her to be ready, but for what? She didn't trust him. A few words spoken in a conspiratorial whisper changed nothing. For all she knew, he was the one to tip Magnus off about her presence in the crowd.

In any case, her fight was not over yet—not nearly over. It had only begun. And yes, Cleo *would* be strong. Just as her father and Emilia had asked her to be.

She would be strong.

She would reclaim her rightful throne.

She would be queen.

ACKNOWLEDGMENTS

Falling Kingdoms would not exist if not for the incredible team at Razorbill and their dedication to getting the world of Mytica into the hands of readers. Thank you so very much to my amazing editor, Laura Arnold, who knows these characters every bit as well as I do—without you this all would have been way less fun and much less organized!—to Ben Schrank for giving me the chance to be a part of it all; to Erin Dempsey for her support from day 1; to Jocelyn Davies for being awesome from the very beginning; to the wonderful Richelle Mead for dinner at the top of the CN Tower when we discussed in depth my fangirl love of vampires and academies; to Shane Rebenschied for the stunning and dangerously beautiful cover art; and to Jim McCarthy, agent extraordinaire.

And thank you to my family and friends who've supported me every step of the way in this breathless journey and who often take me out for lunch and/or dinner when I look in need of a break. This book (and my ongoing sanity) would not be possible without you all in my life! I love you!

CHOOSE YOUR SIDE.

Don't miss

REBEL SPRING

the next epic instalment in
the thrilling fantasy series

May battle commence . . .

Iconic classics
you can't live without . . .

Dracula
BRAM STOKER
Iconic classics you can't live without . . .

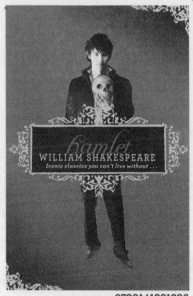

Hamlet
WILLIAM SHAKESPEARE
Iconic classics you can't live without . . .

9780141331829

9780141331836

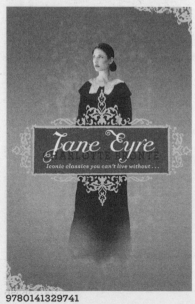

Jane Eyre
CHARLOTTE BRONTE
Iconic classics you can't live without . . .

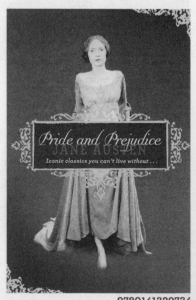

Pride and Prejudice
JANE AUSTEN
Iconic classics you can't live without . . .

9780141329741

9780141329734

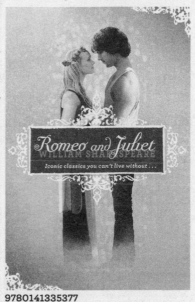

Romeo *and* Juliet
WILLIAM SHAKESPEARE
Iconic classics you can't live without...

9780141335377

Emma
JANE AUSTEN
Iconic classics you can't live without...

9780141335360

Frankenstein
MARY SHELLEY
Iconic classics you can't live without...

9780141334417

The Fall of the House of Usher
And Other Stories
EDGAR ALLAN POE
Iconic classics you can't live without...

9780141336596

He just wanted a decent book to read ...

Not too much to ask, is it? It was in 1935 when Allen Lane, Managing Director of Bodley Head Publishers, stood on a platform at Exeter railway station looking for something good to read on his journey back to London. His choice was limited to popular magazines and poor-quality paperbacks – the same choice faced every day by the vast majority of readers, few of whom could afford hardbacks. Lane's disappointment and subsequent anger at the range of books generally available led him to found a company – and change the world.

'We believed in the existence in this country of a vast reading public for intelligent books at a low price, and staked everything on it'
Sir Allen Lane, 1902–1970, founder of Penguin Books

The quality paperback had arrived – and not just in bookshops. Lane was adamant that his Penguins should appear in chain stores and tobacconists, and should cost no more than a packet of cigarettes.

Reading habits (and cigarette prices) have changed since 1935, but Penguin still believes in publishing the best books for everybody to enjoy. We still believe that good design costs no more than bad design, and we still believe that quality books published passionately and responsibly make the world a better place.

So wherever you see the little bird – whether it's on a piece of prize-winning literary fiction or a celebrity autobiography, political tour de force or historical masterpiece, a serial-killer thriller, reference book, world classic or a piece of pure escapism – you can bet that it represents the very best that the genre has to offer.

Whatever you like to read – trust Penguin.